THE AFTERNOON OF MARCH 30

HE AFTERNOON
ARCH 30
ONTEMPORARY HISTORICAL NOVEL

THANIEL BLUMBERG

PS
3552
.L8424
A68
1984

FIRST EDITION
Copyright ©1984 by Wood/FIRE/Ashes Press
Box 99
Big Fork, Montana 59911
All rights reserved.
ISBN 0-9613338-0-4
Library of Congress Catalog Card Number: 84-90141
Book and Jacket designed by Christen Cody Smith
PRINTED IN THE UNITED STATES OF AMERICA

"A newspaper is a collection of half-injustices" is from *Poems of Stephen Crane*, selected by Gerald D. McDonald and published by Thomas Y. Crowell Company, New York, Apollo Edition, 1971.

The quotation by Doris Lessing is from her magnificent visionary novel, *The Four-Gated City*, published by Alfred A. Knopf, Inc., New York, 1969.

The words of C.G. Jung were taken from an excellent collection, *The Portable Jung*, published in 1971 by The Viking Press, New York.

Readers of this book will find Ralph W. McGehee's *Deadly Deceits: My 25 Years in the CIA* a revealing in-depth study of intelligence issues summarized by the quotation at the start of the March, 1982, chapter. It was published by Sheridan Square Publications, New York, in 1983.

Upton Sinclair's *The Brass Check* is a classic of interest to anyone who wants to understand an era in the history of American journalism. It was, of course, published by the author.

The author hopes that Bill Porterfield and Jim Henderson, two fine writers on the *Dallas Times Herald*, will enjoy seeing some of their good words on these pages. And thanks to Sam Reynolds of *The Missoulian*.

Dedicated to
A. GAYLE WALDROP
and to the memory of
RALPH L. CROSMAN
and
ZELL F. MABEE
who devoted their lives
to improving the quality,
conscience and performance
of the American press

This is a novel. It contains factual references to several living persons, but the characters in the novel were invented by the author and any resemblance to persons living or dead is accidental.

MARCH 30, 1981

Midway through the dark day, a woman turned from the television and looked at me and said, quite sincerely, that she was relieved about one thing.

"What is that?" I said.

"I'm glad it didn't happen in Dallas," she said. "They won't be able to pin this one on us."

As an afterthought, she added, "And thank God, the Hinckley boy is from Colorado."

It was still them against us. We weren't one people, but many, varied and contentious, in siege or under siege, and all the poor woman could think to do was roll up the bridges of the Trinity River moat and lock the windlass.

She spoke too soon, as it turned out. It developed, as almost everyone in the world knows by now, that the suspect, John Hinckley, had spent his school days here in our smuggest suburb, Highland Park, growing up on our snuggest street, rich old Beverly Drive. He had even bought the pistol he is charged as having used from a local pawn shop.

Nov. 22, 1963, comes to mind and won't go away, and doubtless there will be talk of Dallas as a breeding ground for assassins....

— Bill Porterfield, Columnist
Dallas Times Herald
April 3, 1981

Monday was his day off. Otherwise he would have been at the paper and far too busy to have noticed the little item tucked among the big news on television. When Deborah called to tell him shots had been fired at the president, he had first suggested he come down to the news room to help out, but she said all was under control, she'd be fine and wanted to handle it, and God knew he needed the rest. They'd be able to put the story together, lots of time, but if it got too heavy they'd call back and let him know. They weren't even sure if the president had been hit.

The old horse heard the firebells clang. He flipped on the TV to CBS in the living room. Then he turned on the bedroom set to NBC and wheeled it into the living room where he could watch both, quickly flicking back and forth to see how ABC was doing. He watched them all: Dan Rather, whose career got off the ground by the accident of being in Dallas when an earlier president was assassinated; Frank Reynolds, insecure, ill at ease, then flustered and finally collapsing under the pressure, furiously spitting out the words: "Let's get it nailed down—somebody—let's find out!"; Edwin Newman, trying to hold the line for NBC against the other networks' first-stringers. Once again he suffered the wrenching sight, now as American as apple pie, of yet another prominent political figure—a president, or a man who might be president, or a man who many believe should be president—being attacked in front of the eyes of spectators in millions of living rooms, instant replay, slow motion, over and over again. . . .

Quickly—ah, he thought, the news media have never been *quicker* than they are today—came the information that the president had not been shot and that the would-be assassin was a drifter from Colorado, 23 or 25 years of age depending on the network to which you have tuned. Those were just a pair of the mistakes made in the confusion, and the report that the president's press secretary had died, as first reported, was another. He knew a lot of critics, professional and otherwise, were bound to jump on the television journalists for these lapses, but he sat there impressed by the many bits and pieces they accurately fitted together under deadline pressures most critics had never experienced and could never understand. And how can you blame a reporter who is told point blank by a Secret Service agent that James Brady is dead? It was a helluva story, and he thought television did a helluva job in those first few hours after John W. Hinckley Jr. gunned down not only the president of the United States and his press secretary but a Secret Service man and a District of Columbia policeman.

Jonathan Blakely was fascinated because in a life he had left behind he had attended meetings and conventions at the Washington Hilton and knew the layout well. He watched the story unfold, switching from network to network every time a commercial came on. Then, even more fascinated, for he was and thought it likely that he always would be an analyst of press performance—his books and articles had been assigned to thousands of journalism students in colleges and universities all over the world—he started taking notes. It was a ritual with him. Files bulged with notes and cards and clippings and pamphlets and chunks of magazines and reminders and comments and quotations and little slips of paper whose meaning often had been lost as they faded into the past, but the ritual went on. Every time he had moved to a new university, and that was often because he had tried to accept the best of the offers to be a visiting professor, his wife had suggested he throw away the yellowed files and start over. That had been one of the lesser differences between his wife and himself. The white 4 x 6 cards, a pragmatic part of the ritualistic methodology suggested to him during his days as a graduate student, were slugged "Hinckley" as he started taking notes on the possibility that this might develop into yet another case for a nearly completed book devoted to press coverage of death by assassination.

He perked up when Dan Rather informed the audience that the assailant, while now living in Colorado, had grown up in Dallas. Although Jonathan was alone in the house, he hooted loudly. "Dallas! Blakely's Genuine Assassination Profile strikes again!" He relished that tidbit for more than one reason: First, he had grown up in Denver and had several times hiked in the lush, untrammeled countryside that became the Hiwan development and site of the Hinckley home in Evergreen. He had returned often enough to see that outsiders had moved in, taken over and helped turn the memorable blue skies of his youth sticky brown. Furthermore, that bit of intelligence correlated precisely with his private profile of characteristics of political assassins that differed wildly from the cliché-ridden and jargon-infested profiles compiled by what he called "behavioral scientists" (you could hear the inverted commas in the tone of his voice) and the other professional and academic flimflam artists of the psyche.

The notes he made hour after hour grew more desultory until it was time for the regularly scheduled newscasts.

Among the several advantages of living in western Montana, Jonathan had discovered when he came to Placer last summer, is that it is one of the few places on earth where it is possible—if you are avid enough, if you are willing enough—to see each of the three television network newscasts. And not only that, if you've missed a broadcast or want to check an item a second time to make certain that eyes or ears, or both, had not betrayed the mind, you can tune in later to a channel from Spokane. For a news buff whose addiction stretched back to the days when he was ten years old and reading the *Rocky Mountain News* and *Denver Post* from front page to want ads, that was a decided bonus. If you are normal, you don't care that you live in a market where the three network news shows butt up against one another and you get only slightly better than Hobson's choice. But when you have the newsmongering monkey on your back, when you perceive that much of what passes for "news" is more fitting for a book of the grotesque, you need a fix from National Public Radio even before your morning coffee and your daily paper. Then you secretly steal glances at other newspapers during the day and do a mental comparative analysis of two or three television news programs and can't get through the night without a hit of Larry King and the network for news and sports. When something dramatic happens you get an overwhelming case of the munchies, a relentless desire for journalistic junk food—*Time, Newsweek* and *U.S. News & World Report*—artificially flavored, sweetened and fortified with just enough preservatives to keep it from going stale or rotten before it gets into your system and possessed of all the nutritional value of a Twinkie. Jonathan was a news freak, hopelessly hooked even though he had several times taken the cure in Mexico or Morocco or Portugal, skipping newspapers for weeks or months and discovering later that he hadn't missed a thing—that Henry Kissinger and Richard Nixon never really go away. But that didn't stop him from falling right back into his old ways and compulsive habits and reading everything now and then from the *Wall Street Journal* up or down to Shredded Wheat boxes.

When it happened it was beyond the grotesque. For seconds Jonathan Blakely was stunned. John Chancellor, eyebrows raised, informed the viewers of NBC Nightly News that the brother of the man who tried to kill the president was acquainted with the son of the man who would have become president if the attack had been successful. As a matter of fact, Chancellor said in a bewildered tone, Scott Hinckley and Neil Bush had been scheduled to have dinner together at the home of the vice president's son the very next night. And, of course, the engagement had been canceled....

Jonathan went for the phone and got Deborah on the line. "Going okay?" he asked his assistant news editor. She assured him all was going well.

"What's AP got on Hinckley's brother and Bush's son?" he asked.

"What? What the hell you talking about?"

"I'm talking about the brother of the assassin who was going to have dinner with the son of the new president of the United States. John Chancellor just told me. Dan and Frank didn't tell me, but John's real good about society notes. Honest to God,

Hinckley's brother and George Bush's son. Nothing on AP?''
"Nothing yet," she said. "I'll sure watch for it, though. Hey, take it easy. I dig handling this story. Best one I've had so far."
He hung up and poured himself some burgundy. A small flash of anger, one he was familiar with, welled and exploded within him as he thought again of the publisher of the *Placer Tribune* who had canceled the paper's contract with United Press International when it came up for renewal. Jonathan had pleaded with him to renew the contract, pointing out that if UPI lost the *Trib* it would probably close down the news operation headquartered in the state capital and—worse—the Associated Press would not have even the small amount of competition it had from the tiny UPI staff. The publisher had pointed to the bottom line; for established reasons he was known in the bar frequented by his paid staff as "Bottom Line Billingsley," and it happened again. UPI did close down its state newspaper wire and became a supplier to its clients in radio and television. So the *Placer Tribune* had been these last few months supplied only by AP. Its readers paid a large price for the relatively small price the publisher refused to pay for a second news service. UPI was small but gutsy, the tireless underdog who kept punching against its slow-footed heavyweight opponent. Jonathan poured another glass of wine and returned to the television set. But the only matter of consequence, other than assurances that the president would recover, was the sweaty appearance of Alexander Haig, a secretary of state betraying his words of reassurance with a monumental nervousness and a dumbfounding lack of knowledge of the order of presidential succession. Jonathan reflected that William Jennings Bryan had once been secretary of state and that with Haig history had come full circle.

The next morning he searched through the *Trib*. Deborah had done what she would call, with a smile, a "workpersonlike job," but he couldn't find a word about the scheduled dinner. He called her at home.

"Nice job," he said. "Follow up hard on it today."

"Thanks. I thought I did all right, too. Are you into seeing me tonight?"

"With open arms."

"That's what I like to hear."

"Sure is funny, AP not carrying the Bush-Hinckley connection."

"I was hoping for a more romantic response, great lover of truth. Be that as it may, are you positive you heard right? It wasn't just some wino illusion or maryjane fantasy, was it? Maybe Chancellor imagined it all? Hardly anyone watches NBC since Chet died and maybe John was just trying to jazz up the ratings." Seconds of silence passed. "Not funny, huh? Jesus, I'm glad I didn't suggest that you spent yesterday up on one of your green clouds."

"Look, darling Deborah, I would like to impress the following on you. First, Chancellor said it and I heard it. Second, all I had was something called hearty burgundy fortified with sulfur dioxide as a preservative. Third, smart ass, there were no green clouds." Jonathan had frequently regretted telling Deborah and some others on the paper about the first time he had been given some smoke by a friend in Spanish Harlem and nothing happened for about an hour until the THC hit and he was wafted high above the Statue of Liberty on a green cloud. All his friends had agreed that his experience was better than their first turn-on but he nonetheless wished he had kept that nugget of information to himself. "Fourth," he went on as Deborah laughed, "this is no laughing matter. Have you considered how close we came to having the second president in less than 20 years being sworn in on a plane flying from Texas to the capital of the United States? What are the odds on that coincidence? And fifth, now that you've stopped laughing, may I tell you how much I look forward to seeing that gorgeous ass of yours on these premises as soon as possible after you put that paper to bed so I can put you to bed? Is that sufficiently romantic for you?"

"Ummmmmm," she said. "Do you really think my ass is gorgeous?"

"Is Arafat an Arab? Is Bush ambitious? Is Hinckley from Dallas?"

"Jesus, Jonathan, you blow my mind. You're the only man I've ever known who not only can make politics sexy but can make sex political. Even at this very early hour, my bodily juices are flowing and I'm already thinking about tonight."

"I've noticed you are easily aroused. That's one of the many things I like about you. But let's not forget the mundane. Look for that scheduled dinner item. It must have been Reuters or UPI, or maybe one of the NBC correspondents stumbled on it. Anyway, pretty lady, keep looking for it, please."

"See you tonight, O Lothario of the comparative analysis."

"Tonight."

Jonathan, back to his self-imposed assignment, was puzzled. Nothing on the early radio newscasts. Nothing on the TV shows. Maybe it *was* a trip on a green cloud. But no, he couldn't imagine something like that, even if the fact seemed to have disappeared into the thinnest air.

He dressed and walked downtown to the Placer Cafe, putting a quarter into each of the three newspaper boxes inside the door. Over coffee and bacon and toast he went through the papers from nearby towns. Nothing.

Two doors down from the Placer Cafe was Rudy's Out-of-Town News, and the proprietor smiled as he accepted Jonathan's offer to subscribe to eight selected metropolitan daily newspapers, starting with issues of March 31, until further notice.

"It's an investment," Jonathan explained to the man behind the counter who could not conceal his curiosity. "An investment in the stability of our nation. Or if that's too pompous for you, I'm a simple editor of the old school who can't stand stories with unanswered questions. I'm looking for answers."

He returned to his house, checked some more radio newscasts—nothing—and dialed the 800 number of a newspaper in Oregon where one of his former students was on the wire desk. No, she hadn't seen the story and there was nothing in her paper's morning edition about it. But she averred that if the brother of an assassin and the son of a future president were due to dine together, it could have been a meal "second only to the Last Supper in influence on the course of history."

Jonathan then put in a call to Dan Doherty, once a defensive end on his college team and now the head of the Washington bureau of a well-known newspaper. Dan, a free spirit, had never fit into the football coach's philosophy of kill or be killed and as a result lost his football scholarship. Jonathan had talked him into getting a job and staying in school, for which Dan remained grateful. He had done some first-rate investigative pieces for Jack Anderson before tiring of the anonymity and moving on.

"Potomac journalism is something else, Coach," he said after telling Jonathan he was happy to hear from him. "I am now what is known as a personality. Did you ever think I would grow up to be a personality? The principal benefit is that I no longer go to the bathroom."

"I'm glad to see you've not lost your verve working in that nice, cool sewer," Jonathan said.

"How's that again?"

"An old joke, Dan. About the wife telling her husband how she slaves over a hot stove all day while he's working in that nice, cool sewer."

"You been slaving over a hot stove, Coach?"

"Well, in a way. Except that it's more like a hot story." He asked Dan if he had heard of the scheduled dinner.

"Nothing in the *Post*, I'm sure of that. There was a passing mention of it in the *Star*, but I was more impressed with another story the *Star* carried that wasn't in the *Post*. Something about an audit of the company owned by the Hinckleys."

"An audit?"

"Yeah. It was a strange one. The government audited the Hinckley oil company and said it owed two million big ones, or something like that. Come to think of it, it was Hinckley's brother who did the talking. You want to see it?"

"So bad I can taste it. Clip it and send it to me pronto, will you? And anything else you come across."

"Will do, Coach." There was a pause. "Hey, it just occurred to me that I've got one you'll love. It's here someplace." Jonathan heard the shuffling of papers before Doherty came back on the line. "I suspect you saw Alexander Haig in his peerless performance on the national stage just last night in which, while totally out of control, he caveated that the way he conceptualized the situation he was in control. Obviously, he contexted that wrongly."

"As a critic, you have just reaffirmed your impeccable

credentials as a master of the esoteric nuances of Haigspeak."
"Thank you. Well, follow this one, Coach. Front page headline in the morning *Washington Post:* Haig's Actions Again Raise Concern Over His Conduct. Front page headline in the afternoon *Washington Star:* Haig's Role During Crisis Wins Praise." He laughed loudly. "So much for the highly touted objectivity of the news columns in our nation's press. That's one worthy of your files, isn't it?"

"Daniel, you continue to warm my heart. Send me the two front pages, too, will you?"

"Sure. My sensitive nose for news tells me that you are off on another one of your studies, right?"

"Thus far all I have is one big rapidly developing mystery. I'll keep in touch, Dan. And thanks for your considerable help. I really appreciate it. If you hear anything you think I should know, give me a call."

What Jonathan didn't add, what he wasn't ready to tell anyone, was that he also had a hunch. His hunches had been tested while working on the staffs of three metropolitan newspapers and then honed in the years of teaching which required him to read for hours every day and then piece together the lectures that grew, organically, year after year, blossoming with different flowers, always fresh, sometimes weeded insufficiently but still an academic garden for which he made no apologies. At every university where he had been invited to be a visiting professor, students gave him a long standing ovation when he had delivered the last lecture of his courses. He knew he did some things very well—others not so well—and he had learned that his hunches had a rational base that was for the most part a reliable reflection of his varied experiences. He also was perfectly willing to admit that he sometimes saw phenomena that were invisible to the naked eye of others around him. He had never denied the accuracy of one student's evaluation of him as being "off the wall," but he treasured the scores of other evaluations by students who appreciated his lectures on many matters other professors either didn't know or, knowing, kept to themselves.

That, now, was behind him. The two letters on the table next to his chair summed up the imperatives of his new life. One envelope contained a copy of a divorce decree; the other an agonizingly apologetic note from the dean, saying that the request for another leave of absence (without pay) for the coming year could not be granted because blah blah blah. The dean, Jonathan thought, was a clone of Philip Roth's classic television commentator, Erect Severehead; harken ye to the dean: Saddened by the news of the divorce blah blah blah needs of the department blah blah blah budget blah blah class schedule blah blah contractual blah agreement blah blah blah blah blah blah. Just like all those press reports out of Washington all those years that "Our Gang" was in the White House. Well, so be it.

When his wife and son had come to Placer with him last summer the understanding was that he would return to teaching at the end of the sabbatical year. He wanted to spend that year on a newspaper, "hands-on" as all the pooping progressive academicians were now putting it. He had chosen Placer because he wanted the opposite of the crowded, crime-ridden life in East Bay. The *Trib* was happy to have him as a news editor for the year. All was settled.

Until the snows hit and his wife told him on a bleak day in the week between Christmas and the new year that she was taking their son and returning to their home in California. She showed him the thirty-day notice she had prepared for the renters and she said that if he didn't want to go with her or assure her he would return to the university, she would file for divorce. He had sat alone at nights in the stillness of that house and reflected on the gamble he had taken in trying to resuscitate a terminally diseased marriage by the move to Placer. In the parlance of gamblers, a long shot. In cases of calculated risk, he knew, defeat should always be anticipated, which is what made victory—if it came—all the sweeter. The sharp edges of the realized defeat, so painful in the chilling days of January and February, had softened with the first signs of the approach of spring. But this night, on the last day of March, he felt chilled again.

He walked into the living room and sat in a chair before the fireplace. The logs had been set, ready for a match for several days. A cold draft came down the chimney and spread across the floor of the room. He lit a match to start a fire. Crouched before the fireplace, he watched a thin blue spiral twist its way through several logs before disappearing into the black maw of the chimney. He heard the crackle of twigs beneath the logs, a favored sound. He wished that Sarah had enjoyed log fires, but she never regarded the fireplace as anything more than a decorative point around which chairs and sofa could be attractively placed. The ashes, she said more than once, made the room dusty, and fires weren't worth all the trouble anyway.

Once again he sat back in the chair, beginning to feel the warmth of the fire. Now the stillness no longer was oppressive; he had grown, in recent years, to like the combination of warmth and quiet. How many things, he mused with the beginning of a smile, had he grown accustomed to as the years had gone by. And how those years, especially since he turned thirty, had sped by, a burst of existence after the slow, grinding preparation of childhood and youth. Everything is relative, as the sages said, but especially time. Once, when he had turned eleven and had been promised a new suit—a man's suit—on his twelfth birthday, the year had dragged its way into an eternity. Where had the last ten—the last fifteen—gone? A puff, and they had passed.

But no—not quite. Time not only is relative; it is subtle, complex, deceiving, devilish. It has many sides, angles, shapes and forms, determined by the point of view. Some persons have no concept of it at all, whether it involves minutes, hours, days or all the days of one's life. Some waste it prodigiously, then harbor it covetously, often too late and at the wrong time. There! He smiled. See, one can't even describe time without using time in the description. It is elusive, a sprite that dances all around us but we can never touch it. A sprite that peels us like an onion, skin by skin—except that it never gets down to the heart. Always there are several layers left surrounding the heart. That's the problem; that's why time reveals a little bit at a time of every being, but it never discloses all. We live time, we live through time, and often we do not learn—in time.

If the recent years had seemed short, it must be noted at the same time—or rather in the same thought—that the years of his marriage had been long. His life had passed quickly, but the days since that wedding day had gone slowly. That wedding day—what promise, what promises, it had held.

It was, everyone said, a perfect marriage. Only the weather seemed to be against it, for it rained again, the sixth consecutive day, and pools of water had formed in the street outside the small wooden church. He lifted her in his arms and ran through the rain to the car at the curb. Mud covered his shoes and spattered his trousers, but he and his bride laughed along with family and friends who lined the walk to the open car door and then crowded about after they were inside.

"You carried her across the threshold," came one voice. "You gonna live in that car?"

He smiled, waved to them, blew a kiss and started down the street to the foot of the hill. They laughed and waved until they were out of sight.

When they came to a stop sign, Jonathan ran his hand through his black hair and shook the water from it. He smoothed his coat, then turned to his bride.

"Stick with me," he said, "and you'll be in diamonds."

"I'm already in diamonds," she answered. "See?"

She held out her left hand and he kissed it.

Fifteen months earlier Jonathan Blakely had come to the small California college to teach. It was clear from the start that the newcomer, fresh from his doctorate in American Studies, was an assistant professor of journalism on his way up, who couldn't miss in the lushest groves of academe. Students liked him, respected him and showed their appreciation of his classes, his concern and his advice. The self-proclaimed "Young Turks" of the faculty invited him to join their weekly luncheons and promoted a place for him on their most prestigious committees. The head of the college—President Reuben McLendon—awarded him the "Professor of the Year" prize at the commencement exercises.

None of this was lost on the young women of both town and gown. The coeds on the campus smiled when he passed and were warmed by the acknowledging nod of his head. Some would come to his office and speak invitingly to him. Mothers heard of him and hoped their daughters would somehow catch his eye. No doubt about it: Jonathan Blakely was a young man of extraordinary promise.

Marlys McLendon was not one to overlook an opportunity,

and she had prevailed on her husband to invite Jonathan to dinner after the graduation program. What she had hoped would happen had come to pass; there, in the largest of all houses on the hill, the president's home, her daughter charmed this young man with so promising a future. Champagne flowed on the evening they announced they would be married on the Sunday before Thanksgiving. Sarah McLendon, the only child of President and Mrs. Reuben McLendon, home with a degree from one of the Seven Sisters of the East, planning a summer trip to Europe that was unanimously canceled, had caught, quickly, the most eligible bachelor in the college town. They knew he was not wealthy, but no one, least of all the McLendons, believed that Jonathan Blakely would be an assistant professor for long. He was twenty-seven, just right for Sarah, who was four years younger, and the two of them together at parties, at the theater, at the football games were regarded as a most handsome couple. Everyone said it was a perfect marriage.

And still it rained. Jonathan began to think it might be an omen.

"In the Bible it was forty days and forty nights," he said. "We are well on our way toward that. But if we are going to be swept away in a flood I can't think of anyone I'd rather float with. And if we are to be saved on an ark in pairs, I can't think of anyone I'd rather replenish the race with."

A frown crossed the face of Sarah McLendon. "Jonathan," she said, "you mustn't talk like that."

He was puzzled by her response, but the surge of doubt was overwhelmed by another emotion. He leaned close to her ear. "Then," he whispered, "if it is deeds, not words, you want, my dear, then it is deeds you will have."

She did not smile nor did she acknowledge what he had said. He felt a tremor go through her body and he drew her closer. Sarah put her head on his shoulder.

"Oh, Jonathan, when will we get there?"

He wondered whether the voice reflected anticipation or trepidation. "It's not far now," he said.

Soon they were there, in a cabin nestled among the redwoods on the bank of a river, alone. He took her into his arms, and while the rain beat rhythmically on the roof and trickled down the sides of the cabin, making rivulets to the stream, Jonathan Blakely and Sarah McLendon sealed their marriage. Four nights later, in the same cabin, with rain falling as it had intermittently during their entire time there, she told him that perhaps it would be well if he did not love her so much, that she was not as demonstrative as he, that he ought to cool the impulses that did not, in the same degree, well within her. He was baffled at first, then mildly angry; he turned on his side and was awake most of the night while she slept peacefully next to him. Then it was she, for the remaining two nights before the honeymoon week was ended, who first turned to her side after a goodnight kiss. Back near the campus, in a home at the bottom of the hill a few weeks later, she was sick one morning and announced that for the next few months, until she was over first the nausea and then the birth, it would be best if he did not make love to her.

"But Sarah—" he said.

"No," she replied, touching his arm. "I can't. I just can't. Please try to understand, Jonathan."

He tried to understand; he made every effort to understand; he remained kind and considerate and affectionate.

"I love you so very much," he said again a few moments before the doctor entered the delivery room and motioned him to wait outside.

"Yes," she answered. "I know."

In the hours that followed before the birth of his son, Jonathan Blakely nervously and silently prayed for her safety, the birth of a well child and happiness in their marriage. Between his prayers, he wondered why she had not answered, as she had even during the trying preceding months, "And I love you, too."

APRIL

About nine hundred daily newspapers in the United States, comprising the great majority of the journals of influence and circulation, receive and print the news dispatches of the Associated Press.

This means that concerning any event of importance an identical dispatch is printed about fifteen million times and may be read by thirty million persons.

According to the construction and wording of that dispatch, so will be the impression these thirty million persons will receive, and the opinion they will form and pass along to others.

Here is the most tremendous engine for Power that ever existed in this world. If you can conceive all that Power ever wielded by the great autocrats of history, by the Alexanders, Caesars, Tamburlaines, Kubla Khans and Napoleons, to be massed together into one vast unit of Power, even this would be less than the Power now wielded by the Associated Press. . . .

Well-informed men know that the great Controlling Interests have secured most of the other sources and engines of Power. They own or control most of the newspapers, most of the magazines, most of the pulpits, all of the politicians and most of the public men.

We are asked to believe that they do not own or control the Associated Press, by far the most desirable and potent of these engines. We are asked to believe that the character and wording of the dispatches upon which depends so much public opinion is never influenced in behalf of the Controlling Interests. We are asked to believe that Interests that have absorbed all other such agencies for their benefit have overlooked this, the most useful and valuable of all. We are even asked to believe that, although the Associated Press is a mutual concern, owned by the newspapers, and although these newspapers that own it are in turn owned by the Controlling Interests, the Controlling Interests do not own, control or influence the Associated Press, which goes its immaculate way, furnishing impartial and unbiased news to the partial and biased journals that own it.

That is to say that when you buy a house you do not buy its foundations.

—Charles Edward Russell
Pearson's Magazine
April, 1914

Crazy wasn't the exact word. Some people used that word, usually with varying degrees of affection or bewilderment as they uttered it to describe Jonathan Blakely's state of mind at some particular moment. His students had seen him walk into class and immediately launch a furious, rostrum-pounding attack on some malevolence or idiocy or grotesquerie reported by the press or committed by the press. Not quite crazy; more accurately, he was fully aware that he was outraged more easily than almost anyone he had ever known. He would express his own astonishment that the young people at the university or the staffers in the news room, as the case may be, did not share his enthusiastic condemnation of the latest sin of government or corporation or press or whatever. He would express his appreciation when student or co-worker would give even the slightest sign of recognition of the intolerable condition currently under his consideration, but then a gloom ultimately would set upon him.

"Blakely is a tilter at windmills," he once overheard one professor tell another as he walked past an open office door.

"I feel like the nation's most lonesome academic proctologist," he once told the same professors who had expressed admiration for one of his just-published articles. "I am always poking my hand up the ass of America and sometimes I get so excited I forget to put my rubber glove on. Tell me, gentlemen, is there something wrong with me?"

What he suspected was wrong with him was his insistence

that the news media of America begin telling the citizens of America what was really happening in their country. Not the crap reported as those temporarily in the White House jousted for political advantage with partisans in Congress over a bill that had no possibility of getting through the Senate, or the endless other trivialities that filled the front pages and were used to lead off radio and television newscasts. Not the quick one-day brush telling of the latest example of cupidity and criminality of the corporations that control the political, economic and cultural system. Not the silly fascination with matters that would weigh as a feather on the scales of history. Pick a year, he would say, when Lyndon Johnson was president, or Eisenhower or Jimmy Carter, and go look at the microfilm of front pages of the *New York Times*. Then he would quote William Carlos Williams: "Look at / what passes for the new." The real "news" of our time, Jonathan would insist, lies buried in back pages of the established press or is reported only in muckraking periodicals or the quaint publications of those who are genuinely and unselfishly concerned with the course of specific national policies.

"If the national news media told the truth for seven consecutive days about the reasons our nation is going through what it is going through," he would say, "there would be an armed revolution at the end of the week." And he would write that sentence, too, and then, days later, crumple it and score two points in the corner wastebasket.

It had started—his "craziness"—in the late 1950s when, fresh out of college with degrees in history and journalism, he had taken a year to travel around the world. What he experienced first surprised him, then shocked him, then angered him. His professors of history, so concerned with such matters as the influence of bread on the French Revolution, had neglected to inform him that American corporations dominated the economies and, with the help of employees dispatched by the American government, the politics of many of the countries he visited. His political science professors had not once suggested that the Department of State was essentially concerned with protecting the interests of those same American corporations, always being careful to categorize those interests as "our" national interests. Nor had any of his history or political science professors challenged the idea that he had absorbed, primarily by some unrecognized process of osmosis, that those inhabitants of foreign countries who opposed the exploitation of their land and their resources by these same American corporations were communists linked directly to the totalitarian government of the Soviet Union.

In subsequent summers he traveled to Asia and Central and South America and to the Caribbean. He was in Thailand when he read *The Ugly American,* a novel that contained more of reality than all the pap he had read about Southeast Asia in the daily press and newsmagazines of the United States. His own perceptions of the same scenes confirmed Eugene Burdick's thesis that it was not the "beautiful people" of the "Golden Ghetto"—that is, the Americans sent abroad by the State Department—who served our country best, but the "ugly Americans" who live among the native population and come to understand their needs and their aspirations. (To this day, Jonathan is wryly amused by those who either misread or failed to read the book and continue to spread the myth that the "ugly American" is a "bad American.")

In the 1960s he prowled the ancient ruins of Mexico and Guatemala, smoked ganja with Rastafarians in Kingston, fought off an attack of dengue fever in Port-of-Spain while President Johnson fabricated the Gulf of Tonkin Resolution that sounded the knell of death for tens of thousands of America's young men, most of whom had never heard the bells tolling for them on Capitol Hill. He went to Selma as a free-lance reporter; he went back to Mexico to the Plaza of Three Cultures where government troops slaughtered that country's finest young people to make the world safe for the 1968 Olympics; he got out of Prague just before the Russian troops snuffed out the incipient freedom of that tortured nation. He went as a reporter to the steps of the Pentagon in 1967 and into the streets and parks of Chicago in 1968, subsequently writing long articles on the media miscoverage of those two events. He worked for newspapers in three cities, staying only a few months at each when he realized that the immutable law of diminishing returns applied with special force to the jobs of journalism. They were angry years, but they were the most exciting years of his life.

Thus anyone who knew him well also knew that his threshold of toleration for knavery was crossed before most people had even been offended. He could become livid with indignation when some politician—any politician, regardless of party, race, creed, sex or degree of venality, complicity or corruption—would say or support something that was replete with greed, patently false or blatantly hypocritical. He would castigate senators—especially Democrats, who weren't supposed to—who sold out to oil companies or pipeline promoters or wilderness violators or what had once been the railroads. He had no patience for any of the corporate whores who cared not what happened to earth, air, water, fellow man or fellow inhabitant so long as their salary checks continued to be deposited in the bank. He would fulminate against newspaper editors who violated even the least sacred of journalistic principles and he would damn the newsmagazines and other popular magazines as dedicated to the perverse interests of their advertisers, as corporate vehicles of distortion, as promoters of the concerns and interests of the privileged, as panderers to the worst instincts and most undeveloped tastes of the American society. He was known as a knowledgeable but stubborn bastard, filled with idealism and other qualities incompatible in a culture in thrall to Madison Avenue and ruled over by politicians, bureaucrats, industrialists, militarists, flacks, hucksters, shrinks and shysters. Naturally, a lot of people found Jonathan more than a bit too radical for their tastes, too prickly for their consciences, too adamant in the way he insisted that the only salvation for this nation was scrupulous adherence to political, economic and social justice.

On the other hand, when not at the moment outraged or outrageous, he was a witty and loyal friend, generous with requested advice, cheerful on the telephone, a source of anecdotes, information, stories and jokes, both current and classic. He was spectacular on the Frisbee field, both pitching and catching. Many of his friends were younger than he, having once been his students. His male friends generally forgave him his extremism in combating vice and enjoyed his more moderate virtues. Women, especially intelligent women, most especially beautiful and intelligent women, found him an enticing change from the run of men who wallowed in pursuit of wealth and conquest and who only rarely let a foreign idea pass the customs of their mind. Many of the women, he frequently was astonished to learn, thought often of him. He was not quite a man for all seasons, but he was a man who loved all seasons, even when he was experiencing temporary difficulty coping with the pervasive insanity, recognized or unrecognized, that surrounds us all.

The first day of April found him singularly outraged. Back in the news room, he sifted through the dailies from the other cities in the state and the few exchanges the *Tribune* had with other papers, mostly those in the same chain. He muttered and he clipped and he shook his head and he snorted and he uttered profanities directed principally at pork-barreling politicians, tit-sucking bureaucrats and well-known journalists far away in the nation's capital and in the nation's largest city. Deborah, in charge that day of the state desk, was only a few feet away but she could hear his mutterings and sense his growing rage. Knowing that none of his anger was directed at her, she could speak freely.

"I gave it as good a run as I could," she said. "The AP buried the dinner item at the bottom of journalism's hallowed pyramid in a roundup story, where it will either be lopped off for reasons of space or will be read by the faithful few who struggle to get that far. Even then the reader will get the point that it's relatively unimportant or it wouldn't be down that low. You're right, Jonathan, something funny is going on."

"Well, this *is* All Fools' Day," he said as he turned the pages of another newspaper. "But in case you haven't noticed, we have reached a point in our civilization where we not only number our World Wars but we actually celebrate the surrealistic myths that pass for what is important in our lives. That's the reality, Deborah darling, and that's no April fool."

Before she could reply he exploded.

"Hey! There it is!" He turned the front page of a newspaper toward her. "There it is on the front page of the *Gazette*. Somebody else thought it was worth the front page. I'd begun to doubt my sanity—or at least my sense of news values. Just as I thought—it's UPI. The AP had to pick it up from them but they buried it just as you said."

Deborah watched him. "You're grinning, as they say, from ear to ear. You also look like the cat that swallowed the canary. Get that damned smug smile off your face and tell me what's there."

"Baby, it's beautiful," he said. "Thank God for Denver UPI. Listen to this lead: 'Neil Bush, the son of Vice President George Bush, ducked behind the cover of a corporate bureaucracy Tuesday because his name was linked to the older brother of would-be presidential assassin John W. Hinckley Jr.' And listen to the supervisor of corporate relations for Standard Oil of Indiana, Amoco's parent company. Neil Bush is a land man for them. 'At this point, there is nothing to indicate we have any joint ventures with Vanderbilt.' At least he didn't say 'at this point in time.' Then it goes on to give the White House version of what happened—or didn't happen. Here—"

Deborah read the story of the friendship of the young members of the Hinckley and Bush families that had progressed to the stage that they were to gather on a special occasion at the home of Mr. and Mrs. Neil Bush.

"You know, Jonathan," she said, "the more I see of this the more I think you're on to something. It's really peculiar that AP isn't picking up on this story. Or anyone else, either."

Less than five minutes passed before Jonathan's phone rang.

"Dan Doherty in Washington, Coach. I have a dainty dish or three to set before the king. Are you ready? On second thought, let me rephrase that—are you sitting down?"

"Seated."

Jonathan listened silently, but his lips tightened and he nodded his head repeatedly as he took notes. He thanked Doherty, put down the phone and stared at Deborah.

"I'm numb," he said.

"More on the case?"

"Yeah. Several items. First, you know how we've been told that Hinckley was a hanger-on of the National Socialist Party a couple or three years ago and that they kicked him out because he was too unstable even for them? Well, what we haven't been told is that the Nazis also suspected that he was an informer for the FBI, and Dan says there may be good reason for them to think so. Among other things, when Hinckley was arrested at the Nashville airport with three handguns and fifty rounds of ammunition while President Carter was in town, the FBI never reported that arrest to the Secret Service."

"Jesus."

"Let me fill you in on a little history, Deborah. You remember Sara Jane Moore? Well, after they arrested her for taking a shot at President Ford, she kept insisting that she was an informer for the FBI. The interesting part is that the Secret Service had questioned her the night before the shooting and confiscated a .44-caliber weapon, but they didn't detain her because the San Francisco police department had told them that she had, in fact, operated as an informer for them and for what they called two federal agencies. Interesting footnote, wouldn't you say?"

"Exceedingly."

"Dan added a footnote of his own. He says the failure of the FBI to alert the Secret Service to Hinckley's weapons arrest bears a resemblance to the Kennedy assassination in Dallas when the FBI had a fat file on Lee Harvey Oswald but didn't alert the Secret Service. The Warren Commission gave them hell for that snafu. Ready for the next item?"

"I'm fascinated."

"Rightly so. Dan says a guy in the *New York Daily News* Washington Bureau told him that the Federal Aviation Administration sent Hinckley a letter saying he owed a $1,000 fine for the Nashville violation but nobody seems to know what happened to the demand. He wonders who fixed the ticket."

"Someone in city hall, I'll bet."

"Okay, now here's the final item from Doherty. Get this: After the president of the United States comes within an inch of losing his life—literally—the governor of the state of Colorado provides two Colorado state troopers as personal bodyguards for the parents while they go visit their son in a prison that doesn't have any bars. Hell, Deborah, I'm internationally famous for my compassion, but they're pushing me on this one. The plain naked truth for anyone to see is that there are hundreds of old-boy networks in this country and every single one of them goes on a straight line to Washington, D.C."

He stood up and shook his head. "There's more. Two planes were held up for the assassin's parents during their travels—one headed for Washington and one for Denver—and some passengers told Doherty that there was a couple aboard an Eastern Airlines plane who had security men and were getting VIP treatment. Then the airline and the government provided a way for the couple to get off the plane so that reporters couldn't see them or question them. See how they work together even at that level? The same way the corporation and government worked together to get Neil Bush off the hook on the scheduled dinner and the unscheduled quotes before they could rein him in and put out their official line."

"Like my papa used to say, it's not who you are but who you know," Deborah said.

"This gets more infuriating every day. You know how the government treated Oswald's mother? Like shit, baby, like shit. The poor lady was poor. The unconnected lady had no connections. But when somebody who contributes to political campaigns or otherwise oils the wheels of government gets his tit caught in a wringer, if you'll pardon John Mitchell's reference to Katie Graham's bosom, the fucking Red Sea will be parted for him if necessary. You notice how no pillars of the establishment in high commerce or high politics or high courts ever go to jail?"

Donald J. Bitterman, managing editor of the *Placer Tribune*, possessor of a view of the world almost directly contrary to that of Jonathan, looked up.

"If you will stop banging your spoon on your tray," he said quietly, "you might notice that half of Mr. Nixon's White House staff went to prison, a fact that seems to have escaped your ken, Jonathan."

"Bullshit!" Jonathan almost shouted the word. "Precisely my point. Those guys committed felonies of monumental proportions deserving of thirty years on any balanced scales of justice and they're sentenced to a few months at private tennis clubs provided for them and their kind by the United States government. They send Mitchell to the Swanee Sheraton and Haldeman and Ehrlichman get rooms in the federal camp for bad boys in sunny California. Agnew rips off a quarter of a million dollars and goes free while some black guy who netted fifty-five dollars at a filling station is put away for fifteen years in a goddamn two-by-four cage in a medieval state prison. You know, Donald, for a smart guy, which you are, you can be intolerably fatuous at times."

The managing editor grinned. "Gotcha! I cast out a Royal Coachman and you come two feet out of the water to get it. You know, I hate to tell you this, Jonathan, but for a smart guy, which you are, you ought to know it's even worse in Russia."

"In your right ear, Don. What you stalwarts of reaction never seem to get through your heads is that I love this system. Can you hear? I love this system. I despise beyond description the sons of bitches who take advantage of it and corrupt it and degrade it and get away with it. They're the ones who require rehabilitation and never seem to get it." Then he laughed. "All right, I can see I'm not going to change the world from this vantage point. Back to work."

In the days that followed, as Jonathan's newspapers arrived at Rudy's and the mail brought clippings and his phone calls to friends and former students frequently documented his suspicions, he became, as everyone in the news room noted, curiously less outraged. He scissored stories from the exchanges; he quietly took notes when the assassination stories were reported on the television set near his desk; he tentatively replied to questions concerning his progress that he was finding new stuff all the time.

"For instance," he said to Deborah one midnight over Grand Marnier in his living room, "one of the most strained portions of the scenario we have been presented thus far is the contention that young Hinckley is seen off at Stapleton by his mother, flies to Los Angeles, and then a few hours later boards a bus for a cross-country trip that ends in Washington, D.C., the day before President Reagan is shot. That's not what you'd call standard behavior, to put it charitably, right? Okay, now look at this." He handed her a white card, four inches by six inches. Typed there was:

THE ASSASSINATION CHAIN—p. 273
Assassins of JFK, RFK, MLK & attempted assass of Geo Wallace (Oswald, Sirhan, Ray, Bremer):

"Based upon one startling set of circumstances—that all four assassins had been in Los Angeles at one time or another, a million-to-one coincidence...."

"And that book was published in 1976," he said. "Look at this story in the *Rocky Mountain News* that never got on the wire, as far as I can tell. And how about all the unexplained contradictions in that cockamamie tale they put out about how he did it all for Jodie Foster? Those government guys back there have nothing but contempt for the American press and the American public. They think they can get away with anything, and why shouldn't they? They've been doing it since the end of World War Two and they get better at it all the time, with all the practice they've had."

"I think you're on the way to making a conspiracy buff out of me," Deborah said. "But what is it, Jonathan? What do you think is going on?"

"I don't know yet. But I'm finding out something that blows my mind almost every day now. I'm going to stay with this one."

An understatement. He spent his mornings going through the newspapers stacked in his living room, pulling out the pages that had stories related to the attempt to kill the president. He bought the newsmagazines and over morning coffee he circled with a red felt pen the strangely few references to an event that miraculously had failed to change the course of world history; he would jerk out the pages and toss the remainder under the kitchen sink. "With the rest of the garbage," he would explain to visitors. On his days off he spent many hours on the campus, using the university library and the journalism department's reading room to bolster his research. He pecked away at his typewriter and revised drafts and added and subtracted and multiplied and divided sentences and paragraphs.

As April moved toward its end, the events of the afternoon of March 30 drifted out of the news columns and off the airwaves. The president was sufficiently recovered to carry out his public duties. The media promulgated and the public accepted the official versions of what had motivated the feckless drifter and how he had attempted to fulfill his psychopathic fantasies.

Jonathan decided he would wait for the trial—if ever there was one—before going to the white paper of the final manuscript. He showed the blue draft and some notes of additional research to Deborah and to Robert Robinson, the *Tribune's* editor of the editorial page, adding a note that he had many leads still to pursue, especially concerning Jodie Foster, perhaps the most puzzling and intriguing character in this unfolding play worthy of an Ionesco, a Beckett or the other devotees of the theater of the absurd. He remained convinced, as he read the comments of his first two readers in the margins of the preliminary manuscript, that his article was off to a start he would have to finish.

THE AFTERNOON OF MARCH 30
On the morning of March 30, 1981, Scott Hinckley, 30-year-old vice president of the Vanderbilt Energy Corporation, sat in his seventeenth-floor downtown Denver office and listened as representatives of the United States Department of Energy reported that its auditors had uncovered evidence of two million dollars in pricing violations on crude oil sold by the company from 1977 through 1980.

Three DOE auditors, presenting their "preliminary conclusions" of a "routine audit" which had begun on January 2, informed the corporation officials present that the federal government was considering a potential penalty of two million dollars and asked Scott Hinckley to explain the alleged serious overcharges. Scott Hinckley requested "several hours to come up with an explanation."

The meeting ended a little more than an hour before President Reagan and three other persons were shot in Washington, D.C.

The auditors, in the hours after the assassination attempt, decided not to press Scott Hinckley for information "at this time." A spokesman for the DOE in Washington said later that day that "we don't think there is any connection" between the auditors' meeting with Scott Hinckley and the attempt to assassinate President Reagan, "but we can't prove that conclusively."

The Washington Star *reported that the information about the overcharge and the Monday morning meeting was con-*

firmed by what it called "a very, very high-ranking White House official."

Vanderbilt Energy, a Texas corporation with headquarters in Denver, was founded in 1970 by John W. Hinckley Sr. with $120,000 and "no oil or gas production, no leases and no staff," according to its annual report. By 1981 it had gas and oil reserves in eight states and the Canadian province of Alberta. For the 1980 fiscal year, the firm reported a profit of $805,042 on total revenues of $4,875,385. It reportedly operates 204 producing or shut-in oil and gas wells. Only five properties had been covered in the "preliminary closeout" of the audit.

A corporation secretary termed the revelation of the audit "a complete coincidence."

* * *

On the afternoon of March 30, John Warnock Hinckley Jr., 25-year-old younger son of John W. Hinckley Sr. and brother of Scott Hinckley, fired six Devastator bullets aimed at the president of the United States. He was arrested and subsequently incarcerated in what the press described as a "prison without bars," a "campus-like federal prison" with "dormitory-style rooms instead of cells" at Butner, N.C. His assassination attempt occurred only five days after he had parked his car—still carrying Texas license plates—in the garage of his tri-level family home in the exclusive pine-dotted Hiwan Country Club development about 25 miles southwest of Denver. He had checked out of his $10.60-a-night room in the nearby Golden Hours Motel on March 23 and on March 25 he was driven to Stapleton International Airport and seen off to Los Angeles by his mother.

He had visited his family at Christmas and when his parents went on trips he often would take care of the house.

One of his court-appointed attorneys told a reporter that Hinckley might own some stock in the family business but that Hinckley had no control over it and no authority to dispose of it.

The only words the news media reported Hinckley saying in the aftermath of his arrest and at least through the entire month of April were "yes, sir" and "no, sir" in response to a judge, except to describe "his only apparent liquid asset," a white Plymouth Volare.

* * *

Within hours of the attempt on the life of the president, agents of the Federal Bureau of Investigation sealed the contents of John W. Hinckley Jr.'s Park Central hotel room in Washington, D.C., from which he had made two local telephone calls. The official records of John W. Hinckley Jr. at Texas Tech University were similarly sequestered. The Hinckley family residence in Evergreen, Colo., was locked by federal authorities and searched the following morning by the FBI; what was found remains a government secret because a federal magistrate in Denver, at the request of a local U.S. attorney, sealed the search warrant and an accompanying affidavit. A U.S. district judge then denied a request by a Denver television station to allow reporters access to the filed papers, which normally are a matter of public record. Said Judge Fred Winner, propounding an extraordinary thesis that pitted the interests of American citizens against those of the press: "This is a matter of balancing the rights of media against the rights of the defendant and the rights of the government and the rights of the public." He added that the sealing of the documents cannot be done "in perpetuity," and that "somewhere along the line the search warrant, the affidavit and the inventory (of evidence) has to become public property."

No member of the press, as far as can be determined, has seen any of the sealed material. Everything pertinent to the investigation of the attempt to assassinate the president remains in the hands of agencies of the United States government.

* * *

Except for the events in Washington the day before, Neil Bush, 26-year-old son of Vice President George Bush, and Scott Hinckley, older brother of John W. Hinckley Jr., would have dined together in Denver on the evening of March 31.

The dinner party for four was canceled.

Neil Bush, a land man for Amoco Oil, told Denver reporters a few hours before the dinner had been scheduled to take place that he had met Scott Hinckley only once—at a surprise party at the Bush home January 23, which reportedly was 21 days after the DOE had begun what was termed a "routine audit" of the books of the Vanderbilt Energy Corporation. He said he couldn't recall what he and Scott Hinckley might have talked about, or for how long, but he considered Scott Hinckley his friend.

"My wife set up a surprise birthday party for me, and it truly was a surprise, and it was an honor for me at that time to meet Scott Hinckley," Neil Bush said. "To have one meeting doesn't make the best of friends, but I have no regrets in saying I do know him."

The Houston Post quoted Neil Bush as saying shortly after the assassination attempt that the Hinckley family had "given a lot of money" to his father's unsuccessful campaign for the Republican presidential nomination. Neil Bush's wife, Sharon, also said the Bush family knew the Hinckley family because of their large contributions to the Bush campaign. Said Sharon of the Hinckleys:

"From what I know and have heard, they are a very nice family... and have given a lot of money to the Bush campaign. I understand he (John Hinckley Jr.) was just the renegade brother in the family. They must feel awful."

The next day both the Washington and Houston offices of Vice President Bush denied what Neil Bush and his wife had been quoted as saying. The deputy press secretary in Washington told reporters: "We've checked the records and we find no evidence of contributions to Bush from the Hinckley family." A member of Bush's staff in Houston said that Bush's son "probably made a mistake" in saying the Hinckleys contributed to Bush. Neil Bush then denied to Denver reporters that the Hinckley family had made "large contributions" to his father's campaign and refused to talk further with the press. Calls were referred to the White House press offices of Vice President Bush.

The Dallas Morning News, however, subsequently reported

that the senior Hinckley had made a contribution to George Bush's 1970 campaign for the United States Senate, one of Bush's two unsuccessful attempts to be elected to that office from Texas.

In 1978, Neil Bush served as campaign manager for his oldest brother, George W. Bush, who ran unsuccessfully as the Republican candidate for the United States House of Representatives from the district that includes Lubbock, Texas. Neil Bush, who said he lived throughout most of 1978 in Lubbock, which is where John Hinckley lived off and on from 1973 to 1980, said soon after the assassination attempt that he did not know if he had met John Hinckley, brother of Scott Hinckley. "I have no idea," he said. "I don't recognize any pictures of him. I just wish I could see a better picture of him."

George W. Bush said in his home in Midland, Texas, that it was possible his brother met John Hinckley Jr. in Lubbock. He said he also was unsure whether he might have met John Hinckley Jr. "It's certainly conceivable that I met him or might have been introduced to him" in Lubbock, George W. Bush said. "I don't recognize his face from the brief, kind of distorted thing they had on TV and the name doesn't ring any bells. I know he wasn't on our staff. I could check our volunteer rolls."

He said, however, that he had heard of Hinckley's father's oil company, Vanderbilt Energy Corporation.

The comment of a White House spokesman on the Scott Hinckley-Neil Bush dinner engagement: "A bizarre happenstance." A spokeswoman for Vice President Bush: "A total coincidence."

* * *

John W. (Jack) Hinckley Sr., like Vice President Bush a millionaire Texas oilman, moved his family to the idyllic Denver suburb of Evergreen in 1974. He had a reputation as a strict disciplinarian. According to friends, he "set high standards for his children" and the brother and sister of John W. Hinckley Jr. "seemed to live up to them." Sister Diane was head cheerleader and a homecoming princess at Highland Park High School, the most prestigious public high school in the

Dallas area, majored in education at Southern Methodist University in Dallas and married a Dallas insurance salesman. Brother Scott earned academic honors in mechanical engineering at Vanderbilt University in Nashville, Tenn., and Jack Hinckley, according to the Wall Street Journal, was "so pleased with his son's accomplishments that he changed the name of his Hinckley Oil Company to Vanderbilt Energy Corporation." The company is one of an estimated 2,000 to 3,000 high-risk independent oil companies with headquarters in Denver, many of them in anticipation of an oil shale and coal development boom on Colorado's Western Slope, which has been slowed by the Reagan administration. They are known as "Little Oil," to distinguish them from the seven or eight major companies known as "Big Oil."

Jack Hinckley was characterized repeatedly in newspaper and magazine stories and on radio and television as a strong supporter of President Reagan. However, in addition to his contribution to the 1970 Senate campaign of George Bush, the only 1980 presidential campaign contributions cited by a spokesman for the Federal Elections Commission were a $200 contribution by the senior Hinckley in September, 1979, and a $250 contribution by Scott Hinckley the following month to the campaign of John Connally, who at that time was campaigning hard to defeat Ronald Reagan for the Republican presidential nomination.

* * *

John Hinckley Jr. was an avid follower of the Kamikaze Klones, a Colorado rock band described by its leader as "antiestablishment, anti-nuke, anti-system and pro-conservation."

"I used to see him at some of our shows and he was always alone," lead singer Jimmy Murphy, 26, told the Boston Globe the night of March 30. "I haven't seen him since December or January and was surprised we didn't see him at our show in Evergreen last night. I didn't know Hinckley that well, just saw him on the streets and would say hello. We've played a few games of pool together."

Murphy also said: "I know his older brother Scott pretty well *and that's how I met John."*

* * *

Vice President George Bush, transplanted Yankee, son of a partner in a New York investment firm, owner of a Texas oil-drilling company, congressman who had established an unimpeachable record as an unwavering friend of the oil industry, was chairman of the Republican National Committee during the Watergate scandal and a onetime director of the Central Intelligence Agency among his many other appointments. He reportedly spent "15 agonizing minutes" wondering, as Air Force Two returned to Washington from Texas, whether he was about to become president of the United States. His aides prepared him for the possibility that he would be sworn in as president before the day had passed.

Two Bush aides who were on the flight said the vice president gave no indication that he knew about or recognized the Hinckley name. "Frankly," said one of them, "I was with him until we helicoptered back to the Naval Observatory (the vice presidential residence), and I don't believe at that point we even knew the name of who had been charged in this."

Bush's press secretary, replying later to a query from a reporter about "the Hinckley-Bush connection," said: "I don't know a damned thing about it. I was talking to someone earlier tonight and I couldn't even remember his (Hinckley's) name." He was certain, however, that the vice president, if he was familiar with any members of the Hinckley family, "made no mention of it whatsoever." The vice president, he said, "certainly didn't indicate anything like that."

Bush "huddled with U.S. Rep. Jim Wright, D-Texas, the House majority leader... and others," the Houston Post *reported, "but refused to talk with the three reporters on the plane." The Democratic majority leader of the U.S. House of Representatives had been the "host" of the Republican vice president for the latter's Texas speaking engagements. He said Bush "exhibited a demeanor and a strength of character that everybody in the whole United States would be proud of."*

The initially cool relationship Bush had with the man he

challenged in a hard-fought primary campaign for the Republican presidential nomination—especially when he accused Reagan of advocating "voodoo economics"—reportedly had warmed. Only a few days earlier he had won a power struggle with Secretary of State Alexander Haig when President Reagan named him to head the White House "crisis management team."

It was widely reported in the national news media that Bush was in Texas to address an association of Southwestern cattle ranchers and the Texas state legislature. But when the would-be assassin's bullets struck the president and three other men in the nation's capital, Vice President Bush had just finished a luncheon address himself in Fort Worth. Unreported in the national news media was the fact that he had officially dedicated the renovated Hyatt Regency Hotel, owned by Ray Hunt, son of Mrs. H.L. Hunt and the late H.L. Hunt. The hotel also was being dedicated as a national historical site, since it was formerly the Hotel Texas, built in 1921, but not because it was where John F. Kennedy spent his last night on earth. The vice president was introduced at the luncheon by Mrs. H.L Hunt.

* * *

All of the information in the preceding paragraphs was published in various metropolitan daily newspapers. Yet much of it will be news to most Americans. The item about the scheduled dinner of the accused assassin's brother and the vice president's son is probably the single tenuous link between a Hinckley and a Bush that received wide distribution in a portion of the national news media. The rest of the information has been denied to all but a minuscule percentage of the population of the United States.

The reason is simple: With only the one cited exception, the rest of the story never "got on the wire" or was buried deeply in the mass of other assassination news. The Associated Press chose not to "pick up" relevant stories published by its member newspapers—especially items in the Washington Star, the Houston Post and the Denver Rocky Mountain News. United Press International started to cover the story and then *drew back.* The three major national news magazines—Time, Newsweek, *and* U.S. News & World Report—*although certainly in possession of most of the facts of the "connection," chose not to include the news in their columns (except for a typically insipid dismissal of one item by* Newsweek *as part of a derisive sidebar mocking the possibility of a conspiracy to assassinate the president when the investigation had hardly begun). The three national television networks, possibly because of their notorious reliance on the wire services to set their agenda, did not report on the several extraordinary "coincidences" or, in the case of NBC News, did not follow up on John Chancellor's raised-eyebrow report of the Hinckley-Bush dinner. Those daily newspapers of this country that rely almost exclusively on AP and/or UPI for their national and international news had no way of knowing what was* not *being sent to them.*

Two significant and potentially dangerous developments affecting the news media and the people of the United States took place in the wake of the attempt to kill President Reagan:

1) The two major wire services and all of the national organs of news dissemination somehow managed to publish or broadcast hardly a word that did not fit into the scenario rapidly pieced together by the authorities in the hours after the four men were wounded on the sidewalk outside the Washington Hilton. This especially included the successful attempt to keep the American people from knowing of several striking connections between the families of the accused assassin and the man who narrowly missed becoming president of the United States;

2) The major national organs of news dissemination, in a stunning example of the free press of the United States failing its historical obligations to serve as a "watchdog" and a check on the arbitrary actions of government, did virtually nothing to resist what might well be an unprecedented usurpation of the channels of information by law enforcement and intelligence agencies of the federal government. The patently ludicrous—and dangerous—concept of "government ownership of information" propounded by Richard Nixon had become an accomplished—and smoothly accomplished—fact less than a decade after his disgrace. The press of America was fed only what the highest authorities in the administration of justice deemed willing to feed it and only when the feeding served their purposes. This arrogance of the agencies of government was accepted with an alarming subservience by the news media. The vast majority of the citizens of this country, therefore, know only what the federal government, with the inexplicable cooperation of the national news media, decided was proper for them to know about the attempt to snuff out the life of Ronald Reagan. In the process, a classic case of "disinformation" simultaneously was set in motion. Please follow:

Soon after the sickening spectacle of yet another American president or potential president being shot was shown on national television, the first information on John Warnock Hinckley Jr. was hastily promulgated. Eleven hours after the burst of gunfire it was established that he was "a drifter" who "had been taking Valium for some time and had undergone psychiatric therapy," described by his parents, from whom he was "estranged," as "wandering, aimless and irresponsible." He was further characterized as an "emotionless" youngest son of "a fine family" in Colorado, who had grown up in a mansion with amenities "like a machine that dispensed Coca-Cola to thirsty youngsters" in Highland Park, Texas. He was eight years old when John F. Kennedy was assassinated only five miles from his home. He was a transient occupant of seedy motels who recently had left behind an unpaid bill of $55.40, a onetime member of the American Nazi Party who had been thrown out because he felt the Nazis "were not sufficiently militant for him" (documented by a photograph of "Hinckley" at a Nazi rally in St. Louis), who probably had "stalked President Carter" (and possibly Ronald Reagan) and was represented by two court-appointed lawyers. He had been arrested the previous October at a Nashville airport for trying to board a plane with three guns in his suitcase, had paid a $62.50 fine and then had flown to Dallas where he bought a pair of .22-caliber revolvers for $47 each at Rocky's Pawn Shop near the Texas School Book Depository. He had attended Texas Tech University sporadically for seven years, living in one-room apartments and eating junk food, had studied Mein Kampf there, had later lied on employment application forms and had never held any job for long. His motive, finally, was "an unrequited romantic obsession with 18-year-old film star Jodie Foster," featured in the motion picture Taxi Driver, in which a psychopathic hack stalks a politician and plans to assassinate him.

Editorial writers and syndicated columnists leaped out of the blocks with analyses of the state of the nation based on this conglomeration of information, supposition and misinformation. Four days later, however, we were informed that much of what we first had been told was now, as the uneasy ghost of Ron Ziegler would have it, "inoperative." The American public was asked to adjust to a new reality:

The Associated Press, which had rushed us the news of John Hinckley's Nazi connections on the basis of unconfirmed, inconsistent and contradictory claims of two American Nazis, now reported that the accused assassin's membership in the National Socialist Party of America "was the subject of growing doubt" and statements of the two Nazi spokesmen were "being viewed by federal authorities as vague and insignificant." The Daily Oklahoman also reported that federal authorities had concluded that the "Hinckley-Nazi connection may have been fabricated for publicity purposes." And then the man in the Nazi uniform at the St. Louis rally, in two photographs published in almost every country that had sufficient technology to reproduce them, turned out not to be "Hinckley" after all; the AP, which had shelled out $2,750 for the photographs on the unchecked word of a free-lance photographer, explained to its members and readers three days later that the man in the picture had been found and lo, it wasn't Hinckley.

(In addition to its obvious travails in the wake of the assassination attempt, the Associated Press fell victim to a memorable sting by a Los Angeles "psychic" who had "predicted" on a television show "taped in January" that President Reagan would experience "a thud" in "the chest area" during "the last few days of March," and that "someone fairhaired" named "something like Jack Humbly" would be involved. After titillating the nation for a couple of days with a notable lack of professionally sufficient attribution or adequate qualification of the hustler's claims, the AP had to admit that *the forecast details of "President Reagan's brush with death" had been taped after the event.)*

Suddenly, after we have been brought to attention, we discover that the former resident of seedy motels is now represented by associates of the famed and prestigious Washington law firm headed by millionaire Edward Bennett Williams, a former treasurer of the Democratic National Committee and owner of the Baltimore Orioles baseball team. Psychiatrists retained by the parents of the accused conduct tests while the director of the Federal Bureau of Investigation complains to Chicago Tribune *correspondents that agents have been denied access to the prisoner because lawyers hired by his parents obtained a court order keeping them out. Young Hinckley had been supported on his many travels by his wealthy parents—indeed, he had paid his $62.50 fine in Nashville from a roll of $800 in cash he was carrying—and he and his brother and sister, according to 1976 Securities and Exchange Commission records, own 79,437 shares of stock in their father's corporation. Then he is visited by his parents who had been accompanied to Butner, N.C., by two security guards provided by a friend of Hinckley Sr., Colorado Governor Richard Lamm.*

It was at this point that a fresh red herring was dragged across the track being pursued by our baying newshounds.

THE "HINCKLEY-RICHARDSON CONSPIRACY"

The unwillingness of the national news media to explore the intriguing connections that link Washington, D.C., to the luxurious suburbs of Dallas—and now the suburbs of "Little Dallas": Denver—was in especially puzzling contrast to the fervid pursuit of the possibility of a "Hinckley-Richardson conspiracy" that floated for days before disappearing from sight. The news media wallowed in the potentialities of a conspiracy involving still another "drifter and loner" with deep psychological problems—this one, as UPI pointedly phrased it, "from the middle class Drexel Hill suburb of Philadelphia." One Edward M. Richardson, 22, was arrested at a New York City bus terminal on April 7 and charged with threatening the life of President Reagan. The picaresque grotesqueries that followed were worthy of the heyday of William Randolph Hearst. Some selected short subjects:

Federal authorities were searching today for any possible connection between accused presidential assailant John W. Hinckley Jr. and a man arrested here with a loaded pistol who allegedly threatened to "bring to completion Hinckley's reality." (AP)

A number of parallels between Richardson and Hinckley have emerged. Both had apparently been captivated by the 18-year-old Miss Foster.
Both stayed briefly at the Park Plaza Hotel in New Haven, Conn., and sent letters to Miss Foster. Both had recently lived in Lakewood, Colo., just outside Denver.
Both had been unable to find work and appeared to have been drifting around the country with little purpose in the weeks before they allegedly took action against the president.
But federal authorities reiterated Wednesday that they had found no evidence that the two men had ever met. (New York Times News Service)

However, the (New York) Daily News quoted sources as saying the Secret Service was investigating reports the two may once have been roommates. (AP)

An acquaintance, Keith Perry, 17, of Drexel Hill, said he and Richardson were among a group routinely frisked by the Secret Service before a visit to nearby Lansdowne last September by then President Jimmy Carter.
Perry said Richardson remarked: "Wouldn't it be funny if the president got shot?" When Perry asked him why, he said Richardson replied, "He's the president."
A former high school classmate, Peter H. Griffin, said Richardson had a fascination with spectacular crime.
"I remember when Gerald Ford was shot, he got real interested in Squeaky Fromme. He knew everything about it."...

> Richardson's last employer, landscaper Jack Cireale, said he twice was forced to take Richardson home from work early. He quoted the young man as telling him, "I just can't get it together. I need some sleep." (UPI)

> The letter found in the hotel room indicated that Richardson shared Hinckley's "affection" for Foster, said James D'Amelio, agent in charge of the Secret Service's New York office. However, copies of the letter given to reporters in New Haven had part of the text blotted out and the remaining text had no direct reference to the actress; FBI agents refused to explain why the letter was censored. (AP)

> Richardson wrote to the actress that he had attended a Yale student production in which she was performing last weekend, intending to shoot her. But, he wrote, he decided she was "too beautiful to kill." (UPI)

On the same day the AP was reporting that "federal agents can find no connection between the man accused of shooting President Reagan and a man arrested in New York City and charged with threatening the president's life," it nonetheless sent out an extensive "profile" on the latter exploring in considerable detail his penchant for "fantasizing." Like an Escher drawing, the Richardson fantasy was etched into the Hinckley fantasy to become a news media fantasy within a federal law enforcement fantasy within a governmental fantasy within— yes, who-knows-whose fantasy....

As a final note to this journalistic/governmental descent into drivel, ponder three days of coverage, including two front-page stories, starting April 8 in the St. Louis Post-Dispatch:

> A copycat gunman threatened to kill President Ronald Reagan, Secretary of State Alexander M. Haig Jr., Sen. Jesse Helms and teenage actress Jodie Foster because of a "prophetic dream" sent by would-be assassin John W. Hinckley Jr., law enforcement officials say....
> "I will finish what Hinckley started. RR must die. He

(JWH) has told me so in a prophetic dream. Sadly, though, your death is also required," officials said Richardson wrote Miss Foster in a letter hand-delivered Monday to the Yale campus. (Compiled from News Services)

April 9:

Secret Service agents fearing copycat assassination attempts on President Ronald Reagan are investigating similarities between two letters that threaten his life and promise to turn America to the left.

Five days before Reagan was shot, an anonymous letter mailed from Grand Junction, Colo., to The Evangelist magazine in Baton Rouge, La., contained wording almost identical to that of a letter found Monday and allegedly written by Edward Richardson, law enforcement sources said....

David Hail, a spokesman for the Rev. Jimmy Swaggart, who owns The Evangelist, said the letter received by the magazine March 30 said, "Ronald Reagan will be shot to death and the country will turn to the left."

In the other letter, recovered Monday from Richardson's hotel room in New Haven, Conn., the unemployed laborer is accused of writing, "Ultimately, Ronald Reagan will be shot to death and this country turned to the 'left.' "

Both Hinckley and Richardson were in Lakewood, Colo., a suburb of Denver, in early March, but the Secret Service said they have found no evidence of links between the two....

Grand Junction, where the letter to The Evangelist was mailed, is halfway across Colorado from Denver. (UPI)

And April 10:

Edward Richardson, who has been indicted for threatening to kill President Ronald Reagan, underwent psychiatric testing in a New York jail today.

> Richardson, 22, is one of seven men across the country—including one in St. Louis—who have been arrested for threatening the president....(UPI)

No mention in this story of John Hinckley Jr. The "Hinckley-Richardson conspiracy" vanished into the phantasmagoria from which it had been plucked. The coverage was equally extensive on all the television networks over the same period. Deserving of special mention is the New York Times, which front-paged the Richardson arrest and possible conspiratorial ties to Hinckley, provided its readers with three days of extensive coverage of the potential links and then silently let the matter drop. Obviously the agencies of law enforcement and the national news media are willing to engage in speculation concerning the possibility of an assassination conspiracy only when it does not concern people in high places.

MAY

*A newspaper is a collection of half-injustices
Which, bawled by boys from mile to mile,
Spreads its curious opinion
To a million merciful and sneering men,
While families cuddle the joys of the fireside
When spurred by tale of dire lone agony.
A newspaper is a court
Where every one is kindly and unfairly tried
By a squalor of honest men.
A newspaper is a market
Where wisdom sells its freedom
And melons are crowned by the crowd.
A newspaper is a game
Where his error scores the player victory
While another's skill wins death.
A newspaper is a symbol,
It is feckless life's chronicle,
A collection of loud tales
Concentrating eternal stupidities,
That in remote ages lived unhaltered,
Roaming through a fenceless world.*

— Stephen Crane
circa 1894

The editorial across the left three columns at the top of the page didn't look any better to Robert Robinson in the morning than it had when it was pasted up the afternoon before. The publisher had come up with another of his booster pieces that could have been written in the front office of the Placer Chamber of Commerce, the same dreary litany that favored jobs over clean air, preferred a temporarily bustling economy to a healthy environment and offered an invitation to outsiders to add another chapter to the historic rape of the state. The target: the "no-growth do-gooders." Everything except a stab at "bleeding-heart liberals" and the professors up at the university "who never met a payroll." A monument to the thesis that the American press, by and large, serves the interests of the rich, the powerful, the greedy. Always wrapped in the decorative cloak of the flag, tied together with statistics and other lies, presented as an unwanted gift to the legions of readers who long ago had given up reading the tripe on the page with the exception of Robinson's signed editorials, the letters to the editor and Doonesbury.

Robert Robinson, editor of the editorial page of the *Placer Tribune*, sat in his office and stared moodily at his VDT. He needed a satisfactory concluding paragraph for the editorial he was writing. What can you say about the reasons the concrete is crumbling and holes have appeared in the deck of the bridge constructed only a few years ago across the river that runs through the town? How can you word it so the nervous lawyer retained by the paper, who surely would go over this editorial at the new publisher's nervous suggestion, would not nervously conclude that it would be best to delete the final paragraph to avoid any possibility of a libel suit? How can you keep from offending the contractor so that the nervous little business manager, after receiving a phone call, would not go to the publisher with another one of his complaints that Robinson was antagonizing the advertisers? And—as a wave of unease just this side of nausea passed over him—how can you follow an act like that shitty editorial the publisher put in the paper this morning? Too much; too much.

Robinson years ago had won the battle with an earlier publisher by insisting that all editorials be signed, a departure from traditional journalistic practice. Not many papers had followed his lead, but at least it got him off the hook in Placer and throughout the state. No calls this morning about the editorial because readers had learned some time ago to look at the end of the *Tribune*'s editorials to see who had written them before embarking on the journey down the willowy lane of opinion. In the first months after the arrival of the new publisher, Robinson had received calls asking him how he could continue to work on the paper when the publisher contradicted him and how could he stand working for that infuriating fathead and why didn't he quit and start a weekly that the town richly needed, deserved and would support? But Robinson would tell them that the publisher really left him pretty much alone, never asked him to write anything he didn't believe, and as far as the contradictory editorials went—the head honcho back in the middle of the country had firmly established in his annual reports to the stockholders down through the years that his desire for profitable enterprises was several degrees warmer than his concern for journalistic excellence. Nothing would change that, unfortunately, Robinson would say, and he'd continue to plug along. . . .

He wondered again at the combination of circumstances that might explain why he felt so lousy. Nothing he ate, he concluded; it was his life, his whole life, his life until this very moment. The people out there who *don't understand* and, even more damning, *never will understand.* He almost always rejoiced in publishing letters to the editor critical of his editorial positions because they often betrayed a notable lack of information, logic, judgment and mastery of even the more elementary rules of grammar and syntax. But the one in this morning's paper, below the publisher's offensive editorial, bothered him. It was from a prominent politician objecting to an editorial containing a passing reference to a candidate's brochure that included a photograph that "made him look like a politician." Most of the barely literate letter fluffed out the billowing pillow of self-serving pap, but Robinson almost gagged on the line that referred to politics as "the most noble of all professions." Spare us that, sir, he had said aloud as he cleaned up the spelling and punctuation for publication, but this morning, in re-reading it, he experienced added evidence that he wasn't feeling well.

These had been difficult weeks. He thought of the *Tribune* as other staff members thought of their children. This paper had been nourished by him, sustained by his devotion and affection, since he arrived in Placer fifteen years earlier. He had no illusions about the permanence of any material thing and he had long ago recognized the peculiarly evanescent quality of the products of daily journalism, but he could not give fifteen years of his life to this child and not feel the hurt that had been inflicted on it. He shook his head sadly as he turned that morning's issue from the editorial page back to the front page. The paper had gone soft, mushy, under the new publisher and his protégé, brought from another part of the chain to be made managing editor. Even less than the publisher did the managing editor understand the town of Placer. He hadn't been around long enough to understand how it ticks, to develop a sense of place. Fifteen years on the *Tribune* had taught Robinson that the current managing editor, and probably the publisher, would soon depart to become a different cog in the chain's wheel, as soon as there was a proper opening, customarily by a long-delayed retirement, occasionally by a death, celebratorily by a daughter's marriage. The chain was infested with sons-in-law of various high executives. Nepotism, Robinsion had learned, was no more a deterrent to several careers than incompetence or an unfortunate deficiency of intelligence or a lack of experience outside the chain on some newspaper that had a measurable degree of pride, integrity, courage and resourcefulness. He wasn't cynical, he would say, just skeptical.

He rode the surge of desperation and pecked a last graph into the machine. So what if it was one of those "something ought to be done about this" conclusions similar in tone and construction to the endings of scores—hundreds?—of editorials that day in newspapers from Gannett's Maine to Copley's San Diego?

Robinson's eyes and head hurt. He glowered at the video display terminal and pondered the validity of the charge, naturally hardly ever mentioned in the news media, that the VDT is documentably a menace to health. Even the government had been pressured into a study of the cause-and-effect relationship between use of VDTs and cataracts, and he had often written that when the government starts paying attention to a problem you can be certain it is already a serious one. He wondered what had become of the report that the pregnancies of six workers who used the terminals in a British Columbia hospital had resulted in one normal birth, one baby born prematurely, two miscarriages, one baby with a deformed foot and another with severe bronchitis. Now there was a little bit of extra poison in the news room and the hospital; in a few years there would be a terminal for every person in every office and every home, thus equalizing the risks for all. Democracy.

On the other hand (he thought, perversely employing the favorite device of his fellow editorial writers), newspapers as we know them are on the way out, to be replaced by technologically advanced methods of getting our daily information. And with that development will come the technicians to deliver the news. Even more than today the men and women reared and nurtured as news-oriented professionals will be replaced by pretty faces, empty heads and those who have no idea of the ethics and responsibilities that at least have received lip service through two difficult centuries.

He shook his head and sent the editorial slithering its way into the universe of computerdom, hoping that it would not be lost, as it had been more than once, in a black hole along the way. The unholy task done, he leaned back in his chair and rubbed the back of his neck, which also hurt and also Must Have Something To Do With The Terminal. Oh, Lord, how he wished for the time of typewriters, the clatter of the wire service teletypes, the hustle of news rooms of another day. Now the silence and the carpets had transformed Romance into Sterility. What Jonathan Blakely had once said about the couple who had traded the hurly-burly of the chaise lounge for the deep peace of the double bed also applied to newspapering.

Yeah, Jonathan Blakely. He of the vast conspiracy theories. They had talked about it for hours last night. Not that Jonathan was necessarily wrong about how things work in our country these days; as a matter of fact, what had become Jonathan's most recent obsession made a certain amount of sense. He had so informed Jonathan, although he added that he thought it far more likely that the reporting deficiencies in covering the assassination attempt were the result of inefficiency, arbitrariness, ineptness, docility, laziness, inconsistency, superficiality, incuriosity—any or all of these—rather than a conscious effort to spout the official line or cover up uncomfortable information. Nonetheless, knowing what he did of genuine but ignored history, he could not be certain that nothing was rotten in the states back east. And there on the table was Jonathan's new portion of his article on his obsession, given to Robinson last night to read and return today. Now was the time. He walked to the table, picked up the blue sheets of paper in a folder marked "BLUE DRAFT," closed the door of his office and returned to his chair to read.

"THE STALKING OF A PRESIDENT"
The notion that John W. Hinckley Jr. was simply out to shoot himself a president was pounded relentlessly by the national news media for five weeks before finally being abandoned. It began in stories published the day after the assassination attempt when a theoretical link was forged by unnamed law enforcement officials between President Carter and the October 9 arrest of Hinckley at the Nashville airport for trying to board an airplane with three guns and 50 rounds of ammunition in a suitcase:

President Carter was in Nashville that day. A source close to the Reagan shooting investigation said Hinckley had been in Nashville for a couple of days and was heard to note that Reagan had canceled a campaign appearance there scheduled for Oct. 7. (UPI)

The prosecutor of the case, Charles Ruff, was quoted:

"When he (Hinckley) was arrested Oct. 9, President Jimmy Carter was present in that city," Ruff said. (AP)

The April 9 Seattle Post-Intelligencer, under an unintentionally ironic headline ("FBI Defends Withholding Data on Hinckley," which had nothing to do with the sealed evidence concerning the attempt on the president's life but was only a story about Director William H. Webster defending the FBI in an inter-agency squabble with the Secret Service), continued the theory:

At another House hearing, Webster defended a decision by his agents not to pass along to the Secret Service information that Hinckley had been arrested in Nashville Oct. 9.... That same day, then-President Jimmy Carter was due to campaign.... (P-I News Services)

The official speculation was sparked anew by a long April 12 New York Times study based on FBI sources and spread by the wire services:

The Times said the agency's extensive background check on Hinckley since the March 30 wounding... has led agents to conclude that the 25-year-old drifter also tracked Carter.
The newspaper said there was no conclusive evidence linking Hinckley, son of a wealthy Evergreen, Colo., oilman, to Carter, though records of the suspect's travels and eyewitness accounts suggest to the FBI he may have stalked him in Washington in September, December and January. (UPI)

The most interesting paragraphs were in the story of the New

York Times' own news service:

> The possibility that Hinckley stalked Carter is the first major development in the investigation since agents established a motive for Hinckley's alleged attack on Reagan....
> Officials said they believed Hinckley might have stalked Carter in the two hours between the hotel checkout and the airport arrest, but failed to find a suitable moment to attack the president.

On April 16 the "stalking Carter" scenario was embellished by yet another tribe of ubiquitous sources who did not wish their names associated with the information they were dispensing to the public via the news media:

> The Dayton Daily News in a copyright story said it was told by unidentified sources that Hinckley was registered at the Sheraton-Dayton Hotel last Oct. 2, the same day Carter appeared at a town hall meeting in the Dayton Convention Center a block away.
> The newspaper said Hinckley's visit to Dayton lends support to a theory that Hinckley stalked Carter last fall.
> Other reports place him in Chicago Oct. 6 during another Carter appearance.
> The sources said a Sheraton employee identified Hinckley from a photograph shown by FBI agents. They said Hinckley registered under his own name at the hotel Sept. 30 and checked out Oct. 2. He stayed in an eighth floor room. (AP)

For 28 days there were countless other contributions to the theory that Hinckley was "another Bremer"—a reference to Arthur H. Bremer, who kept a journal of his travels and reportedly stalked President Nixon before he shot and wounded presidential candidate George Wallace. (Coincidentally, Bremer was the inspiration for the character in the movie Taxi Driver who allegedly inspired Hinckley.) Then, after almost a month had passed, that "first major development in the invest-

igation" also became "*inoperative.*" On May 6, the Washington Post, *recipient of a special dispensation from on high, reported that an unreleased 1,200-page summary of the FBI's first month of investigations into the assassination attempt concluded that John W. Hinckley "was not stalking Reagan or any other political figure.*" The lead on the UPI story:

> *Federal investigators have concluded that John W. Hinckley Jr. visited Washington several times before the shooting of President Reagan, but did not stalk Mr. Reagan or any other political figure, it was reported tonight.*

The summary by the AP:

> *Hinckley, who is charged with trying to kill Reagan, is instead portrayed in the summary sent federal prosecutors as a confused college dropout who used money from his wealthy parents to wander aimlessly, the Washington Post said in its Wednesday editions.*
>
> *"There doesn't seem to be any information that he was stalking anybody," the Post quoted an unnamed law enforcement official as saying....*
>
> *The summary reiterates previous reports that Hinckley's fascination for actress Jodie Foster was behind some of his extensive travels. Investigators also still believe the assassination attempt sprang from an apparent desire to impress Foster, the Post said.*

Thus, more than a month after the shooting, the "*authorities*" casually walk away from all those suggestive tidbits they had provided the hungry press and the FBI reportedly concludes that young Hinckley had not "*stalked*" President Carter (or President Reagan) after all. The reams of speculation had come to naught and the motivation for the crime was back to square one:

He did it to impress Jodie Foster.

Robinson couldn't get past the idea that what Jonathan was doing was foolhardy. He would tell him so, the next time he had him alone. He knew it would make no difference; there was no way to stop Jonathan Blakely from doing what he made up his mind must be done. The Puritan ethic in large measure was the rope that bound the conclusions Jonathan reached. No need to brood about it, though; when this day was over he would make a special night of it at the Royal. There is no answer to anything, Robinson was certain, but the Royal provided the only possible tentative reply to his needs of the moment.

Robinson often went to the Royal, but he did not enjoy the fraternity boys from the university, the coeds who came with them or in groups, or most of the other men and women who drifted in. What he liked were the people from the newspaper and some of the radio and TV broadcasters. Even they could not satisfy him for more than a few minutes or a few hours at a time, and when he had all he believed he could take of any of them he would depart quickly. Thus would he leave men at the bar or table in the midst of a story; or a glass yet half full; or a woman caressing his shoulders in anticipation of an evening together. Sometimes his departure was silent, perhaps with a nod of his head, and rarely did he offer more than a brief "good night." Then he would go to his apartment and read until the book fell from his hands and he rested in the only kind of full peace he knew. The books provided a kind of pleasure that humankind denied him. He frankly admitted to himself, as he would never admit to the others, that he preferred the good dirty jokes of Aristophanes to the bad dirty jokes of the journalists.

Others, most of the men and, if he had known, most of the women, did not resent his abrupt departures. They recognized that Robinson was "different," and they respected his frequent unwillingness to observe even the rudimentary courtesies of the bar. They liked Robinson, either in spite of or because of his perversity. He was aware that they thought he was his own man and that they admired qualities in him they secretly desired to possess or, in the case of the women, to share. But Robinson knew he was not his own man and he did not like himself as he was. He often wished he could tear himself apart and put the pieces together again; within himself he saw unrelenting contradictions that no amount of alteration could settle, and he had resigned himself to live within the framework he had constructed.

That framework, he often thought, had been beset, then infested, then rotted by termites. What were the names of these little bugs that as far back into his past as he could remember had gnawed at his structure until he was now only a hollow shell? First, if he was to be honest with himself (and Robinson prized honesty to oneself above all other virtues), there had been selfishness. He had learned early, by word and example and the hard, heavy hand of his father, that every smart person looked after number one. This is a bitter world, full of other smart people all looking out for themselves, and if you don't want to be ground up in the grinder and tossed on the garbage heap, you had better be careful. Never trust anyone, never help anyone unless you're sure there's something in it for you. If a man's a man, he asks for nothing and he is very, very careful about giving anything.

Tucker was the name that Robinson remembered best, a name that ran not like a thread but like a knotted rope through his childhood. Tucker the smooth-talker, Tucker the sweet-mouth, Tucker the laughing-man, Tucker the partner of Robinson Sr. They had gone from that grimy town on the Charles, out of the cobbled streets, spurred by a pact sealed in a saloon and dreams of wealth in the west. Something about Tucker had assured Robinson's father that in their case the dream would come true. They set off for the valleys of California, had backtracked into the gulleys of Nevada, had settled in the panhandle of Idaho, where they struck. Their store, opened on guts and credit and a large inventory, was a bonanza. The dream indeed came true.

Robinson had heard the story many, many times. His father would drink the cheap whiskey, sit back in the only chair in the hovel that was their home, and tell the story. Willie Tucker had kept the papers of their partnership in his shirt pocket throughout the lean years of their search, and when the time came to bring forth the papers they did not have on them the words which he had said were written there. Tucker, with the help of a potato farmer turned lawyer, owned the store and the wealth they had won together.

But that was not all he stole from Robinson's father. He took with him, when he went, Robinson's mother.

She had cried as she said goodbye to Robinson and his younger brother the day she left. Her lips trembled and her eyes were closed as she held them, and tears had pressed out from under the lashes. She told them that she loved them but that she could not stay with them or their father another day. He beat her, they knew, and she was afraid of him. She must go, and they must be good boys and help their father, and someday she would see them again. She did not mention Willie Tucker.

When Robinson's father had returned late that afternoon and learned from his children that his wife had deserted him, he went searching for her in a cold, contained rage. Late that night when he returned, drunk, he struck each of the boys repeatedly. With each blow, he uttered, like an oath, the name of Willie Tucker.

Robinson now only vaguely remembered the appearance of his mother, and that of Tucker not at all. Of those years only two vivid memories of his mother remained: The day she had gone away and the night after his brother had been born. He remembered her screams from the bed she shared with his father, with the springs creaking as they had every night, weeping in agony and pleading for a doctor. Robinson was six years old and he had never forgotten those screams or the fact that a doctor never came.

"Don't trust no one," his father had said again and again. Thus, Robinson concluded, had he been made selfish.

Then had come self-pity. He had made the mistake, for a few brief glorious months, of thinking first not of himself but of another person. She had seemed so true, so honest, so dependable, so—yes, he had used the word to her—trustworthy. Reveling in the joys of love, he neglected the axiom by which he had learned to live. And then she had told him that she had met another and would marry the other. He pitied himself, drank himself into a stupor every night, and at twenty-two was certain that he would never love again, or love again in the same way. He had known many women since that first bitter experience and he was right: He never did give himself in love again with the same intensity that had preceded his first, and last, betrayal by a woman.

Later than in the lives of most men had come ambition. He had turned thirty before he discovered that books gave him a profound satisfaction that people could not equal. He haunted the used book stores wherever he went. He read books of all kinds, but he spent most of his evenings studying the intricate patterns of history. The history of man and of other times suddenly had an intimate meaning to him, as if he had pledged membership in a mystic cult whose primary tenet was that all men are products of the past and live, often unconsciously, immersed in the past. He saw the shallowness of his own life, in which he had recognized no history other than that bounded by his own limited anxieties. As he read he stood serenely on Olympus, joined the barbarians in their invasions and plunderings, participated in the unending wars between peoples, suffered under secular and ecclesiastical tyrannies. He went back to the Testaments, and then to the shelves of books microscopically and contradictorily interpreting the Testaments. Doors to new worlds opened for him as he read Thucydides and Livy, Machiavelli and Guicciardini.

He took the short step to the Greek classics, especially enjoying the plays of Euripides and Aristophanes. Then came philosophy. He bought old books by the dozens, but his interests soon settled on Kant, Rousseau, Fichte and Hegel. He responded warmly to the contrary attraction of Hegel; thesis and antithesis, synthesis and thesis, circling and whirling down the centuries, cast light on dark areas of bewilderment that had clouded his understanding. From Hegel he passed inevitably to the tantalizing toughness of Marx.

When he had read the first chapters of *Das Kapital,* repelled at first by the turgid prose, then becoming fascinated as he gazed more fixedly into the eye of that cobra, he experienced a conversion that was almost religious in its intensity. Karl Marx spoke to him, finally, in language he understood, of ideas he had only faintly comprehended, with logic that grasped him and shook him both emotionally and intellectually. He read everything of Marx that he could find; he rummaged in dark corners of libraries for books and essays and pamphlets; he discovered that Marx had been a correspondent at one time for a New York newspaper and he turned pages of the yellowed, dusty issues in the newspaper morgue seeking articles that had been penned by the journalist-revolutionary. The ancient plays of Greece were forgotten, the pallid philosophers of the ages were banished to limbo, and the history he had learned and loved took on a shining new meaning. He concluded that all other views of history were only partially correct and that none of them provided a substantive key to present and future. Now he had a kind of crystal ball instead of a kaleidoscope.

In Marx, he thought, he had found a brittle but brilliant intellect concerned not only with historical and philosophical interpretation but, more importantly, with all the living beings scorned and exploited and rejected by their society. The needs of the people and the revolution of the proletariat, which Marx proclaimed as the aim and goal of humankind, became the end which defined all other aims and goals.

The militant atheism of Marx and the Marxists at first had no appeal for him. He had never devoted much time to questioning the decision he had made years earlier, after going back to the Testaments (and the shelves of books microscopically and contradictorily interpreting the Testaments), that he was an agnostic. He was impressed with what he had found in Marx: Intellectual integrity, sincerity of purpose, a higher morality and a system that would do more than simply repair the cracked and crumbling economic and social structure of the United States. He succumbed to Marx's Eleventh Thesis: "The philosophers have only interpreted the world in various ways; the point, however, is to change it."

His ambition was to help change the world. He had explored the labyrinths of his own unhappy existence and reached the conclusion that his ills, and the ills of all societies which had been organized by man, resulted primarily from man's greed and covetousness. The vicious nature of man had not been significantly softened by twenty centuries of Christianity, aided and abetted by other religions, nor would it change, he concluded, until the economic foundations of life were altered. He smiled whenever he encountered the concepts of "civilized" versus "primitive" societies ("And what, Mr. Gandhi, do you think of western civilization?" "I think it would be a good idea."). The dull comforts granted the laborers by capitalism's benefactors were not enough; the true socialist state offered the best, if indeed not the only, hope of man.

In his reading he went down the avenues, the by-ways, the alleys, the cul-de-sacs of socialism. He studied the writings of Charles Fourier and noted the failures of Fourierism in both Europe and in the Brook Farm experiment in Massachusetts. He found Edward Bellamy's *Looking Backward* a source of ideas he had never approached but he saw in it, too, an example of the kind of utopian philosophy that Marx had warned against. He decided that Fourier, Bellamy, the journalist Greeley and others like them had failed to measure the ruthlessness of the capitalist enemy and had wrongly believed that they could construct a new society within the old one. The only way to attain the necessary fundamental change, he agreed, was to overthrow the old and replace it with a revolutionary classless state dedicated to the welfare of the masses. Then, with the profit motive eradicated, the nature of man, through the years, would be raised to something better, higher and more desirable than it was now and always had been. Such was the guiding article of his faith.

The theory was splendid; the practice left him desolate. He watched in horror as the great lovers of the "workers" fought among themselves for the power and the glory and—most important—the booty. As a reporter he watched the hard, tough organizers of unionism become the fat, corrupt reverse image of the bosses they set out against. Men who started out preaching economic justice ended up willing to seal the miners into a lifetime barren of hope if it would make their own union jobs more secure. He saw the price paid in human misery by those men and their families who valued their individualism more than their wages. He went down into the valley of the Susquehanna, walked in the fog of Scranton and Shamokin and Shenandoah, looked on helplessly as peaceable citizens were shot and beaten, their homes looted and burned out, the cries of "Scab! Scab! Scab!" ringing through the night air all in the name of justice. He developed a deep distrust of those whose passion for justice inevitably evolved into the justice of the figurative guillotine. All revolutions, he saw, carry within their bodies the germs of new and often more deadly diseases. When were we to discover that the nature of evil is no more simple than that of goodness?

He could not write for his newspaper what he had seen in the sooty towns that formed the grimy rings around the coal fields of Pennsylvania. Instead he returned to New York, quit his job and rented a room in a shabby tenement on the lower east side where he could be alone, to ask no questions, to seek no answers, to eat and drink what he had to, to read and read and read. A monumental depression overwhelmed him. He stared into the black abyss, finally did not flinch, resolved that he would forevermore abstain from making moral judgments. He suffered almost unendurably and he was, ultimately, cleansed. He came forth again into the world alone, unwilling to join his fellows on earth but equally unwilling to fight them. He sat in the corner as an observer appointed by no man and responsible to no man. His intuitive ability to project the behavior of others and thereby comprehend the mysterious territories of human motive rarely deserted him.

Now here in Placer he was an observer on the payroll of the Midwest Chain, receiving a salary magnificent for a bachelor. He no longer believed in anything more than the transience of his passage and the need to be as kind as possible to the few persons he knew for whom kindness would help lessen the burden they dragged through life. That night long ago when he had stood in the rear of a Northumberland County union hall until he could no longer stomach the cupidity of an organizer who shouted of the great day coming while lining his own pockets—that night when he had walked out muttering "Workers of the world, unite—you have nothing to lose but your balls," and vomited in a gutter—that night when the cry for a better world went ringing against the rafters in a den of hatred—that night he knew he would be for all time incapable of returning to the world where men and women and children lived in hope.

The knock on his office door jolted him back to now. He slowly rose and opened the door leading to the news room. The man standing there surveying the office seemed to suck up information with his eyes as his head slowly swiveled from one wall to another. At length, apparently satisfied that he had seen and learned all that was necessary at this point, he focused on Robinson.

"I'll buy you a drink," he said. Lines gathered at his mouth and at the corners of his eyes as he offered a modest, practiced, quizzical smile.

Robinson undertook his guessing game. East. Most likely New York City. Probably writer. Maybe newspaperman. Relatively sans malice. Doesn't need a job. Lonely. . . .

"It's too early," he responded. "And I have a page to get out."

The man looked at the large clock on the wall. "You have quite a few hours before that page is due. Furthermore, Mr. Robinson, I'm astonished to hear a newspaperman in Placer decline a drink regardless of the time of day. If this gets out you'll destroy one of the myths by which those of us east of the Hudson sustain ourselves."

Robinson got up, jerked his hat and coat off a hanger on the wall and walked toward the man. "God forbid," he said, "that I take that risk. Especially since you know my name and appear to have the potential of spreading it. I'll have a beer with you."

The man extended his right hand. "Alonzo Schaeffer," he said.

"I'll be damned," Robinson replied, shaking the proffered hand. "I read you all the time. The western star of the paper with all the news that's print to fit."

"I understand you once worked for it."

"Yeah, in the days of glory. And after. You are one of the few who carry on where some of us left off."

"And you?"

"I carry on where everyone left off. Ready for that beer?"

"Lead the way. Oh—"

Alonzo Schaeffer stopped and pointed above the doorway of Robinson's office.

"—I couldn't help but notice that you have a large 3 over your door. None of the other offices in the building seem to be numbered. That seems rather remarkable."

"It's a private joke—in more ways than one," Robinson said. "You prove my point. Hundreds of people have walked into that office but the only ones who ever noticed that number are newspaper people. Like yourself, Mr. Schaeffer. Newspaper people who are worth anything share two qualities in common. They're observant and they're curious. I'm still waiting for the first lawyer to notice that number up there, for instance, and I never expect a doctor or, heaven help us, a politician to pay any attention to it. Practically every new reporter we hire asks about it and I have detected an informal correlation between those who notice it and those who don't and those who are our best reporters and those who aren't. Let's have that beer you promised."

They walked down the steps of the Tribune Building and out on the sidewalk. Robinson guided his visitor to the corner where the Royal was three doors down the street.

"What brings you to Placer?" he asked.

"I'm doing a story. Or rather, several stories."

"That's too bad. You people east of the Hudson, if I may borrow your expression, subsist on myths provided by your paper."

"You don't share the high opinion generally held of the *Times*, I take it?"

"Shit, Mr. Schaeffer—"

"Alonzo."

"Shit, Alonzo, we both know how it works. I left it when I saw it was hopeless and you're with it and trying to do an honest job, from what I read of yours now and then. How long've you been visiting the state?"

"Off and on, a little short of six months."

"Yeah, a little short is right on. You won't get the stories."

"And what does that mean?"

Robinson pushed open the door of the Royal and led the way to the bar. "I'll have a draft," he said. Alonzo Schaeffer nodded to the bartender.

"I came here fifteen years ago," Robinson said. "I've seen a lot of people come and go and a lot of changes. I've written almost an editorial a day since the day I arrived, and I don't write about Afghanistan or even Tuscaloosa. And let me tell you this: Nobody is going to come into this town or this state and six months later write anything about it that makes any sense. Sure you can run your fingers over the skin and find the sensitive parts and the erogenous zones but you won't understand the body. Not in six months. Maybe not in six years. And these assholes who come here from Texas and California bring all their accrued rotten values and they've already started to rot this state."

Schaeffer sipped his beer as if he didn't often drink beer. "I'm not a man who wastes his time."

Robinson took a long, steady gulp. "You're wasting it here."

The bartender filled Robinson's glass. "Your friend here is slow," he observed.

"He'll catch up," Robinson replied. "Lots of men turn to drink when the situation gets hopeless."

The man from New York laughed. "Robinson is convinced I'm on a wild goose chase. I've been told that before."

The bartender didn't smile. "Not by Robinson you haven't," he said. "I wish you luck, but make sure you don't get goosed first yourself."

"Irish wit," Robinson said. "Placer is famous for it. Among other things." He pointed to the sign taped to the mirror behind the bar: LIQUOR UP FRONT; POKER IN THE REAR. The bartender grinned and turned to other customers.

"Even if you get your stories and are satisfied with them," Robinson said, "they'll be buried on page 43. What do people back there care about us out here? Most of them think Placer is just south of the Arctic Circle."

"You'd be surprised to know the extent of the interest the effete east has for your state. That's why I'm here. Some of our readers are enormously interested in what's happening here."

Robinson polished off his beer. "I can guess," he said dryly. "Our friends in the financial caverns."

"Precisely. Can you blame them?"

The bartender returned, filled Robinson's glass, looked with undisguised disapproval at the visitor's half-filled glass and went his way.

"Yeah, I can blame them," Robinson said. "I can blame them for a lot of things. Like what they've done to this state already and what they'd like to do in the future if they could spread its knees. But don't get me started on that. My passion knows no bounds on that subject. I could write a stack of editorials for the next few weeks right here."

Alonzo Schaeffer leaned toward him. "But they wouldn't be printed, would they?"

Robinson worked the glass between his fingers and eyed the other man steadily.

"A little short of six months, hey?" he said slowly. "Okay, now I'll tell you about that mysterious 3 over my door. I nailed it up there myself the first day on the job. It's a personal reminder not to take myself, or anything else for that matter, too seriously. The number 3 represents the male genitalia. It's a sign used by Greek peasants and as far as I can learn by other peasants in the Mediterranean. It helps me to remember what's important and what isn't important. This is between us, right?"

The man from New York nodded.

"What I write in that room isn't important. That's how I get through my life. I pretend sometimes that it's important and sometimes other people tell me I do some good, that I make some difference. My friends even put me in for a Pulitzer last year, but of course it went to a paper in Philadelphia that obviously impressed the judges by actually doing its simple duty. That 3 up there says it all. Hell, Zorba knew where it's at. He knew that the cock is a lot more important than the head and all its agony. He spit on that agony; I spit on that agony."

Alonzo Schaeffer laughed. "I can see why you left New York and came out here."

"Above all, I wanted to go somewhere where I could breathe again. New York is the grayest, most impersonal monument to materialism in this country. The people there have separated themselves from nature. But in all honesty we out here are on our way toward getting civilized, which means that we are almost as ready as those people back east to shove it into the other fellow. To a lot of people back there, including those synthetic robots who run your paper, we're funny little men running around outdoors on another planet. And then they send you here to turn your telescope on us and you guys always look through the telescope from the wrong end and by the gods we do look like funny little men running around outdoors on another planet."

Alonzo Schaeffer laughed again, holding his glass in his hand but not drinking from it. "That's an idea that hadn't occurred to me. But instead of little moon men we could have Indians on a scalping party. Stage coach robberies. Beautiful women ravished by the savages. The leading citizens of Placer getting up a posse. I'll have to work on it."

Robinson twirled his empty glass on the bar. He felt a sharp twinge of familiar nausea coming on him.

"I take it you don't place much stock in tales of violence concerning this part of the country," he said.

"I'm well aware of some unpleasantness in the past. Road agents. Plummer and his boys. The vigilantes. 3-7-77 and all that. It's part of the lore, although I'm not one to..."

But Robinson wasn't listening. He had felt the little wave churn and boil within him and a billowing wall rising to drown his senses. He put a hand on Alonzo Schaeffer's arm.

"Excuse me," he said, rising unsteadily. "I'll be right back."

He walked past the end of the bar and nearly to the alley, pushed open a door with a glazed glass panel and leaned against a wall. He took off his coat and ran a sleeve across his forehead. No one else was in the room.

"Go away," he said aloud. "Go away."

But it wouldn't go away. The memory came back more strongly, more clearly. He was back in the Bitterroots again.

His father, in pursuit of the man who had stolen from him, had brought the boy with him. He had listened in cafes and saloons, in hotels, in stores and on the streets for the name that he had himself uttered hundreds—thousands—of times. He would strike up an acquaintance, pursue it long enough to ask the question that festered deep in his entrails, and if the answer was not the one he sought he would try another stranger. When the possibilities of one camp or town seemed exhausted he would tell the boy to pack, for they were ready to move on. Then the same rounds would begin. The search had taken them around the barren hillocks and sluggish streams of Nevada, through the timbered and craggy territory of Idaho, and had brought them over the awesome mountains and into the gentle valleys of western Montana. At each stop the father would work only long enough to purchase small stores of food and large quantities of cheap whiskey, put some money in an envelope to send to an orphanage that had accepted his younger son, meet a sufficient number of men who could not satisfactorily answer his questions and prepare for the journey to the next cluster of men. The boy often watched silently as his father, in what became a ritual, would talk about the weather, the opportunities for work, the places from which he had come and the places to which he would like to go, and then poise for the only moment of conversation in which he really cared. He would take yet another deep draw of whiskey, run the tip of his tongue around his lips, eye the other man and ask in a monotone:

"Ever hear of a man named Willie Tucker?"

The father knew it was possible that some of the men who thought for a moment and then shook their heads were lying. The camps and framed towns housed men who were quite willing to talk, for most of them were lonely, but they did not relish talking about other men. A stranger might be a friend or an enemy, the friend of an enemy or the enemy of a friend. It did not pay to talk freely on that subject, although little else was forbidden. A man learned the rules quickly and he usually played by the rules. Men would lie, Robinson's father understood, but sooner or later, he also understood, he was bound to find a man who would be able, and willing, to give him the answer he sought.

He met the man at a bar in Darby.

"Tucker? Willie Tucker? Hell yes, I know the lousy son of a bitch. He a friend of yours?"

The father looked quickly at the boy sitting at a table. His eyes darted back to the man with the answer, a big and heavy man. He leaned close to the man at the bar.

"Christ no, he's no friend of mine. I owe him something, and I want to pay him back. You tell me where he is and I'll deliver his balls to you in a bottle."

The man threw back his head and laughed. It was the deep, rich laugh of a man sure of himself, who didn't care about the rules of a game no matter what the stakes were.

"I'd like that," he said. "Hell, that would be a specimen I'd relish. I'd do the job myself, except that I draw the line at murder."

"I don't," Robinson's father said. "Not in this case. Where is he?"

The smile on the other man vanished. The lines on his tanned and rugged face grew taut and hardened. He stared for several seconds at the wiry little man who stood tensely waiting for an answer. He pondered a problem of his own, weighing and balancing several possibilities, and then he made a decision.

"Come over here and sit down," he said.

The father signaled to the boy to stay at the table. He followed the hulk that led the way to a corner table and sat down. The big man's eyes investigated Robinson's father, seeking to size him up.

"I know who you are, Robinson. I've seen you and the boy around. Do you know me?"

The head shook quickly from side to side.

"I'm Washburne Turner. Do you know what I've been doing here?"

Again the head swiveled.

"Look, Robinson," the man said, leaning forward, "I'm taking one hell of a chance, I know, but I need another man I can trust. How badly do you want to get Tucker?"

"I can taste it, mister. I'd go through hell naked to get to him."

"You have any money?"

Robinson's father didn't answer immediately. His mind raced over the potentialities, comparing the likely reactions of the men who held the key to unlock the desperate need that encased him. Yes. No.

"Yes," he said. "I can get money."

"A thousand?"

"A thousand."

"How soon?"

"A week. Maybe two weeks." Robinson's father counted on persons he hadn't seen or heard from or written to in years. One of them would come through. If they didn't, he'd face that after he got to Willie Tucker.

"Okay. I need that amount for a stake. It'll be a loan. I'll pay you back. And I'll take you to Tucker."

"Tomorrow?"

"Yeah, tomorrow. It's the middle of October. The snow's probably started falling where he is. It won't be easy. He lives far back. Far back. It'll take more than a day. We'll leave early tomorrow."

"Shake."

"Right."

Washburne Turner lowered his voice.

"I only been there once. He comes into town to stock up every once in a while. Probably he'll hole up 'til early spring. I bought wholesale in Lewistown, more than I needed, and I sold retail to him. And I delivered. And the son of a bitch didn't pay me what we agreed on. Weaseled on me. That's how I know where he is. Or at least that's where he was a month ago."

Robinson's father couldn't hold it any longer.

"Does he have a woman with him?"

Washburne Turner leaned back and laughed. "Hell, Robinson, he's got more than a woman with him. He's got a tit in each hand all the time. The son of a bitch is dripping money."

"But not just one woman?" Robinson's father persisted.

"Not so I could notice."

That's all Robinson's father needed to know this night.

"I'll see you tomorrow morning."

"You got a horse?"

"I'll get two horses." He pointed a thumb over his shoulder. "The boy goes with me."

"That wasn't in the deal, Robinson. How old's he?"

"Twelve. He won't be any trouble. I'll see to that. Won't open his mouth. He does what I say, and I say he won't be any trouble."

The big man reflected on this development for a few seconds, then he grinned and put out a huge hand.

"Hell, he won't eat much and if it don't snow he won't know it's more'n a camping trip."

They shook hands again and the boy followed his father through the door and down the street toward their hotel. Suddenly he ran into an alley and violently and repeatedly vomited. His father waited silently for him to return. That night the boy did not sleep.

At seven o'clock the three of them were ready to leave town.

They went south and then veered west into the Bitterroot Range. The morning mists that had spread a melancholy cover over them gave way to a burst of sun as they followed the west fork of the Bitterroot and started to climb. The boy leaned over from his horse and tugged at his father's sleeve.

"I don't feel good," he said.

"Jesus, boy," his father said, unable to control his irritation. "I told you to keep your mouth shut on this trip. We'll stop in a little while and maybe you'll feel better."

The horses' hooves beat steadily on the trail and the boy knew his father was balancing his determination to end a search of six years with a reconsideration of his son's plight. Finally the father spurred his horse to catch up to their guide and after a short conversation they stopped. The boy sensed that the big man with them didn't like this unexpected halt, and when he was awakened three hours later the sun was gone and a chill was in the air.

"C'mon, we got to get in a few more miles before it gets dark," his father said. He looked apologetically toward the big man, who already had mounted his horse.

They pushed on and up, past the herds of elk, in scores and hundreds, which fed unmolested near the banks of meandering streams. They brushed aside the limbs of green-boughed fir as they passed under the giant trees. Then they were in a high valley of the range and there was a light fall of snow at a pass, but they moved on until the big man in front of them signaled that it was time to stop. As they made camp along the stream they could feel the crisp, sharp signs of a heavy snowfall to come.

"We'll be there tomorrow before noon," the big man said. "The boy slowed us up some, but we'll get started early."

They sat around the camp fire until long after dark. The wind had risen, then dropped to a lulling whisper. The boy, obeying a silent nod from his father, rolled in his blanket under a tree, several yards from the fire. He could see them, but they could not see him. He watched as his father stood up and went toward his pack. The big man bent forward to light his pipe from an ember taken from the fire.

It was an unintended signal. The boy saw, simultaneously

and in horror, two men leap out of the darkness into the circle of the fire. One man swung high an ax, and in a sharp downward motion split open the head of Washburne Turner. He saw his father rush back toward the man with the ax, then stop short, the top of his head blown off by a charge from a shotgun.

"Where's the boy? Get the boy!"

The boy rolled down the gentle slope, struggling to get free of the restraining blanket. He ran downhill, fell in the darkness, got up, ran again, felt a branch rip the skin and flesh of his face, ran into a tree and fell stunned to the ground. He could hear the crackling of footsteps off to one side behind him. He got up again and ran into a large rock. His hands moved downward, tracing the curve of the rock until it reached the ground. He knelt, then crawled, then pressed his body against the rock, squeezing into a hollow between rock and ground. He shivered with cold and fear as footsteps came nearer. He could hear the men cursing and tripping and falling. They searched for several minutes, uttering oaths and blaming each other for letting the boy get away.

"Goddamnit, Tucker, you should have taken him."

"I was busy, you son of a bitch. Where the hell were you?"

"You said you'd handle him. The little bastard was in easy reach."

"Well, what the hell's the difference. He'll never make it out of here anyway. Come on, let's go."

The boy heard the men return to the campfire. He heard the scurrying about. He heard the whinnying of horses being driven into the distance, then a series of flat, fluttering sounds made by shots being fired within canyon walls. Then he heard nothing more.

Robinson brought his head back sharply against the wall. The nausea was gone, but he felt sweat pouring from him. He walked to the sink and ran cold water over his face and hair and neck. He dried himself with paper towels, took a deep breath and looked back at the door with the glazed glass panel. Then he walked to the window, raised it, and looked out on the empty alley. He placed his hands on the sill and lifted his feet up and through and out. He walked down the alley, broke into a jog and headed home.

Alonzo Schaeffer shook his head and smiled wryly. "It looks as if I've been left to pay the bill," he said to the bartender. "But that was the bargain. Will Mr. Robinson be all right in there?"

The bartender stopped the gyrations of his cloth on the top of the bar.

"Robinson," he said, "will be all right wherever he is."

JUNE

Although meaningful coincidences are infinitely varied in their phenomenology, as acausal events they nevertheless form an element that is part of the scientific picture of the world. Causality is the way we explain the link between two successive events. Synchronicity designates the parallelism of time and meaning between psychic and psychophysical events, which scientific knowledge so far has been unable to reduce to a common principle. The term explains nothing, it simply formulates the occurrence of meaningful coincidences which, in themselves, are chance happenings, but are so improbable that we must assume them to be based on some kind of principle, or on some property of the empirical world.

— C.G. Jung
On Synchronicity

The bedroom, too, was beginning to reflect his life, his primary interest, his obsession. In recent weeks Jonathan Blakely had found it impossible to give his full attention to anything but the attempt to kill the president, and now the stacks of newspapers were growing along the wall at the foot of the bed. Where there had been three fairly equally divided interests in his life—his son, the *Tribune* and Deborah's occasional visits for dinner and overnight—now there was a single driving force that consumed his waking hours. He put in his time at the paper with mechanical competence, his interest quickening only in the occasional item that the AP or the New York Times News Service dispatched concerning The Event. He would stop at Rudy's on his way home to pick up the newspapers characterized in the recent literature of journalism as the "inner ring" of Washington news gatherers of most concern to the executive branch of government. These papers were sometimes anointed as "prestige employers" whose writers are given special consideration in governmental circles because of their ability to dictate what constitutes "news." He would carry home under his arm copies of the *New York Times, Washington Post, Chicago Tribune, Los Angeles Times* and *Wall Street Journal*—to which he added the *Boston Globe, Denver Post* and *Rocky Mountain News*.

The next day he would go through the papers, throwing away the classified advertisements and all the sections devoted to real estate developers, supermarkets, new and used car dealers, merchants of gear deemed desirable by hunters, fishermen, boaters or anyone else the advertising department could appeal to via a special tabloid insert. Out would go the pages sacrificed to the engagements and weddings and other trivial activities of the wealthy and socially prominent, who always were one and the same. He would skim through the sports sections, unable to relinquish that little-boy part of him that had always been happiest on the baseball field, the basketball and tennis courts, the lanes of the track that ran around the football stadium. He was hooked on the gossip of sports, addicted to the drama that took place off the field, as interesting as—or more interesting than—the action that on weekends filled the television screen. So before the excellent sports section of the *Boston Globe* or even the mediocre sports section of the *Chicago Tribune* was tossed into his "garbage pile," he checked the columns that dealt with the Red Sox or the Cubs, the latest scandalous developments in the odoriferous histories of the Patriots or the Bears, even the most recent calamity in the Northwestern University athletic program or the triumphant announcement of the newest Southern Baptist recruit to the basketball glory of the Catholic colleges of New England. Then he would glance at the opinion pages, taking only sufficient time to confirm his conclusion that *New York Times* editorials were concocted from a recipe of one cup Pablum, one cup marshmallow and one cup Stovetop Stuffing, or that the *Wall Street Journal's* daily breaking of wind, at one time presided over by a man with the improbable name of Vermont Connecticut Royster, now was accomplished by someone with a nom de plume whose true name was Neanderthal Temuchin Coolidge. Finally he would pare the news sections down to those pages containing an item related to the near-death of the president. These went into a separate pile in the living room. The bedroom collection would go to the recyclers when there was enough to fill the bed of Deborah's pickup.

And in this bed, as he lay late on this Monday morning, he realized that something had happened to his sex life. Deborah hadn't complained of anything, and she accepted the fact that he had been inviting her to come over less frequently since the obsession had taken hold of him. Theirs had never been a sexual relationship characterized in contemporary fiction as comparable to a dynamite explosion or a railroad train plowing into the end of a blocked tunnel, although it was satisfying in a way both thoroughly appreciated. They had talked for many hours before they agreed that they would like to sleep with each other now and then, would remain totally uncommitted, were free to pursue whatever came into their lives and would continue to live separately. They were gentle and giving and undemanding of each other. When occasionally he or Deborah would say "I love you," they recognized it for precisely what it meant: I have concern for you; I wish you well. They additionally agreed that they would never fall into the trap of those couples who insisted on endlessly discussing "O.R." until it fell apart, tattered, shredded, in pieces. No, they agreed, Our Relationship is for now, for us, not for ever—unless, of course, we change our minds. Both of them knew marriage with the other was not to be their fortune; the meticulous and prudent Virgo was not meant for marriage to the fiery and impetuous Aries.

And his son was less on his mind. The pain of that piercingly cold January day, when Sarah had packed her suitcases and their son in their car for the drive to Berkeley, had diminished in the months that had passed. In recent weeks he found himself considering his son only when the envelopes with the boyish handwriting were in his mailbox and he promptly answered with long and loving letters. Of Sarah he almost never thought at all. But this morning she had briefly fluttered through his mind when he reflected that last night, for the first time since that January day, he had consulted the *I Ching*.

Among the other faults and virtues she shared with her father the university president, Sarah McLendon Blakely had nothing but contempt for the *I Ching* and Jonathan's interest in it. He had learned not to bring up the subject, or any other subject that was "unscientific" or currently under consideration by the liveliest and most curious intellects in the world. She shared her father's view that the authenticity of all ideas already had been settled by the conventional institutions of American society and their established press. Thus he did not in their company mention marijuana, hashish, LSD, police behavior, the prison system, the judicial system, the political system, the social system, the university system, the military-industrial-government complex, open marriage, homosexuality, assassination conspiracies, bodily functions, or—God forbid!—anything related to sexual intercourse. He curbed all tendencies to mock the two major political parties or say an unkind word about the medical profession; he kept to himself his opinions of law schools and lawyers and hospitals and corporations and ROTC and former secretaries of state and recent football coaches and fraternities and sororities and hippies and the underground press and professional nutritionists and psychiatrists, to mention a few of the limitations on his conversational opportunities with his wife, her father, her mother and, especially in recent years, his wife's friends. Sweet Jesus, he had more than once prayed, deliver me from this unto which I have fallen.

He was able to trace with confidence the moment at which his marriage had cracked beyond repair. No cement could fill the void created at a memorable dinner party at the home of President and Mrs. Reuben McLendon. A pall had descended around the barbecue pit early in the evening when he had observed, even before the guests had finished their first glass of wine, that a nation that cut down redwood trees to manufacture patio furniture was in an advanced state of irreversible decline. That was as nothing compared to his announcement at the dinner table, while steadily eyeing the white-haired tenured professor and chairman of the economics department, that a disgruntled state employee had provided Xeroxed evidence that Governor Ronald Reagan, after abolishing the monthly payroll deduction for state taxes so that taxpayers "would feel the pinch," had paid no state taxes himself that year, having taken advantage of the dubious shelters and other loopholes legislated for the sole benefit of the wealthy. The company had sufficiently recovered from that unwelcome datum to move into the living room for after-dinner drinks when Jonathan, brandishing a third glass of Cointreau he had poured himself in the kitchen, had called the dean of humanities a stupid ass or a stupid asshole—the stories subsequently varied—when the ass or asshole had said that Nixon had at least opened the door to China. Jonathan had followed the controversial opening remark with a pungent citation of chapter and verse including footnotes and suggested bibliographical sources, that came down to the fact that it was Nixon, with the assistance of Knowland, the China Lobby and other assorted bunco artists, who had padlocked the door to China for almost a quarter of a century, a period during which the United States was at war for a time with Chinese troops. At that point, correctly sensing the mood of the assembly, he had searched for and found his suit coat near the bottom of the pile on the bed in the master bedroom, somewhat discomfiting the newly hired assistant professor of physical education/defensive line coach and the lady with him, the wife of the aforementioned economics professor, who had coincidentally arrived in the same room before him. Sarah returned home two hours after his arrival and he regarded his decision to sleep in the den as a wise one. Nothing was the same after that.

Sarah's father retired at the end of that academic year and was replaced by a man of private grace but public awkwardness. There were snickers among some members of the faculty at coffee and lunch as they discussed the new president's clumsy attempts to convey friendliness at social functions, at his insistence on hiring professors of high academic achievement, at his resolve to hire deans who were honorable men or women, at his prattling about "academic standards" and the need to abolish what the students termed "mickey mouse" courses. Jonathan regarded him as an extraordinary fluke, a college president with vision, character and integrity who actually cared about the quality of education the students received. It took less than three years for the president to be run off by a baying pack of academic mediocrities, their chief hyena an internationally recognized literary critic. The English department's graduate students saw through him without difficulty; indeed, their private appellation for him was "The Prick." The English professor's lectures were recognized on campus as interesting, witty, charming, sexy, suggestive and original—they became his books—but he would bequeath no more than a casual skim to his examination papers before ascribing a grade based primarily on intuition or a remembered friendly office visit, and he never showed an appreciable interest in the progress or problems of his students. During the internecine warfare that erupted, the unfortunate president retained the support of the majority of the faculty but lost the votes of the majority of the college trustees (read downtown businessmen). Thus the harried president went off to fill a distinguished chair created especially for him at an institution of far greater distinction while a money-grubbing replacement honed his huckstering skills in Main Hall. The fabled groves of academe, no less than his marriage, had grown barren for Jonathan.

He desperately needed sustenance, and the manna came from the state's most prestigious university in the form of an offer that even Sarah couldn't refuse. So they had gone, with their young son, to the hills above Berkeley.

It was there that one of his students insisted that he go to the hungry i in San Francisco to see and hear a woman sing. She was on the same bill with Mort Sahl, and Jonathan was enchanted by her. Half-Apache, quarter-Cherokee, quarter something indefinable beyond her bloodline, she became the lover of his student and the friend of his dreams. She taught him; he taught her. Just as Gandhi had expressed astonishment that no one had told him of the Bhagavad-Gita until he had gone to London, Jonathan was stunned that he had reached the age of 33 without knowing of the *I Ching*. (He felt better when she explained that Confucius is said to have been 70 years old when he took up this first among Chinese classics.) She showed him how to prepare for the ritual, how to cast, how to read the messages of "The Book of Changes." She explained in detail how difficult it was for some people to understand, what it could not do and how it must never be used.

He noted the phenomenon, common to all, that often when we first learn something that impresses us we experience a rash of related references. Thus he smiled one Sunday shortly thereafter when, in a *New York Times* review of a book about Watergate, he read that the "pendular motion in human affairs is no new thing; under other names and with deeper subtleties one finds it at the heart of 'The Book of Changes.' No student of that book could have been astonished at Mr. Nixon's ruin, so soon after his 1972 triumph. Everything that grows, in the organic world of which politics is a part, grows toward its limit." He listened intently and with full understanding when a longtime good friend, seeking to become a produced playwright, had confided to him in a dark apartment overlooking the panhandle of Golden Gate Park, that it was the *I Ching,* with its message of ebb and flow of life, its assurance that this too shall pass, its warning that what we may think are blessings might well be disasters (and more importantly, the other way around), its insistence on reflection and change rather than morbid brooding, that had kept him from committing suicide. Jonathan studied everything he could find written about it for months before casting his first, doing it the honor that the Chinese, who do not take it lightly, accord it.

It was during that same period that he marked a file folder "Strange Deaths (and Other Tales)" and began dropping into it clippings and notes and four-by-six cards. In the years since then he had asked the *I Ching* seven times whether he should assemble his findings for publication and seven times he had been advised that the time was not right. Early on this Sunday morning of Summer Solstice, 1981, when he had returned from work, he had chosen to ask again.

The instructions were clear: "To abstain from action amidst deeds of blood is to accord with the principle of allowing things to take their course." And a reminder that he who strikes blows for the right must be as good an anvil as he is a hammer.

As ever, he respectfully noted the message, meditated on it, put away the books and coins and candles and cloth, and went to bed.

A few hours later, a soft knock on the door brought him to Deborah, laden with a grocery bag and a bottle of champagne.

"Hi," she said. "I thought I would celebrate the Solstice with my favorite recluse. A Sunday brunch of eggs Benedict, toast made from a loaf from the Bread Board, and a bottle of France's finest before we go to work. That is, if I'm welcome?"

He kissed her and apologized for not having invited her over—that day or recently. She said she understood, and together they went to the kitchen. She laughed at the piles of newspapers and remnants of magazines that lined the walls.

"I'm afraid to ask what's new," she said. "But what's new?"

"I just finished another section. Want to read it?"

"Love to. After we drink and dine, okay? Anything about the infamous plea bargain?"

"In another section I'm working on. Those sleazy Washington lawyers are beyond belief. They offer a guilty plea if Hinckley is sentenced as a juvenile. They make the offer a week before he's going to turn 26. The law was intended to apply to defendants under 21, but by stretching the law and your imagination it can be made to apply to someone who's 25 years old. You mark my words, Deborah, those guys are going to bust their balls to see that justice isn't done—that is, if Hinckley lives long enough. He's supposed to be under 24-hour guard and they tell us he tried to 'harm himself' by an overdose of Tylenol. And some people suggest that I'm the one who's making things up. Are you going to make the hollandaise or should I do the honors?"

They laughed, and they laughed more after the celebratory toasts to Solstice, a joint of excellent quality and the good meal they shared. While Jonathan did the dishes, Deborah went to the living room to read another portion of the growing article.

ADD TO "HINCKLEY-RICHARDSON CONSPIRACY" (after NYTimes, "which front-paged the Richardson arrest and possible conspiratorial ties to Hinckley, provided its readers with three days of extensive coverage of the potential links and then silently let the matter drop"):—until June 3, almost two months later, when it reported in the second paragraph of a two-paragraph story on page 26: "Authorities said they could find no connection between Mr. Hinckley, of Colorado, and Mr. Richardson, 22 years old, of Drexel Hill, Pa." Thus did the newspaper of record finally set the record straight.

THE SEARCH FOR "MOTIVE"/
THE DENIAL OF "CONSPIRACY"

The "information" dished out by the myriad of "authorities," "law enforcement officials," "federal agents," "sources," "unidentified sources," "sources close to the Reagan shooting investigation," "congressional and Justice Department sources," "one Justice Department source, who like others asked not to be named," "another source" and similar dodges were what the national news media placidly accepted during this entire episode. (In June, two months after the attempted assassination, United Press International sent a memorandum to its approximately 200 bureaus around the world with this introduction: "United Press International discourages the use of anonymous sources in all stories." The memo restates what UPI, without a trace of irony, says is its "longstanding policy on this subject, which has been debated in newsrooms throughout the country since the Janet Cooke episode." In what UPI called "the only significant revision of the original" earlier memo, reporters are urged to "strive for direct attribution in all interviews and briefings." It was not too little, but for the events stemming from the afternoon of March 30 unquestionably too late. And, alas, it has had not a whit of influence. The deplorable practice continues unabated.)

Furthermore, the coverage bears a striking resemblance to the thoroughly documented use of "disinformation" provided by intelligence agents and others throughout the world. Just as the KGB finds ways to get its propaganda published under the guise of "news" in infiltrated periodicals, so do the CIA and other agencies get stories published in their controlled or penetrated media, including the device of planting in foreign publications stories which are then innocently relayed to American readers by its free press. It was unnecessary in this case to go through overseas channels, however, because the FBI, Secret Service and CIA were in possession of all the essential evidence and could dispense it as advisable or necessary to its pliant press connections. Thus UPI, which had given a good run to the Houston Post exclusive on the Scott Hinckley-Neil Bush scheduled dinner (resulting in front-page play by many of the service's clients and a report on NBC Nightly News), was quickly graced with exclusive photographs of John Hinckley Jr. standing and sitting in front of the White House. The UPI insisted on protecting the source of the gift, leading to variously published disclaimers such as "acquired by United Press International. It is not known when the photograph was taken, or by whom." Another: "UPI would not say when or by whom it was taken or how they got it."

As a result, while the source of the photographs remains undisclosed, the fact is that from the moment the photographs were received by UPI no attempt that can be discerned was made to follow up on the Scott Hinckley-Neil Bush connection that several newspapers had considered sufficiently newsworthy to be given front-page play. Nor was there even a semblance of investigative reporting that explored any of the many other intriguing connections between the family of the accused assassin and the family of the vice president of the United States.

On that note, return if you will to the hours of the late afternoon of March 30, when law enforcement officials, congressional leaders, intelligence authorities, the White House and some journalists appeared to share a keen concern in quickly establishing a motive for the shooting and simultaneously defusing the notion of a possible high-level political assassination conspiracy. Consider the day-by-day official development of Hinckley's "motive," a leitmotif accompanied by a harmonic strain of "no conspiracy" arpeggios, conducted by agents of government as they played the organs of information as if they were instruments of the government's creation.

The first wire service reports were emphatic:

> There was no known motive, no explanation for the savage burst of gunfire that exploded as the president stood beside his limousine. (AP)

A few hours later in an update:

> Both the White House and the FBI said there was no evidence of a conspiracy to assassinate the president.
> "There's nothing at this point to indicate motive or conspiracy," FBI spokesman Roger Young told reporters.
> He added, however, it would be "foolish if you etch that in stone at this point." (AP)

The next day no time was lost in establishing a motive and polishing a stone on which to etch a memorial over the grave of any theory that suggested the possibility of a conspiracy among the influential. First came the hint:

> Sen. Paul Laxalt, R-Nevada, said today that authorities have established a motive in the attempted assassination

of President Reagan, but the senator refused to divulge the details.

Laxalt, a close friend of the president's, spoke to reporters outside the White House after he and other congressional leaders were briefed by Vice President George Bush and several cabinet members, including Attorney General William French Smith.

"It does not appear to be part of a plot," said Senate Majority Leader Howard Baker, R-Tenn. (AP)

"Sources" then added another touch:

> *Federal investigators have found an unmailed letter written by accused presidential assailant John Warnock Hinckley Jr. which indicated "he might go out and do something to get himself killed," Justice Department sources said Tuesday.*
>
> *The sources, who declined identification, said the letter also reflected that Hinckley was in an "I don't care what happens to me" frame of mind.*
>
> *Sources did not say to whom the letter was addressed, nor would they say exactly when it was written. They said it was found in Hinckley's quarters but refused to say exactly which location they referred to. (AP)*

After that gradual buildup, it was announced that the unmailed letter, as all the world now knows, was written to actress Jodie Foster, a student at Yale University.

Quoth UPI: " 'He did it for her,' said one source closely familiar with the investigation. 'She's the key.' "

Announced AP: "Administration and congressional sources, who declined to be identified, said Hinckley's letter spelled out his plans in detail. But they did not elaborate."

And: "Another source said a second letter was mailed, but the source would not say to whom."

And: "Congressional sources said a second unmailed letter written by Hinckley also was found but did not contain hints of suicidal behavior."

Furthermore, the letter "was described by four congressional and Justice Department sources, who refused to be identified," a tacit admission that no reporter had seen the letter. At that time AP expressed an equally interesting uncertainty: "The sources said Tuesday that investigators had found the letter Monday in Hinckley's quarters, apparently at the downtown Park Central Hotel where he stayed the night before Monday's attempted assassination."

"I have killed the president," the New York Times News Service blared that Hinckley had written to Miss Foster in the unmailed letter, qualified by "according to one account provided by sources familiar with the investigation." And, the tale continued, another account from an unnamed source reported that Hinckley wrote, "If you don't love me, I'm going to kill the president." Those two quotations appeared in headlines in newspapers across the land, although they failed to show up in later information concerning the text of the letter supplied by sources, named or unnamed, identified or unidentified, reliable or unreliable, close to the Reagan shooting investigation or far from it.

UPI's "sources" added some curious notes to the unfolding scenario while including the apparently obligatory assurance that no cabal lurked in the background:

> Sources said Hinckley wrote Miss Foster several times in recent months, threatening to kill Reagan for differing reasons. One was a real or imagined snub of Miss Foster by the ex-actor president. The other, according to sources, was a bizarre ploy to win her love....
>
> FBI investigators briefed Justice Department officials and key congressional leaders on the case, establishing, among other things, that there was no evidence thus far of any conspiracy in the shootings.

During the next two days the "sources" and the wire services stressed that last point. FBI spokesman Roger Young said investigators still had "no credible evidence that the shooting was more than the act of one man"; Attorney General William French Smith told reporters that "we do not have any solid evidence that more than one (person) was involved"; Tom

DeCair, a spokesman for the Justice Department, said "we've found no evidence whatsoever to indicate a conspiracy." Thus within three days the law enforcement agencies had succeeded in their two-pronged offensive, piecing together a plausible albeit questionable motive for the attack on the president and allaying suspicions of any act intended to elevate the vice president to the highest office in the land.

But some problems arose when actress Jodie Foster, a spunky young lady, ad-libbed a few lines and didn't quite play the role that either had been assigned to her or was expected from her.

THE "JODIE FOSTER LETTER"
The day after the shooting, Jodie Foster issued a statement to the reporters who descended on New Haven:

> The FBI and the U.S. Attorney's office have asked me to say nothing about John W. Hinckley. But I do wish to say that I have never met, spoken to or associated with him. I will have no further comment at this time. Inquiries should be addressed to the FBI.

The text of the unmailed letter, on which the motive for the assault on the president officially had been established, finally appeared in the Washington Post *three days after it reportedly had been found in Hinckley's Washington hotel room. Some newspapers carried the text supplied by the Associated Press "as reported today by the Washington Post," but others carried a more curious attribution:*

> WASHINGTON (AP)—Here, according to two sources who asked not to be identified, is the text of an unmailed letter to actress Jodie Foster found by law enforcement authorities in the Washington hotel room of John W. Hinckley Jr., the man accused of shooting President Reagan. The date "3-30-81" and the time "12:45 p.m." were written at the top of the letter, the sources said.

The letter, in which the irresponsible drifter and confused college dropout had meticulously included the date and time of day, *immediately began to arouse suspicions among some members of the press*. One need be neither a poet nor a lover to count the ways:

First: The text did not contain the quotations cited by the coterie of "sources" on which the press had chosen to rely and which had been played up in headlines and broadcast throughout the world. This fact alone served to cast doubt on everything else relayed to reporters by those who insisted on remaining unidentified.

Second: The references to "getting Reagan" in the unmailed letter ("There is a definite possibility that I will be killed in my attempt to get Reagan" and "Jody, I would abandon this idea of getting Reagan in a second if I could only win your heart...") caused Jodie Foster to balk. Exercising her free spirit, she disregarded the pleas of the FBI and the U.S. Attorney "to say nothing about John W. Hinckley" and called another press conference after the text was released. Seated in front of the fireplace in the wood-paneled living room of Calhoun College, she wanted to make at least one point perfectly clear:

> Foster acknowledged Wednesday she had received letters signed "JWH" and "John Hinckley," although she said none mentioned violent acts or the president.
>
> Published reports today, however, quoted the unmailed letter found at the downtown Washington hotel where Hinckley stayed the night before Monday's assassination attempt as saying, "Jody, I would abandon this idea of getting Reagan in a second if I could only win your heart."...
>
> "In none of these letters and notes I received was any mention, reference or implication ever made as to violent acts against anyone, nor was the President ever mentioned," Miss Foster said in a prepared statement. (AP)

The authoritative response, deserving of a footnote in the history of this strange case as the "Vague Allusions Construct," is almost on a par with Alexander Haig's memorable suggestion a few years back that a "sinister force" had erased 18½ minutes of Mr. Nixon's tapes. Roger Young of the FBI said

Miss Foster gave agents two letters, having discarded five or six notes earlier. Then this:
"Looking back, one can read in vague allusions in the letters," the FBI spokesman said. "But in no way would reading them alert the reader to a potential assassination attempt."

(Jodie Foster added a succinct personal review of the federal script that had Hinckley acting out the role of the protagonist in Taxi Driver, *a movie characterized by its scriptwriter as "waist deep in Calvinistic notions of worthlessness." Said Ms. Foster: "I'm not really clear if there are any connections" between the movie and the assassination attempt. "As far as I'm concerned, it's a piece of fiction.")*

A few days later a Yale University official let another cat out of the FBI's letter bag by emphasizing that Hinckley had never threatened the president in notes to Miss Foster:

> *The Yale spokesman reiterated that the university had been asked "not to release or discuss the language of the notes, so as not to interfere with the government's prosecution of the case."*
>
> *However, in response to questions about whether the campus police chief, Louis Cappiello, had erred in not giving the letters to the FBI before the assassination attempt, the Yale spokesman said: "The notes were considered harmless and in themselves did not present any violation of local or federal law." (New York Times News Service)*

Third: The text of the hotel room letter contained an introductory clause: "Although we talked on the phone a couple of times." But Miss Foster repeated her firmly held belief that she had never "spoken to" John Hinckley. Faced with the uncomfortable contradiction, patently uneasy authorities dipped once again into their sealed evidence and dug out another favor for the press:

> *Federal officials have found a tape recording of John W. Hinckley Jr. speaking by telephone to a woman believed to be actress Jodie Foster, the woman whose attention he*

wanted to win by allegedly shooting President Reagan....

The tape recording of the phone call, along with one of Hinckley playing the guitar, was found in the Park Central Hotel where he stayed the night before the attack on Reagan, it was learned.

Federal investigators were still trying to make certain Miss Foster is the woman on the short tape recording. Investigators believe the tape may buttress theories that Hinckley's obsession with the 18-year-old actress was linked to his alleged attack on Reagan. (AP)

The flimsy nature of these theories, so desperately in need of buttressing, was clearly revealed in the following paragraph in the Washington Post:

Investigators are working on the theory that the conversations referred to in the letter may have been made by an anonymous caller that Foster never knew by name. That caller could have been Hinckley, and the taped conversation could be one of those calls, sources said.

In building a case for press and public, law enforcement officials have had to do a striking amount of backing and filling. Surely one can be forgiven the notion that the government could buttress many another theory of what lies behind the events of the afternoon of March 30. The same story cited above concluded that "there is no evidence to suggest a conspiracy, but authorities are continuing to check every conceivable lead, officials said." Subsequently, the New York Times quoted the assurance of an FBI spokesman that agents are continuing to gather information to provide "answers for historians, archivists, researchers and those who will come up with conspiracy theories in the future." And the New York Times adds reassurance: "Bureau officials say they are determined to prevent a recurrence of the type of questions that still surround the assassination of President Kennedy in 1963." All good citizens wish the FBI well as it continues to check every conceivable lead.

Fourth: The news accounts of what those in possession of the sealed evidence say is contained in tapes reportedly found in Hinckley's Washington hotel room differ from what Jodie Foster insists is the case. All of these contradictions remain to be explained to the American public and no doubt the most interested spectators will be those skeptical journalists who had the temerity to imply that someone—either the actress or the spokesman for those guiding the case—was not telling the truth. The answer to that question might well prove to be one of the crackers to break open this nutty episode. And even if the contents of the tapes were released, they will leave unanswered questions similar to those raised by the transcripts provided by Richard Nixon of his notorious tapes.

Fifth: No member of the press, as far as can be determined, has seen the celebrated unmailed letter—or even a copy of it—first described as "hand-scrawled" and subsequently as "neatly written on lined paper." Adding to the mystery was the announcement by the Washington Post *that "the contents of the letter were pieced together through a series of interviews with sources familiar with it."*

Sixth: Still another letter by the lovestruck would-be assassin apparently awaits being "pieced together." The day after the president was shot, several news accounts reported that "Hinckley apparently imagined that Reagan had somehow insulted Foster, officials said." One account quoted police sources as saying that a note found in the Washington hotel room disclosed that Hinckley "planned to get even with the president because he believed Reagan had once snubbed the 18-year-old actress." Later stories suggested that a reference to the alleged snub was contained in an earlier letter Hinckley had written to the actress. The nature of the imagined insult has not been disclosed and the drawstrings of the sealed bag were popped open long enough to drop the evidence of the presidential slight back into the dark.

Seventh: The uneasiness of some journalists with the way the authorities were handling the case was exceeded by the anger of a letter-writer to the New York Times *who protested that it was an "outrage to civil liberties that the text of an incriminating but unmailed letter" had been leaked to the press.*

The Warren Commission in 1964 and the House Select Committee on Assassinations in 1979 had sharply criticized the practice of the Department of Justice in leaking information during previous assassination investigations. Obviously the ground rules for news coverage of extremely sensitive political events are in need of clarification.

Finally, in tribute to several reporters of this long and convoluted news story, it must be said that they attempted to provide something more than crazy-quilt coverage. In trying to break through the domestic iron curtain drawn around this event they have managed to indicate to careful readers the contradictions involved in official statements regarding the Hinckley letters and tapes held by the government. Even the most co-opted of American journalists, in the wake of the seemingly endless revelations of law violations, prevarications and cover-ups in the nation's capital, cannot deny that some of those in the employ of the government are not above lying, regularly and consistently, without shame or remorse. The contempt for the guarantees of the First Amendment held by many persons in government heralds a dangerous threat to the liberty of the press. If the national news media fail to serve the interests of the governed and instead serve the purposes of the governors, especially in so important a matter as an attempt to assassinate the president of the United States, it is no exaggeration to suggest that we may discover—perhaps too late—how fragile is our freedom.

She walked out to the kitchen, took the dish towel from him and placed it on the counter, and kissed him long and hard.

"I like you," she said. "I like you very much. I like what you are doing. I like the kind of person you are."

He kissed her long and hard. She knew then that she could ask him the question.

"We still have a couple of hours before we're due at the salt mine. Or is your bedroom too full of newspapers?"

"Never," he said as he picked her up and carried her out of the kitchen. "Never. Never. Never."

JULY

Highland Park is not Dallas... Highland Park is a planned community for the super rich.... The town is not just conservative. It pursues, almost to the exclusion of all other pursuits, the values of a period in American life that may never have really existed except in the hand of Norman Rockwell....

A week before his election, Ronald Reagan needed a backdrop for a final, 30-minute television commercial. He chose the Park Cities, Highland Park and its sister community, University Park. The Young Americans for Freedom and Campus Republicans at Southern Methodist University guaranteed the visuals. Old Moody Coliseum would be packed with young and scrubbed and innocent faces from the 1950s.

SMU cheerleaders and the Highland Park High School band would accent Roy Rogers and Dale Evans and Tom Landry. Red, white and blue balloons would descend on it all. Of all the stages in the land from which Ronald Reagan might make his final appearance before the American people, he chose this one. Facing a sea of faces from Highland Park.

Reagan went to Moody Coliseum on Oct. 30. Seventeen days earlier, John W. Hinckley Jr., who grew up in Highland Park, had bought the gun he would use to shoot Ronald Reagan.

— Jim Henderson, Columnist
Dallas Times Herald
April 5, 1981

Clarence Xavier Toole preferred to drink his beer in the Royal. It was more expensive there than in the saloons that dotted both sides of the streets in a four-block area of which the Tribune Building was the center, but he liked the tone of the place. For one thing, it called itself a Lounge, and he liked the subdued light that played on the red plush seats of the black booths, the extraordinary stereophonic sound system on which "Moon River" and "A Summer Place" were standbys, and the scantily clad waitresses in red and black who brought him the Dos Equis he preferred to what he called the "horsepiss with chemical preservatives and foam stabilizers" that passed for American beer. It was a cozy place, a sexy place, but best of all it was the place where the newspaper people of Placer gathered in their off hours.

He had come to the Royal after a good meal at the Golden Dragon Restaurant, topped by a fortune cookie that predicted "You will astonish a friend." This night, as was often the case, he drank alone at the bar and would continue to do so until the *Tribune* people began drifting in, their deadlines met or past. Then he would join them in one of the booths toward the rear, near the restrooms, or upstairs where tables could be pushed together to accommodate a crowd. This night, however, was a special night because he was just back from Denver.

He was a tall, thin man with a cadaverous face. His shoulders did not extend from the base of his neck at anything approximating a ninety-degree angle; they sloped sharply downward and from them dangled two limp arms. The tips of his fingers at the end of his two spindles reached to his knees when he was upright, and when he was seated they often tapped unceasingly on the table top or on his trouser legs. His eyes were set deep in dark-rimmed sockets and his skin had the sallow look of a man who resented and repelled sunlight. His teeth, when revealed by a wolfish smile, were ragged, pointed, or non-existent in a random order, but those he had were scrubbed to a gleaming white.

Robinson had been the best friend of this collapsed scarecrow of a man almost from the day he had arrived at the *Tribune*. He seldom drank alone with Weenie Toole, primarily because the tapping fingers pounded on the edge of his nerves. But when he saw Weenie on the street or their paths crossed in the office of the *Tribune*, he would always stop to talk to him. Weenie liked to get one of the first papers off the press each night and extract the gist of its pages in the Royal or in his hotel room. When he awoke in the morning he would start in the upper left-hand corner of the first page and read or skim every line, both news and display advertising, in the entire issue. He also would study certain favored sections of the classifieds.

Robinson had given much to Toole. He had given him the nickname by which everyone except Jonathan now called him, a higher degree of acceptance in the downtown community and, rather frequently, a 20-dollar bill or two. In return, Robinson had received a considerable amount of information that often served as background for his editorials.

Weenie did not resent the nickname that Robinson, without a trace of malevolence, had attached to him. He liked a joke as well as the next man and far more than most. In addition to boasting that he knew every story, clean or otherwise, ever told by anyone anywhere, he was the city's undisputed champion of sports trivia, portions of which appeared in a dazzlingly nostalgic weekly column he wrote for the *Tribune*. He also was the city's unofficial historian, possessing not only an encyclopedic memory for names, dates and places, but the kind of insatiable curiosity traditionally associated with journalists that kept his mental files current. As such, he was a friendly adversary of Placer's newspaper and television people; some days the emphasis was on friendly, on other days he could be a more formidable adversary than was comfortable.

Weenie had quickly recognized a kindred spirit in Jonathan, who had a passable knowledge of major events and personalities (as they were now called) in football, basketball, baseball and tennis during the last few decades. When they weren't playing off each other in matters athletic, they occasionally could be found testing each other on punchlines of stories, famous or infamous. When one heard a story that was new to the other, it was the immediate cause for celebration. It didn't happen very often.

"And why is the male alligator man's best friend?" Jonathan would suddenly ask.

"Because if it weren't for the male alligator," Weenie would respond without hesitation, "we would be up to our asses in alligators."

If a newcomer to the group didn't get it, Weenie would insist on a round for the group paid for by the unfortunate who had never heard the beginning and middle of the story. And no matter how many times the others had heard it, Weenie would embellish the tale until the table rocked. Weenie was good.

He had been born in Placer and had lived there all his life except for two years in the mines in Butte and a brief time underground in Idaho. He had gone to the university for three years off and on, taken some history and political science courses and established an imperishable reputation among his contemporaries for the outrageous nature of his behavior at keggers held in a canyon outside Placer and at the annual Foresters Ball and Military Ball. He always had money for beer and sometimes bourbon at the Royal and a meal in one of the two better Chinese restaurants. Rumor had it that he received checks from an annuity provided by one of his ancestors, but Robinson refused to confirm or deny the speculation.

Robinson also kept to himself other colorful adventures of Weenie's journey through life, parts of which were known to a small band of men who lived in the cheap hotel around the corner from the Tribune Building. Occasionally Weenie would drink too much and begin crying, and those would be the times when he would talk not for others but for his own needs. It was during the whimpering finale of a magnificent three-day joust with a series of bottles that Weenie Toole had told Robinson his story. Robinson had lifted the limp and craggy body of Weenie to the hotel, had locked the door over the pleading protests of some of the other residents, and had sat with the bones until they began to stir in the early morning hours.

"Misser Robinson," Weenie had said, "you're old Weenie's bess fren. You're the bess fren a man ever had." Then Weenie had cried, and while the tears rolled into the valleys of his cheeks and over the rim of his chin, he told Robinson why he no longer cared for the body of Clarence Xavier Toole.

He had been a shy, nervous child, closely protected by his mother, especially from his alcoholic and mean-tempered father. At her insistence he had learned to play the piano, and to hear Weenie Toole tell it, he had learned to play well. To run those long, thin fingers over the keys gave him peace and consolation when he had been rebuffed and teased and mocked by the other boys in the neighborhood. He had gradually come to understand that his unmitigated misery was not the result of a single crushing or overwhelming event, but rather was the product of uncomplicated frustrations and disappointments continually repeated. He would play by the hour, day after day, and he was playing on that day a friend of his mother and her daughter came to visit. The girl, about the same age as he, came to sit by him on the piano bench when their mothers had left the room, and she smiled at him admiringly as he played one song after another. He had been greatly disturbed by her body so close to his, for in the preceding months he had been fighting off a growing awareness that he had, as the neighborhood boys put it, "become a man." He was uncomfortable sitting there, and he had become awkwardly confused when the girl, in a quick motion, had put her hand between his legs. There had followed, Weenie Toole told Robinson, some exchange of words, some questions that brought a rush of blood to his head, and then she had placed his hands on her breasts. She had reached into his trousers, and at that moment the mothers returned to the room.

His mother had never let him forget how evil a boy he was.

Five years later he met a 17-year-old girl whom he married

and who asked him repeatedly during the dark hours of the several nights they were married to do again what he had, with repugnance and difficulty, been able to do only once to celebrate their nuptial eve.

"Ann you know, Misser Robinson, I aine never touched a piano and I aine never touched a woman since that time," Weenie Toole said in the hotel room, tears gushing down his face.

Whatever else he was, Weenie Toole was a born detective. He walked around the town and observed. He read and he listened. He kept his eyes and ears on the ready to receive, and remembered almost everything he saw and heard. Robinson believed that if Weenie's nerve hadn't cracked he would have made an outstanding detective or a competent newspaperman. And Robinson was never one to blame a man who had lost his nerve.

Weenie was back from Denver and in his pocket was a folded sheet of paper that he would hand to Jonathan when he arrived at the Royal. He wanted to see Jonathan's face when he read what was written there. This, he knew, was going to be half the fun. The other half had been finding the answers to three questions Jonathan had written on a piece of blue paper when he had made the deal.

When Weenie, toward the end of June, had casually said he was thinking of going to visit a cousin who lived on the outskirts of Denver, he had shaken hands with Jonathan on the secret pact.

"You get one of those cheapo round-trip fares the airlines are offering to keep from going the way of Braniff, come back with the answers to three questions and I'll pay your way," Jonathan had said.

"Good to see you back, Clarence," Jonathan said as he came into the Royal with the managing editor of the *Tribune*.

"Hi, Weenie," said Donald J. Bitterman, the hard-driving, hard-drinking, hard-to-satisfy honcho of the *Trib* news room.

"Nice to be back," Weenie said with a big smile for Jonathan. "Hi, Donaldo," he said with an even bigger smile. If there was one person Weenie especially enjoyed putting the needle into, it was Donald J. Bitterman.

Jonathan knew instantly the trip to Denver had been successful. The fact was confirmed as they walked up the stairs and Weenie nodded vigorously while the managing editor headed for the men's room. As Weenie's body bent and sat and stretched, Jonathan reflected that it was fortunate that Weenie Toole did not have another set of arms and legs, for then he would have resembled nothing quite so much as an octopus. Weenie leaned forward, reached into his coat pocket, pulled forth a folded sheet of paper and sent out a tentacle. "You owe me one hundred and forty-nine dollars," he whispered.

When the waitress who had followed them up the stairs with two bottles of Mexican beer and a bourbon-and-branch had descended, Jonathan opened the folded sheet and read what was written there. Weenie watched intently.

"Ain't that something?" he said.

"I'll be damned," Jonathan said.

"That's approximately what I said three times."

"Worth every cent, Clarence. I'll have it for you tomorrow. Come by the office."

The managing editor joined them. "What are you two Cheshire cats grinning about now?" he asked as he lowered his body, twenty pounds overweight, into a chair at the corner table.

"Clarence here is a natural-born detective. Do you know how he does it, Don? He keeps his eyes moving. Up, down, left, right. Keeps them moving all the time."

"Then how come I stepped in it?" Weenie said as he and Jonathan laughed.

The managing editor groaned. "I can see what kind of night this is going to be." He turned to Weenie. "If you're such an all-fired great detective how about coming up with a bit of research for your column? The last one was long on sentimentality and short on statistics. When you're writing about a game in Bozeman in 1935 the least you can do is include the final score."

"Oh, did I leave that out?" Weenie said innocently. "Perhaps you would be kind enough to give me an appointment so I could go over the ten most important unanswered questions that didn't appear in the news columns of the *Placer Tribune* while I was away? Do you think you could arrange that, Donnie boy?"

"Shit, Weenie, we're not putting out a paper for the author of the unpublished Montana version of the Encyclopedia Brittanica. We're not even putting out a paper for Jonathan's high-domed friends up at the U. We're putting out a paper—"

"—for the condemned men who work out at the pulp mill." Weenie's needle was sharp this night. "You know, I'm still waiting for that investigative report on the health and life span of employees out there. But your predecessor fired all the investigative reporters and brought in that docile bunch you have now, to which you have added your own few sweet things. Why don't you drop by your morgue and take a look at those bound files of the *Tribune* in the late sixties and early seventies when they had a state bureau that reported what was going on below the surface instead of the flatulent stuff that emanates from the state capital these days. And a local staff—may they know some peace on the papers to which they have scattered—that might give you some idea of what a newspaper can be."

"Advocacy journalism, pure and simple. We've grown up and out of that childish shit, Weenie. The function of the press is not to improve the human condition but simply to report it."

"If I felt that way, Donaldo, I'd go to work for ASARCO or Burlington Northern or some fucking oil company and leave the profession to people like Jonathan here." Weenie came on as if he had a pig on the spit. "What do you call what we've had since John Peter Zenger if not advocacy journalism? The advocacy of the status quo, the advocacy of the unrocked boat, the advocacy of the unturned rock because of what might crawl out from under it? The moments of glory of the American press have been few and far between, and this ain't one of those moments. Don't you listen to anything Jonathan's been saying?" He pointed to a folder on the table, with the telltale edges of blue paper sticking out. "What's in there, Jonathan?"

"The latest, collected but uncollated," Jonathan said. "A portion of the whole, an extremely rough draft that deals with Hunts and Hinckleys and Bushes. I keep finding new things all the time. But I warn you, Mr. Bitterman has done everything possible to discourage me from using it."

"Mind if I read it?" Weenie's bony hand was on its way

before the question he asked Jonathan had been completed.

"Don't mind at all. But not for discussion elsewhere. Okay?"

Weenie nodded rapidly and opened the folder. He read while the other two men discussed an item that had come over the wire that night reporting the results of a poll listing 24 professions in order of their reputation for honesty, integrity and ethical standards. Ministers were rated highest, followed by pharmacists, dentists, medical doctors, engineers, college professors, policemen, bankers, television reporters, newspaper reporters, funeral directors, lawyers, stockbrokers, senators, business executives, building contractors, congressmen, local officeholders, real estate dealers, union leaders, state officeholders, insurance salesmen, advertising practitioners and auto salesmen. They agreed that they disagreed with several of the rankings and thought it interesting that journalists were bracketed by bankers and funeral directors. "Between the necessities of life and death," the managing editor said sadly. "Maybe that's exactly where we belong."

Weenie Toole shut out the conversation as he avidly devoured the contents of the blue pages. When he finished, he pushed the folder across the table to Jonathan. "Holy smoke," he said. "That's dynamite. That's very interesting dynamite you have there, Dr. Nobel. You could blow up something with that. And what, pray, Donaldo, do you find wrong with it?"

"I fail to see the relevance," Bitterman said.

"You *what?*" Weenie almost screamed the words, making no effort to suppress his exasperation with the managing editor. "Holy Toledo, Donaldo, does someone have to hit you on the side of the head with a two-by-four to get your attention, you ass?" He turned his head for a moment and winked at Jonathan. "That was a joke, Donny boy. A very old joke. About the guy who explained why his mule was so goddamn obedient." He turned again to Jonathan. "Do you mind if I do the roasting?"

"Be my guest."

"Thank you. It's this way, Don. Right now Jonathan's trying to put two and two together. You say it's coming out five. All he's saying is that maybe it's five, and maybe it's three, and maybe—just maybe—there's something to all of these strange coincidences and connections and contradictions that seem to surround this case. He's saying that he doesn't know what it adds up to yet but goddamnit someone should be pecking away at the calculator. Like the man says, you can't find the answer until you try to solve the problem. That seems to me to be the function of both law enforcement and our fabled Fourth Estate. Right, Jonathan?"

"As the Frenchman with savoir-faire said, *continuez, s'il vous plait.*"

Weenie laughed appreciatively. "Another thing, my good Bitterman, how do you explain the curious fact that no one in the mass media of communications—if you'll pardon the expression—is trying to make any connections other than those provided by the agencies that weigh down the District of Columbia? The press seems to think it is perfectly all right to muck up the life of a movie star like Jodie Foster or some two-bit loony who's transformed into a copycat killer for a few days, but the minute someone with money or political connections seems to come into the view finder they turn and take pictures of the pileated woodpecker perched on the garden fence, if you follow my drift. When was Texas officially declared a safehouse? To put it most bluntly, my righteous right-wing friend, how come Jonathan here appears to be the only journalist in the fair land, in the whole fair land, to be concerned about this unholy business?"

Jonathan couldn't resist. "Just lucky, I guess," he said.

Weenie again laughed appreciatively. "Could you tell me the way to Carnegie Hall?"

"Practice," replied Jonathan.

The managing editor was not amused. "If you two comedians have finished your soft-shoe routine, I'd like to point out that you still haven't answered the question. What's the relevance?"

"Let me try, Clarence," Jonathan said, putting out his arm stiffly in front of Weenie as if he were trying to prevent a child from going through the windshield. "Donald is asking a fair question and he deserves a fair answer."

Jonathan pointed to the folder on the table. "For instance, I think I documented the fact that the vice president is close to all the Hunts. Not just the ones still living, either. There isn't a politician in Texas who hasn't heard—or told—the story about the time old H.L. Hunt invited George Bush to come see him when Bush was running for Congress in 1962, saying he had something for him. Naturally, George's mouth is watering all the way from Houston. Then old H.L. talks about everything but money and when George is getting ready to leave, H.L. hands him a thick brown envelope. George is certain he's really scored until he leaves and opens the envelope and finds that it's filled with a stack of political pamphlets. End of story, but it's clear that the Hunts and the Bushes have known each other for a long time. There's no law against that, and I'm not suggesting that there's anything illegal going on between them. All I'm saying is that under the present circumstances, in which George Bush almost became president, and you have this well-documented Hunt family track record, the matter should be publicly examined. Then add to that the Bush-Hinckley connections, and then pile the Hinckley-Hunt connections on top of that, and you've got a pretty big pile of something, which I'm sure you will agree was never explored in the national press. You may conclude that it's a huge pile of horseshit—that's your privilege. But you also may have a molehill out of which you could make a mountain. It would be the start of what used to be called, in the old days, a Big Story."

"Or a plot for a nighttime soap opera," Bitterman observed dryly.

"It's interesting that you should say that," Jonathan responded. "It's almost a cliché that J.R. Ewing is practically a saint compared to some of the real-life Dallas oilmen. I've seen that comparison again and again in the literature. It's one of the rare instances when television isn't exaggerating."

The managing editor frowned. "I still think you shouldn't screw around with that stuff. It's all conjecture."

"No, Donald," Jonathan said. "That's where I disagree. It's all facts. How you put those facts together is conjecture. And it seems to me that there's not a reporter or editor in America who doesn't engage daily in conjecture—it's the journalist's favorite form of professional masturbation."

"Look, Jonathan, I learned a long time ago that the world is full of strange coincidences and hardly any of them ever add up to a legitimate news story."

"Would you like to add to the list of so-called strange coincidences?" Jonathan leaned toward the managing editor. "Ponder the fact that UPI, which at least started out to report to its clients some facts that didn't fit into the government-controlled scenario and then was given some mighty favorable leaks, came within the well-known hair of going under. If it had folded, the people of this country would have only one American wire service and it would be one that has a 21-member board made up almost entirely of publishers who can look back fondly on luncheons in the White House where they were stroked until they purred. UPI is managing to continue operation, so we have been spared at least for a while a monopoly situation in news reporting, hardly something the founding fathers had in mind. Then mourn for a moment the folding of the *Washington Star*, which was the kind of paper that ran some interesting stories about Hinckleys and Bushes that the *Post* never did tell its readers—all those federal employees. Now the *Star* is dead and the *Post* thrives in a monopoly situation."

"There's the *Washington Times*," Bitterman interjected.

"You've got to be kidding, Donald. The *Star* was a far better paper than the *Post* in many ways. It just had the misfortune of being an afternoon paper in the 1980s. And you know nobody will ever take a Moonie paper seriously."

"Pretty thin stuff, friend," Bitterman said.

"Wait, there's more. And it gets more interesting. The *New York Daily News* carried several intriguing stories the *Times* didn't. The *News* barely got a last-minute reprieve and as of this date is still struggling to stay alive. The *Times* goes its merry way fatter and full of more brassiere ads than ever. Want another suggestive item? The *Los Angeles Times*, with impeccable credentials with the intelligence community, prints not word one while the L.A. *Herald-Examiner* hangs out the dirty linen for all to see. I never thought we'd see the day when a Hearst newspaper would shame a generally respected member of the daily press."

"Still thin, Jonathan," Bitterman said. "There isn't a judge on a bench anywhere who'd give credence to evidence like that."

"I'm not in a so-called court of so-called law, Donald. Not yet, at least. All I'm doing is adding to the long list of startling or suggestive or interesting or pure coincidences that encumber this case and the news coverage of this case. Look, man, when the *New York Times,* the *Washington Post,* the *Chicago Tribune* and the *Los Angeles Times*—the four major newspapers that have established an unimpeachable record of close ties to the FBI and the CIA—don't publish information which other newspapers consider worthy of the front page or a good spread, I submit we have a situation that deserves some scrutiny."

"And who do you suggest should do the scrutinizing?"

"Well, for a starter, I think the professionals ought to do it. The professional societies and organizations of journalism have refused to face up to a problem that didn't exist a few decades ago and that's the infiltration of their ranks by intelligence and law enforcement agencies. We've got to get everyone who is part of the dissemination of news to agree that a new code of ethics should make it clear, with no ifs, ands or buts, that no one can be a journalist and on the payroll of an intelligence or law enforcement agency. They ought to put this policy on a par with the defense of the First Amendment. That's how strongly I feel about this, Donald."

"Are you ruling out patriotism as a quality to be desired in journalists?" The managing editor managed a thin smile as he said the words.

"Donald, I forgive you that question. Stansfield Turner, who is possibly the only man with both an acute intelligence and a sense of decency to serve as director of the CIA, tried to make the same stupid point at a meeting with newsmen a few months ago and he got nailed to the wall by those present. The idea of a journalist serving as an undercover agent seems reasonable to a government man but it is an absolutely intolerable condition to a journalist with any ethical or historical base to his conscience. You can't serve two masters. You either serve the interests of the people, as the press was set up to do in the Constitution and the Bill of Rights, or you serve the government, which was established with all those checks and balances for good reasons. Anyone who doesn't fear the growing power of any government doesn't understand one of the first lessons of history. More people are coming to realize that the government does one hell of a lot of things that aren't in the public interest and a hell of a lot more things that are against the law."

Weenie Toole jumped in.

"You know what the guys who run the government want? I agree with Jonathan. They want the same thing the corporations want. They want a nation of complacent consumers, which we have in large measure right now, but they also want consumers of all the horse manure that they shovel out of the stables in Washington every day."

Bitterman gulped the last of his drink and sucked on an ice cube. "Well," he said slowly, "I for one live in no fear of my government."

"You know, Donald," Jonathan said, "I grieve for you more often than you know."

"And I pray for you more often than you know," Bitterman replied.

"For my salvation?" Jonathan smiled and Weenie laughed.

"No, simply that you'll get your head screwed on straight and stop being so damn paranoid."

The waitress was at their table. "Another round?"

"Not for me," the managing editor said as he stood up. "There's a late movie my wife suggested I watch with her. But I want to thank you two gentlemen for a pleasant evening and one other thing."

"What's that?" Weenie asked innocently.

Bitterman dropped a bill into the tray on the table. "At least you two comics didn't roast that old chestnut about Johnny Fuckerfaster."

The three men and the waitress all laughed, Bitterman for the first time that evening.

"You know, Donaldo," Weenie said, "every time I conclude you have no redeeming social value you come up with something that breaks me up. A lot of the time I know it's unintentional, but you can be as funny as anyone when you put your mind to it. As a matter of fact, the main thing I hold against you reactionaries is your lack of a sense of humor, or in some cases what passes in your eyes for a sense of humor, usually ranging from infantile to juvenile."

"Unlike, of course, the mature, sophisticated, cosmopolitan humor of you two jackasses, hey?"

"Hell, Donny, we think everything—finally—is funny. But you know, I thought of you last night when I saw that Arnie Palmer television commercial. It forms the corner where Wall Street meets Madison Avenue, otherwise known as Jockstrap Junction. There's Arnie, with that unmistakable leer of the locker room, saying 'and believe me, I'm a guy who believes in protecting the old equipment.' I'll bet you rolled on the floor on that one, right, Donald?"

Bitterman paused at the top of the steps. "Weenie," he said, "up yours."

Weenie couldn't resist. The grin flashed wide. "Hey, Donny, one last question. How does it feel to be managing editor of a newspaper that proclaims you can save more than the cost of a subscription by clipping the coupons in the paper and taking them to the grocery store?"

Bitterman stopped his descent. "Weenie," he said after a pause, "up yours all the way to Hoboken."

"Brilliant!" Weenie shouted as he waved a friendly farewell to the departing form.

Jonathan signaled two more to the patient and smiling waitress. She obviously liked being around people from the newspaper. Then he drew the folded sheet of paper from his pocket and looked at Weenie. "Any problems in Denver?"

"As everyone now says, a piece of cake. That's some crazy city down there. Speeded as hell. You call it Little Dallas but it's more like Little Delhi. Dirtiest damn air imaginable. They oughta pass a law that anyone who comes up from Texas has to live in town instead of out in the suburbs."

"Why, Clarence, I do believe you're prejudiced."

"Hell no, I ain't prejudiced. Some of my best friends are Texans." He winked at Jonathan. "I don't have an ounce of racial or religious prejudice in these lean bones, but some of those guys are something else. They're like from another planet."

"I know it's a disconcerting thought, Clarence, but did it ever occur to you that maybe these people have majority control of this planet?"

"It's a thought that's crossed my mind, but I fight it off. It's when I leave home that I realize how close I am to an extraterrestrial. But this was a good trip. What do you think of those

answers and them apples?"
Jonathan read again from the sheet that distinctly showed the effects of being carried in Weenie's coat pocket:

1. How did UPI get those two photos of H in front of the White House that suddenly surfaced after the shooting?
The absolutely solid information I got from "a reliable source who did not wish to be named" is that the photos were part of the sealed evidence taken from the home in Evergreen. They were slipped to a UPI photographer by a Secret Service agent (name on request). Motive unknown. But that's why UPI said that, as a condition of obtaining the pictures, it would release no further details on them.

2. What is the status of the "routine audit" of the Vanderbilt Energy Corporation?
First, Vanderbilt keeps telling the press that the audit began in February, but the DOE says it started Jan. 2, 1981. Second, Vanderbilt and the wheeler-dealer friends of Vanderbilt keep saying it was a "routine audit" and maybe it was, but it sure isn't looking that way. The fact is that the government has come down from the two-million dollar figure being talked about a few minutes before R was shot, but most of these disputes are resolved by negotiations. My source says there's no question that Vanderbilt is going to be billed for more than half a million they overcharged purchasers, plus interest, which could make it somewhere around three-quarters of a million. No small potatoes, no matter how Vanderbilt wants to mash them. Of course, further negotiations could bring down the total.

3. Blakely's Corollary: You can tell a lot about a town by examining its newspaper(s). See if it works, please?
I would say there are two Evergreens, or possibly one Evergreen split somewhere in unequal parts. On one hand you have the Evergreen of the New York Times and the Wall Street Journal, described as wealthy, exclusive, politically and socially conservative and so forth. That's the Hiwan Country Club crowd, in big houses in a development outside town and close to the interstate so they can get to Denver easily to do their business. Then there's the

other Evergreen, made up of earthy, outdoorsy, outspoken types, a lot of them native Coloradans, a fairly ballsy bunch. The weekly paper, as you say is often the case, is closely aligned with the first group. The managing editor is a self-defined "political conservative" and a self-admitted and proud male chauvinist. The paper used to have three pretty good women writers, all of whom fled when this man took over as managing editor. Here, in a nutshell, is what the paper and one segment of the town are like: A lady wrote a letter complaining that the paper printed the weekly horoscope on the same page as the local church listings, causing a "very disturbing emotional reaction." She suggested "I'm sure your attention to this will be appreciated by many." The next week the horoscope was moved to another page.

I picked up two distinct splits in the attitude toward the case. First, the Hinckleys and their friends keep emphasizing how the parents are not in any way responsible for their son's acts. Letters written by friends to the Post and News made the point several times, and the Evergreen paper went even further in an editorial by the managing editor: "We go to the same church. I have ushered you to your seat. I think you have ushered us to ours. . . . What he allegedly did was not because you failed him somewhere along the way, but because of some impulse. . . . You did not fail. He grew to leave the nest. That was your task. You accomplished it. . . ." Downtown, though, the attitude was that young Hinckley had an excessive dependence on his parents and was pretty much a spoiled brat. Everyone at the bars he frequented and the people at the Golden Hours Motel described young Hinckley as "normal," whatever that means in this context. The other split in opinion is more interesting. The Hinckleys wrote a letter to the weekly paper saying that they wanted "to set the record straight." They said that "although John did stay in our home from time to time, he was never a resident of Evergreen." The paper subsequently picked up the line and reported that young Hinckley "never was a resident of the town, but merely a visitor to his parents' home in

Hiwan Country Club." Another editorial later said "only his parents, not the man himself, lived in town." That ain't the way the people around there who saw a lot of him and don't belong to the local chamber regard his residency. The guys around the shooting range where young Hinckley signed in twice (in late December and then the first part of January this year) regarded him as a resident. He also applied for jobs at the News and Post and he listed his parents' home as his address. He may well be a congenital liar, but the residents of the other Evergreen come down solidly that the boy is one of theirs. They're not proud of it. They just shrug their shoulders and refuse to deny it.

Jonathan finished his beer and smiled approvingly at his friend. "What else did you dig up in the mile-high garden?"

Weenie Toole's lips were curled in an especially lupine fashion. "Well, I have what you guys call an update on the governor of Colorado furnishing the two state troopers to accompany the Hinckley parents to visit their son back in April, remember?"

"I do recall going up like a Pershing missile," Jonathan said with a quick laugh.

"Your instincts were right, good friend. It seems that Governor Lamm had met socially with Jack Hinckley on a fund-raising hiking trip to Mount Evans a couple of years ago. And you ought to know that when the protests started pouring in to the governor's office, the chief flack called in the press and said the Hinckleys were paying the air fare for the troopers and therefore the operation was at no cost to the taxpayers. My source said he couldn't find out if the state was reimbursed for the time spent by the troopers away from the duty the taxpayers were paying for. He also couldn't find out whether the rent-a-trooper program was open to the general public. Oh, yes, the governor's spokesperson allowed as how she was unaware of any threats against the parents at the time."

"Good going, Clarence."

"There's a nice little political addendum to that tale which I'm sure you'll appreciate. It seems that Jack Hinckley contributed a lot of money to the 1978 and 1980 campaigns of Congressman Tim Wirth and was a member of the Republicans and Independents for Wirth Committee. That appears to be the way Republican and Independent oilmen funnel their contributions to guys who come on as liberal Democrats. 'Tis true, the bedfellows in politics are strange to the genuine innocents of the world."

Jonathan laughed. "Please, sir," he said as he held up an imaginary porridge bowl, "I want some more."

Weenie Toole rose slightly from his chair, hunched what there was of his shoulders and distorted his voice as he became the thunderous guardian of the workhouse. "What? More? You want more?" He crossed his arms rapidly in front of him, fell back into his chair, and was once again Weenie Toole.

"Try this one on," he said. "But I must preface this pouring with the host's suggestion that I think you'll be amused at its presumption. Nicholas von Hoffman had written a column about the attempt to assassinate Pope Paul and made some passing reference to young Hinckley. It ran in the *Rocky Mountain News,* and shortly thereafter the Senior Hinckley wrote a letter to the paper—here, I made a copy of it—in which he leads off with the following: 'Words cannot describe the pain that was so thoughtlessly inflicted on our family by the unjust column by Nicholas von Hoffman comparing our son John with Mehmet Agca (even before John has had a chance to defend himself in court).' Then he says—honest to God, it's right here—'The inconsiderate hatchet job that Mr. von Hoffman and you did on our troubled son is a cowardly cheap shot.' Now that strikes me as a particularly unfortunate choice of words, wouldn't you say? Then he says: 'It is patently ridiculous to compare John with Mr. Agca. Unlike Agca, our son is not a member of a terrorist group or a political conspiracy. John is simply mentally ill.' Well, that's the *corpus delicti.* No, wait a second—" He had seen a small newspaper clipping sticking out of the copy he had made of the letter. "Here's an answer to Jack Hinckley's letter by a fellow named Joe Ledbetter in Aurora. He quotes the 'words cannot express' part and then he writes one sentence: 'I wonder if the Hinckleys consider the pain and suffering their son has inflicted on our president and the Reagan family and James Brady and his family.' "

Jonathan shook his head and expelled a breath.

"You're pretty damn good, Clarence."

"The way I figure it, there just isn't anybody in the world who doesn't have at least one skeleton in his closet and if I try hard enough there isn't a closet door I can't open."

The hour was late, the beer had been good and Jonathan thought he could take a chance. "What do you know about me?"

Weenie Toole stabbed a pencil-like finger at Jonathan. "Well, for one thing there's Debbie."

"That's Deborah," Jonathan said in mock dismay. "Debbies are cheerleaders, airline stewardesses and corporate secretaries. Where do you never eat?"

"In a place called Mom's."

"Who do you never play poker with?"

"A guy named Doc."

"Who do you never sleep with?"

"A woman whose problems are greater than your own."

"Right. And never get involved with a woman who calls herself Debbie."

"Whatever you call her, she's one hell of a woman. Have it your way. Want another secret exposed?"

"Shoot."

"There are a lot of people—and I mean a lot of people, Jonathan—who think you are maddeningly contentious, opinionated, brassy and at minimum a bit tetched and at maximum a ninetieth percentile crazy son of a bitch. I hope that doesn't hurt your feelings."

"A lot of people, huh?" Jonathan thought about that for a few seconds. "I plead guilty to being intentionally inconsiderate of the feelings of others on occasion, but I try to follow William Blake's suggestion that if you are always ready to speak your mind, a base man will avoid you." They laughed. "You know, Clarence, there was a guy who studied the matter for a long time and he came to the conclusion that anyone who adjusted to the palpable insanity of this world and thereby was regarded as sane was actually insane, and those who couldn't adjust and we call insane are the truly sane ones. Which category do I fall into?"

"Hell, I think you're just plain crazy," he answered without hesitation. Then he added: "Like a fox."

"If I had any more beer I'd drink to that. C'mon, let's go. What did the man having his first intravenous feeding scream at the doctor?"

"It needs sugar in it!"

AUGUST

What is it we find in Montana?
Some people come and look, and laugh and go away.
Some stay for awhile, smiling secretly at these people and their foibles. They depart laughing too.
Montana—backwater. Montana—oddballs who do oddball things. Different. Unsophisticated. Unsubtle. Quirky values.
They don't comprehend what Montanans know.
It has to do with the tie between the people and the land. . . . It has to do with sound and feel. Montana hums. The sound has feel. The sound we hear is from the land, and it takes years of living here to hear it, to feel it enlace your soul.
The land hums. It's a very gentle thing, soft and compelling, hypnotizing. The hum has vibrant beauty. You can feel the beauty of the land.
It both transcends and contains the physical and emotional attractions—the forests and streams, the wildlife and fish, the convenience of life. Fifteen minutes from downtown in any western Montana community and you and the land can be alone.
All that is part of it, but there is more. The hum both enters and enwraps the Montanan. It grips that person and blends him to the land. We are different, even quirky, because we belong to the land we possess. It compels us to love it, and that loving shapes us.
The seduction is subtle and takes years. The consummation even goes unnoticed. When did a newcomer stop being of that, and became of this, and can never return? When did this hum so low and compelling weave its mystic web around one, a network of fragile strands whose strength cannot be broken?
Like love, it cannot be explained. Like love, it's a spiritual and emotional thing. Like love, it cannot be snapped by denial. Unlike love, it cannot rotate into hate.
They go away, these splendid young Montana men and women. They go for opportunity or to "make it" in the world away. Usually they succeed because this land produces strong good people. Often they succeed and return because the land beckons. If they remain away, they yearn for something valuable which they have lost and which no place else can replace.
Natives and transplants alike hear the compelling hum of the land, the gentle summons that causes an echo to answer from the heart.
This isn't our land. This land is its own. We belong to it. It has possessed us, willing captives who hear its hum and must respond with love.

— Sam Reynolds, Editorial Writer
The Missoulian

As Alonzo Schaeffer walked the two blocks to Granite Street between the Old Town Cafe and the O'Hanlon Hotel's coffee shop, he silently formulated the questions he intended to ask Jonathan Blakely. The meeting had been arranged by Robert Robinson ("Jonathan said he has an early breakfast but he'd be pleased to meet you for coffee," the editor of the editorial page had said), and was scheduled for 9 a.m. In Placer appointments were almost always kept punctually, Alonzo Schaeffer noted, a pleasant foible considering the otherwise generally tolerant and easy-going nature of the town. It was not at all like Billings, about which he had written an article that had appeared in his paper three days earlier. That town appeared to belong more to Wyoming than to Montana, and was rapidly filling with junior executives in three-piece polyester suits who were moving in from Texas and Denver to take advantage of the boom times under way with bigger and better ones anticipated. To those young men time was a special, valuable commodity, not to be wasted unnecessarily. Develop, develop, develop; such is the stuff of which fortunes are made. But not in Placer, where things were quiet, the economy depressed, survival taking priority over searches for fortune.

He would be on time and he would be prepared for anything. Robinson had briefed him extensively on Blakely, one of those journalism professors who had questions concerning the current performances of the wire services, newsmagazines, network newscasts and many newspapers. That opinion extended to Alonzo Schaeffer's own newspaper. Uh-huh, included his own, the most distinguished of American newspapers. He was aware that his paper had faults—books had been written about its many faults—but he was not naive enough to think that the profession was ever going to do any better. He was a veteran who long ago had ceased to be shocked by political amorality, who had seen diplomatic deception worked by foreign and American hands with equal facility, who had watched the speculators scavenging in the mealy refuse of human misery, who was accustomed to the servants of corporations successfully getting men to their liking elected to political office so that they could engage in the rawest forms of human exploitation—political, economic, social and sexual. He knew well of bills that exchanged hands, of proffered and accepted bribes, of the threats to destroy those who stood, on principle or in desperation, in the way of power. He had written many stories for his paper on these subjects and almost all of them had been published; reasonable men could reasonably differ about those that had not. And he would be the first to admit, if Blakely or anyone else challenged him, that his stories had fallen like a snowflake on the waters of a rushing river. The fat calf and the sacred cow, who thrived on silence, indifference and apathy, were only rarely corralled and never butchered by the press; most Americans never really rise up against the pervasive corruption in our society. That, however, was not the fault of journalists or journalism, he was certain, no matter how much some critics researched and published and complained.

He also knew that even if the stakes were great in this city and this state, they were even greater more than two thousand miles to the east. He knew that the tentacles of Boston and New York banks had curled around Placer and other cities of this state both before and after the turn of the century, crushing the figures who were giants on their limited stage but mere pawns on the platform of American finance. This, perhaps, was the saddest fact of all: The wars of the copper kings had been personal battles between men who could see and hear and know one another; now the satraps of the conglomerates struggled far from the scene for dominion over the treasures to be won. Who is to blame for "progress"?

He had seen Jonathan Blakely a few weeks ago, on a platform speaking as part of the university's lecture series. He had been impressed by the self-assured informality of the man and with his oratorical ability, with his intelligence and with his courage in facing an audience that included elements hostile to his arguments. He also was put off by an occasional unflattering flair of arrogance, a self-righteous, overbearing air about some of the conclusions, a contentious quality he thought unnecessary. But that was the face Jonathan Blakely either consciously or otherwise presented to the public, and Alonzo Schaeffer many times in his life as a journalist had discovered that men wear masks in public. Some had worn masks even in private, attempting to deceive not only others but themselves. He wondered which of several lines of questioning open to him would be most successful if an unmasking became feasible. He decided, as he stopped to look up at the clock above the sixth floor of the Condor Building, that he would try at least once to catch Jonathan Blakely off guard.

"Placer's Finest Hotel," the sign announced without qualification. The edifice behind the sign was meant to be impressive, and by Placer's standards it was, covering half a block and rising seven stories above the street. It was hardly enough to impress Alonzo Schaeffer, who had wined and dined and slept in the finest hotels of London, Paris, Vienna, Geneva, Tokyo and scores of other cosmopolitan cities of the world. He had chosen to stay in the new motel that sprawled along the river, preferring its plastic poshness to the eminently serviceable offerings of the red-brick hotel. The O'Hanlon had been constructed to look sturdy and permanent, but it also, probably unintentionally, looked forbidding. It appeared to be considerably more than a half-century old, Alonzo Schaeffer guessed, and the heat of the summers and the chilling winds and snows of the winters had darkened the bricks to a point where, also probably unintentionally, the building had acquired a kind of dignity. What probably was intentional, he surmised, was that its architecture unarguably was undistinguished; in Placer the ornaments and filigrees of the east would be out of place. The wooden steps to the coffee shop had once been painted, he noted as he ascended them at two minutes before nine, but the shoes and boots of customers over the decades had scuffed the wood even more deeply than its original exterior. In the east, patina forms; in Placer, exteriors are worn down. That no one had repainted the steps he thought both interesting and significant, for he had walked the silent tiles of a once-thriving department store in Placer, now slowly dying after being taken over by a west coast chain that had covered the resounding wooden floors with linoleum.

A flurry of movement around a chair in the lobby caught his attention. A man who had been sitting there, behind a copy of that morning's *Placer Tribune*, was being asked to leave by two uniformed employees of the hotel. The man had protested briefly, but now was lifting his thin, gaunt frame from the chair and moving toward the exit. He towered above the two men who nudged him, as unobtrusively as possible, on his way, but he could not have weighed much more than half as much as either of them. The man from New York smiled as the barely fleshed skeleton turned for a last word to his escorts before leaving the premises.

The coffee shop hostess greeted him with a warmth that surprised him—yet another contrast between life here and in Manhattan—and led him to a booth as if she had been instructed to expect his arrival.

"I'm Alonzo Schaeffer," he announced to the man seated in the booth.

Jonathan Blakely stood with his hand extended to greet him. He was even taller than Alonzo Schaeffer remembered and there was a pleasing firmness to his handshake. He was dressed casually, even for Placer, his collar open at the throat and chest hair showing where two more buttons down the front remained unfastened. He looked younger than he had appeared when standing behind a podium to deliver his lecture in the university's music auditorium. Except for the hair and the eyes, the reporter quickly noted; up close he could see that the dark-brown hair was streaked with gray and the eyes, also dark brown, were those of a man who was too much in front of a VDT, who read too much, stayed up too late, spent too much time in libraries. Nonetheless, Alonzo Schaeffer thought, eyes that still sparkled with the enthusiasm of youth.

"Mr. Schaeffer, I'm pleased to meet you. Placer is honored. I've read many of your stories."

Alonzo Schaeffer bowed his head slightly and returned the compliment.

"And I'm honored to meet you. Robert Robinson has told me a lot about you. He gave me your article on the '68 Democratic convention in Chicago to read. Very interesting. I'd like to discuss it at length with you sometime."

Jonathan Blakely smiled and motioned the man from New York to sit down. He already had a cup of coffee and he signaled a waitress for another.

"Any time," he said. "I imagine much of it didn't set well with you."

"Perhaps less than you imagine. I have few illusions about the press." He abruptly changed the subject. "I envy you, living here. I like this town. And every time I come through I like it more."

"Yes," Jonathan Blakely said. "A bit rough for the tastes of some, but I like the earthiness. Once you get to know this place and have a taste of it, you realize it has a special sort of flavor. I'm really not one to talk, though," he added quickly. "I came here from California and I'm regarded by many of the locals as one of those who want to Californicate the state. You've seen the bumper stickers, I trust?"

"Yes, I have. I like another one, too—something like NO, LADY, I'M NOT A COWBOY—I JUST FOUND THE HAT."

Alonzo Schaeffer sipped the coffee that had been set before him. He noticed for the first time a stack of newspapers on the seat next to the other man. On the top was a copy of the *Boston Globe*.

"Robinson has been after me for some time to meet you," he said. "He tells me that few, if any, people share the degree of your suspicions toward the east, what you call the orthodox press and especially the eastern orthodox press."

"As usual, Robinson is mostly right." Jonathan Blakely paused for a moment and then picked up the newspaper on top of the pile. "I was reading this paper while waiting for you. I think it's not only the best daily newspaper in the east but in the United States. It's not without its faults, and some benighted publisher a few years ago said it was a paper where the inmates have taken over the asylum, but at least it has made a pioneering start toward what daily newspapers ought to be rather than what most of them are. Care to listen to something?"

Alonzo Schaeffer laughed. "I like the way you push aside the amenities and get to the point. Yes, I'd like to hear it. Do you mind if I call you Jonathan?"

"Not at all, Alonzo. Okay, listen to this. It's a signed piece. Here: 'Washington is home to the world's largest collection of fakers, frauds, phonies, hypocrites, eunuchs and weasels.' Now you know what's wrong with that sentence? It isn't hyperbole. It isn't inaccurate. Every one of those nouns is justified. What's wrong is that it omits the most important word, the most crucial word of all. Crooks. It's all of the above plus crooks. Okay, now here's another part: 'For instance, the United States Senate—a collection of profiles in Jell-O—recently voted 98 to zip not to spend $736,400 on a new gymnasium—only after they got caught trying to sneak the money through earlier in the summer. But going to Washington means having no shame. It means you can never have enough.' Then there's this graph: 'They have people like Jesse Helms, a Bible-bleating redneck who stammers about the cost of welfare fraud and food stamp cheats while he pimps for bigger tax breaks on behalf of industries and corporations that rob more in an hour than an army of welfare cheats could steal in a decade.' And so on."

"You and the man from Boston share an abnormally low opinion of the United States Senate."

"I'm not saying there aren't any decent, informed, sensitive, compassionate people with vision and courage in the United States Senate. There are—the number nine comes to mind. It's a collection of millionaires. Before the Constitution was amended the Senate was reserved for the propertied class, but as usual they found some way to get around the law and they control that chamber with a vengeance. They vote themselves unconscionable salary increases and special privileges granted no other taxpayer while people are dying in and out of hospitals from malnutrition. What everyone keeps forgetting is that there are millions of people who don't vote in every election, and the pundits dismiss them as idiots who don't care enough to exercise their franchise. What the pundits never admit is that most of those millions don't give a damn because they know it doesn't matter which tweedledum or tweedledee gets elected.''

"As a somewhat weary man of the world, Jonathan, I admire your irritation at some of Washington's wretched excesses,'' Alonzo Schaeffer replied. "I would say that our national capital has its share of those individuals. It's about average, I'd say. So what else is new?"

This man becomes agitated quickly, Alonzo Schaeffer thought as the words poured out.

"Right there, right there—that's what I mean. You think Washington is just another average town where good and evil and honesty and dishonesty are balanced in about the same proportions as anywhere else. And I submit that until one perceives Washington as by far—by far—the most corrupt city in the United States of America, it is impossible to report on it accurately. That's one of the primary objections I have to your paper, Alonzo. It's non-judgmental. Sure, it reports about the senators and their gymnasium scam but it never even begins to suggest that it's typical of the standard of morality that pervades the sleazy place. Hell, man, if I'm covering something that would turn the stomach of any reasonable person you can shove your so-called objective reporting out of the sun. You know, every decent thing that's happened in this country in the last two decades has come from outside Washington and from outside the elite media. You name it—the civil rights movement, the anti-war movement, the peace movement, the women's movement, the environmental movement, the good food movement, the hospice movement, the solar energy movement, the nuclear freeze movement—hell, all the movements that could make this a land of milk and honey have been led by people outside the political system and the mass media. Oh, of course all the big papers will come around four or ten years later and support it and *Time* and *Newsweek* will stop knocking it and the politicians will finally get it passed into law, but no thanks, friend, I'm not thanking them. And all the small dailies test the 'validity' or the 'correctness' of their news values by bouncing their front page off the front page of your paper and congratulate themselves if there's some degree of correlation.''

He stopped and put the *Boston Globe* back on top of the pile of newspapers next to him. "End of lecture. Sorry. Let's have another cup of coffee."

This time Alonzo Schaeffer signaled to the waitress.

"I can't say I agree with you, Jonathan, but I assure you that you haven't offended me. Those of us who dish it out, without malice and no matter how objectively, have to expect to take it, too. It comes with the territory. Some newspaper people, especially editors and most especially publishers, are remarkably thin-skinned. There are all kinds of critics. You know as well as I that most men think they could do better than the football coach or drive better than anyone else or are the world's greatest lovers. You certainly try to document the charges you make. And another thing I noticed in your articles is that even when you write about press performance with considerable vehemence, you write more in sorrow than in anger. You can't hide your genuine affection for journalism as a profession. I like that about you."

"You're right. I can't remember when I didn't want to be a newspaperman. And I want you to know that I have a great deal of respect for what you write about this state and this region. You have an admirable degree of understanding of its history and its problems. You do your share of research, too, Alonzo. I wish you well."

Alonzo Schaeffer saw his opening. "Robinson tells me you are working on an article that has to do with the abortive assassination attempt." He said it in such a way that it was half-statement, half-question.

"Actually, it has more to do with the news coverage of that almost successful assassination attempt," Jonathan Blakely said in measured tones.

"Robinson also tells me that you are a conspiracy buff, that you believe young Hinckley might be part of a conspiracy." Once again the half-statement, half-question. He let the words sink in. He watched for some reaction, but none was forthcoming. He pushed a bit further. "Have you finished it?"

Jonathan Blakeley's head tilted slightly. He stared at the man from New York. Then:

"You know, a couple of months ago a former student of mine

who signed up for a four-year hitch in the army sent me a clipping from Germany. It was an editorial in the *Frankfurter Allgemeine Zeitung,* which as you know is a respected conservative newspaper. He underlined a sentence that said that the chain of political murders in America is too long to be written off simply as the work of neurotic loners. And yet every time someone in this country suggests that there are unanswered questions that the government and/or the press are busting their respective asses not to answer, that person can be certain he will be labeled instanter as a kook or a nut or some sort of fruitcake. I'm not even close to being ready to state that there was a conspiracy to kill Ronald Reagan. I was ready to state categorically that there is a conspiracy to cover up a lot of pertinent information connected with that well-publicized event. I'm not sure I want to do it now. The naked truth of the matter is that I'm more than a bit frustrated about the whole thing."

Alonzo Schaeffer frowned. "Frustrated?"

"Yes, frustrated. For almost five months now I've been clipping and pasting and calling up and writing and rewriting and throwing away more pages than I keep and I'll tell you I'm utterly sick of the whole thing. Everyone accepts the cock-and-bull stories put out by the Justice Department with the aid and abetment of the White House and then pushed by the news media. What I know deep down in my guts is that what we have been told are the facts are not what is sometimes redundantly referred to as true facts."

"I'm not bothered by redundancy. But facts always concern me."

"How would any of us know we had all the significant facts of the matter in this case? Suppose—just suppose for a moment—that everything we have been told about the assassination attempt happened to be correct. All the facts, each of them true, would add up logically to a valid conclusion. What do we have? Hinckley is a neurotic punk with an obsession for an actress, so he shoots the president. What's the evidence? A letter no one outside the government has seen, that has been 'pieced together,' and a transcript of a tape the whole of which no one has heard. I'm not necessarily berserk for suggesting that there might be more to it, am I? Now—" He pointed a finger at Alonzo Schaeffer. "—just how do you go about proving a conspiracy? That has to be the all-time, all-American, national champion Catch-22. Not even Joseph Heller would touch that one. All you can do is say hey, what about this? And this? And that? Ad infinitum, ad nauseam. And your paper, sir, is no help. It sets the tone for the rest of the press on the subject of political assassination. It dismisses the possibility, it mocks those who don't, and worst of all it lies its ass off about it."

"Come on, Jonathan, let's document the rhetoric."

"I have a better idea. *You* document the rhetoric. Check your paper's index, Alonzo. Just read the reviews of the books that even suggest there might have been a conspiracy to assassinate a political figure. When you're done, check some of the editorials on the subject down through the years. You'll see clearly enough what I'm talking about."

"I am the first to admit that our editorial writers fart dust," Alonzo Schaeffer said. "But I'll look into it. You may have a valid point."

"Hell yes, I've got a valid point. You know those *Philadelphia Bulletin* ads in *Editor & Publisher*? That's the way I feel. Like the guy who is frantically pointing to an escaped lion or warning of some other imminent calamity that nobody else notices because they're busy reading the *Philadelphia Bulletin*. Except that every time I examine the simile I burst out laughing at the overwhelming irony that emerges."

"There is a recurring thought, Jonathan, that I believe I should mention," Alonzo Schaeffer said as if he were walking through a mine field. "If you feel so strongly that the press hasn't told the real story of this event, why don't you get off your duff and find out what it is? It's all very well for you to sit back with the fruits of your present research in a big bowl, right next to the popcorn, and watch the passing parade, but that's not journalism. That's the effete choice of the gentleman scholar, which I fully understand you deplore as much as I. There's an internal contradiction in what you're doing. If the story is as big as you so heatedly contend, then go get it, man, go get it."

"Touché, Alonzo," Jonathan responded with a smile. "But I set out intentionally to do it, as the song says, my way. I knew I could be faulted for doing only one kind of investigative reporting, but it's the kind I want to do until there's a trial. If everything comes out at the trial then the only complaint I'll have is that the American people were kept in the dark far too long. And if it doesn't come out at the trial, then I'll consider going and getting the story. I don't think the matter requires my urgent attention in the meantime."

"Well, I hear you, but I don't agree with you."

"I chose the way I wanted to go and I choose to wait it out. I got most of my information from reading newspapers outside the elite circle and talking to reporters all over the country. I suggested to a couple of them that they follow up on the leads I had and they chose not to do it. But they confirmed a lot of stuff I've put together. There isn't a piece of information I've written so far that hasn't been available to the national news media, but they also have made their choice not to let the people know about some patently significant items."

"All the more reason you ought to publish your article."

Jonathan shook his head. "No, not yet. Maybe later, maybe never. The timing is wrong. I'll wait for the trial. That's the system—you give everyone a chance to get at the facts in a trial. But they've stalled. They're obviously not ready for a trial. They've got to make sure that everything goes as planned when it finally comes off. That's the way it was in the Moscow trials under Stalin and that's the way this one is going to be—if it ever does come off. The best thing from the government's standpoint is a carefully controlled trial, what is really a contrived trial. The second best thing is no trial at all—something happens to Hinckley. Something stronger than Tylenol. What is nowhere near the third best thing is a trial in which all the reasonable questions surrounding the event are answered. Did you see that story the other day about the FBI's second report to the prosecutor in which they said all the loose ends in the investigation were tied up and no evidence of a conspiracy was found? Well, that's good news, but then they added a statement that they had gone to tremendous lengths to cover anything that would tend to indicate a conspiracy so that when historians look at this event there will be a firm basis to preclude questions that could arise. As a citizen of this nation I don't want to wait for the historians. I want it now—I wanted it five months ago. And don't tell me that the information I want made public would endanger the defendant's right to a fair trial. When it comes to attempts at political assassination the public's right to know takes precedence over so-called premature disclosure—and that's putting it mildly."

"Or as mildly as you tend to put matters on which you feel strongly."

"Touché again. But one of the many reasons I'm so agitated about this matter is that the readers of your paper—if you want it right between the eyes, Alonzo—are aware of nothing but the official line put out by the government."

"All the more reason for you to publish, and soon."

"No, I think not. I have reasons I really don't want to talk about, too. You'll have to trust me on that point. I don't seek publicity, I don't need publicity, and I don't want publicity. I value my privacy a hell of a lot more than I used to. I don't want any crazy phone calls. I don't want any nutty letters. I don't want the IRS or the FBI or the CIA or any other alphabet soup on my table. I've written what I think are the best critical analyses of press coverage in the last few years and I'm through with that part of my life. I don't want to go over the same ground. I'm not trying to hide the fact that I'm discouraged. I like the way I'm putting together a new life and I don't want to screw it up."

"Yes, I understand you were divorced recently."

"That's right," Jonathan Blakely said. Alonzo Schaeffer thought he detected a thought unspoken cross the mind of the other man. Perhaps a second thought unspoken. Finally: "It's a whole new ballgame, as Howard says right before he says I told you so."

Alonzo Schaeffer peered out from under raised eyebrows. He thought he had seen Jonathan Blakely drop his guard. "Would it be possible for me to see some of your research?"

Several seconds passed. "No, I don't think so," Jonathan said softly. "I don't mean to offend you any more than I already have, but the good gray lady you work for is one of the more prominent culprits. Some day, if my piece doesn't get published, I'll be happy to slip it to you for some light bedtime reading." He paused for a moment and Alonzo Schaeffer could see he was weighing something on a mental scale. Then Jonathan smiled and added: "But I would be willing to give you a summary of a section that applies to what we talked about a little while ago."

"That sounds fair."

"It's a section about various kinds of conspiracies. As I already said, I'm not saying there was a conspiracy to kill the president. But I think I've documented what might well be a conspiracy to keep a lot of interesting facts from the American people. And then I think there might be a conspiracy to infiltrate the most important media or otherwise influence the content of what the public is told. I think the total control exercised by the agencies of government in this instance is frightening. And I think the profession is in peril of being deeply penetrated at high levels. Look, the government took a beating from the press in the late '60s and early '70s, culminating in the end of the war in Vietnam and then Watergate. The decline of investigative reporting since then is visible in all the media. Maybe it's a coincidence. There seems to be no limit to the amount of coincidences that people who consider themselves honorable will accept without asking questions. But I add this, Alonzo—maybe it isn't a coincidence. I think the conduct of the press since Watergate constitutes a damning indictment and it's time we admitted it and did something about it."

Alonzo Schaeffer stared at Jonathan before standing up. "I must go. Robinson tells me you're going to be in New York in November. There's a good chance I'll be there most of the month. Give me a call. Perhaps we can have lunch or dinner."

"Yes, I've been invited to speak there. The sins of my academic past are catching up with me. It's a conference to take another look at the peace movement and where it went wrong and possibly right and what it ought to be doing now. I'll give you a call."

"Good. In all frankness, Jonathan, I came here with some preconceived notions. I wanted more than information from you. I wanted to find out what kind of a man you are. I believe I'm getting somewhere on that project."

"That pleases me, Alonzo. I'm sorry I can't be more informative about my article, but perhaps if you keep trying...." He laughed as he reached into his pocket with one hand and picked up the stack of newspapers beside him with the other. "Actually, there are a lot of other subjects on which I can be downright talkative."

"Allow me," Alonzo Schaeffer said as he put down the money to cover the check and tip. They walked out to the street.

"There is something else I've wondered about," Alonzo Schaeffer said. "Robinson tells me you wrote one letter of application and it was to the *Tribune*. Of all the papers in the country, this is the one you applied to first. Why did you want so much to come here?"

"I've been here before, three—no, four—times. On vacations. I fell in love with the place and I haven't fallen out of it yet. You headed anywhere near the *Tribune?*"

"I'd like to walk there with you."

"Good." Jonathan waved his hand. "Look at this place," he said. "Bud Guthrie didn't call it Big Sky Country for nothing. But there's more to it than that. As far as the eye can see, and a lot farther, it's hard land. It was settled by men and women who had to cross a lot of mountains to get here and a lot of them died on the way. This land never gave anything to them without a fight. It even fought back. Take a farmer, or a logger, or a cattleman, or a honyocker or a miner and this land tested him. In Montana, mister, you deserved what you got, because when you got it you knew you damn well earned it."

They walked under a gray sky.

"Look at those clouds. They seal you in a pocket. Here's a town surrounded by mountains. Under you the earth is cold most of the year. And over you a lot of the time you have that cover of clouds. This whole territory was a pocket left almost alone while people went running west to the coast, and then when they finally drifted back to see what they missed they found a lot of little pockets within the big one. You're in one right here. And let me tell you this, Alonzo—this pocket isn't just a physical one. It's cut off from the rest of the world, that's the truth, and it operates under a different set of laws, or justice, or ethics, or whatever you want to call it. You take a man from Boston or LA or Denver or New York—no offense intended,

Alonzo—and you ask him to look at a problem. Then you take a man who's been here a while and have him look at the same problem. That's when you learn the first fact of life about this place. They don't start out here with the same premises and they'll never reach the same conclusion on important matters. Pure logic. And until you understand that about this place, you won't be able to understand anything about it."

Alonzo Schaeffer interrupted.

"Hold on, Jonathan. What you're saying is the same thing Robinson says, that I couldn't write about this place without spending a lot of time here. Frankly, I don't find Placer or Billings or Butte that mysterious. My job is to rove around and move into where I'm assigned or where I think there's a story, and then to write that story. I've been doing that for quite a few years, and I think I've done an accurate, honest job. And if you don't mind my saying so, this isn't the first time I've heard your argument that you can't understand something or some place until you've lived with it or in it for a long time."

"Alonzo," Jonathan Blakely said, eyeing him steadily, "I'm not saying you can't write a story about Placer that's honest and accurate in the way you think of honesty and accuracy. What I say is that I've been over a good part of this whole country and there is no place that lives by a set of values as different as the values here. Sure, there are people here who are like people anywhere else, but they don't constitute a majority. This state has sent more first-class men to that collection of millionaires, racists, drunks and buffoons we were talking about than Idaho, Wyoming, Utah, Nevada and the Dakotas put together. First-rate men like Walsh, Wheeler, Metcalf and Mansfield. And don't forget that this state sent the first woman to the United States Congress and she happens to be, in my opinion, the greatest woman of this country in this century. After you've said Jeannette Rankin, whoever is second on the list is so far down that she's out of sight. She voted against entering World War I and she was the only person in either house to vote against our entry into World War II. I'm not saying I agree with her on that one, but she had principles she stuck by, and that, I submit, is the test of greatness. Courage and vision and principles. And then she came out from the start against our getting involved in Vietnam and explained clearly what it was all about and spoke passionately of the moral culpability of the Dean Rusks and Maxwell Taylors and Eric Sevareids and Howard K. Smiths who were trying to convince us what a noble venture it was to send our young men into that hellhole. If she had been from back east the history books would be full of her, but then if she had been from back east she wouldn't have been the woman she was. And another thing, Alonzo, this state has the most advanced and distinctive constitution in the nation. It barely passed, but by God it passed. The whole history of this place is different. Look—"

They stopped in front of the Tribune Building, but Jonathan Blakely kept on talking. "—Take the town that Daly the copper king built. One day it was a meadow with hardly a human being around for miles. What happens anywhere else when you have a situation like that? Some families move in and they start farms of their own. Then they need a school and a store and a bar and a stable and pretty soon you have a little town. Then it grows and you get a big town. Usually it takes a long time, too. That didn't happen in this state. You had one farm and one family and then in two years you had one hell of a town built around a huge smelter with the highest stack in the world. The historians say that the men who built this state were ruthless, but anyone who wanted something out of this state in those days had better be ruthless or he'd get the guts crushed out of him. You have to understand the history. You want some beaver skins? All right, you come and get them and you fight the Indians and the grizzlies and snow up to your navel and no other white man for hundreds of miles. And when you get them, if you live you get out. You want to grow some wheat? All right, you come here and you get some cheap land or even land for nothing and you farm it. You get some crops when the weather is just right, but then the weather isn't just right for two or three years and you take your family and get out. You want some place for your cattle? Then you bring them here and put them out on all that lush grass. Then you get hit by something like the blizzard of '87 and you get out, with nothing. That's the history of this place. People who don't live here extract its wealth and a lot of other people who live here get beat and go away."

"Do you think that's still true?"

"In most ways. Now it's the so-called energy companies that rape the state and they're just new and improved versions of Rockefeller and Standard Oil ripping off the copper around the start of this century. Unfortunately, the lands they rip off are often agricultural lands. The exploitation of this state by outsiders has never stopped. And the land is still as hard as it ever was. The winters are still just as long and cold. It still beats down damn good men and women who get the hell out."

"You, too, Jonathan?"

Jonathan paused for a moment. "No," he said quietly, "not me. I like the people who stay. You know, Alonzo, there was a newspaperman in the frontier days by the name of Captain James Mills and he once wrote that it was a royal people who occupied these mountains. He said they were a people of courage, self-reliance, industry, thrift, intelligence and charitableness and it was the last-mentioned characteristic that permitted him to stay and be tolerated beyond his deserts. That's the way I feel. I'm planning on staying to fight for this place and I'm planning to die here. This land dares you to get out and lots of good people have gotten out. But I think I've discovered its secret and I think I can live on this land."

Alonzo Schaeffer leaned forward expectantly. "And just what is the secret, Jonathan?"

"The secret, Alonzo, is exactly what I just told you. If you know full well that the land wants to beat you and has beaten so many other people before you, then you stay because the odds are so clearly against you. You stay because there's no place left in this country that is so wondrously beautiful and where you can find a challenge like that."

SEPTEMBER

A bomber carrying nuclear warheads crashes in Spain. All kinds of denials, evasions are made. It can be taken as an axiom that all governments everywhere lie—it is inevitable. Naive people think that conspiracies are seven men around a table in a Machiavellian plot: a conspiracy is an atmosphere, or a frame of mind in which people are impelled to do things, perhaps those things that they could never do as individuals, or couldn't do at other times when the atmosphere is different.

—Doris Lessing
The Four-Gated City
1969

Sunday was the day of rest, recuperation and regeneration. The bodies lay late in bed in the morning, relaxing after a week of work and a roisterous Saturday night, gaining strength for another week of work and yet another splendid Saturday. The beaches were quiet and a soft wind blew out of the Atlantic and up to the hill where pallid clouds served as a cloak over the silence. This was the Lord's day on Fuerteventura.

Anton Wojtas had stopped believing in God many years ago. As a boy scrubbed clean every Sunday in Bohemia he had gone to church, learned the catechism and the rituals, lit the altar candles, and had found the only serenity he had ever known. It ended abruptly when his father, spitting phlegm and cursing the Deity, died in a bed made wet with his sweat, the final oath emerging as a gurgle against all the incomprehensible forces that had made him suffer in an empty and meaningless life. His aunt brought Anton to America, reluctantly and of necessity, to keep him from the mines and the Russians; she took him to Nebraska to live with relatives who had escaped from Czechoslovakia before the Germans had marched into Prague. He carried within him the germs expectorated by his father, not in the phlegm that trickled down to the sheets but in the words that had preceded his death rattle. Anton Wojtas did not hate God; he simply did not believe in Him. What he hated was Communists, and especially Russian Communists. His father, the Russian captain had said, had collaborated with the Nazis. Three soldiers had gone down the shaft that plunged deepest into the bowels of the earth and had brought forth his father. Three days later his father returned, barely able to stagger to the bed, where, three weeks later, he died. Anton Wojtas never wanted to see or hear anything that might diminish the totality of his hatred, which was the ultimate and incontrovertible triumph of his spirit.

This Sunday was to be a work day, devoted to the cause with a sense of urgency and commitment he gave to nothing else. He hauled his short, stocky body out of bed and prepared to meet the visitor whose plane even now was scheduled to be landing at Puerto del Rosario. It meant another assignment that would bring closer the day that the Russian grip on his homeland would be broken and the good people of that land would be free of oppression. Anton Wojtas never doubted that the day was coming and that he was, in his small but significant way, hastening its arrival.

He saw in himself something of the heroic. For most of the forty-eight years since his mother, after expelling a child from her womb for the eighth time and then cradling the tiny Anton in her fitful arms, had died in delirium, he had sensed his peculiar destiny. He prepared his body and mind with deliberate care; the former fueled primarily with meats and potatoes and drawn hard and sinewy by arduous labor, the latter nourished with tracts and pamphlets and books supplied by his father. Both mind and body were taut and tempered to instant readiness, and in the battles that erupted at the mouth of the mines of Czechoslovakia or later in the tapering end of a Saturday night in the bars of Omaha, Anton Wojtas distinguished himself. He established a physical and mental dominion, often challenged but rarely lost, over the boys and men who worked and drank in the same way as he. They learned to respect and sometimes fear the husky Bohunk with the steel-gray eyes and the stubby fists. If he was often one hell of a fighter, he also was one hell of a reader and debater. He planned it that way; he was to be the best at whatever he did, because that way lay power and he needed power to work his will.

Here, on this Sunday morning on the blackest of the Canary Islands, Anton Wojtas experienced the tingling anticipation of important intelligence carried by the visitor. No summer soldier he; when asked to serve, he served gladly, fully. He had given the whole of his life to a cause in which he wholly believed. The time anticipated for so many years was now approaching. The clash of goliaths could be no more than three, possibly four, years away.

His confidence added to his buoyancy on this quiet Sunday morning. He listened to the church bells cutting metallically through the September air, sharply dividing those who heard them as a summons from those who neither listened nor heeded. He heard well and he twisted his lips into fleshly contempt.

"Not for me," he said softly. "You had me. You won't get me again."

He could see his dream flickering into reality: A real chance for another strike at the enemy and another shot in the only war that mattered to him. History—historical necessity—was the centurion whose shield meant he could not lose. There—over there, over the waters he could see from his kitchen window—was the lair of the enemy and when the time was ripe that enemy would be crushed. Anton Wojtas brought his fist down hard on the table and he crushed beneath it the miniature, mortal body of Leonid Brezhnev. When the fist was lifted, the beast had disappeared from the face of the earth. Anton Wojtas was happy and secure and confident.

He looked up as he heard a brisk knock on the door and a tendril of doubt flickered across his mind. He always was annoyed when his reveries, which seemed so real, were interrupted by reality. He found the reality particularly distasteful on this Sunday morning when the dream had been especially vivid.

"Hello, Sebastian," he said.

The Spaniard nodded and walked over to the far side of the table. He twisted a chair around and straddled it, leaning forward with his hands clasped and his elbows pointing to either side of Wojtas. He stared ahead. Wojtas stared back.

"He's on his way," the Spaniard said. "He should be here in about half an hour."

Another silence. The Spaniard leaned back and reached into a pocket of his jacket. He took a large knife from it and flicked out the blade. From another pocket he extracted a piece of wood and examined it.

"I can't stay long," he said in Spanish. "I have to go to church."

Wojtas winced. It was not enough that this man was a cross he had to bear. He also had to bear the man's cross.

"Any time you want," he said flatly. This mother-loving Spaniard could get on his nerves quickly. "Did Luis say what the man looked like?"

Sebastian shook his head and continued to whittle.

"Goddamnit, I told you to always tell me what they look like," Wojtas said, suddenly irritated by another example of the Spaniard's lack of discipline. For three years, ever since Sebastian had come to the far end of this volcanic island with him, he had told him again and again to get a description of any visitor coming in his direction. Sebastian was a fuckup, just as he had fucked up governments of two countries by shooting two Basque separatists in his namesake city in Spain in 1978. He had brought Sebastian with him as a matter of moral imperative, and all he had ever asked him to do in return for the pesetas he provided was to inform him of the arrival and appearance of any visitors whose destination might be the house of Anton Wojtas. And the son of a bitch couldn't even do that. "Is Luis driving the taxi?"

"*Si.*"

The sound of the knife against wood at the far end of the table grated on the edges of his nerves. "Sweet Jesus, Sebastian, don't you ever get tired of chipping on that wood?"

"Never."

"Get tired of it now. Do your whittling on your own time."

Sebastian halted his motion, stared at Wojtas for a moment, and retracted the blade. He returned the knife to one jacket pocket, the wood to the other. He said nothing.

Wojtas was angry at himself. He had allowed his euphoria to be shattered by this everlasting whittler, this fuckup, this refugee from a botched assignment. Three years of taking care of this undisciplined, incompetent mother-lover....

There was a sound outside the door.

"That couldn't be him," Wojtas said, puzzled. "You said half an hour, didn't you?" He got up from his chair, walked to the door and awaited the knock. Then he opened the door. A boy, no more than 10 years old, stepped into the room. He froze in fright as he saw Sebastian.

"I'm sorry," the boy stammered. "I didn't know....I'm sorry...." He started to back out the door.

"It's okay, kid," Wojtas said. "What do you want?"

"Nothing....I just want to leave this....Juanita asked me to bring it to you. It's from the Atlantica...." He stared at Sebastian in terror. "I don't know...."

"All right," Wojtas said. "Bring it here."

The boy swung his right leg around and came toward Wojtas. The leg made a thumping sound as he laboriously maneuvered his way around the table. He placed a wrapped box gently on the table and began to edge his way, sideways, toward the door. Sebastian laughed loudly.

"Hey, boy," Sebastian said, "how come you walk like a crab?"

The boy's eyes projected pure agony.

"I'm sorry," he said. He turned his body through the opening and was gone.

Sebastian laughed again.

"A crab," he said. "Jesus, he makes you think of a crab. The little crab sure wobbled his ass out of here, didn't he?" He reached for his knife and piece of wood and brought them out of their respective pockets.

Wojtas felt a surge of disgust within him. "You didn't have to do that," he said.

"I don't have to do anything, so I do what I please. You're not worried about that little crab, are you? Juanita's little crab...."

"I told you to put that goddamned knife away," Wojtas said. "You're tough, aren't you, Sebastian? You're tough as hell with a little crippled kid. God, you make me sick." He stared at the sullen Sebastian, whose knife remained poised against wood. Sometimes, Wojtas thought with a sigh of resignation, there seemed to be an inordinate amount of shit connected with his life's work. The code of honor by which he lived demanded that he take care of this cipher, but enough is enough. He couldn't take any more of this. The mother said he had to go to church.

"Jesus Christ, Sebastian," he said. "when are you going to church?"

"Now," came the reply. He snapped the knife shut and put it and the chunk of wood back in his pockets. He disentangled himself from the chair and stood up. He challenged Wojtas. "You need me," he said.

"Like hell I do."

"Like hell you don't." Sebastian took out the knife and flicked it open. "You'll find out how much you need me when your visitor comes."

"What the hell does that mean?"

"You'll see."

He closed the knife and left. In the silence that followed, Anton Wojtas felt relieved to be rid of his Spanish charge but he was puzzled by the fact that Sebastian seemed to know something he didn't, and that was intolerable.

"Ah, what the hell," he said, and opened the box on the table. It contained three large pieces of apple strudel. He smiled at the thought that the hotel at which Juanita worked catered well to its largely German clientele who came in hordes, packed in buses, to this end of the island; the Germans, having failed to conquer the world, were now overrunning it as tourists. He thought too that Juanita obviously liked him and that he would like to get to know her better.

He ate strudel and drank coffee and wondered who the visitor would prove to be. Then there was a knock on the door followed by an embrace and a flood of memories. They didn't speak; it wasn't necessary. Wojtas silently signaled toward the beach and the arm that was wrapped around the visitor gently guided him through the door. When they were safely away from the house Wojtas shook his head and smiled.

"I was trying to figure how long it's been," he said. " '63, wasn't it?"

The visitor nodded. "Good old Georgetown."

"Yeah, good old Georgetown. Have you been back? How's Forbes?"

"Several times. The year of the massacre, especially. Forbes has his problems, but he's all right. That's one of the few that hasn't come unglued."

They talked for hours as they walked the beach. The almost twenty years that had passed since last they saw each other melted in the bond that united these two practitioners of a shared profession. They talked of their days together in British Guiana and the years apart, in which they had talked by telephone but never said anything important. They better than most knew the dangers of talking about anything important on a telephone. Any telephone. Anywhere in the world. Every conversation was made with the understanding that their words could be heard or recorded by others who were not necessarily friendly. They made up for the time apart with an affectionate enthusiasm. The visitor would be there only a few hours. Luis waited for him, hovering around the taxi, ready for their return trip.

Anton Wojtas owed much to the visitor. It was he who had recruited the young Wojtas, set him up as an organizer for a fabricated arm of the American Federation of Labor-Congress of Industrial Organizations, and had him dispatched to the steaming edge of the jungle that was Georgetown, British Guiana. It was there that Wojtas was given time to learn the rudiments of his new trade. When the apprentice had mastered the necessary lessons—had become a professional—he was welcomed into the company of other professionals. It was an exclusive company, a dedicated company, and he regarded it as the best of all possible companies.

They walked the beach and talked of times past as the sun arched its way across the dark blue sky.

They talked of how interesting it would have been if the Devastator bullet had ricocheted a fraction differently and if the ailing Leonid Brezhnev went to his deserved reward, thereby making George Bush and Yuri Andropov the first leaders of the world's greatest powers who had served as directors of their respective nation's intelligence services.

They laughed at how far—or not so far—Philip Habib had come—or gone—from those days when he had been one of the government's briefers of correspondents in Saigon at what had been dubbed the "five o'clock follies."

They discussed the errors of judgment that clouded the assassination of Congressman Leo Ryan at an airstrip near the People's Temple encampment in Jonestown as he was preparing to leave Guyana. Wojtas listened intently to the visitor, for he knew that Congressman Ryan had been a co-author of a law that required the CIA to be more forthcoming in its reports to Congress about covert activities.

Shaking his head, the visitor related details of a story published on the front page of the London *Observer* the previous month about the "broken arrow"—code name for an accident involving nuclear weapons—back in July, 1956, at the Lakenheath Royal Air Force Station twenty miles from Cambridge. A B-47 skidded on the runway and burst into flames, engulfing a bunker containing three U.S. Mark 6 nuclear bombs. If the jet fuel had ignited the four tons of TNT that trigger the bombs—at this point his voice trailed off. Only heroism, an incredible amount of luck and the will of God, he said a few seconds later, kept that part of England from becoming a desert.

They talked of the terrible mistake Bill Colby had made by admitting that the company had infiltrated agents into the antiwar movement of the '60s and '70s. And they agreed it was Colby who had brought the wrath of Congress down on the agency, even to the point of ordering it in 1975 to curb all foreign operations not aimed solely at gathering intelligence. "But we're like ol' man river and those waves out there," the visitor said. "We just keep rolling along."

But President Ford had done the right thing, Wojtas said, when he apologized to the family of the CIA research scientist who had committed suicide in 1953 after taking LSD as part of an agency experiment. His visitor disagreed, and he also defended the biochemist in charge of the company's LSD program for destroying all the records of illegal activities. Wojtas said nothing more on the subject.

When the visitor referred to a man in the highest echelons of the company as "a Neanderthal," Wojtas informed him that there are scientists who believe that a tribe of *Homo sapiens neanderthalensis* inhabited the Canary Islands as recently as the 15th century. "You're pulling my leg," the visitor said. Wojtas assured him it was true.

They talked of Hale Boggs and Malcolm X and Dorothy Kilgallen and Dorothy Hunt and E. Howard Hunt and the gangsters around Nixon who were sent to prison much too late—and those who escaped justice. That reminded them of the late H.L.

Hunt and the recent caper of two of his sons, Nelson Bunker Hunt and William Herbert Hunt, whose silver speculations almost brought down the whole economic system. They talked of other capers that hadn't been reported by the press and Wojtas observed that Fitzgerald didn't get to the heart of the matter when he pointed out that the rich are different: In addition to the fact that they have more money, most of them need not fear going to prison. The visitor looked over at him with a quizzical smile.

Up and around a cliff, then down into the square of Morro Hable, a village littered with concrete blocks, the rubble of construction, soft-drink crates filled with empty bottles. A herd of goats roamed the dirt street; two burros, some dogs, a cat sleeping on the remnant of a cardboard crate paid them no attention, but men standing outside the *taberna* watched nothing but them as they walked through the door and sat at a table to drink the rich Spanish wine.

Inside, they talked of women they had known, of wives long since divorced, of children they hardly knew. The visitor told of the girl in a townhouse in Fairfax and Wojtas told of the lovely Juanita, with whom he was sure he would become more friendly in days to come. Then, a bottle of wine emptied, they were back on the beach.

They talked of Sam Giancana and Adlai Stevenson and J. Edgar Hoover and how Lumumba had fallen to his knees and begged for his life when he saw that he had been betrayed. They talked of Allende and Mohammed Mossadegh and Guatemala in 1954 and 1981. The visitor delineated the dilemma of Admiral Bobby Inman and the troubles surrounding Wilson and Terpil. He explained to Wojtas the intricate maneuvers employed to remove from office Prime Minister Gough Whitlam, who pulled Australian troops out of Southeast Asia and denounced Nixon's 1972 Christmas bombing of Hanoi. Wojtas saw clearly that what had been accomplished in more dramatic and violent fashion in Chile and Iran and Guatemala had been duplicated in a society very similar to that of the United States.

The topic returned to Allende and Chile and the importance of the appointment of Judge Barrington D. Parker to preside over the scheduled trial of John W. Hinckley Jr. Wojtas had forgotten that it was Judge Parker who had conducted the spectacular trial of the accused assassins of Orlando Letelier, who was blown up in his car on a street in the nation's capital back in 1976. They laughed as they recalled a tape of a phone call by a man known in clandestine circles as "The Jackal," in which he said that the jury was "so ignorant that one of the best defenses at this time is to throw more shit in and stir it up."

And they talked of recent unhappy matters. Of the two advisors to the head of El Salvador's land reform program who had been shot to death a few months earlier while sitting in the restaurant of the Sheraton Hotel in San Salvador. They had been recruited in much the same way as Wojtas had been in the '60s. The visitor assured Wojtas that the political executions were carried out under orders of a leader of the most right-wing party in that embattled land.

And at last they talked of the new assignment for Anton Wojtas. He would leave by plane the following afternoon, a reservation already confirmed in the name of his officially prepared new passport.

Then, standing behind a dune to shield them from the wind that had suddenly come up, they talked, this time with reluctance, about one more matter: Sebastian.

"There is one final bit of intelligence you should have," the visitor said. "Luis tells me Sebastian was in town last night, in a tavern and in his cups. Luis said he tried to shut Sebastian up, but he wasn't about to be shut up. That is a habit with Sebastian, I understand. And Luis says he didn't tell Sebastian about me. Did you tell him I was coming?"

"I didn't know it would be you. I didn't know who it would be, but I had to tell him someone was coming. He takes care of things at the house while I'm gone."

"Get someone else to do that," the visitor said. "Perhaps your Juanita?"

Wojtas nodded.

"Sebastian saw me today when I passed the Casa Atlantica," the visitor said in a monotone. "I could not possibly like that."

The visitor stared at Wojtas. For several seconds Wojtas contemplated the implications of this unexpected turn in their conversation. He recalled that the visitor had made all the arrangements, three years earlier, and had personally escorted Sebastian to the Madrid airport for the flight to Fuerteventura. His words came out slowly: "You want me to handle it?"

"I think you'd better."

Wojtas nodded again.

They walked up the sandy hill to the house, shared the last of a bottle of Spanish sherry ("This is the only thing I envy you for, living here," the visitor said), and shook hands before moving toward the waiting taxi driver. Wojtas spoke earnestly but briefly with Luis while the visitor settled himself in the rear seat of the Mercedes-Benz.

That night Sebastian, an expert swimmer, dived into the phosphorescent waves lapping the beach of Jandia, as he often did for a short swim before going to bed. The next day fishermen starting a new week lifted his bobbing body from the waters of the Atlantic. There was no mark on him and all the evidence indicated he had drowned.

That night the visitor completed the bumpy 98-kilometer ride to the airport of Puerto del Rosario and boarded a plane for the trip to Las Palmas and then a non-stop flight to Dulles Airport. Late the next afternoon he was back at his desk.

That night Anton Wojtas flicked the switch of the single electric light that illuminated his bedroom, cupped his hands behind his head and looked into the darkness. He experienced once again the rush that was at the base of his addiction to his profession. Tomorrow was Monday and he relished, as he did not always relish, its coming. Monday, then another Monday and then the Monday when the wheel would halt in its turning and a cycle would end. He closed his eyes and he saw Anton Wojtas standing in the sun, multitudes of soldiers passing in review, banners high, a band playing, flowers and flags everywhere, a formation of planes zooming higher, higher, higher toward the sun. He rolled over and was asleep. The next day he, too, with Luis at the wheel made the bumpy trip to the Rosario airport, where he boarded an Iberia DC-9 on the first leg of his journey to Cairo.

OCTOBER

"...the general good requires that no further information be revealed at this time about those who perpetrated the crime."

— *Official Report of the Egyptian government following the assassination of Anwar el-Sadat*

Robinson was uneasy. Perhaps it was the cold, gray October day, the clouds brooding over the hills, making of the big sky a seamless umbrella that shut out the sun. Perhaps it was the accumulation of just such days that had followed monotonously one after another since—when had it been that the sun last shined out of a blue sky? The first week of October, he guessed. Day after day of being hemmed in by clouds. Little wonder he was on edge, more irritable than usual, bummed out.

His sixth sense, the sense in which he took special pride, told him there was more to his uneasiness than the melancholy weather. Certainly the air had seemed more crisp as he walked to the office today and the smell of autumnal spices had given way to the first notice of the oncoming winter, but more than that he had felt in his lungs the musty tinge of smoke that hung in a pall over the town. The pollution now was blamed on the wood stoves that had proliferated in the valley in recent years, and mention no longer was made in the editorial columns to the pulp mill and its voluminous stinking clouds belched hour after hour from its foul guts. On days like this he wished that he didn't work for other men—or at least for the other man who was now publisher.

His sixth sense told him that the publisher privately shared the same wish. How nice it would be—for the publisher—to bring in another mushhead, this time to write the kinds of editorials every day that the publisher inserted periodically, extolling the virtues of motherhood (even when motherhood was not desired), free enterprise (even when the enterprise was solely possessed by a conglomerate), apple pie (even when it had been concocted from apples saturated with pesticides), nuclear armament (even when the publisher's priest was saying almost every Sunday that the nation's nuclear policy was immoral). There had been no words exchanged, no orders from on high, no post-publication memos of late, but the sixth sense had sent the message nonetheless to the brain of Robert Robinson.

Of course, there was more pragmatic evidence. Robinson long ago had pinpointed the principal reason the chain did not have a single outstanding newspaper to point to with professional pride, and that was its personnel policy. The papers did not seek out, and hire, and retain the best. It settled for mediocre reporters, not talented writers; it settled for managers, not leaders; it settled for fair to pretty good papers and a bursting bottom line rather than excellent newspapers and—temporarily—fewer profits. Whenever the word had come back that "we can't afford to do it," he had responded with the intentional cliché that "we can't afford not to do it," but that was long ago. Now the ironic truth was that the editor of the editorial page kept his most important views to himself.

Jonathan Blakely had tried to cheer him up the day before by pointing out that morale was no better elsewhere, that the volume of complaints, gripes, bitches and wails from his friends on newspapers, magazines and broadcasting news staffs across the country had reached epidemic proportions. The malaise that had seized the practitioners of the late 1970s had grown in the new decade into a disease that defied definitive diagnosis. Some said it was the mergers, some the killings of newspapers that died of more than old age. Some said it was the Reagan administration, some that the disappointing last two years of Carter had set off the trend. Some said it was the instability in personal lives, some said it was the unhappy economic times. Some said it was the computers and the dehumanizing technology, some the growing impersonalization of the cities that made reporting seem less significant. Some said it was the threat of nuclear holocaust. Some said they hated working in rooms that never had fresh air. Some had other perspectives, equally subjective and to Robinson's thinking equally valid.

The man who was supposed to have the answers had no reply to the question of what exactly, precisely, had gone wrong.

Then there was Jonathan's strange reaction to the assassination of Sadat. He not only had stopped talking about the shooting of the president of the United States, but had professed a bewildering lack of interest in the numerous and exotic unanswered questions surrounding the slaying of the Egyptian president.

"I am burned out on assassinations," he had responded simply to Robinson's offer of clippings from the *New York Times* concerning the event and its aftermath. "There are all kinds of reasons why Sadat might have been assassinated, of which Islamic fanaticism is one. It beats Jodie Foster, that's for sure."

"Do I detect," Robinson had asked, "some sign of bitterness in that observation? And furthermore, friend, how come you didn't laugh last night when Weenie did his imitation of Anwar saying Bar-bar-ah while being interviewed by Ms. Walters in the reviewing stand as the assassins leapt out of the truck and started firing their machine guns?"

"I was preoccupied," Jonathan had answered, and had changed the subject.

Robinson knew that Jonathan had answered honestly. He was indeed preoccupied, writing a speech to be delivered in New York City the following month. With the trial of young Hinckley nowhere in sight he had stopped his research on that subject and was putting together something more than the usual convention speech, especially since it was a convention of those who were in one way or another connected to the reporting of the war in Vietnam. Jonathan had shown him a rough draft of the speech, whose main point was that the lines between government and media were rapidly being blurred and that the infiltration of the most influential media in various forms constituted a major threat to freedom of the press. Jonathan might be guilty of seeing hobgoblins and bogymen in his scholarly nightmares, Robinson thought, but he also had made some fetching predictions in his time. For one thing, he had forecast in 1970 the rise of an aggressive kind of investigative reporting that would change the course of history, four years before the resignation of Nixon. Of course, he now admitted that he had not foreseen the strength and determination of the counteroffensive by those who rightly feared this newly exercised power of the press. Thus some of the more salutary aspects of the Watergate coverage did not become the achievement by which subsequent reporting would be measured, but became instead the journalistic watershed of a disappointing decade.

He saw Jonathan come into the news room and he called to him.

"Still preoccupied?"

"Not like yesterday." Jonathan came into Robinson's office and sat on a table, his back against the wall. "I finished the mother in the wee-wee hours of the morning. I may add or subtract between now and then, but it's done. As soon as I clean up the copy I'll give it to you for your disapproval. Tell me to get off the limb I've climbed out on."

"Hell, Jonathan," Robinson said with a laugh, "that's your favorite position and your favorite location. You wouldn't be comfortable standing on the ground everyone else is on."

Deborah was at the door. "Is this a private male chauvinist conversation or can an interested spectator join in?"

"Welcome," Robinson answered as Jonathan motioned her to join him on the table. She smiled and declined, sitting in one of the captain's chairs provided for visitors to the editorial sanctum.

"I was just getting ready," Robinson said, "to ask our expert on assassination conspiracies how four to eight men were able to insinuate themselves into a military parade, leap from a truck at precisely the moment that the Egyptian Air Force was staging a spectacular flyover, and with no opposition from the security guard advance to the reviewing stand and shoot President Anwar el-Sadat to death at point-blank range?"

"My files are overflowing," Jonathan said. "When I'm through with the Reagan case I'm hanging them up. I'm done—finished—*kaput*—you hear?"

"But Jonathan," Robinson said in a mock serious voice, "Alexander Cockburn is mighty suspicious about the whole thing and even the *New York Times* says there are what it calls troubling questions remaining about a possible conspiracy. That constitutes a notable first for the paper, right?"

"No, not when it's a political assassination in Afghanistan—or in this event, Egypt. According to the *Times*, the last conspiracy to kill a political figure in the United States involved John Wilkes Booth. Don't get me started, Robert."

"The *Times* even referred to what it called a striking breakdown in security around Sadat. That's a curious fact when you consider that Sadat's bodyguards were trained by our Secret Service and were required to spend a year in the United States in on-the-job training. Nixon started that in 1974, and later the CIA gave Sadat a lot of advanced communications gear to increase his security. It didn't seem to help."

"Leave him alone, Robert," Deborah said. "Can't you see he's burned out on the subject?"

"Yeah," Jonathan said. "I even saw that Haig said categorically that it was Islamic fundamentalists within the Egyptian army who did it. He voiced that opinion when Sadat had been dead possibly two hours. Then that night Kissinger comes on ABC to say that the Libyan involvement was extremely probable, in his words, and that we must assume a plot by Qaddafi. These guys are conspiracy kooks of the first rank when it comes to bullets flying outside the borders of the United States."

"Oh, I almost forgot," Robinson said, delighted at the way Jonathan was coming alive. "The *Times* also wondered out loud in an editorial whether there was truth in Sadat's recent premonitions of a Soviet plot."

"Jesus, Robert, you don't let go easily, do you," Deborah said.

Jonathan laughed. "All right, I'll play Cockburn's game. Sure it could have been the Russians. Sadat kicked them out of Egypt in 1972 and abrogated the friendship treaty with them. The KGB no doubt will extend a warm hand to the man who should henceforth be known as 'Lucky Hosni,' having escaped with only a minor wound while situated to the immediate left of Sadat in the reviewing stand. Of course, you can't rule out Mubarak himself; he would not be the first second-in-command to become impatient. And sure, it could have been Muammar who was behind it; the Libyan radio was filled with calls on the people of Egypt to rise up against Sadat for days before the last parade. That gave some evidence they knew something was afoot."

"I'll tell you my candidate," Deborah said. "It's that exiled General Shazli. He led the Egyptians across the Suez in the 1973 war and when the Israelis outflanked him Sadat fired him. I remember when he was in Damascus and formed a front to take Egypt out of the Camp David agreement. If the conspirators came from within the Egyptian army, as Mubarak keeps saying, I'd take Shazli over the Islamic fanatics any time."

"And he was trained in America," Robinson said. "Good nomination, Deborah. I keep coming back to the Al Tekfir Wal Hijra, the official favorite conspiracy target, or the Moslem Brotherhood, who tried to get Nasser once in Alexandria. That's Alexandria, Egypt, not Virginia. If it had been Alexandria, Virginia, it would have been the work of a lone neurotic gunman who couldn't make it with girls and had trouble keeping a job. And every time I keep coming back to the Islamic fundamentalists as the likely conspiracy I have to think of the Saudis, who finance them, along with the Iraqis. And you can't rule out the PLO or the Syrians. It was joy unreserved in Beirut and Damascus when the news was announced."

"That's right," Deborah said. "And did you notice how everyone went about their business in Egypt as if it didn't matter to them? There were more tears shed on the TV networks in New York than in all of Cairo. I recall when Nasser died the Nile almost overflowed as the multitudes poured out their grief."

"The difference in the reaction to Sadat's death in Egypt and this country, I suspect, is the result of the American mass media overlooking a lot of stuff that the State Department and the Pentagon and the White House wanted overlooked," Robinson said as he sifted through his clippings. "They liked to gloss over Sadat's less glamorous first marriage and the way he kept the children of that marriage out of sight. And while the American press made much over the beauteous Jihan, the lady was mightily disliked by Egyptians in the millions. She and her husband had been accumulating enemies for a long time. It wasn't just the Islamic fanatics he was throwing into prison. Not much was written in this country about his crackdown on the Coptic Christians. As a matter of fact he cracked down on a lot of people, including some journalists who had strong democratic instincts, which was out of character for the benevolent dictator Baba Wawa assured us he was. And he wasn't even in his grave before his house out near the pyramids was bulldozed until not a sign remained in the sands around the inscrutable sphinx. Also, there's the matter of his brother."

"Ah-ha," said Jonathan. "The plot thickens."

"Well, actually he's Sadat's half-brother. Esmet Sadat and his family are estimated to be worth sixty million dollars, which isn't bad for a bus driver who was earning a hundred bucks a month back in 1973. I've seen stories in the British papers about how hated he and his three sons are."

"Wait a minute, Robbie," Deborah said. "I've been thinking about what you said about the Saudis as possible conspirators. It took them two weeks to get back the Grand Mosque of Mecca when their very own Islamic militants took it over a couple of years ago. They wouldn't be supporting the Egyptian Islamic fundamentalists, would they?"

"The Saudis move in mysterious ways. You have to remember that Sadat was the ultimate traitor, the man who flew to Jerusalem and made peace with the Israelis. The Saudis will deal with anyone. They dealt with Nelson Bunker Hunt and William Herbert Hunt in the great silver caper, didn't they? Which reminds me, I was reading an account of the silver scheme the other day and I came across a sentence to the effect that reporters in Saudi Arabia aren't permitted to ask impertinent questions and I thought about how far down the same path our native reporters have gone in the past few years. But I digress."

"Khomeini," Deborah said.

They looked at her.

"Sure, Khomeini. The ayatollah said a thousand times that Allah should take Anwar. And don't rule out Israel."

"Israel?" Robinson shook his head. "The Israelis are the least suspect. They couldn't possibly prefer Mubarak to Sadat."

"But Robbie, the men of the Mossad move in ways so mysterious they make the Saudis look like they're running an open society. They could know all kinds of things that would explain why Sadat had to be eliminated."

"Okay, okay," Jonathan said, sliding along the table until his feet hit the floor. "You still haven't named the real conspiracy. It's—are you ready?—the CIA."

"Of course," said Deborah.

"Of course," said Robinson.

"No, I'm not exactly kidding," Jonathan said. "You remember how Sadat boasted a few weeks ago that he was helping supply the Afghan rebels with American arms? When I read that I had the same icy feeling I got when I came across the statement President Kennedy made the month before Dallas—that he was going to splinter the CIA in a thousand pieces and scatter it to the winds. Sadat obviously had lost his bearings when he committed that dreadful indiscretion to an American journalist. I had a hunch he wasn't long for this world, one way or another."

"Come on, Jonathan," Robinson said. "All of this is worth at least a speculative footnote in your article, isn't it?"

"No," Jonathan replied. "I told you, I've had it. When I'm done with this piece I'm done with the subject. I'm going to write long and ponderous essays on people I have known and places I have been. I'm going to write it for my son and whatever grandchildren he may give me. And that's the truth."

Deborah got up from the chair and smiled at Robinson. "On that solemn note, we bid you farewell, Robbie. Come on, Jonathan, it's terminal time."

Robinson laughed. "I take it, then, that you are accepting the guilt of the dedicated assassins who are now in jail and who will be shortly tried?"

"And no doubt shortly executed," Jonathan said. "Nice and neat. The hand of the thief is cut off but the hand of the one who prospered most from the heist remains in possession of the loot. It's an ancient Arab custom that has been improved and refined by our contemporary establishment."

"I further take it that you don't dismiss the possibility that other sinister forces may be behind this assassination?" A second passed. "Too?"

"The pregnancy of that pause was not lost on me, Robert," Jonathan said, smiling. "Yes, too. The unfortunate Anwar presented a target so large that we'll probably never know who really pulled the trigger. And I repeat: I'm out of it. Thirty, man, thirty."

Jonathan and Deborah returned to their desks and began their part of the job of getting out the next morning's paper. A few minutes later she was back at his desk, staring fixedly and silently at him as she dropped an item from the *Washington Post* wire in front of him and walked away....

WASHINGTON—John W. Hinckley Jr. reportedly wrote he was in conspiracy with others when he shot President Reagan and also described in writing purportedly fictional co-conspirators, apparently thinking he could trade the "information" to make a favorable deal for himself.

A Justice Department spokesman said Tuesday a continuing FBI investigation into the March 30 shooting "has developed no reliable evidence of a conspiracy." The Justice Department and the U.S. attorney's office in Washington refused to comment on a report by a Washington television reporter that Hinckley allegedly concocted the conspiracy scheme. The report also said prison officials intercepted letters from Hinckley to "co-conspirators."

Hinckley's plan was discovered last July when guards at the federal correctional institution at Butner, N.C., found writings about the alleged conspiracy among Hinckley's papers during a routine search of his cell.

Those documents, which have been the subject of hearings in U.S. District Court in Washington for two days, were seized by prison authorities and turned over to the FBI. Copies of the documents have been kept under seal at the court in Washington.

Hinckley's lawyers contend the search that uncovered the alleged conspiracy documents was illegal because Hinckley had a right to expect his personal papers would be kept private. They want Judge Barrington Parker to prohibit the government from using the documents at Hinckley's trial. The government contends Hinckley was told that his cell would be searched.

Jonathan looked toward Deborah, who was nodding her head, her lips pressed together. He nodded back a thank-you and returned his thoughts and activity to the terminal in front of him.

But late that night at home, in front of his typewriter, he experienced again the wrenching intuitive suspicion that the American people were not being told about matters that they had every legitimate right to know. He thought, as he had often since the evening of March 30, of *Catch 22*, which he regarded as the most inspired American novel of this century. When Joseph Heller spins his tales, no matter how hyperbolic, incredible, ludicrous, lunatic, apocryphal and unbelievable they may be, the reader believes—*believes*—if the reader understands how things work in the military, which is simply a microcosm of the way things work outside the military. Heller had taken the insights of Sherwood Anderson, who had brought the insights of Swift and Blake into the twentieth century, and made clearer than ever the truth that if one lacks a sense of the grotesque, one never opens perhaps the most important lock to the human experience. And Jonathan believed to the depths of his being that once that lock was opened, the hidden doors of perception awaited the key.

At that moment he realized he had not smoked in months. He got up from the chair in front of his typewriter, turned the lights low, started the stereo and poured a hearty measure of Grand Marnier before relaxing in the big easy chair in the corner of the living room. He had no desire these days for grass, the set and setting not being right. Nonetheless, he thought it ironic that the policies followed by the dunces in the federal government had made unnecessary for many those risky and often unsavory trips to Mexico and the more surrealistic lands of Latin America. The United States was now harvesting perhaps 20 percent of its own marijuana, according to official estimates. It had become America's fastest-growing crop in more than one sense. Even some of the good farmers of Nebraska and Iowa were setting aside well-hidden acres. Strange, when you stared at it long enough, how almost everything seemed to be in control of the crazies....

...Jonathan, Jonathan, there are questions you must not evade....Why am I doing this? Why do I have this obsession? Why do I appear to be the only person alive thus possessed? Am I seeing clearly? Is it all simply a matter of coincidences that have no significance? Why won't I let go of it—or, far more important, why won't it let go of me?...You have noticed, Jonathan, have you not, that people sometimes look at you as if you're a bit weird, right? And most of them have stopped asking you questions about the article, haven't they? Could it be that this whole thing—yes, you can't believe you ate the whole thing, can you? —is something that could prove to be embarrassing? Humiliating? Jonathan—a laughing stock?...

...No. Even if it all turns out to be nothing more than coincidences—even if all the questions are satisfactorily answered—it should not have been left to me—or anyone else—to ask the questions. The press should ask the questions—always. And the press should get the answers—always. When that stops happening, we are in trouble—deep trouble. And it's happening more and more all the time....

...I keep thinking of Camus, of what he believed, of what he wrote, of what he did with his life. And what does it mean to be "the best man for the world's fight"? Do you close your eyes to what you are doing and justify the so-called good life so long as the consequences of your actions remain invisible to you and your wife and your children and your friends? Or do you speak out and damn the consequences? Hell, man, that one's easy. You do what you know you must do....

...Hinckleys....

...Jack and John and Scott and JoAnn....Diane down in Dallas....Hunts and Bushes and Bradys and Reagans....*Und das ist nicht alles*....

...The firm of Edward Bennett Williams and the court of Barrington Parker....It's hard to take lawyers, it's tough to shake judges....

...Parker? Yes, Parker—and Foster, too....Jodie! Jodie! What did you do? How do you fit and what does it mean? When will the press and the regime come clean?...

...The *Times* and the *Post* and the *Post* and the *News*. Another *Post* for other views....*Times* and *Newsweeks* and *Rolling Stones*. *U.S. News*, Kamikaze Klones....

...Robert. Clarence. Deborah. You've stuck by me....You, too, Doherty, back in D.C.....The guys from Montana in New York AP....Good gray Alonzo, I'll soon see....

...Scott Simon on NPR....Good reporters every-

where.... The best to all of thee....
...Hey! Maybe we can get this one for the Gipper!... Enough....
...Arianne....I think of Arianne....The lovely Arianne....The beloved Arianne....I have always loved thee, Arianne, since I first set eyes on thee....

Jonathan Blakely sipped the last of the liqueur, waited until the stereo shut itself off, turned on the lamp next to his typewriter, and as the clock slowly struck three sat down to write:

INSTEAD OF A TRIAL....
Among the other tiddlywinks snapped into the cup that runneth over in this saga of the grotesque:

* *On September 20, the* Washington Post *reported that it had received and verified an unsolicited letter from Hinckley asking that he not be called a "drifter" in future news articles about him: "I may have done some drifting in the fall of '80, but in the years prior to this, I was not roaming around the country." The son of a millionaire oilman added: "You and the other journalists make it sound like I was some kind of a hobo or something...." In a separate note, he told the newspaper: "My attorneys are trying to hold the press coverage to a minimum and therefore will have nothing to do with reporters." Neither his attorneys nor Justice Department officials nor the U.S. Attorney's office in Washington were willing to comment on the letter.*

...You know, you can close your eyes and hear the cadences of John W. Hinckley Senior in that letter. Same style, same concerns, same attitude toward the press. Also coming through loud and clear is the one thing all the shrinks agree on: Young Hinckley's stunning lack of remorse for the enormity of his crime. And there's no question, mentally ill or not, that he's a liar of extraordinary proportions. He lied repeatedly on his application forms for various jobs; he lied to the people he knew at the Golden Hours Motel; he lied to his family again and again; and here he is on the front page of the *Washington Post*, which spreads his wretched drivel. It's infuriating, especially after months of silence from him and everything pertinent to his crime sealed from the public (except, of course, that which has been chosen to be leaked).

...Not a drifter? Okay, as Dan Doherty put it together from his personal "usually reliable sources," which will have to do for now, starting in 1976: Texas Tech student Hinckley leaves school in April for Hollywood....By September we know he was back in Evergreen....In February, 1977, off to the West Coast again....In three weeks he's back home, then to Texas, then to Nashville, then back to Lubbock for the 1978 summer session at Texas Tech....Then he's off to Dallas, home for Christmas and back to Lubbock in 1979....In 1980 he was home "for a few weeks," then to Dallas with his sister—Lubbock—home—New Haven—home—motel in Denver—Lubbock—Washington, D.C.—Columbus, Ohio—Dayton, Ohio—New Haven—New York City—Lincoln, Nebraska—Nashville—New Haven—Dallas—Washington, D.C.—home—Washington, D.C.—New York City—New Haven—home—New York City—home—New Haven—New York City—Golden Hours Motel—home—Los Angeles—then the bus to Washington, D.C....And Dan says there are probably a lot of other places Hinckley drifted to but this is a fairly well-documented itinerary and suits the purpose for now....I'll see if a more complete account of his travels shows up for the article...Sure would like to know what he was doing in Dallas and Washington all those times and especially to whom he made those local phone calls the day of the shooting....

...That part about his lawyers wanting to keep things quiet was interesting, too. Good old Superlawyer Edward Bennett Williams—that's what *Time* calls him: Superlawyer Edward Bennett Williams. His firm is at present turning the old trick of delaying the trial as long as possible; let the public interest wane—as public interest inevitably wanes—and the odds go up for the accused. Lots can happen to improve your chances the longer you keep the litigation going. Hell, it's October now, and *U.S. News & World Report* was trying to explain away the delay last August. "The Hinckley Case—Why It's Dragging" was the title. Funny thing about that piece—it appeared in the magazine dated August 31, 1981. Now almost everyone knows how the newsmagazines date their issues ahead so that readers will think the news is fresher than it really is. A fairly harmless deception, compared to the infinite number of other deceptions in each issue. But the lead of the story was that 10 weeks after Pope John Paul II was shot in Rome, his attacker was sentenced to life in prison while 20 weeks after Reagan was wounded "the man accused of shooting him hadn't even been indicted." Unfortunately for the magazine, Hinckley was indicted on August 24. (Could there be someone at the magazine who tips a secret agency on its upcoming contents? Jonathan, Jonathan, how could you suggest such a circumstance?) . . . . Another funny thing: Hinckley was indicted on the same day that Mark Chapman was sentenced to 20 years to life in prison for killing John Lennon. Gaze upon the contrast: Chapman, remaining silent as to his motive, except to read aloud in court the famous passage in "Catcher in the Rye" where Holden Caulfield keeps the kids from falling over the cliff, while his lawyer insists to the last that his client was not mentally competent when he pleaded guilty to the crime. And the judge rejects the lawyer's contention that the killing was an insane act and insists it was "an intentional crime, a crime carefully planned and executed; he knew what he was doing." Oh, Justice, when expelled from other habitations, find thee some dwelling place.

. . . Hinckley also told the *Washington Post* that while he wasn't a drifter, he "would have traveled to Budapest to find Jodie Foster." This whole Jodie Foster *schtick* was on my nerves months ago. . . . Temper, temper. . . . We'll get to her.

. . . First, let's take care of those two sterling periodicals, *Timeserver* and *Newsweak* (will it become *Newspeak* in 1984?), which not only published Hinckley's twaddle but actually solicited his views.

* *The* Washington Post *turning over its front page to the claptrap propounded by this would-be murderer was bad enough, but as nothing compared to the spectacle presented by its sister publication,* Newsweek.

. . . I'd love to make that "its hooker-sister, the frilly, frothy, trendy Newsweek."

When the barely unsuccessful assassin jauntily offered to "answer by mail a typewritten list of 20 questions, none dealing directly with my case," the editors of Newsweek *decided it was an offer they couldn't refuse. While Presidential Press Secretary James Brady still struggled to regain the use of the brain that John Hinckley Jr. had shattered with an explosive bullet more than six months earlier, that newsmagazine submitted*

... What belongs there is a period.

xxxxxxxx *that newsmagazine played its version of the "20 Questions" game with a defendant pleading insanity whose views on gun control and everything else asked*

... **have approximately the same weight and odor as the wind broken by a bean-eater.**

have neither relevance nor news value. And the kid from Evergreen certainly knows how to rub their noses in it; he told Newsweek: *"I'm not granting interviews to any other publication." But lo,* Time *magazine received the same offer from the media-manipulating punk and promptly assumed the same position, subsequently*

... after an easy labor

delivering an issue with only one page devoted to Hinckley compared to the two pages delivered by Newsweek *on the identical date. Unfortunately for* Time, *Hinckley ignored its questions and penned an essay on Jodie Foster.*

... Bad breath, *Time?* A touch frigid, perhaps? Was he put off by your exceptional interest in herpes (in contrast to your mind-boggling indifference to the various kinds of cancer caused by several of your advertisers?) Professors of journalism: Profess about editorial decisions that not only turn punks into heroes but serve to set up the next victim(s) of death by assassination. Profess concerning the floodgates that are opened by such decisions, in which "journalists" beg for the attention of this little scoundrel whose sole claim to our attention is that he almost murdered the president. Of course you expect it from the *National Enquirer* and the like—that's the small price we pay for liberty of the press—but not from publications that claim to be honorable or pretend to be responsible. And Don Bitterman, among others, wonders why I can't take seriously these two parodies of what a responsible newsmagazine should be in a nation that in its First Amendment to its Constitution established the press as a bulwark against the excesses and tyranny of government.

... Now, to Jodie:

> * *A few days later in September—precisely six months to the day of the assassination attempt—those in possession of the sealed evidence informed us that one of the famous Washington hotel room tapes did indeed contain the voices of young Hinckley and young Foster talking to each other on the telephone. Transcripts of two conversations were leaked by unidentified "law enforcement officials" to—nota bene—the United Press International. Why they were suddenly made available was not explained. Neither reported conversation contained any reference to the president or to any violent acts, "law enforcement officials said." The transcripts and the tape provided for broadcast on radio and television contradicted the unequivocal statement by the young actress shortly after the shooting and later repeated even more firmly that she had never "met, spoken to or in any way associated with one John W. Hinckley." When questioned by a UPI reporter about the obvious discrepancy, she said federal officials had requested her not to discuss the case. "It's not anything I can talk about," she said.*

... Shee-itt. If you don't mind, Jodie, I intend to talk a lot about it before I'm through. All of this fishy business remains to be explained to the American people, and no doubt among the more interested spectators will be those skeptical reporters who made it clear that either the actress or the government was not telling the truth.... Click! There's someone reaching once again into the bag of sealed evidence in the District of Columbia and handing transcripts of tapes to someone from a wire service. How's that for a little Polaroid shot for the albums of those who still think a measurable amount of honor can be discerned along the slimy banks of the Potomac?

...Asterisk....My ass to risk: In the days after the shooting we were told by those famous reliable sources that two—count them—tapes were found in the Washington hotel room. One was of Hinckley speaking by telephone to a woman believed to be Jodie Foster; the other of Hinckley "playing the guitar." Then in May, UPI told us that Hinckley "tape-recorded a monologue last New Year's Eve," and that "these tapes were also found in Hinckley's Washington hotel room." Will someone please count the tapes again?

...You know, there's another mighty peculiar thing about what the FBI found in that Washington hotel room right after the shooting. The *Washington Star* reported that agents were seen leaving with eleven suitcases and boxes. Could that have been a typo? Here's a guy who flies from Denver to Los Angeles, spends a few hours there, turns around and goes across the country on a bus and ends up in a D.C. hotel room with enough stuff to fill eleven suitcases and boxes?

...Which reminds me: When the *Washington Star* folded, leaving the scene to the *Post,* it was more than a local event—it was a national disaster. Somehow I've got to slip a brief diagnosis of the multiple ills of the *Washington Post* into this article before I finish.

...Now for today's news:

* *On October 21, the wire services got around to telling the American people that last July John W. Hinckley Jr. reportedly wrote that he was part of a conspiracy to assassinate the president of the United States and that he had written letters to his co-conspirators that were intercepted. Here is the way the* Washington Post *transmitted that information to the newspapers that subscribe to its wire service:*

> WASHINGTON—*John W. Hinckley Jr. reportedly wrote that he was in conspiracy with others when he shot President Reagan and also described in writing purportedly fictional co-conspirators, apparently thinking he could trade the "information" to make a favorable deal for himself.*

There, good readers, is a textbook example of how the press all too frequently adopts the official stance of whatever authority is in charge of releasing information. In the lead paragraph, the co-conspirators claimed by Hinckley are instantly "purported" to be "fictional," and the statements of the accused assassin are instantly dismissed as a ruse "apparently" to obtain "a favorable deal for himself." The authority? The government. The second paragraph makes that clear, along with much else:

> *A Justice Department spokesman said Tuesday a continuing FBI investigation into the March 30 shooting "has developed no reliable evidence of a conspiracy."*

...Jesus, sweet and loving Jesus, I can't stand this. Bet your boots, and whatever else you can beg, borrow but not steal, at odds of 10 to 1 if necessary, that this batch of evidence never sees the light of day. If ever you needed documentation for the thesis that the American press and public have reached a state of unparalleled passivity, this is it. The government is in the process of controlling what we may know, limiting what we may find out, legislating what we may believe. No question about it—I've got to rewrite that New York convention speech. Take out some of the history of the reporting on Vietnam and put in more recent history.

...I'm too tired to go on with this. And I haven't come to my notes on Judge Barrington Parker yet. That's an interesting collection.

...Judge Barrington D. Parker of the United States District Court for the District of Columbia: 66 years old, short, bespectacled. His left leg amputated above the knee in 1975, the result of being struck by an automobile while crossing a street in

Washington. Likes historical fiction—especially James Michener—progressive jazz, classical music.

...But: (1) He is both black and a Republican, a combination that arouses mixed emotions in many whites and a single strong emotion in almost all blacks who vote; (2) He was appointed to the federal bench by Richard Milhous Nixon; and (3) He subsequently has been involved in a series of widely publicized cases in which he became noted for his controversial decisions. Another federal judge, describing himself as "a longtime friend," says that Parker "has no hesitancy in coming forth with unpopular decisions."

...Well, there was his decision on May 31, 1979, that President Carter had exceeded his constitutional authority in seeking to propose wage and price guidelines, described as a victory for the plaintiffs—nine member unions of the AFL-CIO—and "a significant defeat for President Carter's anti-inflation program." (His decision was reversed on appeal).

...Then there was the case of California's lieutenant governor, Edwin Reinecke, who in 1974 had been convicted of lying to the Senate Judiciary Committee during hearings to consider the nomination of Deputy Attorney General Richard Kleindienst (who later was to get a suspended sentence) to replace John Mitchell (who later was to be convicted of a felony). Reinecke (yea, verily, his boss was Ronald Reagan) lied about his role in the infamous case involving the charge that the International Telephone and Telegraph Corporation offer to underwrite the 1972 Republican National Convention was connected with the settlement of a government anti-trust suit under terms highly favorable to the conglomerate. The judge could have imposed a five-year jail sentence and a $2,000 fine on Reinecke. But Judge Barrington Parker gave him an 18-month suspended sentence and one month's unsupervised probation.

...Oh, Jonathan, it's late.... But there's the Helms case. It's 1977, and the former director of the CIA, Richard Helms, pleaded no contest to two charges of failing to testify "fully, completely and accurately" before the Senate Foreign Relations Committee in 1973. Helms testified that the CIA had not covertly supplied money to opponents of Salvadore Allende to block his election as president of Chile. A Senate investigation concluded the reverse and found that Helms had lied. The Justice Department argued against a criminal indictment of Helms for perjury, contending that a trial would require disclosure of confidential material that might "compromise national security" or "create diplomatic embarrassment for the United States." Judge Barrington Parker, before passing sentence, told Helms that "if public officials embark deliberately on a course to disobey and ignore the laws of our land because of some misguided and ill-conceived notion and belief that there are earlier commitments and considerations which they must first observe, the future of this country is in jeopardy." He then proceeded to protect the future of this country by giving Helms a suspended two-year sentence and a $2,000 fine.... There are spectacular footnotes: The lawyer for Helms was none other than Superlawyer Edward Bennett Williams, the man himself. (Nail it down, Jonathan; it's the Superlawyer's lawyers who were subsequently hired by Hinckley's parents). Standing before Judge Parker, Williams pleaded for a lenient sentence, saying that Helms "would bear the scar of a conviction for the rest of his life." After Parker passed sentence, Williams told reporters outside the courtroom that Helms would "wear this conviction like a badge of honor." Helms eagerly agreed with his lawyer.... Then more than 400 former and perhaps present CIA employees gathered at a country club in Bethesda, Maryland, gave Helms a standing ovation, put two wastebaskets atop a piano and quickly contributed far more than enough to pay his fine.... I remember reading the story and thinking that November 4, 1977, was the night a faction within the Central Intelligence Agency declared war on the elected and legitimate government of the United States....

... And then there's the trial involving the murder of Orlando Letelier on a street in Washington, D.C. The judge: Barrington D. Parker. The director of Central Intelligence: George Bush. One of the many unanswered questions of that trial: How do we square what the evidence indicates with what Bush told federal investigators? One certain fact: Before the trial of John W. Hinckley Jr., reporters should read the transcript of the trial of the accused assassins of Orlando Letelier, presided over by the same Judge Parker....

...And how did Judge Parker become the judge for this trial of international interest and significance? "In another sharp diversion from regular courthouse procedure," as the *Washington Post* flatly put it, his name was randomly selected as presiding judge for the Hinckley case from a stack of shuffled cards that bore the names of fourteen federal judges who were available. "That selection process normally is carried out by a court clerk," the *Post* went on, but "the more elaborate procedure" in the private chambers of the senior judge was meant to ensure that it was "perfectly certain there's no question about the correctness of the draw." Thus was the card bearing the name of Barrington D. Parker turned over....

...And....

Jonathan Blakely's eyes closed involuntarily. He opened them long enough to turn off the lamp and walk to the couch, where he pushed a pile of newspapers to the floor, lay down, put his arms around a pillow and dreamt of Arianne.

NOVEMBER

It is my belief that the establishment—that elusive but very real force in American life—has of recent weeks opted decisively for Ronald Reagan. I also believe he will be elected President. The reasoning behind that conclusion may be a bit perverse, however. I am convinced the establishment has decided that authoritarian controls must be imposed to get the country out of the mess in which it finds itself; that there is no other way to preserve the power structure. In short, it believes that democracy is doomed in a world of shrinking resources and rising expectations, but that the structure which surrounds it can survive if we abandon some of our freedom.... As controls began to be imposed, people would not grasp what was happening until it was too late....

> — *Carey McWilliams, Editor/Writer*
> *Written shortly before his death*
> *on June 27, 1980*

Alonzo Schaeffer was on time, pulling up to the curb in front of the hotel on 28th Street that had seen better days, most of them more than three-quarters of a century earlier. Jonathan, who had been walking the streets of Manhattan appraising the schizophrenic nature of the urban condition, opened the door of the BMW, shook hands, slipped into the bucket seat and relaxed.

"Nice seeing you again, Alonzo."

"How did it go?"

"About as you might expect. Barry Zorthian did a reprise of his four years as master of ceremonies at the Five O'Clock Follies in Saigon and Gloria Emerson called him a brilliant and determined liar and Barry said he didn't have to justify himself to Gloria and Gloria said that Barry shouldn't even have been invited to speak at a conference like this. Ellsworth Bunker doddered in—I'm glad I don't have a head full of his memories— and Daniel Ellsberg gave additional evidence that he remains a deeply troubled man. And there was Marilyn Berger and Bernard Kalb and Bill Bundy and Dave Dellinger. I could drop names all over the place. And the usual clutch of academics, including the classic sellout who wrote a book aimed at establishment hearts and was promptly appointed director of some institute subsidized by government grants. In other words, just like any other conference held in New York City."

"I'm glad to see that you remain unchanged," Alonzo Schaeffer said, laughing. "I thought a brush with the big town would shake off some of that provincialism that encrusts you. How did your talk go?"

"How can one tell? I laid it on the line, as I told you I would. The applause ranged from polite to enthusiastic. I got out of there alive, at least. Let's talk about it over dinner. Where are you taking me?"

"To a little Italian restaurant in the Village. Some might call it quaint. I've been going there for years."

"Sounds good."

As they drove the narrow streets and crowded avenues on the way south, Jonathan once again was plagued by an insistent question for which he could find no rational or reasonable answer: Why did these people stay here when they could go westward, away from the stifling, enervating swarms of humanity who infested this largest of all American cities? The only answer that made sense to him was that they had never been anywhere else where they could make some comparisons. He sought counsel.

"Why do all these people stay here, Alonzo?"

"I think, strange as it must sound to you, that they like it here."

"Mmmmmmmmm. Not very many of them act as if they like it here. Most of them seem to be unhappy. Hurried, hassled and unhappy."

"I can't deny that. I rather like coming here for short stays, but I'm always glad to get back west. It's a nice place to visit but..." He looked over at Jonathan and smiled. "I can't believe my eyes—there's a parking place." He swerved into the open spot. "It's only about six blocks from here."

Ah, the Village. For many years, during his occasional visits to the wonderland of the great white way, where the mouth of the media bids good evening to Mr. and Mrs. North America and All The Ships At Sea, Jonathan had stayed in the apartment of a friend on Hudson Street. The relationship had cooled—and the apartment no longer was offered—when he had asked his host, a theater director, what his greatest ambition might be. "To win a Tony," his friend had replied, and Jonathan had burst out laughing. Honors, honors, honors everywhere. Everyone finally could be famous, anointed with a sacred oil that evaporated in the second beyond the consecrated person's allotted moment in the sun, but the honor always could be hugged as proof of one's having passed this way.

He told Alonzo that story as they walked to the restaurant. The reporter, who had won far more than his share of journalistic prizes, looked at him quizzically and then brought the subject back to the conference.

"I saw in this morning's *Washington Post* that Ben Wattenberg spoke at the conference and disagrees with your view that the government lies excessively."

"Oh, bullshit, Alonzo. Wattenberg is to societal studies what the Harvard Medical School is to health research. He's been peddling his disinformation for so long that his meanness is taken for insight. All he does is manufacture statistics that the establishment is panting to hear. He's a direct descendant of that flack with the title of Assistant Secretary of Defense for Public Affairs who defended the government's 'inherent right to lie' back in 1963. If your paper wanted to perform an overdue public service it would start on January One and list the name and occupation of every public servant—elected, appointed or hired by the federal government—who was investigated and found wanting, was convicted, was in a drunken brawl or was snorting shit, took a payoff or in other numberless ways proved unfit by any respectable standard to be paid with funds provided by taxpayers. Run it every day for a year, in goddamn agate type if you want, and at the end of the year, when the readers saw how long the lists were, they'd demand a whole set of concrete prisons to house all the politicians and bureaucrats and other thieving bastards who betrayed the public trust. Then you could consider another list of those other adepts at misprision who bilk the taxpayers by shilling for corporate weapons makers and the other corporate merchants of death who have the rest of the citizens of our nation by the well-known tits and balls. Hell, the way it is now, the revelations are so routine a lot of papers don't even run the stories or they end up in their News Digest on page a hundred and fifty-nine."

They entered the small Italian restaurant and took a table in the corner. Jonathan stared at the menu.

"Would you be good enough," he said, "to recommend a dish

before I order the veal scaloppini?"

The other man laughed. "That's what I like most about you, Jonathan," he said. "You keep an open mind on all subjects. Your selection, in this case at least, is beyond reproach." He ordered the two dinners "with the usual wine" and handed the menus to the waiter.

"You certainly have a thing about the government, don't you?"

"No more than millions and millions of other people out there," Jonathan responded. "And let's not confuse the issue, Alonzo. The Constitution and Bill of Rights are magnificent. The system is splendid. It's the people who have violated the system and corrupted it who stink to high heaven. I had a city editor once who said that there are two statements that always should be regarded with suspicion. One is 'The check is in the mail' and the other is 'I'm from the government and I'm here to help you.' "

Alonzo Schaeffer laughed. He saw that Jonathan was still high from the adrenalin pumped into his system by his public address a few hours earlier. He listened.

"Did you catch the story about John McCloy saying that the government owed neither reparations nor apology to the 120,000 people of Japanese ancestry who were put in concentration camps during the next-to-last World War? American citizens, too, even as you and I. McCloy was assistant secretary of war at the time and he said it sends him up the wall every time someone suggests that an apology is owed. You know, that's the kind of mind and conscience that boggles the imagination. You can't rehabilitate someone like that. He's hopeless. And that guy was high up in the hierarchy."

"Don't forget, Jonathan, that we've had some damn good ones serve in the State Department, too."

"Oh, I don't forget that. But the non-McCloys only rarely rise to positions of influence. Let me tell you a little pertinent tale about something that happened last July. We got a story over the wire about two men who resigned their $50,000-a-year government jobs in what your paper described as a very rare act among Washington bureaucrats—they left over a matter of principle. They couldn't stand the way the manufacturers of infant formula urged mothers in poor countries to bottle-feed their babies. And then the United States cast the only vote in the United Nations World Health Assembly against a code that would curtail that kind of marketing. They had seen how their government put corporate greed above the lives of the babies who die from this form of undiluted criminal avarice."

He paused. "And then, Alonzo, a few minutes later we got another story over the wire about Robert McNamara, the corporate genius in charge of the war in Vietnam for about eight years before he slipped out the side door to become president of the World Bank. In the news story he absolutely refused to break his thirteen-year silence on the conduct of that war. And you know what he said? He said that as an international servant—whatever the hell that is—it is inappropriate for him to talk about national politics—past, present or future. And then he added that even if he had not been an international servant, he wouldn't wish to complicate the task of his successors. Man, he's the terror of our times. Here we are getting tangled up in a new Vietnam in Latin America and the expert on all the follies of Vietnam doesn't want to say anything that might be considered critical. There is a special place in hell reserved for people like that, as the old saying goes."

"All you're proving is that we do have all kinds—good and bad—in the high echelons of government."

"Hey, no question. We're just dickering over statistics. I'm just talking about who's in charge, who's in control, who's on first. The guys in the State Department who turn the burners up and down, on and off all the time. Iran, Afghanistan, Cambodia, Vietnam, Thailand, El Salvador, Nicaragua, Mexico, all over Central and South America—it's a cinch to cite chapter and verse. And tell me this, Alonzo: How come weeks go by without a story on Iran in your paper?"

"Very simple. After the hostages were released, Khomeini closed the door on American correspondents."

"Precisely my point. The experts on Iran point out that the French press, for instance, has no trouble whatsoever finding out what's going on in Iran—and printing it. But the minute it becomes White House policy to put a low profile on a country, the press follows that policy like a little puppy following its master. Look, Alonzo, the people who run your paper are not unaware of what's going down in Iran. Their foreign affairs writers shuttle back and forth between jobs on the paper and jobs in the State Department. It's a monumental journalistic disgrace. They're supposed to put their wiliest foxes in charge of the chickenhouse, but lately you can't tell who is the fox and who are the chickens. Are we supposed to believe the fairy tale in which the chicken is transmogrified into one of your cute little front-page foxes?"

Alonzo Schaeffer made no attempt to hide the fact that he was miffed.

"You seem to have a notable lack of respect for the integrity of anyone not yourself, Jonathan. Have you noticed that not-too-attractive quality about your personality?"

Jonathan laughed. "Hey, Alonzo, don't get touchy." He reached out and put his hand on the other man's shoulder. "I try to dish out compliments to anyone who deserves them. I'm well aware of the fact that no one can get too much approval. I number among my friends and acquaintances a lot of people in the profession who have integrity. Like you, Alonzo. You just weren't listening when Ken Kesey said the goal of all of us should be to transcend the bullshit. You simply have a constitution that can absorb a lot of compelling facts and not let it bother you."

"May I remind you that I resigned from Henry Luce's shop when I couldn't tolerate the Vietnam war coverage? And I wasn't the only one who quit as a matter of principle. You know, Jonathan, I finally have figured out why you go off the tracks so often. Would you be interested in my analysis?"

"Very. Anyone or anything that helps me along the way is appreciated."

"All right, here it is: The reason you get derailed so often is that you can't bring yourself to believe that there are men in high places who actually want an arms race, who actually would like to go to war with the Soviet Union, who actually believe a nuclear war can be won. That there are men who lie with a straight face or cheat every chance they get, or take advantage of their fellow man without a qualm, who don't give even a passing thought to the suffering of the poor or the elderly or the unemployed, who couldn't care less what happens to your precious wilderness or to wildlife or plants or trees or anything else that stands in their way on this earth. Far from holding their noses, they love the smell of the money that crosses their palms. They don't give a damn about who gets tortured, or who dies or who gets killed so long as it's done out of their sight. There are men in high places who actually plot the terrible suffering and deaths of our young men on battlefields that have nothing to do with the security of our nation and who think it's proper to destabilize other governments or assassinate the leaders of governments they don't like, without giving a thought to the fact that if it's all right for us to do it to them, it might be all right for them to do it to us. Do you follow me?"

"Hey, Alonzo, you don't think I'm that naive, do you? Of course I know those guys are out there."

"Yes, my friend, but you don't really accept the fact. *Accept* is the operative word. You say all those things, but then you act as if you're the only person in the vicinity who is aware of those truths. You never say 'So what else is new?' "

"And I hope I never do. Fuck those sycophants who mock anyone who is in earnest."

"See? My analysis is correct. You refuse to accept the fact that human nature is such that under any system, in any society, within any culture there will be individuals who will not follow the ethical or moral values you prize so highly. And please don't suggest to me that it's possible to create such a society. Utopia is nonsense spelled sideways. Jonathan, it simply isn't going to get any better, and the day you accept that fact—and I repeat that *accept* is the crucial word—that will be the day you become a happier man."

"I'm not so sure." He sipped the Italian wine Alonzo Schaeffer had ordered. "This is a far cry from that fountain water they package and import from Rome and huckster on the airwaves. Look, Alonzo, I'm not trying to solve all our problems by pointing at the villains. But I think one of the best ways to make this a fairer society is to say that villainy is being practiced and that we ought not turn our heads and say it doesn't concern us. That's the happiness of the schmuck with his head in the sand and his buttocks high in the air."

"But you're standing on the brink of cynicism."

"Oh, no, Alonzo. I stand where I've stood ever since my eyes were opened—on the water's edge of skepticism."

"Well, as long as you don't plunge in you'll be safe. The undertow can carry you out to cynicism." He leaned back as the waiter set their plates on the table. As he picked up his fork he looked across the table at Jonathan and smiled.

"If I may change the subject, I believe you will be pleased to know that you have a fellow bather at the water's edge of skepticism in regard to the attempt to assassinate our president. Does that surprise you?"

" 'Tis the millennium. What's happened?"

"Two things. First, I took your suggestion and checked my paper's record on reviews of assassination books. You're right. It's a stunning record of amazing consistency. Hostility rampant no matter which book."

"Ah-ha."

"The orchestration was made even more obvious when an early edition review that was favorable to one assassination book was pulled from later editions. That takes a quick, firm hand on the throttle."

"Ah-ha."

"The second thing was the coverage of young Hinckley's suicide attempt the other day and his claim that he was part of a conspiracy."

"Ah-haaaaaaah. You noticed."

"I did indeed."

"You're ready."

Jonathan reached for the manila envelope he had been carrying and now was on the floor under his chair. He opened it and drew out three sheets of blue paper that he handed across the table.

"I'm waiting for the courts to decide on the disposition of the papers found in Hinckley's cell before I write about it," he said, smiling broadly. "But that was certainly curious—Hinckley claiming he was part of a conspiracy. That's about the only opinion he has that wasn't given a run in the media, as you noticed. But try this short section at your leisure. Over coffee, perhaps?"

"Now," Alonzo Schaeffer replied.

THE TWO "SUICIDE ATTEMPTS"

Turn now to the two reported attempts of John W. Hinckley Jr. to take his own life while he was supposed to be under 24-hour guard.

The first, on May 27, 1981, was described as "an attempt to harm himself by swallowing an overdose of the aspirin substitute Tylenol." That was the first we heard that the 24-hour watch Hinckley had been under since his arrival at the Butner Federal Correctional Facility "had been discontinued after a short time," but now we were informed that it had been reinstated. Nonetheless, there was a second attempt, on November 15, after he had been transferred to the stockade at the Fort Meade army base in Maryland. This time he reportedly tried to hang himself with an army field jacket. (That was an especially poignant touch, since in Taxi Driver *the DeNiro character puts on his army fatigue jacket and sets off to find the politician.) The Reuters account of the second attempt, selected by the* New York Times, *said that Hinckley "suffered some injury to his neck muscles that could lead to complications." Then:*

> *The Justice Department statement said that Mr. Hinckley apparently stuffed cardboard into the lock of his cell door to prevent federal marshals from rescuing him. But a marshal forced his way through a window and cut him down, the department said.*
>
> *Mr. Hinckley was suspended for three to five minutes before he was pulled down and remained on the floor for 30 minutes before he was taken by ambulance to a hospital.*

The Associated Press, in a later summary of the incident, provided an additional tidbit when it reported that Hinckley was able to jam the lock of his cell with cardboard and tie himself to a window when a guard "who was watching him from an adjacent room turned away to let another guard in." Furthermore, the guards "had to reach in the window from an exercise yard" to cut down the prisoner, and Hinckley *"was suffering from acute lack of oxygen when he arrived at the hospital 30 minutes later, after guards cut his cell open."*

His officially announced and intriguing condition: *"With the exception of a short lapse of memory surrounding the circumstances of the attempted suicide, clinically, John Hinckley's mental capacities are intact. More definitive testing is required to determine if there has been any long-lasting effect."* The additional medical tests on the prisoner were planned *"to determine whether he suffered any permanent brain damage."*

Either the demonstrably fertile imagination of young Hinckley or the fecund brains of the Department of Justice had succeeded in devising three plots that surely would have drawn smiles of admiration from Agatha Christie: Death by Overdose of Tylenol; Stuffed Cardboard to Foil Rescuers; and Brief Turnaway of Guard During Twenty-Four-Hour Security Watch. But in this tale, as should be clear to all, no scenario is too grotesque for our consideration.

(For another example, it was at this point that the spokesman for the Department of Justice delivered himself of one of the many memorable utterances associated with the entire Hinckley affair: *"It was because he was under 24-hour watch that the attempt was unsuccessful."*)

As Stephen Crane has said, now this is the strange part:

Hinckley's father was interviewed by the Baltimore Sun. He was reported as saying that his son's attempt to take his life came as no surprise, that he had warned Justice Department officials two days before the suicide attempt that his son was in *"total despair"* and should be under closer surveillance. When Hinckley's father requested closer supervision of his son, the Baltimore Sun pointed out, *"the younger Hinckley was supposed to have already been under a 24-hour watch that included closed-circuit television monitoring by senior inspectors in the U.S. Marshals Service."* An even more significant accusation by the senior Hinckley, however, was that the Justice Department had not revealed the full details of what had happened in his son's cell. The Justice Department refused to comment on the senior Hinckley's charges. Once again we have an instance of government ownership of information that belongs to the people of the United States; once again we have an instance of the benign press of the 1980s failing to follow up and get the story behind the story that its editors were certain to select as the top news event of the year.

The government spokesman, however, did announce that the prisoner had been moved to another cell and all of us were assured—or, more accurately, reassured—that the U.S. Marshals Service "had placed added security around the new cell."

On the basis of the established record, alas, no one could be certain that Hinckley would not "try" again. The pattern is clear. Some might see a subliminal message woven into the fabric of the pattern, but that is an arcane skill not widely understood in our society.

Alonzo Schaeffer shook his head.

"What you're suggesting is that the Justice Department was playing politics with this case."

"Hell no, I'm not suggesting it—I feel like screaming it from the top of your fucking Empire State Building. Look, who's in charge, finally? None other than Attorney General William French Smith, longtime friend of the president who's been through the political mill. He claimed outsized write-offs on an oil and gas shelter and took a huge severance payment from a company on whose board he served. He was forced to kick in on the tax break and he reportedly returned the severance payment. That's the man in charge of the nation's criminal justice system. In the old days the president would pay off his campaign managers by appointing them postmaster general, but since Nixon peddled the United States Post Office they now become director of the CIA, for God's sake, or attorney general. Mitchell went to jail, Kleindienst was convicted, and now we have Smith. These boys play political hardball the way Pete Rose plays baseball, except that these guys come into second base with their cleats high. And you expect me to anticipate an impartial investigation into the shooting? Come off it, Alonzo. Who's being naive now? Wherever there's law, there's politics. And wherever there are lawyers there's rancid politics."

"You have a point," Alonzo Schaeffer said. "That's the same William French Smith who approved the merger of the *Seattle*

Times and the *Seattle P-I* when his own antitrust division turned thumbs down on it. Nobody wanted the merger except the owners of the two papers, so they could milk the advertisers the way the San Francisco sheets do. It was a damnably weak case they had."

"Weak isn't the word. They had no case. A lot of publishers wanted to buy the *P-I* and keep a competitive situation there. The *Times* is a house organ for Boeing and the *P-I* is classified as a failing newspaper—but what newspaper run by the Hearst Corporation isn't either failed or failing? That was a nice favor from the attorney general of the United States to two newspapers and a chain that will repay the favor many times over, you can be sure. That's justice as meted out by the man who runs the Justice Department. The stench is overwhelming."

"I don't often quote Francis Ford Coppola, but he was on the mark when he said that men of power and the criminal in our society are distinguished only by their situation, not their morality." Alonzo Schaeffer stared for a few seconds into his wine glass, then added: "Actually, there's more honor among the mafia than in some of the gangs we've had in the White House in recent years."

Jonathan took several more sheets of paper from the envelope.

"Here," he said. "You're really ready. Last August I told you about the pages I'd written about conspiracies involved in this case. Here's the brew the witches concocted."

THE THREE "CONSPIRACIES"

Nothing on these pages is meant to suggest that there definitely was a conspiracy to elevate Vice President George Bush to the presidency. What is clearly documented on the preceding pages is that the American public has been denied a substantial amount of pertinent information concerning those "extraordinary coincidences" connected with the events of the afternoon of March 30. The answers to the many questions raised here may be revealed satisfactorily in a public trial of the accused or, failing that, in an opening of all the evidence that has been gathered and sealed by the government. How persistently the news media push for this to happen may well be the litmus by which this possible conspiracy could be tested.

* * *

But there definitely was a conspiracy in this case, as these pages also have documented. It was a concerted attempt on the part of the Department of Justice and other agencies in the executive branch of government to control the release of information concerning the attempted assassination. The law enforcement agencies, with the acquiescence of the courts, sealed a large amount of evidence that normally would be part of the public record and unquestionably should be known by the public in a situation that strikes at the stability of our political processes. Furthermore, those who control the sealed evidence have intentionally leaked portions of the contents to suit their purposes, a procedure that does nothing to inspire confidence in the system of justice or the performance of a free press. In the process they have firmly established the principle of government ownership of information that historically has been open to both press and public.

This successful hustle of the national news media by federal agencies is all the more remarkable because it has been so unremarked on. The principal organs of news dissemination, with rare and noteworthy exceptions, have been seized by a timidity that contrasts starkly with the gutsy investigative reporting in the early 1970s that broke through the government/corporate/military complex in a way unparalleled in American journalistic history, even by the renowned muckrakers of the first decade of this century. Sadly, the times now are such that only an occasional reporter was able to slip into a story a note that obliquely questioned the government spokesmen who had usurped control over what the American people were to know of the near-death of their president.

And then we were put through the spectacle of the family of the defendant and their justly famous lawyers—and ultimately the defendant himself—arrogantly assuming the position of providing only that information they wished to provide. Some fuss has been made, here and there, about the news media's "invasion of privacy" of the Hinckley family in Evergreen, Colo. The truth of the matter is that the press accepted the family's refusal to answer questions of legitimate public interest while giving extensive publicity to their views emanating from "press conferences" conducted by next-door neighbors and formal statements issued from the offices of their distinguished attorneys. The Hinckleys have every right to remain silent in the face of the journalistic inquisition, but they morally relinquish that privilege when they "go public" of their own accord and actively seek to promote their opinions without facing the fair questions reporters might raise.

Less than 48 hours after the president was shot, the attorney and family friend of the Hinckleys announced he was delivering the "final statement" from the parents of the accused. Nonetheless, the Associated Press subsequently distributed verbatim a five-paragraph release issued from the office of "prominent criminal lawyer Edward Bennett Williams" and signed "JoAnn and Jack Hinckley." The gist was that their son was "a sick boy," and they complained that they had "seen certain press reports that we believe to be inaccurate." They did not elaborate, however, nor did any members of the family, as far as can be determined at this writing, relent in their refusal to be interviewed, except by the friendly and understanding Wall Street Journal, *which asked Scott Hinckley none of the questions crying for an answer or even any of the questions raised earlier in its own news columns. Thus the national news media, in addition to permitting representatives of the federal government to take possession of the press's constitutional and imperative role as gatekeeper of the news, allowed the attorneys for the defense and even the next-door neighbors of the accused assassin's parents to control what the public was to be told of the motives of the defendant. The overbearing nature of this circumstance was made complete by the wretched excess of a neighbor's assurance that "arrangements will be made to feed the press"—a "feeding," incidentally, that never took place. And the kid-glove treatment accorded the Hinckleys by the national media contrasts vividly with the relentless pursuit of less patrician parents and relatives of other political assassins.*

Similarly, the vice president, his press agents and members of his family have not been forthcoming on matters related to the attempted assassination. For examples, the press let them brush off the Scott Hinckley-Neil Bush scheduled dinner and the fact that the vice president's son and daughter-in-law appeared quite certain that the Hinckleys and Bushes were old friends—a friendship that included Hinckley contributions to the vice president's campaign coffers. The vice president's press agents put out the story that the kids were mistaken and that they had checked their records "and we find no evidence of contributions to Bush from the Hinckley family." The media sucked in that marshmallow and found it sweet. But the truth is that Jack Hinckley contributed to the United States Senate campaign of George Bush 'way back in 1970.

On March 18, 1970. They do seem to be old friends.

The problem comes down to a press corps that in the 1980s no longer asks the questions that should be asked. Access, the golden key to "success" for journalists on the Potomac, is rarely endangered these days by introducing a subject that might touch a raw political nerve. Thus we read an unblushingly adoring paean by a Hearst columnist to Vice President Bush, written shortly before the afternoon of March 30, concluding with the observation that President Reagan likes Bush because "he is loyal and he keeps his mouth shut," and that they work well together because, quoting Bush's press secretary, "After all, they are both gentlemen."

When Scott Simon, who had done a long report on John Hinckley Jr. for National Public Radio, was asked why he thought no reporter had probed the relationships between the Bush and Hinckley families, he thought for several seconds before replying: "That may be something gentlemen just don't ask gentlemen."

Perhaps the press, far from being arrogant and imperial, as some unfriendly critics and well-burned scoundrels have suggested, has under the circumstances been far too gentlemanly.

* * *

The third "conspiracy" is a subtle canard fostered by politicians, furthered by the media and accepted by much of the public. It is that a political assassination conspiracy in our country is so unthinkable that no one should waste time thinking about it. This in the face of overwhelming evidence to the contrary and the fact that approximately as many persons now believe the Warren Commission Report as believe in the tooth fairy. As recently as 1979 the final report of the House Assassinations Committee concluded that the murders of President Kennedy and Dr. Martin Luther King "likely" resulted from conspiracies not fully explored by either the Warren Commission or the FBI. The stench that marks the trial and the trail of James Earl Ray to the Tennessee penitentiary does not go away. Unanswered questions remain in the killing of Robert Kennedy and Malcolm X and the shooting of George Wallace. And, of course, now the near-assassination of Ronald Reagan.

On the surface, the performance of both the national news media and the agencies of government seems frustratingly inexplicable. But gradually, as the evidence accumulated, at least a partial explanation began to take form. First came the hints:

Here comes Andy Rooney (pure onomatopoeia, that) to assure us the day after the assassination attempt that "it didn't represent any political movement, any plot or conspiracy." No, sir. "No one was trying to overthrow the government and put a junta in charge—although don't bet you won't be reading a book suggesting that in the next 10 years." And he goes on to describe the best of all pollyanna worlds: "The best thing for all of us would be if [Hinckley] were found to be mentally incompetent of knowing right from wrong. It would reduce the crime to one of no significance at all, and then if Reagan, press secretary James Brady and the two police officers could recover successfully, we could all put the incident out of our minds and go back to work." (Don't think for a moment that those Philadelphia lawyers in Washington won't try to make andyrooney's dream come true.)

From Los Angeles, hear ye an excerpt from a story on the Academy Awards ceremony, which had been delayed one day by the shooting: "It is interesting that I did not hear a single suggestion that it could have been a conspiracy or even politically motivated. It was presumed immediately to be the act of some dreary nobody who wanted to be somebody by touching a celebrity."

Another columnist, the day after the crime: "There is one difference between the Kennedy assassination and the wounding of Reagan. Conspiracy theorists had a field day trying to link Oswald with a plot to kill Kennedy, but it's highly unlikely they will be able to convince any segment of the public that John Warnock Hinckley Jr., 25, of Evergreen, Colo., was working with others who wanted Reagan dead."

And then, as manna, a column contributed to the Boston Globe *by an assistant professor of sociology at Harvard. It was written in the hours after the shooting when all he had was a great deal of misinformation, and he unwittingly supplied the undeniably logical conclusion:*

> *For no matter what the true responsibility may be, the very identity of the assassin has the potential to discredit a movement or political organization or bring shame upon some social group or family....*
>
> *That's why probably many Americans felt a certain relief in learning that the accused assailant of President Reagan comes from a homogeneously American background, had some mad obsession with an actress and might as easily have killed Carter as Reagan. The less rational his motivation, the more politically isolated and meaningless the act.... The insanity of the lone assassin protects us from messages that other circumstances might suggest and that might be far more dangerous to the traditions of an open and tolerant society.*

Those "messages" and those "other circumstances" do not become less dangerous by averting our eyes. Quite the contrary, an open and tolerant society will perish once the curtain of secrecy is lowered by those in power and the press does nothing to raise those black drapes.

Alonzo Schaeffer handed the pages across the table. He spoke softly.

"I must say, Jonathan, that you are the most haunted man I know. Every now and then I perceive a note of hysteria in your writing, but I can't deny that you have put together a case that is utterly reasonable despite its obvious haunted quality."

"The fact is," Jonathan said, "I'm haunted by something else." He put the sheets back in the envelope and tucked it under the chair. He took a deep breath. "Right from the start we began to see a lot of stuff written about how the parents of the assassin weren't responsible for the acts of their son. I didn't bring it up; lots of writers got into the subject. And when a friend of mine—you remember Clarence Toole—went to Evergreen and did some investigating for me, he told me the local paper had two obsessions of its own. One was to impress on its readers the notion that John Hinckley Jr. never *really* lived in Evergreen. That 'really,' Alonzo, is in italics—my emphasis. Oh sure, they say, he always used that address every time he was asked his home address and—oh, admittedly, he spent a lot of time living there off and on—but, well, uh, he was just a shiftless drifter from this red, white and blue All-American family. At that point I say listen good, buddy, because if his home address wasn't there it was nowhere. You see, Alonzo, the ultimate truth about victims of that obsession is that in their eyes the lad had no home address. And that means the lad had no home."

Jonathan paused and shook his head sadly.

"You know what his father told him once? 'You can't come home, John, we've had it.' It was the *Wall Street Journal* that reported the speculation by psychiatrists that when Hinckley fired the shots he was symbolically attacking his father and namesake. Have you noticed that he was the second son and yet he's the one carrying his father's name? Then we have the statement of young Hinckley's roommate in the freshman dorm at Texas Tech who said Hinckley talked a lot about how his father was going to give the family business to the older brother and that he was going to be left out. Somehow I believe all those shrinks who've examined Hinckley when they say the same thing—that the guy has shown not one sign of remorse or acceptance of any personal responsibility for his actions."

"I'm listening," Alonzo Schaeffer said. "And the paper's second obsession?"

"The second was that the parents had no responsibility in all this. The editorials were adamant on that point. Well, Alonzo, this is the moment that I confess to you that I've had a subobsession that haunts me almost as much as my obsession itself. Here's what it is: One of the wisest women I've ever known once told me that she was absolutely certain about very, very few things. Then she said that of the following she was positive: Our Children Are What We Taught Them To Be. That's what she said and I've never forgotten it. And I think she meant that to apply in a more general sense, too—that we're all responsible for what the children around us do. I don't think any of us can easily dismiss our share in the creation of an assassin who subsequently has become a media star."

"Jonathan, we both know why the establishment press just runs its fingers over the surface of events. The media aren't simply part of the corporate structure—they're the foundation. I agree with you that there hasn't been a significant step forward in the quality of news presentation since most newspapers appropriated the best perceptions of the alternative press and made them their own. Even the *Chicago Tribune* shows signs of trying to put out a paper that isn't dedicated to the memory of Colonel McCormick's wildest hallucinations. Television news is even worse. It's worse than it was when Huntley and Cronkite were doing it. It certainly is jazzier, but everyone's substituting graphics for content these days. Look at *USA Today*."

"Yeah. And please don't think that I'm under the illusion that those guys who run the big news operations will ever listen to a voice that comes, for instance, out of the still mountain air of Montana. All the voices they hear—or, rather, listen to—come from the throats of people just like them, who are so mired in their environment that they can't see it clearly. It's McLuhan's fish multiplied by the metropolitan populations of the United States."

Alonzo Schaeffer leaned back as the waiter brought the Cointreau he had requested with a silent signal.

"Well, what about your speech today? You said we'd talk about it over dinner, but we've talked about everything but that."

"No, not altogether," Jonathan replied. "I didn't mention the unpleasantness of last March but I certainly had it in mind when I wrote the speech. What I did was recapitulate the dismal record of the mass media in reporting the antiwar movement of the '60s and early '70s and then I suggested that the reason now is much clearer. We subsequently learned a lot about the infiltration of the media by the intelligence and law enforcement agencies of the government."

"I trust that you documented the charges."

"Fully. Or at least as much as has been revealed, and that's more than enough although I suspect it's only the famous tip of the infamous iceberg. The revelations that the FBI had journalists on their payroll. The revelations in 1973 when the CIA admitted it had 40 full-time reporters or free-lancers on the payroll, and five of them were with general-circulation news organizations. The later revelations that many persons working for the American news media since World War Two also served as salaried operatives for the CIA while performing their duties as reporters. Carl Bernstein has put the number of American journalists who took on secret assignments for the agency at more than 400. Even your paper has reported that between 30 and 100 were paid for such work and that more than 50 news organizations were either owned or subsidized by the CIA. We've been victimized by a lot of disinformation, which is an impolite euphemism for deliberately attempting to deceive the people of the United States whether it's practiced by agents of the KGB or the CIA. We also know about the twelve full-time CIA officers who worked abroad as reporters or non-editorial employees of American-owned news organizations and in some cases were hired by the news organizations whose credentials they carried. And the corruption of the book-publishing industry is sickening. Up until 1967—man, that's almost 15 years ago—the CIA had been behind the publication of more than a thousand books, and they refuse to tell the citizens which ones. It's all in the Church Committee reports. And the Pike Committee—"

"But all that has been published, by your own admission."

"Of course. How else would I know about it? That's the goddamn irony of the whole thing. Bill Colby says in 1975 'We do not at this time employ any regular staff member of a U.S. daily newspaper.' That's a classic. 'At this time,' he says, ruling out past and future. 'Employ,' he says, but what about payment for services rendered? 'Regular staff member,' he says, but what about correspondents or—more important—management? 'U.S. daily newspaper,' he says, but what about papers abroad whose so-called news could be picked up and spread here? And how about the two major wire services that supply the bulk of the information to the channels of the national news media? And then you get Stansfield Turner telling the American Society of Newspaper Editors just last year that he saw nothing wrong with recruiting journalists for spook work."

"I remember that."

"And I hope you remember that when he caught a lot of flak from journalists who refuse to serve as prostitutes he seemed surprised. He said it was only being patriotic. As I'm far from the first to point out, the fact that Turner failed to grasp that the issue is integrity and absolute independence is appalling. And you can imagine what's happening under Casey. He's under so much stress he can't even play a round of golf without four men with submachine guns surrounding him. What kind of craziness have we come to?"

"We have come to a kind of craziness that is well reported to those who read."

"Sure it's reported, but not a single professional journalistic organization has delivered a clear statement that secret commitments are decidedly unpatriotic. And it seems to me that the lords of the press owe the public an unequivocal statement that they will do everything possible to prevent any conspiracy with the agencies of government. And I think you and I and the other people in the news rooms deserve no less an assurance from the top levels that the news isn't being poisoned by subversives who seek to destroy what should be a free press in a free society."

"But there already are such provisions that relate to conflict of interest in the wire services and newspapers that I'm familiar with," Alonzo Schaeffer protested.

"Not enough, Alonzo. They're in the most general terms, like prohibiting secondary employment if it compromises integrity, or some such evasive directive. Only the UPI, to my knowledge, specifically forbids working for the CIA, FBI or any other governmental intelligence or law enforcement agency, and deplores covert or clandestine cooperation. And as I've shown in the Hinckley case, there is more than one instance of peculiar reporting by UPI along the way."

"How about codes of ethics?"

"The statement of principles revised a few years ago by the newspaper editors doesn't even touch the subject. And that's the most famous—or infamous—code we have."

Alonzo Schaeffer pondered the point.

"Could you," he began hesitantly, and then finished quickly, "entertain the possibility that you are making a mountain out of a molehill?"

"No way," Jonathan answered. "I'm not suggesting that a large number of persons in management positions in news organizations are corrupt or even corruptible. All I'm suggesting is that some of them have not been above a bit of unethical cooperation with some agencies of government at the expense of the citizens. I'm not seeing ghosts or goblins, Alonzo. The spooks are there. We've already been penetrated. And man, when you've been penetrated without consent, that's rape. We've been raped, and nobody is willing to testify against the bastards."

"We've muddled through all these years," Alonzo Schaeffer said as he gave the waiter the sign that he was ready for the check. "We'll muddle through again."

"That's the attitude that bothers me, Alonzo. I can't get out of my mind two sentences in a review of the movie *Absence of Malice* in the *Columbia Journalism Review*. It was written by a former *New York Times* reporter and Pulitzer Prize winner. The first sentence said that the ranks of journalism are littered with the unscrupulous, the conmen, the intelligence agents who use journalism as a cover, the hustlers who spoil its reputation. The second sentence said that's the price we pay for our freedom. Well, I'm glad to see that the reviewer included the undercover agents as part of the scum attached to our profession. That's the good part. But it's nonsense to regard undercover agents in journalism—or journalists who are undercover agents—as no more dangerous than the other scam artists in the media. It's pure mockery to suggest that spook-journalists do no more harm than the schlock merchants. Those guys are the opening wedge of those in government who want to establish authoritarian control or secret control over the channels of information."

"Well, I'm sure you're right about some of those in government," Alonzo Schaeffer said. "The frontal attack on the Freedom of Information Act shows this administration's hostility toward the public knowing what the government is doing. Not one respectable bit of evidence has been supplied to show that the security of the United States has been threatened by information revealed by the press in its use of the Act. Quite the opposite, our democratic institutions have been strengthened by revealing how the government secretly and often illegally and frequently contemptuously operates against the public weal."

"We're in a whole new ballgame, as they say, Alonzo. Political power isn't as powerful as it used to be. Watergate showed that. Economic power has taken over. But power is in the process of moving toward those who control information. And that is a fact well recognized by those who would like to turn our country toward a totalitarian state."

"You're really not very sanguine about the future of our republic, are you?"

"Not the way we're heading. I remember the '60s too well. The press barely provided a safety valve for legitimate and constitutional dissent that time, but that's when the Fifth Estate was born: People in the hundreds of thousands assembled in the streets and petitioned their government for a redress of grievances. It was pretty peaceful that time, but we won't be that fortunate next time, if there is a next time." He paused as the waiter put the check on the table. "Some of my friends claim to see a grass-roots movement growing very rapidly and think it could become a force in the next presidential election if some courageous and charismatic man could be found to take the lead. I'd like to say man or woman, but we still have many notable prejudices in this land of the free, I'm afraid. And I'll confess this to you: I feel like the animals who know that a storm or an earthquake is coming."

"If you want some even more unsettling news," Alonzo Schaeffer said, "our number one muckraker tells me the Pentagon brass are going to push for lie detector tests for their employees. And I have it on unquestionable authority that the president will issue an executive order in a few days authorizing the CIA to operate within the United States."

"But that's strictly forbidden by its charter. You've got to be kidding."

"I wish I were. You're absolutely right about one thing at least, Jonathan. These guys mean business. They make the Nixon gang look like clumsy amateurs—which, on second thought, they were. Remember when John Mitchell said this country was going to be turned so far to the right you wouldn't recognize it? They didn't quite get it done—Watergate saved us—but this is a lot of the same old gang who don't plan to make the mistakes Nixon made."

"Then it's not just a showdown with the Russians these guys are aching for. They mean to have a showdown with anyone who doesn't approve of their abominable foreign policies when the time is ripe. Chile was the dress rehearsal. They ran their maneuvers in Chile. Only instead of the stadiums being filled, they'll open the gates on the concentration camps Tom Pettit once showed us on television."

"Oh, I don't think so. Not in the United States of America."

"Well, I'll say this: If we're lucky, we're in for the most bitter confrontation between the press and the government since the Zenger case, and that was more than 50 years before the Bill of Rights. If we're not lucky, the press will approve of the clampdown, with the usual few exceptions, the way the vast majority played ball with Joe McCarthy and Nixon and all those House Un-American Activities Committee crooks who ended up in prison. You know, Alonzo, what gets to me more than anything in this whole study of the assassination attempt is the indescribable arrogance of those with wealth and power."

"It's nothing new," Alonzo Schaeffer replied. "It goes all the way back to the Federalist Papers and their argument against guaranteeing a free press outside government control. The only difference is that it's not currently fashionable to hold such a philosophy publicly, but you can be sure that there are millions of Americans—especially those in the bureaucracy and industry and the military—who would welcome a clampdown on the press. Alexander Hamilton didn't pull his punches. He regarded freedom of the press and the whole Bill of Rights as nonsense. He regarded the mission of the Constitutional Convention as securing for the rich and well-born their distinct, permanent share in the government. At least that's the way I remember his words."

"That's close enough."

Jonathan reached into his pocket and pulled a bill from his money-clip.

"It's Dutch, as we agreed, right?"

"Right." Alonzo Schaeffer placed his American Express card on top of the restaurant check.

"Gold," Jonathan said. "Why, that means you are in very select company—those whose finances and credit rating place them in the nation's top five percent."

They both laughed. Then Alonzo Schaeffer spoke.

"You know that old warning about never eating in a place called Mom's? Well, I never eat in a restaurant that doesn't take the American Express card. I feel that's the minimal protection I can provide for the gastrointestinal tract."

They both laughed again.

"I'll have to remember to add that to the list for Clarence Toole," Jonathan said. "When I get back...."

It was snowing the next day when the plane landed in Placer, and as Jonathan drove in the night from the airport to his home near the university a melancholy settled over him. He felt very much alone.

DECEMBER

*Whatever earth expected
to be doing on this night,
it turns more slowly
as I turn to you.*

*We dress for the occasion:
you in purple, I in red.
The fire turns all we give it into gold.
Time turns more slowly
though the year recedes.*

*I take food from your hand,
wine from your mouth.
We smoke. We dance.
The ceremony grows.
What we will be can wait
for what we are.
Earth turns more slowly,
when I turn to you.*

*Our bed is on the hearth tonight.
The gods are kind.
We worship all of them,
not knowing which to thank.
Time stops.
The year turns over
as my body welcomes you.
The year has nothing more to do.*

—Barbara Farquhar

Alone he awakened. Alone he washed and brushed and shaved and dressed, walked quietly through the silent house and sat down at the kitchen table. Coffee is the breakfast of the man alone, and he drank it as does the man alone, thoughtfully. He wondered whether he would spend the rest of his days on earth alone; he wondered if he could reconcile himself to being alone, accepting it as the lot of all beings; he wondered whether being alone, in essence, was the mortal preparation for the most lonely act of man, dying. He wondered, and for every question there were, as always, several answers.

He had chosen to be alone, ever since that autumn morning when Deborah had turned to him, kissed him again and again and pressed her radiant body against his, and nothing happened. He had explained that he liked her, cared for her, in many ways he loved her. She had asked him to spare her the next line—"but I'm not in love with you"—had laughed, had said she understood, had kissed him and wished him well. And they had thanked each other for the good past few months that they had agreed were to be without commitment, without strings, without ties. They were still loving friends at work and when she showed up at the Royal one evening with the new sports editor he rejoiced for and with her. He had sought no replacement. He was wed to his article, embracing it with a passion that surprised him. But that, he thought with the first smile of the day, was one of several secrets of his research he would manage to keep to himself.

He saw the two letters on the dining room table, decided to reread them and carried them into the kitchen. He would need a third cup of coffee, so he ground the beans and poured the hot water. As usual, there was good news and bad news. The good news in the first letter was that he would not be expected to attend the funeral. The bad news was that the required dealings with the funeral directors had driven his former wife, already shattered by the death of her father, to the verge of hysteria. The bad news in the second letter, mailed in obvious agitation two days later, was that she had decided that their son should remain in California for the Christmas and New Year holidays to ease the pain of his grandmother during this most difficult period. The good news was that she promised to free their son for a visit to Placer during his summer vacation from school.

He was reminded of the single aspect of his years of university teaching that he most missed—the time between quarters or semesters. That was when he had spent long hours with his son, tying tighter the bond between them. It was in those days, as they gave each other undiluted attention during almost all their waking hours, that he offered the boy choices of things to do, areas to explore, places to see. It had been the growing being who had guided the way along paths he freely chose, not the man pushing and molding his offspring into something that would fulfill his expectations. He was certain that if he had three sons they would be notably different from one another, having been encouraged to follow their natural bents. It was a gift he passed on from his own father and mother, whose children had each followed a self-chosen way of distinctive interests, always blessed by patient, forgiving and loving parents.

One of the several certainties of his divorce was that he refused to engage in competition for his son's affections. He was willing to wait until his son grew into a man and would be able to form his own valid conclusions. In the meantime, the boy was no worse off than he would have been if his parents had continued the charade and remained together. The house that was now so quiet had been a battleground on which the boy was at least as much a major casualty as his warring parents. He was better off this way.

Or, Jonathan Blakely wondered, was that a rationalization to ease his conscience, to repel the gnawing knowledge that he once had said 'til death do us part? The boy, too, had said wistfully that he wished they had stayed together as a family, no matter how bad it had been or might become. And there had been that plaintive phone call from the faculty friend on the campus where he had met and married Sarah: "Why did you leave her?"

He started. Bullshit! He wasn't going to fall for the total middle-class bullshit trip of guilt, succumbing to that despicable trait embedded in the unexamined lives of millions of victims of this society's warped values! Not he. Not I, said Jonathan Blakely and he turned to ponder the more acceptable conclusion that the bleakness of the winter had served to demoralize him.

That was it. The bleak winter combined with the information that his son would not be with him. Add to that the fact that his research notes piled up but he could not break the block that prevented him from translating the raw material into prose. Include the remembrance of something he had read somewhere that for at least six months after a divorce one shouldn't make a major decision because one is not oneself. Add to that the arrival in recent days of the first detested invitations to enforced conviviality of the season, to be climaxed by the one offer he couldn't refuse—the annual newspaper staff blast so accurately immortalized by one former reporter as the "Tribune Toilet-Hugger." Yes, and even add to that the passing of his father-in-law.

Surely the death and burial of Dr. Reuben McLendon was not a source of sadness to him. He had disliked the old man in ways his former wife had been unable to understand and she had attributed the inability of the two men to become warm friends to the fact that they were so much alike. He brooded over her belief that her father and he shared some common attributes: sometimes arrogant, unconsciously condescending, even unknowingly inflicting hurt on others. They were both intelligent and knowledgeable, she admitted, but they both were positive they had the answers to most of the questions confronting humanity. Thus their incompatibility was no surprise to her. She had once compared her husband's visage, during an unhappy moment in their marriage, to "the same martyr look that comes over my father." He knew the look and he resented the comparison. Thus this morning he puzzled once again over the damning proposition: Suppose she was right?

Enough! He walked to the window, noted the dark overcast sky, the motionless trees, the pall of smoke that hung low over the city. He rejected the idea of an overcoat, hoping that the brisk walk to the Tribune Building would warm him sufficiently. He methodically placed the empty coffee cup in the sink, turned off the kitchen light, and went out the back door into Placer's dawn.

At this hour he rarely saw anyone, and that was one of the reasons he liked to go early to the news room. This was the time of day when he could think most clearly; ideas, he had long ago discovered, had sharp edges on them in the thin aftermath of sleep before too much wakefulness had blurred the outlines. It was also the time of day when he was least likely to be forced into observing the social banality of greeting other persons. If an occasional citizen crossed his way on this early walk, he always had found it possible to continue his thoughts uninterruptedly, while nodding his head in the direction of the passerby. Why he could do this acceptably in the beginning morning and not later in the day was one of the several minor mysteries of social man he was prepared to acknowledge as a blessing.

His thoughts, as usual, turned to his latest research.

He had stumbled serendipitously on the intriguing history of the Federal Correctional Center at Butner, N.C., where John W. Hinckley Jr. had been confined for more than four-and-one-half months after his arrest. It was supposed to be "the prison of the future" when it was opened in 1976 after a stormy controversy. A protest campaign mounted by civil rights and civil liberties organizations, churches and prison-reform groups charged that the prison was to be used as an experimental center for "behavior modification," psychosurgery and "aversion therapy," involving sensory deprivation, extensive use of drugs and other questionable procedures. The Bureau of Prisons reportedly changed its plans as the facility neared completion, more than two years behind schedule. According to statements by authorities, the center became a "medium security prison and diagnostic center." The national news media reported that

Hinckley "underwent extensive psychiatric tests" there. All of this constituted yet another "strange coincidence" surrounding this most unexplored of attempts at political assassination in our time.

Further adding to the mystery was the statement of the defendant's father in an interview with the *Baltimore Sun*. Jack Hinckley had complained bitterly about the treatment his son was receiving in prison. The response, the *Baltimore Sun* reported, was that "Justice Department spokesmen refused to comment on that charge or on what therapy Hinckley has received while awaiting trial." The nine words following "or" awakened in Jonathan's mind an unanswered question of monumental proportions.

His instincts told him he was on the brink of other discoveries and that he was right in exploring the—shall we say?—colorful aspects of the special prison at Butner, N.C. Listen to thy inner voice; everything you need to know is within thee. So be it.

He plodded on, step by step, beset with the notion that all his work and writing was for naught. The wasteland of television had provided a model for the book publishing industry, now firmly in the grasp of corporations which manufactured books the way they manufactured everything else. Other corporations marketed the products in their bookstore chains and at checkout stands. Yes, they called books "the product." The purveyors of books, no less than the operatives of the television networks, had separately arrived at their beloved bottom line: Maximum profits come from "blockbusters." A publisher in Boston had said it well: "When it comes to fiction, anything that's not 'm.o.r.'—middle-of-the-road—or doesn't already have a track record, is in trouble. You can't blame the chains for doing what they do best in terms of their own corporate strategies." So schlock predominates. He continued his writing and research knowing that even if his work were published it would reach only a small audience. Like mehitabel, he would say "wotthehell wotthehell there s a dance in the old dame yet" and go back to polish another paragraph. It had come to pass in America that not only the food supply but the literature itself was dispensed in supermarkets. And the lovely lady in the bookstore in the middle of the block has become a rarity, the likes of her driven out of business by the new chain store on the corner, opposite McDonalds. He smiled in silent remembrance of the late Marshall McLuhan, who saw coming everything that has arrived.

The smile vanished as another thought came out of nowhere—Jonathan was certain that some thoughts do come out of nowhere, being there before one knows how they got there—and he said "Never!" out loud. Never, if a book of his were published, would he go on a book-promotion tour. "It's demeaning and degrading" was what Theodore White had said the other day. "You have to strip yourself threadbare like a piece of fabric." And then, like almost all Theodore White proclamations and conclusions, it was followed by a *non sequitur:* "But it's necessary because we are living through a period of cultural discontinuity in the United States—look at the arcades with Atari guns." Good old Teddy, adding another muddled interpretation to the pile he has created down through the years, a creature of unmatched talent for inaccuracy (the critiques would comprise a body larger than the original), ineptitude (*Breach of Honor* being an unintentional denunciation of everything he had written previously) and ass-kissing ("You may be sure, Mr. President, etc...."). Thus he volunteers to strip in public, bemoaning his fate as if the purpose of the book-promotion tour wasn't to promote the sale of his book. When a man accepts that which is demeaning and degrading, by his own admission, Jonathan thought on this dreary day, how nice it is not to be Teddy White.

He entered the Tribune Building and walked up the flight of steps to the news room. He nodded to the switchboard operator who, busy on a call, smiled back to him. He picked up a copy of that morning's paper and sat down at his desk. The local news, as it had been every day for months, was botched in one way or another: A well known avenue had become a street in the hands of a recently recruited reporter who had taken two journalism courses in a community college in a nearby state; a story had ended with a colon, the final quotation having been dropped "for lack of space"; a councilman's name had been spelled incorrectly; the temperatures listed under high and low had been reversed (again); the corrections column attempted to put right two errors in yesterday's paper that never should have been made in the first place; and—oh, to hell with it! He could not bring himself to care about those news pages that were the responsibility of others, and he was hardly cheered when he turned to the sports section, dominated as it had been every Monday morning for months by the Camel Scoreboard. The publisher had furnished some fuzzy rationalizations to the outraged sports staff, who quite properly asked when the front page would be bordered by the Burlington Northern and the editorial page framed with artwork furnished by the hucksters in the employ of Atlantic Richfield. The hilarious account of the publisher's enraged reaction when he passed the news room bulletin board had raced along the grapevine; a sports writer had posted a variation of the old joke about a man and a woman who, having established what the lady was, were simply dickering over her price. Nor had the fact that scores of other dailies across the country had declined the offer to prostitute their news columns lessened the shame of the wretched seduction of the newspaper for which he worked.

When he turned to the editorial page even Robinson's impassioned editorial deploring the latest act of avarice by the power company seemed flat to him. The fight that Robinson insisted had just begun had in reality ended the day the governor accepted the invitation of the president of the power company to use the company plane to fly to a conference in Washington, D.C. The story had been broken by a state bureau reporter of another newspaper and Robinson had seized it and squeezed it for all it was worth, but of course nothing changed. The governor had turned on his most oleaginous smile for the television cameras and in his most unctuous tones had explained that he had saved the taxpayers' money and that he "couldn't be bought by a plane ride." What was left unsaid until Robinson said it was that the whore could not be deflowered. Jonathan read Doonesbury and rejoiced that there was at least something provided by a national syndicate that was relevant and made sense.

Not that Robinson, in his way, didn't make sense. It was just that the brave words, lined up magnificently in battle array, were only the vanguard of a paper army; the trenches behind

Robinson, filled with eager and hearty troops in a decade past, now contained a loyal few and the refuse of deserters. The guidons of the vanished army lay in the mud, trampled by those who had run to the rear or, worse, had gone over to the enemy. And General Robinson, if the truth were told, also was tired of the battle, but he refused to capitulate and suffer the ignominy of surrender. His choice—if he were free to make one—would be to take his horse and retire to the secure and comfortable confines of his estate, to live out his time in remembrance of glories past and the bittersweet nostalgia for those halcyon days when the sun was high and both the man and the horse were stallions.

But that was not Robinson's way. He would not give up the attempt to marshal the forces yet another time for a new battle, another victory that would inevitably be one of Pyrrhus. So he fought his good fight, a lone voice in the figurative wilderness while the literal wilderness was being threatened with seismic bombs so that the barbarians from Texas could destroy even more of what remained of genuine civilization.

Jonathan turned back to the front page to savor the one small shining light of this otherwise dark December. He had managed to jerk a story that had been dummied on page 33 and put it where it belonged. With earlier deadlines than the old days (another doubtful bit of progress bequeathed by the new method of printing in which Gutenberg had been replaced by Dow) the pages toward the back of the newspaper had to be laid out and pasted up and prepared for the presses early in the day. As a result, some of the better news stories often were put into those pages and Jonathan had learned from experience to keep a watchful eye on the selection. He remembered well the dictum of one of his journalism professors who had cautioned his students to read the pages near the classified advertisements carefully because that is where newspapers, if they haven't killed a story, bury it alive.

What he had saved from that fate and put on page one was an item headlined "Former director of CIA criticizes new rules." It not only was unquestionably the most important story of that day but one that clearly demonstrated the extremely dangerous path on which the administration was embarked. The fact that the warning came from the only director in the history of the CIA to condemn the blackest arts routinely practiced and approved by his predecessors gave it even more credence. Criticizing the presidential decision to allow the CIA to conduct covert operations within the United States, in violation of its charter, Stansfield Turner pointed out that the CIA "is not trained to operate within the constraints of American law." That, he said, was the role of the FBI "and they're well trained for it." Buried in the story was the decision to do away with the requirement that the CIA director clear any "highly sensitive" intelligence with the National Security Council, thereby giving an even freer hand to the current director and, at least equally dangerous, his successors. Stan Turner, it was obvious to Jonathan, may have only a hazy understanding of the functions of journalists, but he had thorough knowledge of the tendencies of intelligence agents.

Jonathan recalled how the CIA had abolished its public affairs office three months after the assassination attempt and had cut its staff of fourteen dealing with press and public inquiries. Representatives of the news media protested, with no success. The man who had been in charge resigned, correctly pointing out that the office had succeeded in creating more understanding of the agency's functions by answering questions of legitimate concern. His replacement was a vice president for corporate communications. Jonathan heaved a sigh and returned to his more private matters.

Even the clock on the wall was silent in the still news room. He considered the time when clocks on the wall ticked, when there was a clatter and bustle and flavor to editorial rooms of newspapers before the technology of offset lithography altered the appearance and, inevitably, the content of newspapers everywhere. The machines of the wire services, now infinitely quieter, were in a separate room. The carpeted floors and the soft-ring telephones gave a funereal tone to the place where once the aspiring cubs knocked over the pastepots and bounded across the wooden floors in their haste to get a story. The television faces of the video display terminals soundlessly took orders; when he had started as a newspaperman, the old Underwood had talked back to him as he typed. He thought of the savor of life that had evaporated in this dark winter, all of his yesterdays lighting the way to dusty death, all of his tomorrows crouched ready to creep in their petty pace to the last syllable of his recorded time.

Letters, letters. He stared at the pile of letters on his desk. He thought of the letters he had opened and consigned to a trash basket on all the days of years gone by, with little changed. How few letters changed anything—at least anything important. Some do; men and women, young and old, continue to write them, to tell, to ask, to amuse, to sadden, to break news, to break hearts, to break lives. And in the meantime he gazed into the black chasm of despair, contemplating the seconds...the minutes...the hours...the days...of life...the life of all in the world...his life....

He shuffled through the top few envelopes of his mail, listlessly noting the return addresses and then the contents of each envelope. This one he would pass on to the publisher for action (action, he thought: the involuntary formalized redundancy epitomizing the structure of most lives); that one predicted enormous economic suffering unless more publicity was given and more attention was paid to a bill now before Congress (the problem, like all problems, will pass); the next offered alternatives (all paths, sir, lead to the grave); the next contained a closet bigot's confidential warning based on unimpeachable rumor, unquestionable hearsay and unmitigated ignorance (let there be light, the Lord commanded, and the evil tongues began to wag); a bulletin from the national headquarters of a political action committee decrying policies from Franklin Delano Roosevelt through Richard Milhous Nixon to James Earl Carter (hindsight, as usual, casting a brilliant light on the fallacies of the past); then a "news release" from a gaggle of mining companies opposing the passage of an initiative limiting their right to leave behind radioactive uranium mill tailings (vote, wretches, so that Mother Earth might empty her bowels more expeditiously); several more of similar content down to one from New York, a reprint of a speech written by a public relations practitioner and delivered by a chairman of the board, imploring that urgent steps be taken to prevent a break in the market (ah, yes, ye that live off the labor of others, the nervous sweat of speculation smells not so sweet). When he lifted the next envelope from the pile he did not open it. He dropped it in the wastebasket.

It had uncovered an envelope with handwriting he instantly recognized. A blue envelope, a blue stamp, the address handwritten with blue ink. All was Libra blue.

He fumbled as he opened it.

"Beloved:"

Nine lines.

He folded the note, placed it back in the envelope, put it in his shirt pocket. The news room was no place to regard such matters.

He walked to the park by the river and sat on a bench. The morning rush hour was beginning and there he was safe from the fumes expelled by the stream of automobiles going in both directions as the new day began. Two graceful women jogged by him and they all smiled in the passing. His smile continued as he took out the note and slowly read each word again.

"Joyous news!" the *I Ching* had told him when he cast it a week earlier on a lonely Thanksgiving day. He had learned many lessons from the Book of Changes through the years; in his depression he had for a while lost track of one of the most important: that life is ebb and flow. He was back on track now.

They had written to each other periodically—every six months, a year, sometimes more—since she had graduated from the university ten years earlier. He had not been able to bring himself to write of his divorce, certain that he had no right to interfere in any way with her marriage even though she had made it clear that hers had become as unsatisfactory as his. But she had received the news from a friend and now she wanted to see him. He rejoiced.

She had rented a house on the Oregon coast for a week and was driving there—alone—the day after Christmas. If he could—"Darling, if you would..."—join her, she would await him. Please let her know.

The days raced by. Jonathan worked extra shifts, trading off with Deborah, who gladly exchanged free time during the partying period for work during the drab days that always depressed her between Christmas and New Year's. He even accepted a few invitations to the pre-Christmas parties, showing up after the paper was put to bed and joining in the cocktail chatter, drinking wine, smoking grass and hash, parrying questions about his article, rescuing a female sports writer from passing out at the office party, taking her home and putting her chastely to bed. He knew he would soon be free for those precious days after Christmas.

On the day of Winter Solstice he cast the *I Ching* as the sun rose at 8:20 a.m. The message again warned him that now was not the time for publication. "In a struggle with an enemy of superior strength, retreat is no disgrace.... If, out of a false sense of honor, a man allowed himself to be tempted into an unequal conflict, he would be drawing down disaster on himself.... Think about alternatives and prepare for any eventuality.... No situation remains for long."

As the sun set at 4:51 p.m. he drank a lone but not lonely toast to the reunion that approached. He tossed the coins and consulted the Book of Changes on the approaching reunion: Very strong forces were coming together in the days ahead, not without some difficulties, but a loving, creative, growing time for both of you. Do not fear, although "misfortunes" always come; life is cycles; the changing seasons provide us a way to learn and understand the order that should be in our lives at all times.

During the eight hours and thirty-one minutes of the day that was in light he had walked and meditated and ate fruits and drank juices and cleared his mind and body until a glowing peace was his. He was ready for reunion. "I've never seen you so happy," Deborah said the next day. "That's because I've never been so happy, smart girl," he said, and then he was gone from Placer.

He drove to Oceanside, arriving as planned just after dark. The lights were on in the house on the cliff overlooking the ocean. His heart pounded as he knocked on the door and pushed it open. He looked up and she was there, at the top of the stairs, wearing the same white blouse and same lustrous black skirt she was wearing when he first saw her ten years earlier. She fondled the newel post for seconds, then let her hand skim over the bannister as she descended. It was as if her hand were moving lightly down his body. He watched, caught his breath, and in three quick steps met her and crushed her in his arms.

This is a first time, like that other first time. Lips on lips, tongue on tongue, then her breasts arch and his cock stiffens against her.

"God, I love thee."

"And I adore thee. Come."

He lifts her and carries her back up the stairs. Then they are naked, length of body against length of body, touching, feeling, feeling the other's feeling, breathing, caressing, kissing, and all the time remembering, remembering over the years, over their years apart, now together, now shuddering, now ready, now oh so ready. His finger finds her nether lips and gently strokes her hooded part. She moans and kisses and lifts to him so that his hand can come under her. "Now," she says and he is there, poised over her there, then touching there, then in her there, then all is there. They are what they have always known themselves to be: two parts of one.

The two rested, drank wine, heard the chimes at midnight, slept the night through. Then came the days of walking the beaches, going with the tides, gathering the bread freshly baked at the bakery and the food freshly taken from the sea at the wharfside market. Long and gentle talks of all the days since they had parted. They toasted the new year in and their old lives out.

They soon would marry.

JANUARY

NEAR THIS SPOT

ARE DEPOSITED THE REMAINS OF ONE

WHO POSSESSED BEAUTY WITHOUT VANITY

STRENGTH WITHOUT INSOLENCE

COURAGE WITHOUT FEROCITY

AND ALL THE VIRTUES OF MAN WITHOUT HIS VICES.

THIS PRAISE WHICH WOULD BE UNMEANING FLATTERY

IF INSCRIBED OVER HUMAN ASHES

IS BUT A JUST TRIBUTE TO THE MEMORY OF

BOATSWAIN, A DOG

WHO WAS BORN AT NEWFOUNDLAND, MAY 1803,

AND DIED AT NEWSTEAD ABBEY, NOVEMBER 18, 1808.

— Inscription by Lord Byron
on a monument to his
Newfoundland dog
1808

Arianne Blakely passed in seconds from disorientation to recognition; as usual, she awakened not slowly but almost at once. She lay wrapped like a mummy in the Swedish down quilt that was one of the many new things in her life since she came to live with Jonathan Blakely. She smelled the coffee that Jonathan brewed, and smiled at the remembrance of his words: "I shall bring thee coffee in bed every morning of our lives together." She pulled her arms free and reached for the new bathrobe on a stack of newspapers at the foot of the bed, got her arms into the sleeves, then stood up and wrapped the robe around her body. The fabric brought memories of chilly mornings in the shadow of the Colorado mountains, a fire in the stone fireplace, her mother and father alive, her life uncomplicated. She sighed, wondering whether she would ever not need the memories she so carefully hoarded. Others, she knew, saw her differently—aloof, perhaps cold, always in command of herself and the situation. Well, my girl, you put that Arianne together and you can't blame people for seeing her. But Jonathan—oh, Jonathan—knew better.

"I have to pee," she said as she brushed by him.

"You're all alike," he said. "Coffee in thirty seconds."

When she came out she pulled the bedroom curtains apart before climbing back into bed. Snow had fallen during the early morning hours and the scrape of snow shovels sounded in the dulled, padded, echo world that snow creates. She could see the clock tower on campus against a white sky unbroken by blue, and she imagined the students wrapped to the eyes, sexless, hurrying toward a new day's collision with facts and figures and—if they were lucky—someone who would expose to them a new idea or test a concept long held. It was Jonathan, eleven years earlier, who had taught her of Locke's "received hypothesis," the bane, the deadly poison, of our existence. She heard him coming toward the bedroom, carrying two cups of coffee, the morning elixir that warmed hand, body and heart.

They kissed.

"Is Mrs. Blakely happy?"

"Mrs. Blakely, thank you, is very happy."

It was she who had suggested, with perceptible tentativeness after they agreed there was no question about their future together, that they go to Las Vegas to be married. He had laughed.

"Vegas? Really? That's the soft underbelly of America."

"No it isn't, Jonathan. That's Orange County. Vegas is a genuine up-front town. What you see is what you get. There's precious little hypocrisy there. I've been thinking about it and there are a lot of good reasons why we should get married there. Are you listening?"

"A good part of me is ears."

"Good. In the first place, it's perfect for anonymity. A marriage license listing in the Las Vegas papers, where listings run on and on, would be of interest to no one we know. For a guy who doesn't list his number in the phone directory, it's the ideal way to keep some people from being too sure about your private life. I love the way you guard your privacy, Jonathan. Except for the people you care about, you keep whatever you're doing to yourself. I remember when we were seeing each other at Berkeley that no one seemed to know where you lived or your phone number."

"Discretion is the only way to keep this damnably nosy society out of your private life. A hell of a thing for an aggressive journalist to say, but I've never gone out of my way to make news. What else?"

"Second, we could see Sinatra. He's there."

"A strong and persuasive point."

"I thought that one might please you. Third, I would like to see your unseemly boasts about your system at the black jack table put to the test."

"As I have seemly contended, it hasn't failed me yet. With you beside me in the wilderness it couldn't miss."

"Fourth, I have someone I'd like to be there as a witness—someone who's never been to Vegas and would appreciate the garish, tasteless, campy style of the place. A woman of the earth who would love to spend a couple of days in an impossible electric fairyland. I owe her, Jonathan—she's the one who heard about your divorce and told me. It would be beautiful to have her there for our wedding. She lives in Tucson and it would be an easy flight for her. And you could invite anyone you wanted...."

They flew off to Vegas on a Monday morning after four hours of sleep, landed at McCarran, rented a car, went into town, bought a license, arranged for a minister of the Congregational church to prepare for the ceremony, had lunch, drove to the airport to welcome her friend, settled her in the hotel a few doors down from their Scheherazade Suite, returned to the airport to welcome his son, picked up her friend on the way to the church for the wedding, and then feasted on their specially prepared wedding dinner at the front-row table nearest Sinatra. A final celebratory bottle of champagne before the guests went to their separate rooms, and he called her for the first time Mrs. Blakely.

"I really like her, dad," his son had said. "And thanks for the most exciting day of my life."

"So far, buddy. Only so far."

The next day he cashed the $1,000 he had brought in traveler's checks—the amount he was prepared to lose if his system went wrong—sat down at the far end of a black jack table in a Strip hotel where dealers used a single deck, and a little less than seven hours later cashed in his chips. He had enough to pay for the plane fares, hotel bill and a celebration into the night. The next morning the four of them joined in a tearful, happy time at the airport. That afternoon Jonathan was back at the news desk of the *Placer Tribune.*

And last night he was back with her in their house near the campus and this morning he had brought her coffee.

"Is there anything I can do to make Mrs. Blakely happier?"

She thought for a moment. "Yes, as a matter of fact, there is something you could do. But I warn you, although it's a small thing I'm asking for, it won't always be so."

"Well, as Shakespeare put it, 'tis a small thing, but 'tis mine own."

She punched him on the arm. "You need make no apologies in that category. No, Jonathan, what I want is—I don't think you are at all ready for this...."

"Come on, come on."

"A Newfoundland."

His mind raced from Lewis's dog (or was it Clark's?) to Nana in Peter Pan to Lord Byron's Boatswain.

"Ummm," he said. "They get big, don't they? I mean *big*."

"Is that asking too much? Is it too much to take on me and a Newfie in one fell swoop?"

"You mean right away? You mean I don't even get a year or two to get used to the idea?"

She laughed. "All right, I get the message. It is too much to ask. Forget it."

"No, don't forget it. You knocked me flat on the canvas, but the count has only reached seven. I'm getting up. A bit dazed and confused, but I can weather this."

"I warned you."

"I didn't think you packed a wallop like that. You don't see many Newfoundlands around. Do you have to go to Newfoundland?"

"Oh, there are puppy farms here and there, but I don't think they're doing credit to the breed. And we don't have to go to Newfoundland, smart ass. How does a little town outside Seattle grab you? There's a lady there who breeds beauties, and she even has some Landseers."

"You're sneaky, you little sneak. You've been studying up while I wasn't looking. What's a Landseer?"

"Real sneaky. Landseers are black-and-white Newfies. Otherwise known as Supernewfs. The lady says that black Newfies will bring you the morning paper, but Landseers will read it on the way in."

"That's what we really need around here—another news

freak. Okay, okay. Look into it. And since there are only two things a bed is good for, and you're not doing either one at the moment, how about getting up and getting going?''

At the bathroom sink there was barely room for her to stand. Her elbow brushed the shower curtain and the back of her calves rubbed the toilet bowl when she bent to brush her teeth. Old houses in university towns seem to meet the same fate—dissection. Someone years ago had turned this large closet into a bathroom and had rented out one of the bedrooms. She brushed her hair, then patted lotion on her face and body, smoothing breast and knee, hypnotically, a morning ritual. What did Jonathan see, she wondered, to look so closely and approvingly? What she saw in the mirror added up to what she was accustomed to: pleasing, perhaps, but not fascinating. Breasts too small, legs too straight, ass a bit too fleshy. Yet Jonathan loved her ass, *loved* her ass—"I," he had proclaimed years ago on the beach at Big Sur, "am an ass man"—and he had refused to consider her contention that his ass was nicer than hers. No matter how she saw herself she knew that men did come at her; they must see something. The problem, however, had been what she saw in them, which had not been much these last few years. After first love—like all first loves, he was totally wrong—what then? Two or three men she had once thought would be important had been allowed or encouraged to drift away from her, without regret on her part. Then Jonathan. Then two more experiments—one unsatisfactory, one disastrous—before her husband, now her ex-husband. And now again, at long last, Jonathan.

Flashbacks. She loved them. The novelist's device, so much discussed at the writers' conferences she had attended and the insufferably smug writers' program from which she had been graduated at "The Harvard of the West" (indeed!) with a master's degree. (What you had learned of lasting value, innocent Arianne, is how down and dirty the real world of commercial publishing can be.) And in the real world of her life flashbacks were the frosting on the cakes of fantasy and memory and reverie—sweet and just desserts. She laughed out loud. Now she could have her cake and eat it, too. Ten-and-a-half years of remembrance, a jar of rosemary he had given her in the top drawer of her dresser, so that hardly a day passed without her thinking of him—and them together....

...''Oh, Arianne, that's Professor Blakely! It has to be. He's one of the best lecturers on campus. Everyone flips over him. Well, almost everyone. I had a class with him last spring. Now I go just to listen to him. He talks about things the textbooks never touch. When he tells about it and documents every point, it all makes sense. He's got some wild theories he throws out, too. What did he say to you?''

''He just asked me what I'm majoring in, that he hadn't seen me around. I went into the Journalism Library to read some magazines between classes and he walked in to get some newspapers. I told him I was in English and he looked at me as if he thought that was too bad and then he smiled and left. That's all that happened.''

''Oh, is it? Oh, is it? You couldn't wait to know who he was. You're smitten. Well, join the club. He's married, Arianne, and he has a little boy. Tough titty for you. Hey!—''

Her roommate must have caught the look on her face.

''—I didn't mean to be so sporty about it. I'm sorry, Arianne. Really.—''

She could see the light bulb above her roommate's head flash on.

''—Look, he's lecturing this afternoon at one, if today's Wednesday and we're not in Belgium. Come on, Arianne, I'll go with you if you're afraid to go alone. We'll sit in back. He doesn't mind if you're not registered for the course if you sit in back.''

Later they were walking through the campus gate, past the tables set up by students, former students, non-students, graduate students, students who had graduated, students who would never graduate, and some who would never be students. It was the glorious autumn of '70 and although the rabid campus protests and demonstrations of the '60s had somewhat subsided, there still was excitement aplenty for her. The sweet smell of grass—which for many had replaced the sweet smell of success—surrounded them as they walked up the steps of the imposing old building that was a center for noontime agitation, past a bearded orator who denounced in a scatological frenzy the latest transgression of the despicable Nixon, and into a misshapen room where rows of bolted-down chairs rose steeply away from a platform. The seats were filling rapidly and she didn't see on the faces of the students the customary look of anticipated boredom. The talking stopped when he came in.

He strode in abruptly. He looked taut and preoccupied under the fluorescent lights. As she studied him, she guessed he was in his early thirties. He wore rust-brown corduroy pants and a brown v-neck velour shirt; clearly he was not a suit-and-tie lecturer. He was tall and lean and paced the platform with a big cat's grace, but performing as a cat would not, aware of himself. His dark hair was showing traces of gray. His voice reflected what she thought was an admirable confidence as he raised it and lowered it as part of the orchestration of the major points of his lecture. She had trouble listening to him and watching him at the same time, so she watched and let what he was saying go past her. She allowed part of her mind to look for wrongness in him, but there was none. She ran imaginary fingers down his back, feeling for the shape and texture of him under his clothes. A sensation, like liquid heat, rushed from her head to her crotch, stunning her. *It does! It does!* She always said that for her it starts in the head, and it does. She looked at the line where his shirt covered his belt, then lower. She closed her eyes and now she listened.

"The greening of America." She had never heard that expression before and she was fascinated as he explained that the new book had much to say for the aspiring journalist. He drew large graphic strokes of what he deemed the significant sections and, his voice going soft and sad, dismissed what he regarded as the silly irrelevancies of an otherwise seminal work. Seminal, semen, seed. She loved that word and—oh, sweet Lord—she loved him. This was a class unlike any she had been in; none of the *explication de texte* that drove her up the walls of her English classes; none of that pedantic neutrality so dear to those professors who refused to profess; none of that unspeakable banality and emphasis on the obvious of the sundry bores who declaimed themselves behavioral scientists. He was saying something about how he hoped he had given them their tuition's worth this day when the bell rang.

"I'm going to speak to him." Her voice came out of a cave, a sound she didn't recognize. Her roommate touched her, questioningly, but she shook her head. "We'll talk later." She walked down the steps, a weakness behind her knees, and sat down in front of the platform.

He was surrounded by students, a few of them looking hostile, she saw with surprise. Two young men—she guessed they were seniors—arguing determinedly that J. Edgar Hoover had a right to order his agents to engage in illegal acts. The others, both male and female, looked as if they wanted him to put their world back where it had been an hour earlier. Now she could study his face more clearly: dark brown eyes, bushy brows, thin lips, a long and sensual nose. She liked the wisps of hair on his chest that emerged above the vee of his shirt; even more she liked the fine black hair that began on the back of his hands and went up his arms under the shirt. She felt the universe slowing, as if permitting itself finally to be comprehended. This conversion of abstractions—space, time, motion—into presences that pressed against her glowing skin—was it truly love? Whatever it was, the absence of sound told her they were now alone with it.

"I saw you sitting there in the back row," came the voice. Then closer as he came down the steps from the platform and stood before her: "Well, what do you think? What do you think of the mad orator who tears away the veils from subjects which are generally kept hidden from little boys and girls? Some of my sedate and respectable colleagues do not approve. But what do you think?"

What she thought was that she wanted to be where she was more than any other place in the world. Then she thought again. "I think you are the most interesting professor I've ever heard." The words, she feared, emerged with a perceptible quiver, and when she heard his words she knew that she had crossed a line that was now behind her.

"And I think you're the most beautiful woman I have ever seen."

He put out his hand to her and helped her out of the seat. "Do you have time now? Could we talk? In my office?"

He walked beside her down the hall, up a flight of stairs to the deserted third-floor hallway and into his office. He told her that he wished she had been at his Monday lecture when he had gone through *The Greening of America* chapter by chapter, demonstrating that parodies were inevitable but that parts of it burst with ideas that never had been expressed so well. He closed the door of his office and stared at her before he spoke.

"Don't tell me your name—not just yet. It doesn't matter right now. What matters is that I'm so nervous I probably will go on blathering about the lecture instead of talking to you about what's really important and what's really important is that you are here in my office. I've thought of nothing else since I saw you in the library yesterday and nothing like this has ever happened to me before—I swear—and I meant what I said about you being the most beautiful woman I've ever seen."

Of this she was certain: She must be honest with him always. "I'm so nervous I'm shaking." A pause. "You're married, I know."

"Yes." That very quickly. This very slowly: "We're playing with fire. I know it. Do you understand you're playing with fire?"

She nodded and took the three steps she needed to reach him. His arms went around her and she expelled a rush of breath before his lips came down on hers and her neck snapped back. She ran her fingers along his neck, listening to her body. Warmth moved through her. She felt faint. *Trust him, trust him.* Her arms tightened around him.

He lifted her into his arms and backed into the chair at his desk, holding her on his lap. She felt his hand move down the front of her and she parted her legs to receive it. "Oh, God," he said, and she thought he might stop. He mustn't stop—no!—and she raised her body to press against his hand and opened her mouth to receive his tongue, wanting to be penetrated wherever she was empty, feeling his erection under her, wanting, wanting. "Please."

She didn't know she had said it until she heard it. His hand unfastened her jeans and she lifted away from him as he pulled them down and off, taking her shoes with them. She felt him tremble against her when his hand touched the wetness between her legs, and she too trembled as a wanting welled inside her, making her nipples hard, her consciousness dim. There was no sensation in her body except where it touched his or was touched by him. She felt him tugging at his belt, getting his body free. She stood and pulled her panties off and waited for his clothes to come away. He sat back in the chair and pulled her down on top of him, his hands cupping her buttocks and pulling her hard against him. With her knees pressed against the back of the chair, she felt him push into her. She buried her face against his throat, letting him move her. His penis felt sharp where it touched her, as if it were a knife that could open her. But it wasn't pain. It was... "Oh, Jesus." He pulled her closer. "Oh, Christ, oh, Jesus." He lifted her. "Oh, God." She took his shirt in her teeth, then let go. "Oh, Jonathan." And she kissed him and kissed him and kissed him as the spasms took over her body and she felt his liquid spurt into the center of her. "I love you," she said, and they rested tight together.

Their breathing slowed. He stroked the back of her head, ran his finger over her ear and along the jawbone to the tip of her chin. He touched her lips lightly with his, and before he kissed her again he said, "And I love thee."

She remembered every moment of that day. And the times together that followed in gentle rhythm, broken only by the fierceness of their passions when he crushed the seedlings of any doubts that had grown within her in their days apart. For him, as she listened, there were never any doubts. He told her on that first day that he would not divorce, not at least until his son was old enough to understand and able to cope with the parting that divorce would bring. He asked nothing of her but what she willingly wanted to give, and she accepted this condition joyously. She was to receive her degree in a few months and until then she wanted nothing but to be with him every possible moment. He was sleeping alone in his basement den, an arrangement both husband and wife had agreed would make their marriage possible and their lives bearable. They would stay together for the boy, and their limited social life made it easier for them to continue their marriage. They went separate ways along paths that had diverged years before.

Jonathan's way included her. Their likes and dislikes, revealed in the afternoons or evenings or weekends in which he could reasonably be away from home or office, first amazed, then amused them. They shared a love of ocean, of beaches, of sun (he Aries more than she Libra), of seafood, wine, brandy and liqueur, of music, of poetry, of quiet walks and uninhibited play. He never laughed at her awkward first tosses of the plastic friz and rejoiced as he coached her over the weeks into being the lithe and lovely quarterback who could deftly lead him into the corner of the end zone for the winning touchdown as the last seconds ticked off before the final gun. They romped naked on the shore below Pacifica, danced down Oak Street in the rain after seeing "A Man and A Woman," celebrated the memory of William Randolph Hearst by inadvertently leaving traces of their lovemaking on the bedspread in a guest house at San Simeon, dropped acid supplied by the fabled Owsley himself in a field overlooking Bodega Bay. They drove often to Sausalito and Mount Tamalpais, occasionally to a discreet faculty member's discreetly hidden house in Mendocino. And then it was June.

It came too suddenly for her, disorienting her although she had known that in June he would be off to work on a newspaper in Oregon for the summer and she would begin the travail that leads to a master of arts degree half way across the continent. She listened, not wanting to hear, as he explained that they would have to return to the places they were before they had met, that he could not ask her—and she should not ask herself—to go on with what they had had these past few precious months. His little boy, his little boy. He would not leave his little boy....

Who could say that he was wrong, as she often had thought in these ten years that had passed? Ten years apart from him, including eight years of marriage that never had been quite right and inevitably turned quite wrong before she began the process of ending it the day after she learned of Jonathan's divorce. My God, she thought, it has been less than two months since I wrote that letter to him! Her personal message to the world: Never Despair!

Here she was, in a town much like the one in which she had grown up, starting a new life with a man she knew was right for her, winnowing the seemingly endless possibilities for the future. She felt as if she had grown up at random and had drifted over the years like a gull. Now she was resting on a wave, an undulation of the surface, and Jonathan was being carried along evenly with her. What a mystery and what a miracle that they should at long last be together. There were so many what-if-you-had-nots, even more what-if-I-had-nots. It had been a fantasy for her, yet all the time something surely had been pulling them closer; she sensed it there, waiting to be seen if only she could turn her head quickly enough. Now there were many things she knew neither she nor Jonathan wanted in their lives. She would guard against those assaults of a culture that sought to govern their actions and limit their choices. No need to worry about Jonathan; no one she had ever known had more faith in the potentialities of the human spirit when freed from the devices of small and miserly men. Together they would make a life worth living, of that she was certain.

While Jonathan was at the *Tribune* she plucked book after book from his shelves, probing the places his mind had been. She was surprised at how many of his books exposed and denounced the myths that a society—or a profession—employs to disguise its real history. She read Upton Sinclair's bitter criticism of the press of his time, Stephen Crane's poems and stories and "pills," and the many books about William Randolph Hearst to understand better why neither he nor his descendants were able to publish a newspaper that merited respect. She read Ferdinand Lundberg's explanations of why the press often fails to serve the public interest and the books of George Seldes, a man who saw American journalism with perhaps the clearest eyes over two decades. She read A.J. Liebling and, at Jonathan's suggestion, went to the library at the university to see what he called "the single most despicable obituary printed in my lifetime," that in *Editor & Publisher* after Liebling's death. She agreed. Overtaken by serendipity, she read randomly in the bound volumes of *E&P* and was appalled at its decline from an astute and honorable critic of press performance in the 1930s and 1940s to a shifty apologist for the fattest and least responsible cats of the industry in the subsequent decades. In the hours toward midnight, before Jonathan returned home, she caught up on the life and times of "Petroleum V. Nasby," the timeless relevancy of the philosophy of "Mr.

Dooley," and the observations of archie the cockroach and his friend mehitabel the cat, *"toujours gai toujours gai."* It would take months to read all the books in that house that she wanted to read, and she was on her way. She noticed, too, that on those shelves were books by Kazantzakis that she had recommended to him in those ten long years that they had been apart.

On this night, when she heard the steps on the porch and went to the door, she greeted a snowman.

He had walked the fourteen blocks from the Tribune Building in a soft snowfall and he shook off most of the flakes that had accumulated on him before he kissed her.

"Jonathan, you've just got to start wearing an overcoat."

"No need for one. This is the banana belt compared to Buff-a-lo, Chi-ca-go, Caleve-land or Dez Moinz Io-way. I'm tempted to say something about cold hand, warm cock, but I know you wouldn't approve. And I wouldn't blame you."

"Well, the first thing I'm going to do is make you some hot tea."

"And the second?"

She laughed. "The second thing I'm going to do, after your lips are no longer blue, is kiss you again. You can take it from there."

"At your service, sweet Arianne."

He sat in one of the two large overstuffed chairs, listening to the sounds of crackling fireplace, Sinatra singing, water pouring into tea kettle, cupboard doors opening and clicking closed. The surge of happiness he felt in the first moments of his return began to recede, and in its place came an overwhelming contentment, the realization that he belonged here more than any other place on earth. This had become, in the winter of his discontent, his cave; here he had found warmth.

"Rose hips tea to warm thy innards," she said. He had been so deep in his thought that he had not heard her come into the room.

She sat in the other large chair and picked up a folder filled with blue sheets on the small table between them. "I read your draft of this section this afternoon."

He eyed her silently, waiting.

"Jonathan, it's scary. It's really scary. My first reaction was that I didn't want you to publish it. I think it's good. Damned good. Of course, I'm biased as hell, but I like everything you write. You know what I like best about your writing? It's a kind of indignation, a lot like Liebling's, that runs along just below the surface, because you want the world to be fair and logical and it's the farthest thing from either. And what you're saying frightens me. Am I right to feel this way?"

"Absolutely. I get scared sometimes, too. Not exactly scared, but a kind of jitters, more like the butterflies before a game or a speech or something you're not sure about how it's going to turn out. And only God knows how this is going to turn out."

"I'd be less than honest if I didn't tell you that sometimes I wish you'd forget the whole thing. You're driven to carry this through, I know. I understand that, even if down deep I don't really understand why you're so driven."

"I've always been that way," he answered. "Even when I was very young I got angry when the world wasn't fair because I wanted more than anything for the world to be fair. There was always a little voice somewhere telling me it ought to be, and I still hear that little voice." He leaned forward and looked intently at her. "I think I know at least one of the many reasons the world isn't fair. It's because we have had a lot of practice, and a lot of encouragement—and a lot of that encouragement has come from the press—to avert our eyes from the dark side of our national character. A story came in tonight on AP about the number of guns confiscated from passengers in airports all over the country. Which airport do you think had the most?"

"Dallas."

"Of course. And Los Angeles was second and Houston was third. And get this: The number confiscated at the Dallas airport was more than twice—more than twice—the number confiscated in L.A. And the Dallas airport has led the nation in the number of weapons seized for the last three years. You take the ten most bizarre shooting stories of the year—any year, practically—and seven of them will be in Texas. The only place that's more corrupt is the District of Columbia."

"I think you're right. The stories that keep coming out of there day after day turn my stomach."

"You remember when that plane went into the Potomac? Exactly one guy jumped in to save a woman who was drowning. The press proclaimed the glory of the American spirit, but just one guy jumped in. That, I submit, is the precise percentage of heroism, courage and selflessness that pervades the capital of our country."

She came to sit on his lap and they kissed.

"Enough of that. Ask me what I did today." She grinned widely at him.

"Oh-oh," he said. "It's that sneaky look I know so well. What is it?"

"I called Bothell, Washington."

"Do I see something looming large in our future?"

"You do indeed. But right now he's a beautiful Landseer puppy. The lady says he's exactly what we want. He'll be ready in a few days."

Jonathan nodded. "So will I," he said.

That was why, late in January, they were driving in a blizzard on Interstate 90, a bundle of black and white fur on the seat between them. They eased by the stalled semis on Snoqualmie Pass, skidded into a service station to see what could be done about the ice-clogged windshield wipers, explained to the concerned highway patrolman that they had to get back with their puppy that night. Then they were out of the storm, back in Montana, the car radio telling them the sun was out in Placer. She carried the little Landseer into his new home.

That night they talked about what his name should be. He said he had thought of one. She said she had thought of one and that she had a story to tell. It was how she admired the overwhelming choice of 55,000 Montana school children who had voted to select an "official state animal." A large majority chose the *Ursus horribilis,* praised as strong, courageous, independent, lovable, magnificent, wild, untamed, mighty, intelligent, brave, proud, adventurous and fiercely unpredictable—all the characteristics the students said aptly describe Montana and its people. Of course there were a few adults who opposed the selection of the grizzly bear, an animal who is ferocious when aroused and who resists man's encroachment and the resulting defilement of its habitat; the protests of those adults were drowned in a wave of approval.

As with so much else, the coincidence of their separate conclusions found Jonathan and Arianne tumbling in laughter and love at the growing miracle of their oneness. Their puppy would be named Bear: To please her, because his breed shared so many virtues of the animal who roamed their rocky mountains; to please him, in honor of the warm and witty and intelligent press secretary to the president of the United States, known by that affectionate nickname to family and friends, shot through the brain and now a suffering and barely surviving innocent victim of John W. Hinckley Jr.

FEBRUARY

There was a candidate for district attorney, William Travers Jerome by name; a man with a typical "Evening Post" mind, making an ideal "Evening Post" candidate. He conducted a "whirlwind" campaign, speaking at half a dozen meetings every evening, and stirring his audience to frenzy by his accounts of the corruption of the city's police-force. Men would stand up and shout with indignation, women would faint or weep. The boy would sit with his finger-nails dug into the palms of his hands, while the orator tore away the veils from subjects which were generally kept hidden from little boys.

The orator described the system of prostitution, which was paying its millions every year to the police of the city. He pictured a room in which women displayed their persons, and men walked up and down and inspected them, selecting one as they would select an animal at a fair. The man paid his three dollars, or his five dollars, to a cashier at the window, and received a brass check; then he went upstairs, and paid this check to the woman upon receipt of her favors. And suddenly the orator put his hand into his pocket and drew forth the bit of metal. "Behold!" he cried. "The price of a woman's shame!"

To the lad in the audience this BRASS CHECK was the symbol of the most monstrous wickedness in the world. Night after night he would attend these meetings, and next day he would read about them in the papers. He was a student at college, living in a lodging-house room on four dollars a week, which he earned himself; yet he pitched in to help this orator's campaign, and raised something over a hundred dollars, and took it to the "Evening Post" candidate at his club, interrupting him at dinner, and no doubt putting a strain on his patience. The candidate was swept into office in a tornado of excitement, and did what all "Evening Post" candidates did and always do—that is, nothing. For four long years the lad waited, in bewilderment and disgust, ending in rage. So he learned the grim lesson that there is more than one kind of parasite feeding on human weakness, there is more than one kind of prostitution which may be symbolized by the BRASS CHECK.

— Upton Sinclair
The Brass Check
1919

THE POLLS FOR "NUMBER ONE"
The attempt to kill President Reagan was voted the "top headline story" of 1981 by the newspaper and broadcast editors of both the Associated Press and United Press International. It was regarded as a bigger story than the freeing of 52 American hostages by Iran after 444 days of captivity, the assassination of Egyptian President Anwar Sadat and the attempted assassination of Pope John Paul II, which finished second, third and fourth in both polls. As such, the quality of the reporting of the event of March 30 merits more than ordinary scrutiny.

Of special interest is the fact that the UPI editors, who selected not only the "top headline stories" but the "most significant stories" of the year, chose the attempt to murder the president as only the ninth *"most significant story." Apparently the editors accepted the official line that the shooting was nothing more than a senseless act by a deranged drifter who had lived in squalor in his one-room rented apartment in Lubbock or his cheap motel room outside Denver, was estranged from his family and smitten with an unrequited love for a young actress. Obviously, they were influenced by the circumstance that the attempt to end the president's life was not quite successful, thereby lessening its significance; if the president had not survived, the story would have been first in significance not* only in the United States but almost everywhere in the world. Or, again, the balloting editors may have remembered the fabricated picture presented to us of a wisecracking president walking into the emergency room of the George Washington University Hospital, getting off some extraordinarily quotable quips to his wife, his doctors and his nurses, and generally being reported, as one journalist wrote, as if he were "a man having a few stitches taken in a minor wound."

Examine the last-mentioned possibility:

It was not until a week after the crisis had passed that we learned that the 70-year-old president had been far more seriously wounded than we had been led to believe, that his blood pressure was low and falling when he entered the hospital, that he was in great pain and acute distress, that he had difficulty breathing and that he fell to one knee in the emergency room. Nonetheless, on that Monday night of March 30 after the operation on the president, we were told by the hospital's eloquent and telegenic spokesman, Dr. Dennis O'Leary: "He was never in any serious danger. The bullet was not really very close to any vital structures." When the crisis had passed, however, the good doctor/spokesman admitted that he had made his statements to the press and public "as upbeat as possible without damaging my credibility." Thus we discover that the president's blood loss was 3.7 quarts, not the 2.5 quarts that Dr. O'Leary reported, and that eight units of blood were transfused, rather than five units as stated at the news conference. And another doctor was quoted as saying that President Reagan "definitely was in a life-threatening situation." Still another doctor: "The loss of blood was so rapid that in my opinion a 15-minute delay in getting the president to the hospital could have made a big difference and might even have been fatal."

More sugar coating on the placebo prescribed by Dr. O'Leary was washed away when we were informed that an explosive bullet had entered the president's chest, ricocheted off his seventh rib and penetrated three inches into the lower left lobe of his lung; a hospital X-ray, according to one account, showed "a small, slender metal fragment shaped almost like a comma in the shadow of the heart."

Ultimately, the American people were informed of the truth of this aspect of the most recent attempt at political assassination. But how would the UPI editors have voted for the "most significant story of 1981"—and how would the course of world history been changed—if there had been an infinitesimally different angle of ricochet of one of the bullets fired by John W. Hinckley Jr.? Or if the bullet taken in the stomach by Secret Service agent Timothy J. McCarthy had found instead its intended mark? Or if the bullet that came to rest intact next to President Reagan's heart had fragmented into four pieces, as did the bullet that lodged in the brain of White House Press Secretary James S. Brady?

"Significance"?

The new president of the United States would have been George W. Bush.

"Significance"?

Let it be here suggested that many facts of "significance" never reached the general public.

Robert Robinson looked out the door into the news room. It had all the pizazz of an insurance agency. Each employee in the room with a Visual Display Terminal, carpet underfoot, a pervasive mortuarial silence broken only by the occasional ring of a telephone. He remembered when the news room throbbed. That's what he missed, day in and day out. When he started newspapering it was a bit past the time of "The Front Page" but the news room still throbbed. It was *exciting*. It was *interesting*. It was *romantic*. Terribly, *terribly* romantic. Even the secretaries who worked there and the people who emptied the waste baskets and mopped the floors thought it was someplace special; it was as if they were part of the excitement, the interest, the romance of getting out the paper. And down below were those huge presses starting up, and then picking up speed and then the throbbing, throbbing, throbbing as those papers rolled out and up and along and were met by men who grabbed them off the rollers in fifties as each fiftieth copy came along marvelously askew. Then the papers were in the hands of the men of the circulation department, a proud bunch, glad to be in a job that was something more than the dreary routine of so many of the men they drank beer with. Then the loaded trucks, with the name of the paper on the sides, moving out, one after another in convoy, like a field artillery battalion moving up to the front.

And what had he come to? Before reading Jonathan's latest three pages he had just finished editing the monthly column of Harry McGillicuddy, a local millionaire who had made the bulk of his fortune from clearcutting several of the forests within a couple of hundred miles of Placer. A man with a heart of stone, so that he could assure his readers that his heart neither would nor could bleed for any cause, he had a head to match. He referred often to his wife, never conscious of his disdain, occasionally bordering on contempt, for what he often implied was the lesser sex. He had also managed to raise a daughter who had dared to run for public office as an anti-feminist, finishing, after spending an affordable portion of her father's fortune, fifth in a field of five. In the Republican primary. Strange pair, that.

Robinson looked back at the three blue sheets on his desk. He would have to tell Jonathan about that piece he hadn't thought worth mentioning in one of those Washington magazines some time back. President Reagan, according to the article, had gone through an unpublicized medical crisis a week after he was shot; his temperature went up to 102, his color worsened, his white blood count went up, he was spitting fresh blood and the persistent high fever led doctors to debate operating on his bullet-pierced lung a second time. Dr. O'Leary had not leaped for the microphone to announce those developments and nothing like that had come over the wire to the *Tribune.* He penciled a note on his desk calendar to remind him to tell Jonathan.

He knew that another reason he had not mentioned the article was that Jonathan had canceled his subscription to one of those Washington magazines after a former student had sent him a copy of an article he had submitted to it. The article had been set in type, the editors were enthusiastic about it and it was scheduled for an early issue—until the publisher, the wife of a syndicated columnist, had ordered it killed unless the references to Henry Kissinger were taken out. Robinson had a good amount of sympathy for Jonathan's strong feeling on the subject, especially since he had experienced the pleasure 15 years earlier, shortly after joining the *Tribune*, of canceling the dreadful column of the husband of the Washington publisher. But he would run McGillicuddy, of course, for he remained one of those old-fashioned editorial page editors who believed in the concept of a "fighting balance." He ran columns on all sides of issues, unlike those papers and magazines that favored columnists who shared their editorial viewpoint. Interesting, too, how the right-wing boys—the Buckleys, Buchanans, Kilpatricks *et al.*—and their somewhat more moderate conservative colleagues had come to outnumber those dissatisfied with right-of-center policies in the opinion market. And the canard that the news media have a liberal slant continued to thrive in the wonderland of American journalistic criticism. That had to be one of the major hoaxes the political right played again and again despite overwhelming evidence to the contrary. Robinson was amused. In every election this century, save one, the Republican candidate for president had enjoyed the support of a majority—frequently a vast majority—of daily newspapers and of all three newsmagazines since their inception. That one election, in which Candidate Goldwater presented a greater threat to the status quo than Incumbent Johnson, demonstrated where the interests of most newspaper—and all newsmagazine—publishers rested. Last night Weenie Toole had called to the attention of Don Bitterman one of the better political jokes of our time after LBJ beat Goldwater in 1964: The Democrat says you vote for Goldwater and in six months we'll have half a million soldiers in Vietnam; the Republican votes for Goldwater and sure enough, in six months we have half a million soldiers in Vietnam.

Bitterman hadn't heard that story, and it was a pleasant change from the needle Weenie usually put into him. As a matter of fact, there had been considerable needling, almost always amiable, at the gathering for dinner last night at the Blakely home in which Arianne, a cook and baker of extraordinary talent, had her first experience of dining with seven persons in varying degrees on the news side of the newspaper business.

The Blakely guests had been Donald and Elaine Bitterman (she an occasional columnist and vacation substitute in what the *Tribune* called its Life Style section, although the front door of the Tribune Building still provided directions to the "Society Department"), Deborah Delaney (former assistant news editor, now putting out the weekly television and arts tabloid), her cohabiting friend Arden Rosenberg (a recent addition to the "Toy Department" who had provided a needed touch of sportsy verve to that section of the paper), and Weenie Toole (weekly master of sports nostalgia and expert on every section, page, column, paragraph and line made available to subscribers of the *Placer Tribune*). And himself. He'd had a very good time.

The evening had started with an enthusiastic sampling of Schwennesen's Cherry Wine, concocted with cherries that repaid their organic nurturing with an exploding flavor. Weenie Toole, who once had defined a wine connoisseur as "anyone who doesn't drink it from a bottle in a brown paper bag," described this wine, with pinkie raised, as "a pleasantly versatile wine, complex in structure, of great dimension and breed, its fresh, fruity bouquet and pleasant, natural tartness balanced by a slight trace of residual sweetness, comparable to a wine I recall savoring in a quaint little inn outside Innsbruck, fitting to be served with the assorted fine cheeses provided by our lovely hostess." There had been a toast to happiness of the host and hostess, delivered in a stentorian imitation of Chet Huntley by the irrepressible Weenie, who had known the late newscaster as a boy in Whitehall. There had been some good-natured ribbing about the choice of Las Vegas for the nuptial vows of the Blakelys.

"If you promise not to laugh," Jonathan had said, "I'll tell you one of the reasons we went to Vegas. We wanted to see Sinatra."

"Sinatra?" Robinson had smiled approvingly. "I've seen him three times and he's in a class by himself. The best one-man show I've ever seen was Sinatra at the Sands back in the '60s, and he's still number one. Jesus, the guy's now—what?—67 or so. He's incredible. He stays young—in his way, I admit—but by the gods he stays young. He's earned his money. He's like Dick Hugo, too. Hugo writes the best poetry being written in this country and he's a lot like Sinatra—a renegade in his fashion. Gutsy. With Hugo, everything he feels hangs out. He's the most open person I've ever known. Sinatra is closed off-stage, but when he comes out there in front of you he gives you everything he's got."

"We loved him," Arianne said.

"I haven't been impressed with his private life for a few years or that entourage he seems to think he needs," Robinson said, "but I'm not perfect either. The Kennedys ruined him."

"The Kennedys?" Arianne looked over at Jonathan, who shrugged his shoulders and then pointed to Robinson.

"Sure," Robinson said. "Let's look at the record." He did that line in his Al Smith voice, which he remembered hearing on the radio as a child. "Everyone who knew Sinatra in his early years, with Harry James and Tommy Dorsey and then his first movies, told me you couldn't hope to meet a nicer guy. A really decent young man with a remarkable modesty considering his talent. Everything he stood for—politically, I mean—showed intelligence and compassion and admirable instincts. He worked his ass off to help John Kennedy get elected, and then when the Illinois ballots were safely tucked away and Nixon conceded, that whole Hyannisport crowd crapped all over Frank. That Cape Cod clan didn't like his Italian friends, some of whose methods of assembling wealth resembled in many ways the old Joe Kennedy techniques. Hurt him deeply, I heard. So he adopted the famous Kennedy motto: Don't get mad, get even. He switched some of his friends, to the likes of Spiro Agnew and Ronald Reagan. He went downhill as a person."

Yeah, it had been the Kennedys all right, Robinson thought. That reminded him—last night:

"Tell him your joke, Don," Elaine Bitterman urged her husband. "Go on. You're always telling me the ones Weenie and Jonathan tell."

The managing editor shrugged uncomfortably. "It's a bit sick. I warn you of that."

"All the better," said Weenie. "Sickness is in the mind of the beholder. I've always agreed with Sam Goldwyn that anyone who'd go to a psychiatrist ought to have his head examined."

"Go on," said Elaine Bitterman.

"All right." Donald Bitterman looked uneasily at the others. "It goes like this: Do you know what President Reagan wrote in a note to John Hinckley?"

The company waited expectantly.

"He told Hinckley that Teddy Kennedy was dating Jodie Foster." . . .

. . . Robinson looked out the window at the snow drifting on Main Street. A blizzard forecast, a blizzard beginning; it was a hard Montana winter this year. The calendar on the wall, on which he recorded the high and low outside temperatures each day, proclaimed that the thermometer had not gone above the freezing mark on 29 days since the start of the year. But that was good, that was great. Only the hardy would come to the state; only the hardy would remain. There were, of course, those who fled to Arizona and points south during the colder months, but even they were excused by friend and neighbor who knew the tortures of cabin fever. It was better this way; the Eagles had sung the requiem: "Call it paradise/Kiss it goodbye."

The phone rang. It was Arianne Blakely. He told her what a great dinner she had prepared, what a splendid time he'd had the night before.

"But Jonathan's worried," she said. "He thinks he may have offended Elaine—perhaps even Donald. He often feels that way the morning after. He has that kind of spell instead of a hangover. Assure him, please, when he comes in, that he didn't cross the line. Will you do that?"

Robinson laughed and said he would. Poor Jonathan, he thought, always willing to tell you precisely what's on his mind—often when not even asked—and then suffering the tortures of the damned who can't keep their mouth shut. He knew why Jonathan was uncertain in the light of the new day. . . .

. . . Late in the evening, when the company was deep into the bottle of Grand Marnier, came what those present were likely to remember as "Jonathan Blakely's Nine Scenarios." The subject surfaced abruptly when Elaine Bitterman, all innocence, had asked Jonathan to relate some of the strange coincidences and unanswered questions her husband had periodically mentioned, offhand and disbelieving, during the eleven months since the president had been shot. Robinson recalled with a smile how Jonathan had reluctantly agreed and then had turned to Elaine's husband.

"Well, for starters, Donaldo, there is that intriguing coincidence related to one of your favorite bugaboos, the Trilateral Commission."

Donald Bitterman's head jerked sharply toward Jonathan. "What's that about?" His question reflected his sudden concern, for there was one passion the managing editor shared with his political opposites on the far left—an abiding belief that the Trilateral Commission was the principal instrument of the Rockefeller conspiracy to control the world.

"Well," Jonathan said, "Vice President George Bush just happened to meet with the Trilateral Commission the day before the assassination attempt, at which time he introduced former Japanese Premier Takeo Fukuda—you remember him, surely, from the reeking scandals that rocked his extraordinarily corrupt party for several years? And Reagan himself was scheduled to meet with the Trilateralists in the Oval Office when he finished his speech at the Washington Hilton that very day. That very afternoon of March 30, Donald. How's that for coincidence?"

Bitterman eyed Jonathan suspiciously. "How come you never mentioned that to me before tonight?"

"Why, Donald, I didn't think it was important. You're not one of those conspiracy freaks who hops on every coincidence that comes along, are you?"

"Go on, go on," Elaine Bitterman insisted.

"Off we go, so fasten your seat belts, ladies and gentlemen," Jonathan said. "The first scenario necessarily must be the one that has been formally, officially and authoritatively presented to us: That a virtually penniless drifter with a brief history of so-called mental problems shot the president because of an unrequited infatuation for a young actress. We are even beginning to see it in the press as unattributed but confirmed history—you know: 'Hinckley, who shot President Reagan in an effort to impress Jodie Foster.' All other possibilities have been dismissed. I'm examining that scenario in detail in my article, but the gist is this: First, what's the evidence to support this thesis? Primarily, a letter Hinckley purportedly wrote in his hotel room before going out on his mission. No member of the press, to the best of my knowledge, has ever seen that letter. It was pieced together—those are the exact words—by the *Washington Post* from various sources. It took the authorities three days to arrange for this text to be pieced together and the leaks during those three days were wildly inaccurate compared to the ultimate version. Then there was a reference in the letter that Hinckley was going to 'get Reagan.' Now pan the camera over to our actress friend, Alicia Christian Foster, Jodie herself, the bare-bottom child in the Coppertone ads at the age of three, who also was blessed with a magnificent head. She was a remarkably precocious youngster, was nominated for an Oscar at the age of fourteen and was graduated at the head of her class of thirty from a prestigious bilingual school in Los Angeles, delivering her valedictory address in French. She is no dummy. Now zoom in for a closeup: There she is, telling the press that the FBI told her not to talk and that she didn't want to jeopardize the prosecution, but she wanted everyone to know she had never met or spoken to John Hinckley and that in his notes to her he never once mentioned President Reagan. The Yale authorities back up her story. She even calls a press conference to repeat and emphasize those points. Then when some tapes of Hinckley talking to her on the phone are released—months later—she says it's all something she can't talk about. And the press lets her off the hook. In all the millions of words written about Jodie in this affair, her contradictory and puzzling statements have never been reconciled. And there's another thing: We have her statement that Hinckley had never mentioned the president in his notes to her. Contrast that with the statement of a government spokesman the day after the shooting that Hinckley believed Reagan had insulted Jodie and this suggestion was contained in a letter Hinckley earlier sent to the actress. Incidentally, I've not been able to find out what the purported insult might have been, although much was made of that so-called evidence in the first days after the attack to bolster the whole he-did-it-for-Jodie shooting script. And consider this, too: Two days after the shooting an FBI spokesman says that Hinckley made several phone calls to Jodie but that Hinckley either spoke only briefly or did not get through to her, and six months later they bring out these tapes of rather lengthy conversations between the two. What we need is a repeal of the Jodie Foster Rule—that's the rule that says when federal officials tell a private citizen not to talk to the press, the press accepts that muzzle. There was once a time when the press would have gone after her and got the answer to the question that bears so strongly on this attempt to kill a president. That isn't even investigative reporting; that's elementary stuff in Beginning Reporting. Or at least it used to be. The press of the '80s obviously has forgotten the immortal words of a Chicago newspaperman who said he came to either get a story or get a footprint on the seat of his trousers.''

''Are you suggesting that the tapes of Hinckley talking on the phone to her were faked?'' Donald Bitterman's voice dripped incredulity.

''No, Donald, I'm suggesting that half a year after the event—almost to the day—the FBI furnished the text of the tapes to UPI out of the blue. I'm suggesting that Jodie Foster and the government can't both be telling the truth. And I'm suggesting that the major piece of evidence presented to us thus far to bolster the infatuation-with-Foster theory is a pretty raggedy pair of pants.''

Weenie Toole laughed and quickly explained: ''Our friend Jonathan is referring to the words of a now-forgotten sage who observed that more girls have said no because they had on raggedy pants than for any other reason.''

Jonathan pressed on:

''Okay, here's another part of the tale that hasn't been given a ride in the press. You know all that baloney concerning Hinckley and *Taxi Driver*? Well, what Hinckley did parallels far more closely a book called *The Fan*, which he allegedly packed around with him. It's about a psychotic young man, precisely Hinckley's age, who has a father who tells him to take on the responsibility of supporting himself, refuses to send him money when he pleads for help, won't listen when he begs for an advance on his inheritance, and sends him to a psychiatrist. The son promises his parents that all their disappointments in him will be replaced by news of him so astonishing that they will hardly believe their ears. He writes a succession of letters to an actress and insists that the two of them one day will be husband and wife. He feels no remorse after carving up a woman's face with a knife. He leaves a love letter to the actress to be found after a shooting. The parallels are eerie. Oh yes—the character in the book signs one letter to the actress 'The Man You Have Been Searching For' and Hinckley keeps a journal titled 'The Diary of a Person We All Know.' "

"I read that book," the sports writer said. "It's by Bob Randall. They made a movie out of it, too. Do you remember that photo of Hinckley sitting in front of the fence outside the White House? Well, there's a shot in the flick of the punk sitting across the street from the apartment of the actress he's infatuated with, and the same kind of fence is in back of him. I wonder if Hinckley saw that one during his travels."

"That's interesting," Jonathan said. "And we shouldn't overlook another book reportedly found in Hinckley's Washington hotel room that seems to be more significant than the *Taxi Driver* movie. It's a book by Eliot Asinof called *The Fox Is Crazy Too*, in which a criminal repeatedly escapes punishment by feigning insanity and fooling the shrinks who examine him."

"Somehow you'd think more attention would have been given to *Ordinary People*," Deborah said.

"I haven't seen it," Jonathan responded. "What was it about?"

"Talk about parallels," Deborah said. "It's a story about a family living in a suburb similar to Evergreen—you know, big house, country club, lots of vacations, all the status symbols that surround the Hinckleys. But the family is falling apart because of the pressure of psychiatric treatment for the younger son—just as the Hinckleys are reported to have marital problems stemming from a disagreement over how to handle their younger son. The boy tries to commit suicide after the death of his older and more successful brother. Eerie parallels."

"Yeah, and eerie ironies," the sports writer added. "The flick wins the Academy Award for best picture of the year and Timothy Hutton gets an Oscar for best supporting actor playing the younger son. Then the awards presentation is delayed twenty-four hours because the younger son in real life shoots the president."

"This is all very interesting, I'm sure," Elaine Bitterman said tentatively, "but it doesn't really have much to do with the case, does it?"

"It's only part of a scenario, Elaine. Just chalk it up to a series of unimportant coincidences," Jonathan replied. "But try running this up the flagpole, Elaine, and see if it makes you want to blow reveille: After his arrest, John Hinckley was rushed to the federal facility at Butner, North Carolina, where we were told that mental competency tests are conducted for federal courts. Well, the other side of that unflipped coin is that Butner was the scene of one hell of a battle against its opening in 1976 because it was going to be an experimental prison where new inmate programs would be tested. Please remember that Hinckley didn't say a single reported word except to answer a judge's routine questions for weeks after the shooting while the whole Jodie Foster mini-saga was worked out. What a nice place to get John Hinckley to see that he did it to impress Jodie Foster, hey?"

"Preposterous," Donald Bitterman interjected.

"Oh, I don't know," Jonathan quickly replied. "Some of the government shrinks don't think so. I have it on excellent authority that at least one of them believes the whole Jodie Foster thing was implanted in Hinckley's mind by the defense's headshrinkers after the arrest while they had him at Butner. Don't forget they had him there for close to five months. Arthur Koestler wrote about the Russians' success with that sort of thing about forty years ago and the crude techniques of that time have been refined remarkably since then."

"All right, Sherlock, we get the point," Donald Bitterman said. "What do you suggest as replacements for the accepted theory?"

"Scenario Number Two: The audit. Here are auditors from the United States government—by coincidence on the very morning of the day of the assassination attempt—telling the Hinckleys that they had uncovered evidence of pricing violations on crude oil sold in the preceding four years. Vanderbilt Energy, they say, owes the government two million dollars. By a happenstance that sum is approximately what the *New York Times* estimated to be the wealth of the Hinckley parents. The older son says he'll need a few hours to come up with the answer to why the company has overcharged to that extent and a little more than an hour after the meeting breaks up the younger son tries to make George Bush president of the United

States. Now all that remains to be found out is whether John Junior—who apparently was spending a lot of time at home while the audit was under way—knew about it. It's a variation of the old Watergate question: What did John Hinckley Jr. know about the audit and when did he know it? Then you call in Seymour Hersh to discover whether John Junior knew his brother was palsy-walsy with the son of the man who would be president—''

"But the brothers weren't close," Elaine Bitterman said.

"Oh, no? Then why did the *Boston Globe* report that the leader of a rock group in Evergreen said he expected to see John Hinckley at a gig the night before the assassination attempt and that he met John through Scott? And isn't it more likely, rather than less likely, that Hinckley knew about the audit and about the budding friendship of his brother and Neil Bush? Hell, I'm not saying that's the way it was, but it makes at least as much sense as the Jodie Foster *shtick*."

"Why didn't the papers follow up on that?" It was the sports writer who was curious.

"I'll tell you why," Deborah said. "Jonathan showed me what he was writing right after it happened. Neil Bush says he'll give one statement to the press and that's all—and the Denver reporters let him get away with that. Since no one could get to the Hinckleys, that whole part of the case got buried."

"Worse than buried," Jonathan said. "The audit never got any play in the national media, so hardly anyone knows about it. But consider the fact that in the days that young Hinckley was planning and executing his crime, the Department of Energy was under heavy fire from what the AP described as skeptical members of the House Energy Subcommittee on Investigations. Representative Albert Gore subsequently warned against what he called white-collar crooks manipulating the zealots at the budget office to fix the cases against them. At the same time there was Bob Whittaker, a Kansas Republican, telling the other members of the Subcommittee that he had been assured by President Reagan that his administration will work aggressively to punish those guilty of oil overcharges and potential criminal violations. I suggest it is possible that President Bush's policy might be otherwise. Which allows me to segue into a couple of preambles to Scenario Number Three. Ready? First, I took Bear"—he pointed to the Landseer Newfoundland puppy lying at Arianne's feet—"to our veterinarian the other day for some shots and we got to talking about political assassinations. The vet, who is a very honest conservative, says when it comes to a political assassination the first question should always be: Who profits most from it? The second preamble is that it's strange, is it not, that every political figure who has been assassinated in recent years—the two Kennedys, Malcolm X, Medgar Evers, Martin Luther King—was someone who sought to change this land for the better. All right, I saw that look, Elaine; let's say they were trying to change the status quo. Who and what have profited beyond the dreams of avarice from those assassinations? John Kennedy is killed in Dallas and is succeeded by a Texan. Bobby Kennedy is killed in Los Angeles on the day he's won the California primary and is a cinch for the Democratic nomination in Chicago. Nixon, who would have been trounced by Bobby, subsequently beats Humpty Dumpty. Reagan almost dies and another Texan stands ready to be sworn in on a plane flying to Washington. And don't forget that Dr. King was in the process of tying the tragedy in Vietnam to the civil rights crusade and was at the moment by far the most powerful threat to the establishment. So who profited the most? Lyndon Johnson, Texas, Richard Nixon, the militarists, the oil companies, the conglomerates, white men rather than black or brown or red or yellow men, rich men rather than poor men, and those who polarize our people rather than those who seek to bring us together in some degree of humanity and some sense of brotherhood. Are those facts or are those figments of a distressed imagination?"

"I notice," Donald Bitterman said, "that you conveniently omit the attack on George Wallace from your soft-shoe song-and-dance routine. How do you fit that in?"

"I exult at your question, good Donald," Jonathan said as he moved toward his desk, riffled through a stack of white note cards and pulled one out. "Listen not to me, but to *The Official Associated Press Almanac 1973*, pages 44 and 45:

The May 16 election returns from Michigan and Maryland

were even more pleasant for the Alabama governor. He had won 51 percent of the vote in the Michigan primary, his first majority in a northern state. McGovern received 27 percent, Humphrey 16 percent. In Maryland Wallace had also won, his 39 percent a clear victory over Humphrey with 27 percent and McGovern with 22 percent.

The news, however, was anti-climactic. Wallace had been shot the day before the primary by a 22-year-old misfit from Milwaukee, Wis., Arthur Herman Bremer, at a rally at a shopping center in Laurel, Md. Bremer's choice of Wallace as a target had apparently been of no special consequence. Bremer had also stalked President Nixon at an appearance in Ottawa, Canada.

"I love those last two sentences," Jonathan said with a wide grin. "Notice how the official version bears a striking resemblance to the case currently under consideration. Notice how in the recent instance the FBI first said Hinckley had stalked Carter and then on second thought concluded that he definitely had not stalked Carter and now there are hints that they're swinging back to the position that he did stalk Carter. That makes the choice of target apparently of no special consequence, as the AP so charmingly phrased it."

"Well, what does that prove?" This was Elaine Bitterman jumping to the defense of her husband. "McGovern was the one who profited by Wallace being knocked out of the race."

"Oh my God, Elaine." Heads swung toward Deborah. "McGovern had the Democratic nomination in his pocket regardless of Wallace. If Nixon's hoodlums could have picked a candidate to run against it would have been McGovern. But if Wallace ran again as a third-party candidate he would drain millions of Nixon's votes and take away a lot of Nixon electoral votes, especially in the South. Tricky Dick probably popped champagne corks on the day Wallace was shot. It was Nixon who was assured of re-election by Bremer's bullets."

"I'm not so sure," Elaine Bitterman responded with a trace of tartness. "I think Nixon would have won anyway."

"All right, granted he might have won anyway, but he surely profited most from having Wallace out of the way."

"Long preambles, friend," Donald Bitterman suggested.

"Yes, Donald, but necessary to understand Scenario Number Three, which is the Bush-Hinckley connections. Note that I put that in the plural. No need to belabor the Scott Hinckley-Neil Bush relationship, which the national news media barely touched and then dropped like the hot potato it is. But what about the Bush press agents saying that their records showed no contributions to their man from the Hinckleys when the opposite was the truth? What about reporters shying away from asking Bush if he knew Jack Hinckley or how well any members of the Bush family knew any members of the Hinckley family—as I urged several of them to do? What about the press repeatedly characterizing the Senior Hinckley as a strong supporter of Ronald Reagan when the fact of the matter is that both Jack and Scott Hinckley contributed to John Connally's campaign at the very time Connally looked like the best bet to stop Reagan's bandwagon? What about that story in the *New York Post* that said flat out that Jack Hinckley raised funds for Bush's unsuccessful campaign to wrest the Republican presidential nomination from Reagan and that the two families maintained social ties? In that same story the reporter even suggested that young Hinckley might have been a familiar face to officials involved in Reagan's visit to the Washington Hilton. It's well established that the drifter drifted into Washington several times. And no one has explained those two local calls he made from his hotel shortly before the main event or the fact that before he left the hotel for the last time he asked at the front desk whether he had any phone messages."

There was a pause. "Don't forget the Bush-Hinckley connection in Lubbock," Arianne said.

"Yeah, that's a rather big one," Jonathan responded, nodding appreciatively at his wife. "Bush's son George ran for Congress in the district that includes Lubbock. He went through close to half a million bucks trying to get elected, which was $120,000 more than the Democrat who whomped him. Neil Bush was his brother's campaign manager and spent a lot of time in Lubbock where John Hinckley lived during the entire campaign while attending Texas Tech. There appears to be no end to coincidences...."

"And that's exactly what they all may be—just coincidences," Elaine Bitterman said.

"Fair enough, Elaine," Jonathan said. "But wouldn't it be nice if all the coincidences were satisfactorily explained instead of lurking in the background and forming the pattern of a possible cover-up? I might even get over my obsession that all this funny business really does add up to something more dreadful than any of us might contemplate."

"Any more scenarios?" Donald Bitterman asked Jonathan impatiently.

"Most assuredly," Jonathan said. "Where am I? Oh, Scenario Number Four. That has to be the Hunt-Hinckley connection—or possibly even the Hunt-Bush-Hinckley connection. Where should I start?" He reflected on the matter. "Okay, I'm talking about the Hunts of Texas. I'm talking about the two sons of the late H.L. Hunt. You remember H.L., I'm sure, as the man whose name was frequently mentioned in connection with the assassination of President Kennedy, especially the failure of the Warren Commission to follow up on several leads linking him with Jack Ruby. Both J. Paul Getty and the Associated Press saluted H.L. as the richest man in the world. He was a man who paid no attention to the law and lived by his own rules. He was, among other things, a polygamist who had three families—two of them secret—sired fifteen children and left seventy living direct descendants when he died in 1974. He was a crackpot. He—"

Donald Bitterman interrupted. "How far back into ancient history do you intend to take us, professor? What's the point?"

"The point is that no examination of the events of March 30 could be complete without an understanding of the relationships between Hunts and Hinckleys, and it is an involved scenario requiring considerable explanation and a degree of patience on the part of those who are not impressed with history, Donaldo. Bear with me, please, while we turn to two of the fifteen H.L. sired, namely Nelson Bunker Hunt and William Herbert Hunt. They are the ones, along with assorted other family members, who shook the foundation of the nation's financial institutions in 1980 with their Byzantine attempt to manipulate the silver market. The great silver caper involved two of the richest families on earth—the Hunts and those high in the government of Saudi Arabia. They finally were bailed out by the banks and agencies of the United States government. Now for the connections you await with such intense and ill-concealed interest, good friends. Nelson Bunker Hunt resides in the exclusive Highland Park section of Dallas where he was a neighbor of the Hinckleys for several years. John W. Hinckley Jr. attended schools with a daughter of William Herbert Hunt. Hinckley also spent time in Dallas, where his sister lives, off and on after the family moved to Evergreen. I think the Hunts and Hinckleys might have been acquainted."

Donald Bitterman interrupted again. "What is this—guilt by association, Senator McCarthy?"

"No, Donald, let me finish. By coincidence, earlier on the same day that President Reagan was shot, a federal judge in Dallas temporarily blocked the Securities and Exchange Commission from taking scheduled depositions from Nelson Bunker Hunt and William Herbert Hunt in a continuing investigation of the 1980 silver crash. The most interesting statement that day came from the SEC counsel who argued against the temporary restraining order, saying that the public must know its government is able to go forward and ferret out all the facts. With President Reagan in office the Hunt brothers faced a minimum of a hard year of tough litigation with no assurance they'd come out of it scot-free. A government headed by old friend George Bush would be infinitely less likely to go forward and ferret out all the facts. And George had just finished a luncheon address in which he was introduced by Mrs. H.L. Hunt when he heard that he had best fly back to Washington. While I'm at it, let me call your attention to a footnote that won't go away. The press went out of its way to report that Bush was in Texas to address some cattlemen and the state legislature, but nary a word about the fact that when the shots were fired in Washington he had just accommodated another son of H.L. Hunt—Ray—by helping dedicate his hotel as a national historical site. Ray Hunt, in addition to having served as chairman of the Young Men for Bush in George's ill-fated 1970 U.S. senate race, was named by H.L. Hunt in his will as sole executor of the old rogue's estate. Sometimes I think the press has dedicated itself to keeping the people of this nation from knowing how things really work."

"C'mon, Jonathan," Donald Bitterman said.

"All right, Donald, retain your faith, but consider another dogma. Forget for a moment all the drifter-with-an-obsession reportage we were subjected to. Let's look at the situation prior to March 30 through John Hinckley's eyes. First, he knows he's likely to survive the presidential assassination attempt. He knows a Puerto Rican was killed trying to shoot his way into Blair House to get at Truman, and Oswald was gunned down by Ruby. But all the rest survived the shootings at the scene. He figures if he is shot down, that'll serve his father right, but he'll likely survive. And what's waiting for him? All the resources of papa's substantial bank account will be put at his disposal. He knows he'll get the best lawyers money can buy. He'll be famous. And most important of all—he probably thinks he'll get off."

"Why would he think that?" Donald Bitterman asked.

"For several reasons, but most importantly because of a trial involving Nelson Bunker Hunt and William Herbert Hunt in Lubbock, Texas, while Hinckley was living there."

"What's that all about?" This time it was Elaine Bitterman who interrupted.

"Back in September, 1975, while Hinckley was living in Lubbock and going to Texas Tech—that was the semester he switched his major to history—there was a spectacular trial in which two of the late H.L. Hunt's three families patched up their enormous differences to help keep Bunker and Herbert out of prison. They were on trial for illegal wiretapping and a subsequent charge of conspiracy to cover it up by bribing prospective witnesses not to testify. Bunker reportedly had told a wiretapper who expressed concern about criminal and civil action if they were caught that he wasn't worried about that prospect, adding that the family could take care of any legal problems that might arise. The two Hunts hired a Denver public relations man to polish up their image for the trial and their lawyers pulled out all the stops—Herbert even broke down and cried on the stand. The whole thing was characterized as a Texas-style private-enterprise version of Watergate. The Lubbock jury, of course, was quick to find them not guilty on the wiretapping charge. It was quite a show, and one can't help wondering how much Hinckley read about it or, even more interesting, whether he attended the trial. And one is led to surmise how much influence Bunker's statement after the trial might have had on the impressionable lad. I have it over here—"

He arose and went to his desk. He came back with a set of white note cards.

"—and here it is. This is what Bunker told the press: 'If we'd been just ordinary folks, Herbert and I would have been in real trouble. We can afford it. But my heart goes out to all the ordinary people, poor people, middle-of-the-road people who can't afford to hire counsel to defend themselves. The government can call out a whole array of talent to prosecute a case, but many defendants can only afford to plead guilty or nolo contendere.' If you stare at those sentences long enough and then at a blank wall, a picture emerges. Hinckley also might have noticed how seven months later the government dropped the obstruction-of-justice indictments against Herbert and then Bunker was allowed to enter a nolo contendere to the charge that he 'did knowingly misbehave'—what, pray, would we do without lawyers to amuse us?—and was fined one thousand dollars. Yes'm, just the facts—one thousand dollars. Does that tickle any funnybones?"

"You have a thing about the rich, don't you?" It was the voice of the managing editor of the *Placer Tribune*, whose salary was icing on the cake left him by both his father and grandfather.

"Not at all, Donald," Jonathan replied quietly. "Not nearly the kind of thing Scott Fitzgerald had."

"Some of his best friends are rich," said Weenie Toole.

"Indeed they are," Jonathan said to the smiling skeleton. "And I like very much what some of them do with their money. Nonetheless, I don't kid myself about others among them. Our literature is filled with speculation on the ways the rich are different from the rest of us, but no one ever mentions the most significant difference—that it's infinitely more important for them to have a government friendly to their specific interests, their legal positions, their bank accounts and their tax obligations. For example, Mr. and Mrs. Nelson Bunker Hunt paid a total of less than ten dollars—nine dollars and sixty-five cents, to be exact—in federal income tax for 1975, 1976 and 1977."

"If I recall correctly," Robert Robinson said, "the Hunt brothers also were involved in a soybean caper a few years back. Didn't they try to corner the market and then get away with the illegalities with a slap on the wrist from a federal judge in Chicago?"

"Precisely," Jonathan said. "And believe it or not, Bunker has tried to corner the world horse-breeding market. No kidding. He pretty much succeeded in buying and building a monopoly on blood lines by using secret, deceptive and unethical means to purchase the best blood stock. The horsey set in Kentucky had to take special steps to counter his practices. They thought it was great when he was buying all those horses, but one day they woke up and discovered they were facing the prospect of buying from him—and at his prices."

"He had a corner on politics in some circles, too," Arianne added.

"That he did," Jonathan said. "We all know that on the fateful last morning of John F. Kennedy's life there was a black-bordered full-page advertisement in the *Dallas Morning News* sarcastically headlined WELCOME, MR. KENNEDY, TO DALLAS. It was filled with the kind of venom that has given the place the title of 'City of Hate.' Bunker Hunt peeled off some green bills from a fat roll he was carrying to help pay for that ad. Back in those days he also was associated with the International Committee for the Defense of Christian Culture, which had been founded by an ex-Nazi, and he's also peeled off a lot of green bills as one of the largest contributors to the John Birch Society. More recently he has become enchanted with the bloodcurdling Guatemalan general, Efrain Rios Montt, who proclaims that the innocent as well as the guilty will have to die to save Guatemala from communism. At any rate, I find the Hunts far more relevant to a study of political assassination than the giggling Ms. Foster."

Weenie Toole was out of his chair and on his way. "Hold it, Jonathan, because I can't any longer. Don't say another word until I return."

A few minutes later, when Weenie and others had taken their

places in the living room, Jonathan resumed.

"For Scenario Number Five I offer you evidence of a criminal conspiracy of some sort, especially that of the still-unexplained Nazi connections. You may recall that Hinckley showed an unusual interest in Hitler and the Nazis and the Auschwitz death camp, according to one of his Texas Tech professors. He paid $30 for a two-volume *Mein Kampf* in a Lubbock book store. He wrote a letter to the student newspaper in 1978 saying that the American Nazi Party could become more dangerous than an atomic bomb and should not be underestimated. He shares the Nazi hatred of blacks and Jews. And then days after the shooting the director of the FBI said it still hadn't been confirmed whether Hinckley had been a member of the American Nazi Party. I haven't come across anything since then that offers an answer to that significant unanswered question."

Jonathan paused and smiled broadly. "On the other hand we have one of the American Nazis saying that he thought Hinckley was an undercover federal agent trying to stir up trouble. I hasten to add that I give little credence to that opinion. However, under the same heading of a criminal conspiracy one must include organized crime. The evidence there, I admit, is slim—but interesting. People wondered why the would-be assassin chose a .22-caliber gun, even with explosive bullets. Well, in recent years a .22-caliber bullet in the head has served as the calling card of organized crime."

"Yeah, interesting—but slim," Donald Bitterman said.

"I said it first, Donaldo," Jonathan responded. "But add the fact that young Hinckley was seen off at Stapleton Airport by his mother, flew to Los Angeles and then a few hours later boarded a bus for a cross-country trip that ended in the nation's capital. The FBI said it believed Hinckley did not have any checked baggage when he left Denver and therefore probably didn't have a gun. The FBI speculated that he went to get a gun, but his 20 hours in L.A. are not accounted for. What was it all about? Was it to get a gun? Last-minute instructions? Or what? Also in this category, how was Hinckley able to buy the Devastator bullets in Lubbock when they are supposed to be available only to law enforcement officers with proper identification? How did he do that? Those bullets were developed to enable sky marshals to shoot hijackers without the bullet also penetrating the aircraft's outer wall. The police like them for undercover work where firearms have to be small. And then you have the strange case of the fixed ticket—"

Arianne broke in. "You really shouldn't call it that, Jonathan. It's more accurately the case of the botched baggage."

"Amendment accepted," Jonathan said. "You all noticed that much ado was made about the FBI failing to inform the Secret Service of Hinckley's arrest in Nashville when he tried to board a plane with three guns in his baggage, right? That's an offense subject to a civil penalty of up to one thousand dollars for each of the three weapons seized at the airport. The authorities said a follow-up letter sent to Lubbock was returned with the notation that the addressee had moved, but an alert reporter promptly pointed out that on the Nashville police form Hinckley had given his Evergreen home address. Silence. Thunderous silence followed."

Silence in the room, too, as Jonathan sipped the orange liqueur and smiled at Arianne.

"The professor is now ready to move to Scenario Number Six—the Synfuel Scenario."

"Sinful?"

Donald Bitterman delivered a blazing glance to his wife. "Synfuel, sweetheart," he said, and everyone but he laughed.

"The Synthetic Fuels Corporation is also exceedingly sinful, Elaine," Jonathan said. "In addition to the huge expense—enough to relieve a tremendous amount of hunger among our citizens—and the ruinous environmental devastation, the process gobbles vast amounts of water and emits intolerable amounts of air pollution. So if you consider all that and the wasting of taxpayers' money as sins, the people behind this ripoff will roast in hell for centuries to come. The Corporation went into business just a few months before Reagan was elected and Congress authorized it to spend almost eighteen billion dollars in the first round of an eighty-eight-billion-dollar boondoggle. Let me say that again so that you won't minimize the significance of this scenario: Eighty-eight billion dollars. Now hear this: The deadline for submitting the applications for federal aid was March 31—the day after the assassination attempt. And guess who dominated the sixty-one proposals submitted? Why, it was that rapacious bunch of Texas energy conglomerates, led by Tenneco of Houston with bids for three major synfuels projects, including one to devastate a part of Montana. And there was Transco of Houston and Texaco, Exxon, Mobil, Union, Phillips, Sun, Standard Oil of Ohio—"

"All the big boys who don't want to take on a job involving their own money were standing in the welfare line for a government handout," Weenie Toole said.

"Right. Now all of this gall is divided into three parts—"

"Beautiful," Weenie Toole said softly.

"—and the first part is the Synthetic Fuels Corporation itself. It immediately was beset by unmitigated corruption, even by the standards practiced in Washington. The House Government Operations Committee said in plain English that the Corporation's board of directors at their discretion simply dispensed with compliance with the law. They also approved salaries for their officers far beyond anything paid other federal employees. I'm sure it will be a continuing scandal until Congress puts an end to the whole damnable project—but don't hold your breath. The second part concerns President Reagan, who had campaigned against the Corporation that Carter put together. He dismissed Carter's entire board a month after his inauguration and was taking his sweet time appointing a new board. The word was out that Reagan's policy was to let synfuels sink or swim in the realm of private enterprise, with little or no federal help. In his budget cut request to Congress shortly before he was gunned down by a kid who spent most of his life among Texas oilmen, Reagan proposed to rescind several billion dollars for building six government-owned demonstration plants to test new technologies, yet another decision that could not have been pleasing to the bandits above the Rio Grande. The one thing the energy conglomerates don't want is to slow up this gravy train or to junk the whole fiasco and use the cash reserves to lower the federal deficit, as some of our more responsible representatives have suggested. Please note that the seven directors of the Corporation that Reagan subsequently appointed are strong supporters of his free-market approach and are on record as opposing subsidies to the energy conglomerates which eventually will use the technology to reap huge profits without being forced to make heavy investments. The pitiable Stockman had much to say on this subject in the famous *Atlantic* article that a *Washington Post* staffer thought was too good for his paper. Finally, don't forget the recent words of our Western Montana congressman who said that it is his frank judgment that oil companies run Washington, D.C. Which brings us to part three, involving our good old Houston oilman, the vice president of the United States, who if given the opportunity would have that Corporation grinding out billions to his Texas oil friends quicker than you could say pushy preppie. It would have been his second act as president."

"Let me! Let me!" Weenie Toole exclaimed. "What would have been his first act?"

"Thanks, Clarence," Jonathan said. "His first act as president of the United States would have been to fire William J. Casey as director of the Central Intelligence Agency. Which brings me to the next scenario, a conspiracy involving the CIA—"

"Ye gods," said Elaine Bitterman, "can't anything happen without the CIA getting blamed for it?"

"If the truth were known," Robert Robinson said, "the CIA gets blamed for things it has done in approximately the same measure as it doesn't get blamed for things it has done. Go ahead, Jonathan."

"You didn't let me finish, Elaine. This scenario involves the CIA, the FBI and all the intelligence and law enforcement agencies of government. But once again I must beg your forbearance as I engage in the provocation of citing historical fact. Let's look at the trail left by the current director of the CIA, whose sole intelligence experience was as an OSS spy during World War Two. First, back in 1972 when Robert Vesco offered to give two hundred thousand dollars secretly to the Nixon re-election campaign in return for special treatment from the Securities and Exchange Commission, it was SEC Chairman Casey who met with Vesco's representative two hours after the donation was delivered to Nixon's representative. Vesco, you may recall, was charged with looting two hundred and twenty-four million dollars from four mutual funds. What we're talking about is big-time stuff. Then we have the fact that Casey refused to put his holdings in a blind trust as his predecessors—including Bush—had done when they took over the CIA. Casey also is one of six persons with broadest access to secret government data on international economic developments and has played the stock market with notable success. All of that is in addition to other shady deals with which he has been charged. Only a few weeks after the assassination attempt a federal district judge in Manhattan ruled that Casey and other directors of a firm had knowingly misled potential investors by failing to inform them that about sixty-eight percent of the money being raised was to repay loans to the company officers and directors. Then just last month we had the investigation of Casey on the charge of failing to register as a foreign agent while he was a private lawyer serving the Indonesian government. He was helping find out how the Indonesian government could change its laws so that—here we go again—American oil companies that buy Indonesian oil could regain the lucrative credits the IRS had revoked in 1975. He met with top officials of the Treasury Department and IRS several times, but we can all be sure that Reagan's longtime friend, Attorney General William French Smith, will find some technical loophole for Reagan's campaign manager to crawl through. Casey also failed to list all his business holdings and legal clients in the disclosure documents required by law."

"Big Oil is big trouble," Deborah said.

"Now we come to the Max Hugel affair. He's a New Hampshire sewing-machine importer and a protégé of the late William Loeb, one of the four or five worst newspaper publishers of our time and a strong Reagan supporter. To the astonishment of almost everyone, including Barry Goldwater, Hugel was appointed by Casey to head the CIA's clandestine services. Unbelievable as it may sound, Hugel was to be in charge of our nation's covert operations. He resigned quickly, however, when the *Washington Post* reported that he once had slipped inside information about a firm he headed to two Wall Street brokers so that his company stock would go up. Now a funny thing happened on the way to the 1980 New Hampshire Republican primary. Loeb wrote in his *Manchester Union Leader* that the victory of George Bush over Reagan in the Iowa caucuses had all the smell of a CIA covert operation. Those were the exact words—had all the smell of a CIA covert operation. There are those in the CIA or now semi-retired from the CIA who would very much like to have George Bush as president of the United States. But that was not to be, and it was Reagan's campaign manager who was appointed director of the agency. Obviously, that has not set well with Bush supporters in or now out of the CIA. I think it's safe to say that there is an internal split of monumental proportions in the agency, and one that will have to be resolved shortly. My outstanding source in this area suggests that barring unforeseen events the deputy director will soon resign. Keep tuned to the evening news and read all about it in the *Placer Tribune*."

"I don't think Barry Goldwater was ever angrier than he was over the Hugel affair," Arianne said. "He put a lot of pressure on Casey to resign."

"Right," Jonathan continued. "Things looked very dark for Casey. But he pulled out of it—such things are endlessly arranged in the District of Columbia—and he survives. That cat has used up several of his nine lives. What I'm trying to suggest in my clumsy way is that these men are not what could be termed, even with utmost generosity, a law-abiding, highly ethical, scrupulously honest bunch."

"Which may be exactly what we need to fight those communists, terrorists and murderers on the other side," Elaine Bitterman said.

"That point of view is held by others and it has merit," Jonathan replied. "Not much merit, Elaine, but merit. I don't happen to agree with it. I think if we have something good to give to other countries—like democracy—you don't have to sell it. You just put it outside the door at night, as Dick Gregory used to say, and they'll come and steal it. What's happened is the politicalization of the CIA, especially since Nixon's appointment of Bush as director. But let me make another point: Reagan had put the CIA on a collision course with the FBI. When the word got out that he intended to give the CIA authority to infiltrate and influence domestic groups and organizations for the first time in its history, the FBI had to try to protect its turf. That kind of work had been limited to the FBI. Reagan was playing the hardest of hardball. The Senate Intelligence Committee couldn't get him to give them the time of day when they voiced their extensive concerns about this horrendous step toward an American Gestapo or KGB-type of intelligence service. Which brings me, finally, to the most pressing reason of all to include the intelligence and law enforcement agencies in this scenario: If there was a conspiracy of any kind behind Hinckley, they among them know it, and they among them are covering it up, and they among them are keeping it from the citizens of the land of the free and the home of the brave—I thank you for your attention."

Donald Bitterman exploded. "Holy Toledo!" he said as he stood up and looked around. "How could something like that be covered up? What are you on—opium? That's got to be the craziest pipe dream I've ever heard. If that's the best you can do, I'll stick with the Jodie Foster scenario."

"Relax, Westbrook," Weenie Toole said. "Sit down and enjoy the show. It isn't often you get a performance like this."

"Thank you again, Clarence," Jonathan said as the managing editor sat down. "Out of deference to some in the audience I will make the rest short and sweet. Or bittersweet, if you prefer. Scenario Number Eight is the Hinckley Conspiracy. After all, he wrote to that effect in papers seized in his cell last July—that he was part of a conspiracy—but the good judge in charge of his case and a majority of the good judges above him are making sure that the evidence is sealed forever. That way we'll never know, will we? So be it."

"Hinckley's crazy," Elaine Bitterman said.

"If we grant that, Elaine," Jonathan responded, "what does that make AP and UPI and *Time* and *Newsweek* and all those other publications that devote pages to the wacky opinions of the *meshuggener?*"

"I don't know what that means," she protested.

"It means crazy, Elaine. Crazy as in this entire crazy case."

"Well, he is," Mrs. Bitterman insisted.

"Only when it suits his purposes—or those of his lawyers," said Weenie Toole.

"I just don't put much stock in assassination conspiracies no matter what you say, Jonathan. Not here in the United States."

"You and the *New York Times*, Elaine," Jonathan said.

"You're in good company. However, Spiro Agnew, one of your favorites until he got caught with his hand in the White House cookie jar, says when he was vice president of the United States he received a veiled death threat from Alexander Haig. Agnew said it scared hell out of him. Why do you think he called his book *Go Quietly...Or Else?*"

"Please, let us put an end to this bickering," Weenie Toole said.

"An excellent suggestion," Donald Bitterman said. "What's the ninth symphony?"

"How appropriate that you chose to word the question that way, Donald—another example of synchronicity for our collection," Jonathan replied. "The Ninth Scenario is unfinished. An unfinished symphony, to use your word, Donald. It's a melody we haven't yet heard; it's a song we'd sing if only we could get to all the sealed evidence; it's a tune that keeps going in and out of one's mind, a lost chord that perhaps one day we'll hear again. It's a scenario beyond our ken, so dank and dark and sable that perhaps we ought to leave the dragon in its den. I want no part of it."

Arianne spoke quietly: "You may think Jonathan is putting you on, but I assure you he isn't. He's deadly serious. One of the reasons he holds off publishing his article is that it might provide the key to a door that is best left locked. That's all I can say."...

...Robert Robinson realized that he was staring at the editorial headline he had punched into the VDT minutes earlier. Well, he would get on with it. The voice of the *Placer Tribune*—muted, indistinct (and often irrelevant) as it might be—must arouse the rabble daily. The commandment was writ large in stone, discovered and brought down by some journalistic explorer in the nineteenth century who had climbed the mountain, because it was there, in days when journalists still climbed mountains.

He would write about how President Reagan was correct to pull back on synfuel production, how he should treat the nuclear power industry with the same kind of benign neglect, and how wrong it was to starve research and development money for solar energy, conservation, small hydropower and other technologies which, together, could provide America with a wide assortment of weapons for beating all threatened energy crises.

"Jonathan," Elaine Bitterman had said last night as they put on their coats to go into Montana's February night, moon glistening on snow, "I honestly think that you are making something very complicated that actually is quite simple."

"Yes, simple," Robinson said quietly to himself. And then he thought that everything is simple once all the answers are known to all the apposite questions, and all the reasons for all the actions are clear, and all the locks on all the hearts of mankind are turned with the right keys at the right moment. Then, certainly, is everything simple.

MARCH

The CIA is not now nor has it ever been a central intelligence agency. It is the covert action arm of the President's foreign policy advisers. In that capacity it overthrows or supports foreign governments while reporting "intelligence" justifying those activities. It shapes its intelligence, even in such critical areas as Soviet nuclear weapon capability, to support presidential policy. Disinformation is a large part of its covert action responsibility, and the American people are the primary target audience of its lies.

> — *Ralph W. McGehee*
> *Deadly Deceits: My*
> *25 Years in the CIA*
> *1983*

The sun rose orange over the Atlantic. First came the color, then the tip above the horizon. Anton Wojtas propped the pillows behind him and cradled the sleepy Juanita with his right arm. Then half the ball, now red-orange, was visible over the horizon. They watched silently as the minutes passed, a ritual they both had come to cherish when either of them awoke near sunrise. Then the circle was above the water and shone full for another day on Fuerteventura.

"This is a special day," Juanita said.

"Every day that you are with me is special, *querida.*" Wojtas spoke in tones that he had never used before.

"No, Anton," she said. "Today is very special. You are well again and in a few days I will be well. It is a sign. Today is the Equinox."

"The Equinox." He repeated her words as if the significance escaped him, as if he were asking a question.

"Yes, the Spring Equinox. We primitive people care about such things that you civilized people pay no attention to."

"I caught the way you said *civilized,*" he said. "Okay, what do we do that's different today?"

"For one thing, we pay respect to nature. We observe the fact that this is a special day. We consider that there is an order to the universe and that there truly is a new order in our lives."

"Okay," he said. "We'll make today a special day."

Her words struck him as an intriguing coincidence, for a peculiar lack of order had overtaken his life since his return to his island home which, he confessed to himself, more accurately was his island hideout. It wasn't that his life had taken an uncomfortable turn for the worse, the usual reason among mortals for increased introspection. Far from it. In all the important ways he was happier now than he had been in many years. And he was far from certain why he had been so surprised to find himself jolted into a wrenching examination of the life he had chosen so unreservedly decades ago. It was a combination—a synergistic catalyst—of several gnawing uncertainties that had festered within him in the months since October, even before Luis, his Mercedes-Benz beside him, had warmly greeted him at the airport. It had begun, he realized, when he was sitting by the window on the sixth floor of the Cairo Hilton, overlooking the Nile, and had been overwhelmed with the realization of the number of generations who had made their way through the years of recorded history. Somehow that had led him to reflect on what he had done and was doing with his brief span on earth. Then, with Luis in the taxi heading south, taking him to the far end of the island that now had become for him the far end of the earth, he stared moodily at the few houses along the way where some kind of cactus was being cultivated—"for the camels to drink," Luis had once told him, laughing—and wondered why he had picked this place to live. When Luis stopped at a *taberna* it was a pack of Winstons he came out with; Avis had been at the airport and Coca-Cola was in the bars. America is everywhere; America precedes you and follows you wherever you go. Here he was going to the end of the earth, where he felt safe, where his friend in Rabat who understood such matters had told him three years earlier he would be safe. "Morro de Jable," his friend said. "I'll spell it for you." He had written it down and "for sure," as his friend, like Sadat, said all the time, he had felt safe here.

But what he had once regarded as the perfection of this chosen isle for his purposes and for his home had, with a suddenness that had startled him, become considerably less than perfect. Yet the only changes around him had been for the better. His puzzlement lessened when he realized that in his ruthless pursuit of a fixed goal over the years he had denied himself a sense of irony that now seized him and unsettled him and—he caught the irony of the word—destabilized him. So much had happened so quickly in what had been a placid paradise that he still was in the process of sorting the broken pieces and putting together those he wanted to keep in his life.

With Sebastian out of his life and Juanita in it, the thorn was gone and the rose was his. Juanita had taken excellent care of his house during his absence. She had swept it and scrubbed it cleaner than it had been since he rented it three years earlier, when he gladly volunteered to pay several thousand extra pesetas a month to the grateful landlord so that he could assure himself of tenancy for as long as he wished. She had fresh flowers on the kitchen table, fresh fruit atop the refrigerator, fresh sheets on the bed she shared with him on the night of his return and every night since. She had decided that she liked this American, that he needed a woman and that she was to be his woman. He did not resist, nor did he ever find reason to regret her part in his life in their time together. It was he who had insisted after a time that she quit her job at the hotel and move in with him. He did it in full knowledge of the fact that the invitation, of necessity, included her young brother. That, too, had made a difference of considerable consequence in the life of Anton Wojtas, twice married, twice divorced, twice a father of children who long ago had turned their backs on him.

The boy, fatherless, idolized him. His inclusion in the household, at the outset an obligation, became quickly a blessing. The three of them were seen often on the beach or working in the garden that had been planted behind the house or, with Luis as a fourth, at the cinema or in one of the restaurants not yet overrun by tourists. Then Anton Wojtas paid the fare and the fee of a physician recommended by the cultural affairs officer at the American embassy in Madrid. The examination of the boy's right leg and the prescribed treatment in the following weeks had remarkably increased the young fellow's mobility. He still limped, but no longer so badly. The gratitude of both Juanita and the child blossomed into an unreservedly expressed love which, to the astonishment of Anton Wojtas, he found himself unreservedly returning. He recalled that it was Dostoevsky, one of a select few Russians, living or dead, that he admired, who had said that hell is the suffering of being unable to love. In years past he had pondered the validity of that observation, but now he was freely admitting to himself that the other side of the coin certainly was true in his case. In loving, *in being loving,* there was more joy than he had ever known.

"Simon," Juanita had said, "was named for Bolivar. Our father taught us that Simon Bolivar was the greatest leader in the struggle to liberate South America from Spain. He hoped that some day Simon would help to liberate the Canaries from Franco."

That had been the opening shot of what developed into an all-out attack on the foundation of beliefs that had sustained Anton Wojtas through the long years of service to his country, to his principles, and to his desires. The salvos that followed were devastating. He would retreat, gather his forces for a counter-attack, only to be shelled into submission once again. His own artillery, he discovered, most often exploded harmlessly off-target, while Juanita's interdictory fire made a shambles of the supply lines that had served him so well for so long.

"Was Franco that bad?" He had never challenged the hypothesis he had received, that Francisco Franco's dictatorship, emerging from one of the most brutal and bloody civil wars of this century, was also a triumph for the interests of the people of the United States of America.

"Anton, Anton," she said almost sadly. "You are an innocent. You are an innocent among innocents. You are like most Americans, innocents who were led into Vietnam and now are being led into a more terrible war, lambs to a slaughter. You are a good man, Anton, a strong man, a proud man. But you are still innocent."

Thus began the tale of living under the iron fist of Franco. Parts of the story stretched for hours, now and then over many days. Much of the history he knew well, but it sounded different as it came from her. It is one thing to "know" that Franco's armies had overthrown a freely and honestly elected democratic government chosen by a majority of the people of Spain; it was another matter to *understand* that stark fact. He had "known" of the decisive support of Franco in the civil war by the Catholic church that he long ago had abandoned; now he *understood* the transformation—still resisted, of course, but a transformation nonetheless—of the Catholic church that she cherished. Of course he "knew" that Franco came to power with the support of Hitler and Mussolini and continued to support the enemies of the United States during the Second World War; now he was beginning to *understand* that no fascist can ever be regarded as an ally of his beloved country. Most of all, he came to understand what he had made no effort to comprehend in years past: that Franco had wounded, perhaps mortally, the Spanish spirit.

"That's what I can never forgive him for," Juanita said. "He made the Spanish people an unhappy people. Even here on the Canary Islands. Almost half a century under that bastard, that monster. And he so destroyed the spirit of the people that we had to wait for him to die before we could begin to breathe again. The Portuguese rose up and drove out their monster, but we waited for ours to die. And we thought he would never die. Do you remember how he hung on? He was obscene even in his death. When the announcement finally came, my friends and I closed the curtains and drank to his death. Can you believe that? Our priest was there, too. He wouldn't raise his glass to that toast and he would not drink to that toast, but he was there and he drank with us. I will never forget that."

Another time: "The truth you avoid, Anton, is that the new America is nothing like the America that was loved and admired all over the world. The Statue of Liberty was the symbol of freedom. Now your symbols are the soldier and the adviser"—the word sank with sarcasm—"and the helicopter and the bomb. The truth is that your country has become the very thing it was founded to oppose."

A few days later: "I can't believe what goes on in your country. Your generals and your politicians sit around and talk about how they can win in El Salvador. That's not the question they should be debating. The question is what right does the United States have to kill people in El Salvador?" Her voice took on a sharper edge. "As a matter of fact, what right does the United States have to tell people anywhere how they should live? When did God appoint your generals as His guardian angels? I wonder when your government will understand what those Maryknoll Fathers were saying in Guatemala—that they were helping the Indians against the junta not because they had read either Marx or Lenin, but because they had read the New Testament."

The next morning, as she read a newspaper published in Madrid: "Here's another one of your politicians who says he doesn't care what foreigners think of the United States. It never seems to enter their heads that every time they talk about another country it's the Americans who are foreigners. I used to see that kind of tourist all the time in Las Palmas. The *norteamericanos* who got mad at the waitress who couldn't speak English. Or wouldn't speak English."

"I thought you liked Americans."

"Oh, I do," she answered quickly. "The Americans I meet are almost always good people. Especially your young people. But what your government does is wicked. I can't understand why the American people let their government do the things they do in other countries."

"Hey, Juanita, come on. It's the freest country in the world. What are you talking about?"

"Sure, free for you. Not free for me. What I'm talking about is your foreign policy. It's all wrong. Do you know what it's like living in a country that's run by Francisco Franco? Do you know what it's like, with his soldiers and his police and his torturers? What do you think made it possible for Franco to stay in power all those years? It's the Americans—no, no—it's the American government. If the American government had stopped giving Franco all that money he wouldn't have lasted a year. He was the most hated man in the world on these islands."

"I think you give the American government too much credit—or too much blame."

Her eyes flashed. "Oh, do I? Anton, let me tell you...."

And tell him she did. He listened while she told him of her father, a school teacher with a fiercely independent spirit who knew more about the history of the United States than most citizens of the United States. Of her two brothers—one older, one younger—who inherited from their father, as did she, their passion for liberty. Of her boyfriend, sought by Franco's secret police after leaflets had been dropped from a highway bridge into the army camp below, calling on the soldiers to revolt against the Franco dictatorship. Not once, but many times, that young man had returned to drop the incendiary broadsides to the assembly ground below. But one time too many; he had been identified and had gone into hiding. He went for a time to Barcelona, but he missed the Gran Canaria and Juanita and thought he could come back safely. He was wrong, as they knew instantly when they returned from a movie and walked into her family's apartment on a warm night in Las Palmas seven years ago. They saw sitting there her father and two brothers—which they expected—and three armed men—which they had not. Her friend turned toward the door that had been slammed shut behind them. The police started shooting immediately, killing her friend and wounding her. Her younger brother rushed at one of the officers who picked him up and hurled him against the wall. He had been crippled ever since. They took her to the police headquarters, stripped her naked, applied electric shocks to her body and beat her until she lost consciousness.

"They wanted the names of our friends. I never told them. When I finally got back to the apartment my father and my older brother were gone. They had been taken to a prison. They're dead. I know they're dead. And what had they done? All they wanted was to be free. The police said we were Communists. None of us were Communists. We're Catholics and we want nothing to do with Communists. So I took my little brother and we came here. To get away from all that, if they'll let us."

Then she said it:

"What I suffered, what my family suffered, was the doing of the American government."

He did not speak. He waited, his eyes asking the question.

"We checked on the policemen." The fire was gone from her voice. "They had been trained on Tenerife by some of your American experts on secret police training. They learned all the newest tricks. That must have included how to throw a little boy against the wall and how to apply electric shocks to the genitals. I screamed, Anton, I screamed. I heard others screaming."

Over the weeks, Juanita fought a war of attrition.

"You do not tell me what you do and I do not ask you. I accept that. But I know this much, Anton—you hate the work you're doing. You did not hate it when I first met you, but now you have come to hate it. Is that right?"

He would not answer. He would turn his back to her and gaze for minutes in silence at the ocean, as if the waves held an answer for him—and thus for her. She would persist.

"Anton, I want you to be happy. We were so happy these last months, before you changed. I don't know what it is. Is it me?"

He would shake his head, silently hold her in his arms.

"If it is not me, then it is your work. Then you must stop your work."

He would shake his head violently at this, and walk away.

"What is so hard, Anton? We need little to live here. Is it that you no longer wish to live here?"

Finally he would answer, softly. "Juanita, stop asking questions. I have a problem. I'll work it out." This time he took her hand and together they walked the beach of Jandia.

After dinner, as they sat on the beach on the way home, a star shot across the sky and disappeared. Anton Wojtas thought of the blessed cord of gravitation whose pull held together those heavenly bodies in the same way that the events of his life had been held together by the powerful cord of logic. Now that logic was askew, the cord had snapped, and he felt himself hurtling into a new and unexplored plane.

What he had come to know, and could not bring himself to tell her, was that he had learned there was a limit to that which he had believed was limitless. A man can call up only so much fortitude. Every time he had summoned up his courage it had meant one less time he could call on that reserve. It was not, as he had thought, a commodity that comes in an endless stream; there is just so much of it—the amount varying in every human being—but once it goes it is gone. Then—of this he was not yet certain, of this he still thought much during the day and often during a sleepless night—one could go to pieces. And that, for Anton Wojtas, was a condition he could not bring himself to face.

He subjected his life to re-examination. After his experience in British Guiana—in which one of the more important lessons he learned the hard way is that the American ambassador doesn't really want to know about covert operations—he spent two years on special assignment with an American magazine. That was followed by six months at a World War II naval training base in Virginia. There on "The Farm," as it was known, he learned the finer points of clandestine operations and the more arcane techniques of paramilitary and quasimilitary undertakings. He was given a code name and was assigned to WH—the Western Hemisphere—not generally regarded as a plum. He found himself surrounded by a number of former FBI personnel who had been brought into the CIA when the agency took over Latin American operations from the FBI after the end of the Second World War. He also concluded that he did not rate a more choice assignment because of his ethnic and academic background; the smooth and polished graduates of the Ivy League drew, it seemed to him, the more interesting capitals of the world to start their move up the ladder. Nonetheless, he worked hard and effectively.

At his second post he provided a heavy-drinking newspaper columnist with a weekly column that required little more than the addition of the journalist's famous byline. He was a major contributor to the organization of a disruptive demonstration when the new Soviet ambassador reported for duty. He arranged for a fabricated and extremely incriminating document to be planted in the suitcase of a local labor union organizer returning from Cuba. During the remainder of his two-year tour of duty in that country, he did not see the organizer again.

Now that he looked back on those early years of service, largely in Central and South America, he had to admit there was little of the heroic in them. He enjoyed master-minding some of the extremely successful propaganda campaigns, entertaining and paying off bureaucrats and politicians, provoking dissension within groups trying to reform the government or overthrow a dictator. He admitted to a bizarre pleasure when tapping telephones. Best of all, of course, was his contribution to the capture and slaying of Che Guevara. His ascendancy in the agency was then assured. With the exception of a lethargic term in Bangkok—"to civilize him," another case officer confided—he was on special clandestine assignments.

During this entire period only one aspect of his job had caused him concern. Some of the station officers, less dedicated than he to the proposition that all else was secondary to the international struggle against the Soviet Union, relieved themselves of derogatory observations about company policies and often openly hooted at official explanations that emanated from the State Department. On one occasion a forgery prepared in another Latin American country was so incompetent that its many deficiencies were widely reported in the American press, but he noted that the author was promptly dispatched without reprimand to another station where his cruder talents were subsequently employed with desired effect. He learned, of necessity, to accept the incompetence of some agents who were only a shade this side of stupid. Well, he concluded, it takes all kinds.

Then three years ago, caught in one of the periodic maelstroms of internal agency politics, he opted to join in perhaps the most sophisticated and hazardous undertaking in the history of western intelligence. They crossed over to an operational realm that the KGB long ago had made a part of its standard procedure. The demands of these last three years, and the entirely different demands that Juanita placed on him since his return from his assignment in October, had taken their toll. It was in this time of muddled uncertainty that he had received notification that Luis and his Mercedes would be required once again at the airport.

He had taken an instant dislike to the visitor. "Beware the ides of March" had raced across his consciousness when he noted the scheduled arrival date and hardly a minute had passed after the man clambered out of the Mercedes, Luis already uncharacteristically silent and grim, before Anton Wojtas felt like punching the fat face. He recognized the visitor instantly as an agent who had been borrowed from the Army Special Forces—a process known as "sheep-dipping"—nine years earlier. The dolt had committed one of the more embarrassing intelligence blunders of recent years, resulting in the death of an innocent Moroccan in Norway who had been mistaken for Abu Hassan, the charismatic head of Yasir Arafat's intelligence unit, Squad 17. The Palestinian, regarded as the mastermind behind a series of successful assassinations, unsuccessful assassination attempts, media-mesmerizing hijackings, deadly car-bombings and the most spectacular terrorist achievement of all—the seizure and slaying of nine Israeli athletes at the 1972 Summer Olympics in Munich—ultimately met death in Beirut in 1979 when his automobile passed a booby-trapped Volkswagen. Wojtas had seen some of the Mossad reports on his visitor after the 1973 debacle in Norway, and he did not blame the Israeli intelligence agency for its anger or its conclusions. Yet here was the fat-ass on this day in 1982.

The visitor seemed amused at his surroundings and had almost laughed as he said "Nice place you have here." As they walked on the beach he listed some of the deficiencies of Luis as an airport greeter and then he turned the conversation to Juanita.

"That's some gorgeous *chica* you have there," the visitor said. "I take it she does more than clean house for you, right? Couldn't help but notice her condition. If she kicked her shoes off she'd be the way our daddies told us we should keep them." He laughed loudly.

Wojtas didn't laugh. "You don't approve?"

"Hell, it's not a matter of approving or disapproving of the *chica*. I'm just not too fond of women in general. Especially in our business." He looked at Wojtas and grinned. "But don't get me wrong—I'm no fairy. It's not that I can't love the ladies, I'm just not fond of them. Like the man says, put a sack over their heads and turn them upside down and they're all the same. I don't have much respect for their minds, but that doesn't keep me from admiring other portions of their anatomies."

"It seems to bother you that she's a Spaniard." Wojtas didn't like anything that was being said, but he especially didn't appreciate the way the visitor twice had pronounced *chica*.

"Well, to be frank with you, it's the kind of Spaniard she is that I don't like. I saw the poop sheet on her. She has a lousy background, and you know that as well as I do."

Anger welled higher in Wojtas. "She doesn't know anything," he said.

"She'd better not."

He stopped at the water's edge, literally and figuratively. He wanted to go no farther with this visitor. He asked him for the latest intelligence and for his assignment. He was perplexed by both.

Obviously, the official for-his-eyes-only reports he was receiving periodically were no longer telling him what he needed to know. More accurately, what he ought to know, what he had to know. What the fat dolt had told him did not fit with his understanding of the situation. He had been on a "media fast," suggested by Juanita—a vacation from newspapers, magazines and radio. The stereo had become his source of information as Juanita ordered records by the half-dozens from a mail-order house in New York. As he watched the waves breaking on the beach, he resolved to subscribe to the *International Herald Tribune* and to request the issues published in the preceding six months.

The assignment suggested by the visitor was even more perplexing.

"No," he said. "Not Mulcahy."

The visitor looked at him quizzically. "Is that what you want me to tell them?"

"That's right. Jesus, what are we coming to?"

"What we're coming to is the nitty-gritty. If you can't stand the heat, get out of the kitchen. If you're in some sort of mid-life crisis, I can tell them that, too."

"No, I'll tell you what to tell them." It irritated him almost beyond endurance to take this kind of crap from a proven, documented incompetent. "You tell them to talk to the admiral. He knows exactly how I feel. You tell them they can go ahead on this, but not with me. Mulcahy is out of bounds for me. Tell them I'll be right here if they want me to take on something else. But tell them I'm available only until the middle of the summer. Through July. Is that clear?" Anger welled again. "Is that goddamn clear?"

The visitor smiled.

"Nothing could be clearer," he said.

"Let's go back."

Wojtas did not invite the man to stay. When they reached his house he called to Luis, who returned the visitor to the airport although his plane was not scheduled to leave for seven hours.

Juanita was washing dishes when he walked through the door of their home. The record on the turntable was his favorite. She had told him that he was "Ulysses," and on this day the words on the record meant even more to him. He was looking out the window at the ocean, his back to her, when he heard her come into the room.

"I'm thinking of retiring," he said.

Silence.

"That's what I told him."

Silence.

"He agreed to pass the word."

Silence.

Wojtas turned around and saw her staring at him. He knew what she was waiting for.

"Just one—maybe two more times. Then I'm finished. We can go where we want. I won't leave you any more after that."

Tears welled in her eyes and she shook her head.

"No, Anton, that's what you say now—one or two more times. Then you'll say another time. No, Anton, you should do it now. No more times." The well of tears flowed as he came forward and took her in his arms.

"You have to understand, Juanita. Listen. You have to understand. One or two more times and that's all. He agreed to tell them that. Do you hear me? He agreed."

He waited for her sobs to subside. His eyes, he knew, would have to tell her. He put his hands on her head and lifted her face.

"All right, Anton. I understand," she said. She kissed him, salty from her tears, and they clasped hands and walked out to the beach.

The awesome truth, naked and unblushing, that with Juanita's insistent help he had finally forced himself to face, stood confirmed by the words of his visitor and the nature of his declined assignment. The distance between his youthful idealism and his subsequent acts had gradually grown larger. The gap between what he now believed and what he practiced had become intolerable. The enemy, masters of deceit as they had been called by a man he once revered, ultimately were neither better nor worse at the art and science of deception than he and his colleagues. What the dedicated minions of the enemy sought to impose could not possibly be worse than what was being done by the thugs who ran the oppressive juntas he had helped to bring into being or sustain in power.

He held Juanita's hand as they silently walked along the deserted beach in the wind that swept large waves toward them. He thought of the suggestion of his visitor that perhaps he was suffering a "mid-life crisis." That had to be pure baloney; guys who have lived much of their lives in a state of crisis of one kind or another don't have a mid-life crisis. He dismissed the fathead's notion. But there was another notion that took its place: Was he truly in love? That was a possibility he could not so easily dismiss. Juanita was unquestionably the most knowledgeable, the toughest and yet the most loving woman he had ever known. He never experienced an uncomfortable moment in her presence and she responded warmly to his embraces whenever or wherever. She spoke English with only a few limitations that were rapidly diminishing, and he treasured the way she moaned her endearments in both Spanish and English when they coupled, especially when they lay on a blanket behind a sand dune under the blackest skies he had ever seen—black velvet studded with stars. Here was a remarkable woman who had come with her little brother from the Gran Canaria, with its poinsettia trees, bushes of geraniums and exotic plants, to this volcanic island, gray and black and seldom green—a few cacti and fewer palms—with soil that turns red as one goes south from Rosario, then blends into dunes covered with patches of spiky grass and the soft sand of the long beaches that stretch to Morro Jable. And she had come from a place where there were many Americans, tourists and transients mostly, to a spare place where there were few Americans but many jobs at the new hotels financed by foreign corporations to cater primarily to the German tourist trade. An extraordinary woman indeed. And now he heard her voice.

"You want to turn on?"

He nodded, smiling for the first time since the hour before the visitor had arrived. They turned to walk back to their house.

He remembered the first time she had asked him that question in the troubled days after he had returned from Cairo. He had pondered her question for several hours. His restlessness, the inexplicable new mood that had descended on him, goaded him toward affirmation. "It's better for you than alcohol," she added with an assuring smile, and when he thought about that contention he was forced to the brink. His way through life had been oiled with alcohol so that he could slither and slide through the difficult hours of later afternoon and early evening, like almost all the men who practiced his profession, like millions of others in all the lands of the occidental world. Still, he was apprehensive. She responded to his doubts softly, seriously, with assurance that he wouldn't have a "bad trip," that he had nothing to fear because the *keef* brought out only what already was in his head, that it was a blessing provided by nature that he too long had denied himself. He reflected on the proposition, said yes to her, and that, he was convinced, made all the difference.

Now she was with him again in the living room of their home. She reached for a jar that was disguised as an orange candle—itself a gift she had made for him—and turned the lid. She extracted a bud and loosened it with thumb and forefinger. Only a few leaves were required for the thin paper that she rolled into what he had come to call, wryly and appreciatively, a "needle joint" because of its appearance and effect. Then she lit three joss sticks of flowery scent and slowly flicked through their collection of stereo records. He was aware that the records were the only additions to his rooms that he had provided; all else that had transformed his house into a place of color and scent and sound and beauty had been brought there by her. In the English she had learned in Las Palmas, she "laid" the gifts on him. "To lay" equalled "to fuck" in the world he knew so well; "to lay" meant most often "to give" in the world she had entered and was opening for him. He was conscious of the fact that he was smiling.

"You like?"

"I like very much," he answered.

As she had done so often in the days since his return, she selected and then stacked three records on the turntable. He had cautioned her, as he had heard through the years, that stacking the records "ruined" them, "warped" them, "wrecked" them, but she would have none of it. That, she responded, was a myth propagated by the fluttering aesthetes of the world (the words were his; she had acted them out). Let them, she added, jump up to change or turn the record after every spinning; she preferred (and he, too) the phallic attachments that allowed them to have music interrupted only by the machine's whir and click and plop of another record. Three records had she selected, and on the top, the last to fall, was the one he liked best.

He lay back on the pile of pillows she had made and stacked in one corner of the room—"canary yellow," she had said, "in honor of the place where I found you"—and lit the joint. He sucked in the smoke along with cooling layers of air between his parted lips, as she had taught him, and swallowed it as if he were drinking water. "It's not like smoking cigarettes," she had said. "You take it here," patting his stomach, "not in your lungs." Then: "As close as possible to here," patting his cock. He handed the joint to her and when he exhaled, finally, no smoke escaped. Thrice more they repeated the extraction. He had barely put the roach in an ash tray before the music swelled and enveloped him in a wave that lifted him and carried his body out of the house high above the clear blue water of the beach at Jandia. Minutes passed and he was on the beach as another wave crashed over him and amid the swirl of sand and salt lofted him once again and pulled him shoreward until he rested in no more than a foot of water. The waves undulated and broke over him with a gentle sigh of silken spray. As he lay there, the water receded and he looked full into the sun that burned in a cloudless sky. Burned—and then exploded. Silver flashes of electric pressure, a long, loud rumble that pounded in time to the music, a gathering from within a volcano, a surge, a thrust upward, an eruption, a hot fiery molten river pouring forth from the cone, a coming, a climax, a stream of lava rolling down the slopes, running toward the sea, lava, lava, lava—

"I love you, I love you, I love you." Her voice came from the clefts of the canary yellow pillows. "*Te quiero, te quiero, te quiero.*" And Anton Wojtas said the same words to her. . . .

Cataclysmic. That was the word that came to him a few minutes later as he fell away from her. Not just today, not just now, but what had happened to him and was continuing to happen to him in the weeks since she had been with him. Juanita, Juanita—she of the long legs that made her as tall as he, the hands with tapering fingers that set him aglow, the lovely high breasts, the cascading black hair, the round beautiful face—Juanita, Juanita. He whispered the words of love again to her.

It was three days later, in the afternoon, when Anton Wojtas felt the first dull ache in his arms and shoulders. Then he began to sweat. He shivered and vomited. Juanita took his temperature and helped him to bed. Two hours later she made him get out of bed so she could change the sheets soaked with his sweat. She told him not to worry.

"Dengue," she said. "Dengue fever. It will pass. It will leave you weak for a time, but you will be all right."

She sent Simon to summon Luis and go to Puerto del Rosario for medicine. They returned in the dark and she administered the dosage with a cup of tea. She sat next to the bed and placed cold cloths on his forehead, replacing them when they were warmed by his brow. He reached out to touch her, to thank her, to show how much he loved her. He closed his eyes and she was gone.

The apparition was there. It taunted him, sneered at him. It asked him the question again and again. *Where had it gone wrong?* It demanded that he no longer evade the question. The apparition became a beast—stark, defiant, roaring. It tortured him and he tortured himself. He wanted the question to go away, unanswered, unsatisfied. But it would not. The agony grew as the time passed. The thought came again and again that the agony would never go away, that he would always be like this in an unending hell. When he thought he could stand the agony no longer he begged the beast to let him go. The beast, yellow liquid flowing from the pustules that covered its body, said nothing. All right! All right!—he screamed the words—I'll answer the question. The beast subsided and the apparition, silver and blue, reappeared. *It had gone wrong,* he said, *when he had accepted the most uncomplicated of political deceits: The end justifies the means.* This was the failure for which he now blamed himself, now tortured himself. If he had been strong—as he had always thought himself to be—he could have survived infinitely more than the petty trials of conscience through which he was passing.

Peace came to him. Then the furies silently assembled. He knew they were there, at the foot of his bed. He did not need to open his eyes, for he could see them clearly. Slowly, gleefully, they began to taunt and tantalize him. Then they began to wrap him in bonds. But I gave him the answer, he said. Go away. They laughed and shrieked uncontrollably. They delighted in an eerie, fantastic, orgiastic dance, and he could feel the bonds drawing tighter. Suddenly, in a panic, he realized that he was bound so tightly that he could not move. He pleaded with the furies to let him go; had he not been tortured enough? Then they became quiet, and they spoke to him in reasonable tones. They wanted no misunderstanding at this point, they assured him. He must know what his choices were, and he must abide by his decision.

We will cut you free on one condition, they said. You must promise only that you will settle for the weakness you have chosen, without regret, without remorse, without questioning, without bitterness. He shook his head violently. Give up everything to which he had devoted the whole of his life? No! He had never settled for anything less than victory and he would not start settling for less now. No!

All right, they said softly, that is one choice. Then we offer to cut you free on another condition. You must promise to continue what you have been doing, without regret, without remorse, without questioning, without bitterness—and without guilt. But we warn you that if you ever fail to meet this condition, we will return and bind you again, even more tightly. He shook his head slowly. I can't promise that. I'm not strong enough. No, I cannot accept that condition either.

The furies came very close to his ear. They spoke in a whisper. We will turn our backs, they said, and you will find a knife in your hand with which to cut your own bonds. Yes! he shouted. That was the choice he wanted! But you must let us finish, they whispered. Once you have cut your own bonds you must live with whatever befalls you. They winked slyly. We want to be fair, they said. Let us assure you, they said, that the tortures you already have experienced are nothing—*nothing!*—

compared to the tortures of the damned who have cut their own bonds and then have been sorry. Do you fully understand? Give me time to think, he said. Oh, take all the time you like, they said, but in the meantime we shall keep you bound.

Finally he cried, Is there no other choice?

Yes! Yes! Yes! they shrieked. Yes! Yes! Yes! You may take the knife and instead of cutting your bonds with it—you may plunge it into your heart!

Anton Wojtas opened his eyes and saw the ceiling and felt the dampness of his pillow. He turned his head toward the door. An apparition there had taken a shape barely discernible as it stood framed in the doorway. For a few seconds it stood there, breathing deeply and swaying uncertainly, its lips silently moving, its eyes staring deeply· into his. Come in, come in, the message played its way slowly across the outer edges of his mind, come in and torment me, torture me unto death, no peace even to the grave, come in and follow me, prod me, tell me how wrong I have been, how I wronged so many, how I failed, how I never loved, how I can never hope to keep the love I have found....

"Anton." He heard. "Oh, Anton, Anton, Anton."

The apparition moved toward him. He turned his body and his arms came out from under the sheet to encircle her. She moved convulsively in his embrace, sobbing out his name over and over again, covering his face with kisses, then resting her cheek against his face. The minutes passed, the sobs ceased, the two racked bodies became still. He took her head between his hands and searched deeply into her glistening eyes for some trace of the answer to the question still numbing his mind. When all he saw in those eyes was anguish, an unspeakable reply to an unspoken question, he forced his lips to move.

"What is it, Juanita? What's happened to you?"

She was on her knees at the side of his bed and she stared silently at him. Then he could feel her pressing against him, twisting her body slowly, then pushing herself away from him. She stood unsteadily and took two heavy, difficult steps back from the bed. As he watched, she bent slightly and began lifting her dress. His eyes followed the rising hem, grew large, closed tightly for an unendurable moment, then opened fully. She held her dress with one hand at her breast, and her other hand moved slowly in an arc away from her waist until it rested at her side. A towel, dripping blood, fell to the floor. The outline of clotted, blackening blood ran down one leg. Tears welled again in her eyes and coursed down her face.

"Your fever did not break for three days. I thought I might lose you," she said. "I lost him instead."

He felt a warm rush to his head, his mouth opened involuntarily and his tongue pressed between his lips. He closed his eyes and his head moved slowly from side to side. His left hand pulled back the sheet and his arms stretched toward her.

"Juanita, *querida*, come to me."

The dress tumbled down her body as she moved toward him. He lifted her gently and drew her against him. The sweet odor of his sweat and the moist salt of her tears overwhelmed his senses of taste and smell. The tears gathered into a stream and then a pulsating cataract that swept over him and drowned all thoughts except the vast love he felt for her.

He became conscious of another stream that had in the minutes before flowed red from her body, draining into a small pool that now lay warm and moist between them. But he knew that they would come through this; they would dam the flow, the pool would dry, and they both would be well again. She was here with him, in his house, in his bed, in his arms, weeping, her tears cleansing, her warm blood sealing them together. He turned toward the window and saw the red glow left behind by the setting sun.

The next morning the sun rose orange over the Atlantic. When Luis came, they were still in bed, and he made eggs and toast and coffee for them. He had brought the mail and a box of newspapers. Anton Wojtas glanced at the return addresses on the letters, opened one and read it, and put them on the table next to his bed. Then he began to read the papers from Paris, slowly and carefully. He pieced together the news stories from country after country, noting datelines and bylines, reading between the lines. By early afternoon, when Juanita walked with him to a deck chair in the sun, he was smiling and joking with Luis.

"You feel better," she said. "I'm so happy you feel better."

"I've counted all my blessings," he said. "A letter and the

newspapers told me what I wanted to know."

"What was in them to make you feel so much better?"

He smiled again. "The answer to my problem." He raised his hand, palm toward her. "You said this is a special day, *querida*. It is. No more questions. We are celebrating the Equinox."

In the days thereafter, as both of them healed, she asked no more questions, pleased to see him regain his strength, delighted to watch him sleep through the night, ecstatic at his affectionate tenderness for her. It was, she told him, a miracle. When she was alone, she thanked God for the miracle.

But it was, he could not tell her, a miracle he thought more likely wrought by his Satan than by her God. That morning of the Equinox, in the newspapers Luis had brought, he had discovered, in a blinding flash that melded the pieces of his shattered mind, a truth that had been hidden from him in the preceding weeks of uncertainty and anxiety. The answer had come.

Four choices had the furies offered him. He had quickly rejected the first and the second. There had followed the nightmare of the penultimate decision which was to decide his ultimate fate. And now, in sunlight, he knew he had chosen rightly.

APRIL

*"If the law supposes that,"
said Mr. Bumble, . . .
"the law is a ass, a idiot."*

—Charles Dickens

AT LONG LAST, THE TRIAL....
The trial of John W. Hinckley Jr. opened on April 27, 1982, one year and 28 days after he assumed the police firing stance on the sidewalk of the Washington Hilton and pumped explosive bullets into the bodies of the president of the United States, the president's press secretary and two officers of the law.

For more than a year the evidence of the assassination attempt had remained sealed from press and public by the government and the courts; for more than a year a series of incredible "coincidences" related to the violent event remained unexplained; for more than a year legal maneuvering and delays by both the United States Department of Justice and the high-powered associates of famed criminal lawyer Edward Bennett Williams in Washington's most prestigious law firm had postponed the trial again and again and again. In addition, for much of a year the two reported "suicide attempts" by the accused remained, as the press reported, shrouded in mystery, and the contents of an admission by the defendant that he was part of a conspiracy had been sealed from the public and ruled inadmissible as evidence in the trial.

What, precisely, had happened?

In the first days after the shooting, a spokesman for the Justice Department was quoted as saying that the trial might be delayed as much as three months for psychiatric tests of the accused. The court-ordered examinations to determine the would-

be assassin's mental state, he said, had "stopped the clock" on the legal process and "supersede Hinckley's constitutional right to a speedy trial." United Press International quoted him as adding, "I would assume that the defense is not in any hurry to come to trial," a remark that the wire service did not suggest was uttered with a smile or intended to be ironic, especially in the light of subsequent delays initiated by the prosecution as well as the defense. Under normal circumstances, the grand jury would have issued an indictment within 30 days after the case had been referred to it three days after the crime was committed. Again, if standard procedures had been followed, no later than 10 days after the indictment an arraignment to charge the suspect would have been held and a trial scheduled. As we all know, nothing even close to that happened in this case.

Late in June, inexplicably at the government's request, an extension to the three-month commitment period was granted by the court, giving the medical staff at the Butner facility a fourth month to do its work. On August 1, the date allowed by the court, the psychiatric report was filed by government psychiatrists. The court immediately sealed it from public disclosure. On the same day the spokesman for the Justice Department said there were no immediate plans to move Hinckley and it was not until August 17 that he was transferred to the Quantico Marine Base. Thus Hinckley spent four-and-a-half months in an institution near Durham, North Carolina, that originally had been designed to practice experimental methods of behavior modification.

In the last week of August—almost five months after the shooting instead of the maximum of 40 days customarily allowed—the accused, having been ruled competent to stand trial, was indicted. The federal grand jury charged him with 13 counts, including attempting to kill the president and assault with intent to kill Press Secretary Brady and two law enforcement officials. He faced possible life imprisonment on several of the charges. His defense lawyers were given until September 28—another month—to decide how they would argue the case. Judge Parker, obviously in no hurry to bring the matter to trial, granted the request of Vincent J. Fuller, chief defense attorney, that the psychiatric evaluation of Hinckley be continued for yet another month. No date was set for the trial, but reporters speculated that the earliest possible date was late October.

NBC Nightly News reported that Hinckley's parents wanted to avoid a trial and were urging their son to plead guilty so that "personal problems would not be made public." Nonetheless, young Hinckley spurned his parents' wishes and pleaded not guilty in what the New York Times described as "a firm, clear voice."

On September 28, as scheduled, Hinckley's lawyers officially admitted in papers filed in U.S. District Court that their client was indeed guilty of firing the shots and then revealed the strategy they would undertake. "That these four men were shot and grievously wounded... is not in any dispute," they stated. "That the defendant held the gun and fired the shots that wounded these men is similarly not in any dispute." They said they would raise the insanity defense as the "only real issue" at his trial and asked federal prosecutors to agree to a formal stipulation that their client fired the shots. "Such an agreement," we were told, "would eliminate the need for a trial on the basic elements of the case, and leave only the question of Hinckley's mental state at the time of the shootings." The government was given until October 16 to respond to the defense filings and a hearing on the issue was scheduled for October 30 before Judge Parker who, we were informed, would preside at the trial.

An additional indication of the strategy of the defense lawyers was revealed when they also argued that the trial should be "bifurcated"—necessitating the empaneling of two separate juries—because the emotional impact of the prosecution's evidence of the shooting would be so great that a single jury would not be able to consider objectively the psychiatric testimony that would be presented in the second trial.

"Inevitably," contended the lawyers, "there will be the kind of patriotic wrath that any American must feel when the president of the United States is subjected to such a violent attack.... And, predictably, there will be a desire to make an example of John Hinckley in an effort to deter others from following in his footsteps."

(Let the record show, please, that the hired lawyers do not believe that one of the functions of the system of justice is to deter others from engaging in political assassination. Even more insulting, their words suggest that those who do thus believe are guilty of an unnatural desire. Such is the sophistry to which citizens are subjected by the high-priced mercenaries available to those who can afford to pay their price.)

On that same September 28—two days short of six months since the crime—the defense lawyers got around to asking the court to prohibit as evidence statements Hinckley had made to law enforcement officials after his arrest although the lawyers acknowledged that Hinckley had waived his right to remain silent. They also contended that statements Hinckley made during a psychiatric examination held shortly after his arrest should be excluded because he already had admitted he was competent to stand trial and objected to the examination.

After all this, the Associated Press reported that the trial now was "unlikely to begin before December."

On October 10, Judge Parker demonstrated how wrong the press can be by scheduling the trial for the last day of November. On Halloween, however, the New York Times reported in a one-inch story on page 13 that Judge Parker "was likely to agree with a request by government prosecutors to postpone the trial" until January. Sure enough, on November 14, in another one-inch story at the bottom of page 10, the New York Times reported that the trial would be postponed to January 4. The reason? The judge "felt it would be difficult to impanel a jury over the holidays."

The following day John W. Hinckley Jr. reportedly attempted to commit suicide in his cell, a story unto itself.

Jonathan looked at the mass of clippings and notes that remained in the folder. This was not an easy matter, piecing together the complex legal maneuvers—all because Hinckley was not brought speedily to trial, as was his right and, more importantly, the right of the people of the United States who still knew only the flimsiest information concerning the assassination attempt.

He plucked from another folder the section on Hinckley's two "suicide attempts" that he had written in November and tucked them under the pages he had just written. He began a new section:

THE SEALING OF THE "CONSPIRACY" EVIDENCE

Late in July, on the day after a spokesman announced that the FBI's second lengthy report to U.S. Attorney Charles F.C. Ruff had concluded that Hinckley had acted alone and that "the FBI had not found any information that this attack was a conspiracy," guards took from Hinckley's cell evidence that indicated he was indeed part of a conspiracy.

Seized were some sheets "of almost illegible handwritten notes bearing on alleged criminal activity," according to one news story. Another reported that "sources" said the notes "mentioned an apparently nonexistent assassination conspiracy." That Hinckley had written he was part of a conspiracy was confirmed by "a Justice Department source," but the FBI, after investigation, announced it had concluded "that there was no reliable evidence of any conspiracy."

On October 19, Hinckley sat silently through seven hours of courtroom testimony about "a mysterious document taken from his cell in July," according to the New York Times. *The contents were not revealed in newspaper accounts, but one guard—a Donald Meese—reportedly said that "something in the document had caused him concern about possible danger to Mr. Hinckley and to unspecified others." The chief correctional supervisor at the Butner facility testified that he had taken the papers from a large envelope in Hinckley's cell because they were "contraband." He defined contraband as "something that a prisoner should not be in possession of."*

Three Butner guards testified that the papers were found in the course of daily searches of the cell for potential weapons or evidence of suicidal tendencies—measures ordered after Hinckley's "suicide attempt" in May. Judge Parker warned the guards not to disclose the contents of the papers in open court and ordered them to give secret testimony in closed session, in the words of the New York Times *"to prevent the press and public from learning the contents of some handwritten papers" taken from Hinckley's cell July 27. Defense lawyers said the material they sought to suppress contained Hinckley's "most private (if not secret) thoughts about his legal situation," and that guards had violated the Fourth Amendment prohibition against "unreasonable searches and seizures."*

On November 17, two days after Hinckley reportedly tried to take his life for the second time, Judge Parker ruled in a 34-page opinion that the federal officials who interrogated Hinckley after his arrest had violated his constitutional rights. He also ruled that guards who had seized Hinckley's diary and what were variously described as "two to four pages of handwriting, folded in half or in thirds" had violated the Fourth Amendment rights to privacy of the prisoner (who was at the time under 24-hour surveillance by guards and television monitors). All of this evidence protested by the defense was sealed from press and public and the prosecution was told it could use none of it in the trial.

The government took until mid-December to appeal Judge Parker's ruling, claiming that statements in the hours after the shooting were "critical" to their hopes of proving Hinckley was sane when he shot the president. They argued that the evidence, even if illegally obtained, in this case should be allowed to rebut Hinckley's insanity claim. The appeal meant that the trial, scheduled for January 4, now would be postponed "for several weeks."

It took until February 23, 1982, for a three-judge panel of the U.S. Court of Appeals for the District of Columbia to rule that the handwritten notes and the oral statements obtained from Hinckley constituted "tainted evidence" that had been obtained illegally and therefore could not be used by the prosecution.

The prosecution suffered yet another blow when U.S. Attorney Ruff told Judge Parker that because of the delay in bringing the case to trial he was withdrawing from the case. He had been in charge of the case from the start.

Late in March the government asked the full 11-member Court of Appeals to reconsider the "tainted-evidence" ruling. It was at this point that the defendant's father told the **Rocky Mountain News** *that his son had been denied his rights to a speedy trial. "The Justice Department is dragging its feet," said*

John Hinckley Sr. "We've been ready since November." Scott Hinckley, who had succeeded his father as president of Vanderbilt Energy Corporation while his brother awaited trial, agreed.

On April 5 the Court of Appeals, by a vote of 7 to 4, with "no explanation" turned down the request for a full-panel review. The Justice Department announced it would not seek a Supreme Court review. Thus were the issues that had arisen in the hours after the shooting and in late July finally resolved. The government asked Judge Parker to set a trial date. Done: April 27.

THE BARGAIN COUNTER OF JUSTICE

Attention must be paid to other aspects of the strategy employed by the lawyers of the accused. In late May, less than two months after the shooting, the defense lawyers offered a guilty plea in the case if the government would recommend that Hinckley be sentenced as a juvenile under the Federal Youth Corrections Act. Under this proposed arrangement, announced by "legal sources who declined to be identified by name" and confirmed by "one Justice Department source who declined to be identified," a convicted person can be released at any time the authorities decide that the defendant's anti-social tendencies have been corrected and he or she no longer poses a threat. The law was established to govern sentencing of defendants younger than 21, but allows federal judges broad discretion in sentencing adults between the ages of 21 and 26. Unfortunately for the internationally prominent Washington criminal law firm, this was too much even for the Justice Department to stomach, especially since the lawyers had taken their own sweet time to study their client's birth certificate. Alas, they gave the government less than a week until Hinckley's 26th birthday to reply to the proffered plea bargain. To no one's surprise, nothing more was heard of this tortured ploy.

Nor has anything yet been heard of another ploy attempted by the attorneys for the defense. Last November Attorney General William French Smith rejected a second offer by the defense lawyers for a plea of guilty to specified charges. If the plea bargain had been accepted, Hinckley could have been sentenced to life in prison, making him eligible for parole after *serving 10 years. For reasons unexplained, the offer was not reported in the national news media.*

Jonathan stared at his notes. That last item was from Dan Doherty in Washington, D.C. The scene of the crime. Actually, and more accurately, the scene of the crimes. Even more accurately, the scene of some of the worst crimes being committed in the United States of America. Dan assured him of the accuracy of the information, but he said he couldn't get official confirmation and he was damned if he was going to fall into that trap of "sources who refused to be identified." Dan thinks it's about time the press of the 1980s started reporting what the reporter has good reason to believe is true and then add: "The Justice Department (or whatever) refused to comment on this item of public interest (or would not confirm the information which, under law, is supposed to be a matter of public record)." Or other devices designed to unfrock the anonymous bureaucrats, politicians, flacks and authorities who block the public from knowing what the government is doing.

The next item among his notes also was a gift from Dan Doherty. When the envelope had arrived, he had thought for a moment that it was empty, but when he slit it open and turned it upside down a clipping fluttered to the table. Written with a red felt pen was the message:

"COULD THE FIX BE IN?"

The clipping was from the *Washington Post*, page 7 of the March 6 issue, with the headline: "Law on St. Elizabeths Commitments Overturned."

Jonathan remembered that he had burst out laughing when he read it for the first time; was there no "coincidence" too strange to be brought into this case by those associated with law and justice? Now he was of a more sober mind as he read the item again. A two-to-one ruling by the United States Court of Appeals for the District of Columbia had overturned a statute providing for mandatory commitment of federal defendants to St. Elizabeths Hospital when they are found not guilty by reason of insanity. This meant that Hinckley, if he were acquitted, would be released from federal custody unless the government undertook separate proceedings for his commitment. Call in not the clowns but the Keystone Kops as we then would be provided the spectacle of Hinckley offering prosecution evidence from the trial that he had been sane while the government presented defense testimony that he had been insane.

Also of special interest to Hinckley and his lawyers and others unspecified:

"The decision yesterday may also strengthen the Hinckley defense argument that the prosecution should be required to prove that Hinckley was sane when he shot Reagan and the three others. Trial judges in the Washington federal court have had to decide whether the defense or prosecution should carry the burden of proof on a case by case basis since the law is unclear in this federal district."

How convenient for Hinckley and his lawyers. How nicely things were working out for them as the case dragged on and on....

"Mail call," Arianne said as she brought the almost-daily collection of letters, bills, appeals from organizations that promise to do well with your contribution, appeals from charities that promise to do good with your contribution, magazines seeking your subscription or pleading for renewal or threatening to send no more after the current issue, and mail-order houses of various sorts. "Three of the same brochure from Shopping Universal," she said. "What could you have bought from them?"

"Absolutely nothing," Jonathan replied. "They bought my name on three lists I'm on or something like that. Do you ever get the feeling that if the senders of junk mail paid their fair share of the postal expenses we could reduce the outlandish rates for newspapers and magazines? There was once a time when a prevailing doctrine of the Congress was to encourage or even subsidize the spread of ideas and different points of view, but now the government discourages the dissemination of information and serves as a delivery boy for the mail-order houses. Incidentally, did you know that young Hinckley once planned to go into the mail-order business?"

"Really?"

"Yeah. He applied for a business permit in Lubbock to open up a mail-order shop called 'Listalot.' Like everything else he's done, except for one thing, he failed to follow through on it."

She stared at the blue sheets next to the typewriter. "Is that what you're writing now?"

"No." He handed her the scarred first draft and went to the kitchen to brew some tea. He took down a jar labeled "Evening in Placer" and put the kettle on the burner. When he returned, with two cups of tea, she had finished reading the pages he had written. He handed her the clipping Dan Doherty had sent and silently indicated that he sought her opinion.

"I'll tell you what I think, my darling," she said after reading about the decision of the United States Court of Appeals in Washington. "I think what you should be writing is not another article about press performance. You've done that several times, Jonathan, and there's no mountain there for you to climb. What you should be writing is a novel. Look at what you have: It's an extraordinary combination of an Agatha Christie detective story and intrigue in the highest levels of government and journalism. All you need is an international spy or two and you'd be in John le Carré's backyard. And all of yours is true. You could turn it all into fictitious names and you'd have one hell of a *roman à clef.* How's that for a dust-jacket testimonial? And like most dust-jacket testimonials, provided by a very good friend."

"I'm not sure I could write a novel."

"You can write a novel. I'm certain of that. I read them all the time, as you well know. You've got something to say. Something very important to say. Something very, very important to say. Do you read me?"

"Loud and clear. I'll think about it. In the meantime, I'm stuck writing the rest of this article. I think it's interesting on its own, or will be once this insane trial ends. A novel, you say? In the parlance of another world, I'll get back to you on that at some point in time."

Arianne had come to know him well enough to let the matter drop. A few seconds passed. She moved to new ground:

"There is something, though, that bothers me about what you're doing, Jonathan. You've always stood against the press prying into people's private lives, invading their privacy, especially when the only purpose is to sell more copies. You've made it quite clear down through the years what you think of Murdoch newspapers and magazines like *People* and *Esquire* and the newsmagazines that are just as trendy, glitzy and superficial. I still remember you quoting something at Berkeley about how literature is judged by its mansions and journalism by its tenements. The thought just won't go away that you may be accused of invading other people's privacy just like those cheap sensation-mongers."

"A damn good point, beloved, to which I've given a lot of thought myself. The answers are these: The private lives of the Hinckleys ended the moment one of them committed an act so monstrous that it almost changed the course of history. George Bush as president is something far different from Ronald Reagan as president. Bobby Kennedy as president would have been something far, far different from Richard Nixon as president. Sirhan Sirhan didn't just kill a man. He took away from the rest of us—millions of us—our electoral privileges, and under our system that is equivalent to taking away one of our most cherished freedoms. The right of the American people to know everything there is to know about this assassination attempt takes precedence by several hundred miles over the privacy of the principals involved. Furthermore, as I have proclaimed from lecterns from sea to shining sea, no elected official and no person hired by the government should be above journalistic scrutiny when their private lives encroach on their public duties. And all the angels of the universe know I'm not engaging in this self-torture for money. I happen to care about the United States of America and I happen to care about such old-fashioned ideals as justice. Especially justice, because that's what primarily distinguishes our nation from those dictatorships so beloved by so many in government agencies. I'd just like to help make sure that the next time there is evidence of an attempt at political assassination the press doesn't cover it up or pretend it isn't there. Hey, let me lay it right on the line: The next time might be the last time. The scariest thing of all is that the next round of conspirators could be nothing but heartened by the way this miserable affair was handled by the press."

"I'm glad I pressed your button."

"Oh, I'm just getting started. Hell, I don't know that there was a conspiracy behind Hinckley. What I do know I intend to lay out there and the press and public can do what they will with it. Then I'm going to take a few weeks off for making virtually uninterrupted love to you in exotic and erotic locales. And then I intend to write a nice, pleasant book that perhaps someone will publish and sell two hundred and eighty-seven copies. At the same time I intend to build a house of wood in the woods overlooking a lake for us and the Bear and whoever comes along to live with us happily ever after."

"A synopsis of which I approve with all my overflowing heart." She kissed him. "How's that? Did that curl any important hairs?"

"My entire pubic area came to attention. Hey, move it. There's a more immediate project I need to work on. I've got to put together some more pieces of this puzzle so they make some sense. Get the hint?"

She kissed him again and was gone from the room.

He continued to sift through the folder marked "TRIAL DELAYS/SUICIDE ATTEMPTS." When he came to a note concerning the performance of George Will on a television news analysis program, he paused.

Consider George Will. This bland, cold, unfeeling syndicated columnist who drifts in and out of *Newsweek* (along with others of his kind) and has become a glib "television personality" typifies what passes for news commentary and analysis in the eighth decade of the American century. He is fundamentally satisfied with almost every aspect of our society, our culture, our condition. He refuses to examine the ethical basis of the problems that confront us. He stands defiantly on the wrong side of the ramparts, armed to the teeth (a dagger is there, ready for a turned back) in defense of the status quo. When the government has done something wrong in George Will's eyes, it is only because the administration wasn't militaristic enough, did not lie with sufficient plausibility, or did not protect the interests of the powerful, the wealthy or the jingoes with appropriate vigor. Then there's David Brinkley, long over the hill, the target of hoots and howls from the NBC television newsmen and crews for many years because of his inability to conclude a commentary without reference, however oblique, to the inequities of the national tax system. After this Brinkley foible had been called to Jonathan's attention in 1976, he had noted that three out of four Brinkley commentaries did indeed touch on this obsession. And Jonathan carried within him the bitterness that in the 1960s not one of the television or radio commentators opposed the government's war in Vietnam, although approximately 40 percent of the citizens who voted on the issue in disparate geographical locations voiced their opposition. The pack of jackals, led by Eric Sevareid, taunted, ridiculed and attacked those who demonstrated their opposition to the policies of the military-industrial-governmental complex. Of course there now was Bill Moyers, the lone exception to the dreary litany provided by other commentators, his born-again consciousness repentant for the sins he committed in the service of the Johnson White House. He now provided the sole incisive television examination of Washington's passing parade, led by costumed clowns.

What about "60 Minutes," you say? Oh, that quartet is ferocious in pursuing some of the despicable con men and scam artists who thrive on the fringes of the commercial world but they rarely touch the corruption and law violations on a grand scale by those in government or the monumental illegalities of the conglomerates; indeed, look at who sponsors the program. Jack Anderson? Once a voice in the journalistic wilderness crying out against the vices of the powerful, he has been co-opted by the very forces that once came within an ace of murdering him. PBS? Nixon won that war; the "non-commercial" network has been riddled with commercials by one corporation after another, "fund-providers" for the programs that question not *quo vadis*, and only rarely a distinguished documentary of the kind that once was its pride.

But George Will—fresh in Jonathan's mind was a delicious moment on the Larry King radio show one dark night earlier in the week. Will, as is his wont, was demonstrating his enthusiasm for Socrates, exclaiming that here was a font of wisdom who never, never had been wrong on any subject. A couple of phone calls later a gentleman courteously asked Mr. Will if he agreed with Socrates on the subject of slavery. There followed some of the most painful seconds of dead air in the annals of broadcasting before Will lamely responded, "Uhhhhh.... no." Larry King broke his own record for precipitous interruption with an almost frantic announcement of the location from which the next call was coming.

Jonathan winced as he saw the next item in the folder. It was a quotation from the *World Almanac* of 1976 reporting that the two attempts on the life of President Ford had "spurred criticism that intensive media coverage of the president's activities and glamorization of the would-be assassin exacerbated the possibility of further assassination attempts." The media had progressed not a whit on either score; the nightly invasion of television screens by a Ford, a Carter or a Reagan on the flimsiest of pretexts—followed by front-page coverage the next day in the elite circle of newspapers—has made the pseudo-event a staple of "news" coverage. As for the charge of glamorization of would-be assassins, the space given to the opinions of the pampered punk now on trial was a damning indictment of so-called respectable publications that can't distinguish between sense and sensation. He would so write, he assured himself. . . .

THE PRESS AND THE DELAY

In one of the few instances in which a member of the national print media questioned the delay in bringing the accused to trial, U.S. News & World Report *wondered, 20 weeks after President Reagan was shot, why "the man accused of shooting him hadn't even been indicted." Headlined "The Hinckley Case—Why It's Dragging," in its issue dated August 31, 1981—five months and a day after the crime—the magazine reported that a 1980 survey showed that 96 percent of criminal cases in federal courts were completed within 100 days as required by the 1975 Speedy Trial Act. But—aha!—the 100-day rule is waived in cases involving sanity tests, the magazine pointed out. That accounted for a three-month delay—described as "the usual period" for psychiatric tests—and for what might be described as "the unusual period" involved in the extension to four months granted by the court. The remaining five weeks of delay before the indictment received no accounting. After so satisfactory an answer to its own question, the magazine saw no need to raise the question again in the* subsequent eight months that passed before the case was dragged into a courtroom. The reader is left to wonder what excuses the magazine would have given for all the additional delays sought and granted to both prosecution and defense teams by an amiable judge.

Then there was Newsweek. It addressed the matter of unprecedented delay in its April 5, 1982, issue—more than a year after the attempt to kill the president. It reported that the case was put on hold for four months while the defendant's head was examined, and confessed: "That is an unusually long period." Then it added, with what the reader is asked to assume was a straight face, that "lawyers speculate that it was granted to prevent the defense from appealing on the grounds that the doctors were hurried," a sentence that tempts one to add "and the cow jumped over the moon."

The rest of the delay? Easy, in the gospel according to Newsweek: "The skirmishes over Hinckley's statements—and some papers that prison guards seized from his cell and which the court also suppressed—has been going on since September." Note how Newsweek makes no reference to the reported contents of the seized papers; note how Newsweek glosses over the fact that the problems never would have arisen if Hinckley had been brought to the bar of justice within a decent interval; note how Newsweek makes no reference to the delays caused by the prosecution, the defense and the judge.

Still more: "There is good reason to build in delays in notorious cases, lest trials be held in an atmosphere of hysteria," as if a trial held in the summer of 1981 would have been more hysterical than the one that ultimately was convened.

Newsweek's conclusion: "Justice delayed may be justice denied but it takes a celebrated case before anyone cares to complain about it anymore." That silly sentence deserves examination on two counts: First, the law of the land demands that justice not be delayed and the lessons of history demonstrate that in this case justice delayed might well produce no justice at all. Second, the fact that Newsweek didn't care to complain (and still wasn't complaining) during the more than a year that passed before this tortured prose found its way into print does not mean that "anyone" hadn't complained. It may constitute news to Newsweek, but there are many persons and publications concerned about the flaws of the American system of justice as practiced, to use Newsweek's idea of syntax, "anymore."

(For instance, the Denver Rocky Mountain News, more than a month before the trial: "The law's delay in the Hinckley case is already an affront to the ordinary person's notions of justice. If the case turns out as his lawyers hope, it would amount to one of the worst miscarriages of justice in the nation's history." So much for the manure spread by Newsweek.)

Equally discouraging to those who are dismayed by the press becoming first the sweetheart and then either the wife or mistress of government in the 1980s—after all, no banns have been posted—has been the decline and fall of our land's most publicized investigative reporter. Along in January, 1982, came the "Premiere Issue" of The Investigative Reporter, "Editor and Publisher/Jack Anderson." On the cover was a dramatic but inaccurate drawing of John W. Hinckley Jr., gun in hand on the sidewalk outside the Washington Hilton, and the announcement of the featured piece: "The Day Reagan Was Shot" by, of course, Jim Bishop. Packed with pablum, it added nothing to the official version of the event. A second article, "Who Is Trying to Kill President Reagan: A Look at Three Life-Threatening Plots," embraced the already discredited "Hinckley-Richardson Conspiracy" and two other ludicrous tales, precisely the kind of mongering that justifies the ridicule heaped on many crackpot conspiracy theories. A disaster, the "Premiere Issue" was not followed by a second issue, although in a letter to subscribers Anderson announced that "we have now concluded negotiations with a corporation, which will underwrite the magazine." The projected corporate solution, however, failed to materialize. If this is the state of the art of investigative reporting as practiced by the most widely acclaimed practitioner of them all, the good citizens of our land require divine intervention far more than they realize in mundane matters related to governance, liberty and justice.

Jonathan did not feel up to coping with the next two items in the folder. Somehow, he thought, he would weave them into the tapestry on another day. Perhaps they were worth no more than a footnote? Consider:

1. There's the *New York Times* asking in an editorial after more than a year had elapsed since the shooting, "Why Rush the Hinckley Case?" Oh, why indeed, Good Gray Lady? Hear her: "Is it another example of inordinate delays in the legal system? No." Enough. Enough. He smiled as he recalled the time he had told Alonzo Schaeffer that his paper's editorials were third-rate compared with those in several other metropolitan dailies and Alonzo had waved his hand impatiently and said "Fourth-rate."

2. There's Vincent J. Fuller, chief defense attorney, in a court in Washington using almost verbatim the same arguments employed in a *New York Times* editorial a few days earlier. Which comes first, O ye sages of journalism, the chicken or the egg? Does the lawyer have the editorial writer's ear or does the lawyer scoop up the editorial writer's droppings? Either way....

He chose to move on.

TELEVISION AND THE DELAY

As the anniversary of the assassination attempt and the scheduled trial drew nigh, Hinckley returned to the news in full force. Probably the most zealous attempt to observe the anniversary was made by Ted Koppel on the ABC "Nightline" of March 30, 1982. Koppel gracefully pointed out that the man who fired six shots at President-Elect Franklin Delano Roosevelt in 1933, killing instead the mayor of Chicago, was electrocuted two weeks after his indictment and 33 days after the crime was committed. Koppel then spent most of his time that evening trying to make sense out of a bewildering Harvard law professor and a barrister whose tongue was so forked that he not only mumbled contradictions of his own fuzzy positions but absolutely refused to reply to Koppel's repeated, occasionally desperate, question of whether the unprecedented delay in bringing the case to trial served to "undermine our faith in the legal system." Finally, under excruciating pressure from Kop-

pel, it was admitted that the vast majority of such cases come to trial within six months and 97 percent of them within a year. This performance was actually equalled by the new Chief Bloviator of American Communications, George Will, who observed that the long delay in bringing the accused to trial was "clearly the model of a civilized society," an observation only slightly less ludicrous than some of his other ululations. If this half-hour performance on the late-night screen constitutes a valid example of the state of the art of in-depth television news reporting, this nation desperately needs an Elmer Davis, the likes of whom has not been seen or heard since the passing of the heyday of radio news analysis. An Elmer Davis would have broken this case wide open by the first of June.

A few days later, along came John Chancellor on NBC Nightly News to comment on the preposterous delay in bringing the case to trial, scheduled to begin the following day. Chancellor, following Koppel's lead, succinctly pointed out that it took the Italian courts only 10 weeks to convict the man who tried to assassinate Pope John Paul II. Furthermore, the Egyptian government required only five months to convict the men who murdered Sadat, Chancellor added bitingly, conceding that by comparison "the appearance of justice has been damaged" in this country. The primary deficiency of this sound editorial judgment was that it took Chancellor only a few hours less to decry the situation than it took the government to bring the accused to trial. Where, one might properly ask, was Chancellor when we needed him—nine months, six months, three months earlier?

The men who had fired the shots at President Roosevelt, Pope John Paul II and Anwar Sadat had indeed received swift and sure justice, as our television mavens had informed us. But that analysis did nothing more than skim the surface. Deeper:

President Garfield died September 19, 1881. His assassin was hanged less than 10 months later.

The assassin of President McKinley was executed 45 days later.

The man who tried to shoot his way into Blair House to assassinate President Truman was wounded, recovered and was convicted in a little more than four months.

Jack Ruby was found guilty of slaying Lee Harvey Oswald less than four months after the assassination of President Kennedy.

James Earl Ray was arrested June 8, 1968, and charged with killing the Rev. Martin Luther King. Although he changed lawyers before the trial, he was sentenced nine months and two days after his arrest.

Sirhan Sirhan's trial started seven months and two days after he killed Robert Kennedy.

Arthur Bremer, who shot and seriously crippled George Wallace, was sentenced less than three months later.

Sara Jane Moore, who had fired one shot at President Ford that was deflected and injured no one, after psychiatric examinations was adjudged legally competent to stand trial less than two months later although she had been hospitalized for mental treatment seven times in the previous 25 years. She was brought to trial less than three months after the event.

Lynette Fromme, a follower of Charles Manson, was arrested September 5, 1975, for pointing at President Ford a gun that did not even have a bullet in the chamber. She was indicted on September 10, pleaded not guilty September 19, was ruled mentally competent to stand trial September 23 and the trial began November 4, less than two months after her arrest.

He stopped. Oh, counselors, trained in our law schools to serve corporation and state—but not justice. What hypocrites they are taught to be, what twisters of truth they learn to be....

But no, he couldn't let himself give in to those sentiments, however true. The problem at hand was literary. Should he include in the article the other notorious murder cases, not involving political motivation or implication, that were brought to trial with dispatch? Should he mention the especially pertinent case of Mark David Chapman—Texas born—a former mental patient, who originally pleaded not guilty by reason of insanity to the charge of shooting John Lennon to death? *Six-and-a-half months* elapsed between the murder and the start of the trial. Against the advice of his lawyer, he changed his plea to guilty and was sentenced to a long prison term. The judge rejected the contention that the killing was an insane act and said it was "an intentional crime, a crime carefully planned and executed; he knew what he was doing." A description that applies with remarkable accuracy to our little friend from Evergreen....

Should he include the case of Edward M. Richardson (What! Dear Reader, you mean you do not remember him?), the figure blown into a fatuous three-day sensation as half of a "Hinckley-Richardson Conspiracy" by a press that refused to explore several of the "strange coincidences" that popped up in the days following Hinckley's attempt to change the person who heads our government? It took only *three months and six days* to bring him to trial and sentence him to a year in prison and five years probation. This resident of "the middle class Drexel Hill suburb of Philadelphia." This man who had fired a shot at no one. His lawyer told the judge that his client was involved in "intense marijuana use and some use of L.S.D." The newspapers that delivered this information didn't say what the various members of the press who exploited this ridiculous nonstory for three days had been on....

He was tired. Far too tired to deal with the item that had been misplaced in the folder and was intended for the section describing the indescribable delays in bringing Hinckley to trial. He closed his eyes and saw the picture: There's Vincent J. Fuller again, standing in the court the day the judge finally had set the trial for April 27, asking for still another delay until the first week in May so that the lawyers for the defense could have more time to "prepare" their expert psychiatric witnesses. *So that the lawyers for the defense could have more time to "prepare" their expert psychiatric witnesses....*

Jonathan Blakely gathered the blue sheets and sought Arianne. He found her in the living room, two glasses and a bottle of red wine on the table.

"Long day?" she asked.

"Long day," he said as he sank into the easy chair. "I couldn't take it any more. The problem is that there is no English word to describe the last note I came across. Even *chutzpah* is too weak."

"What's that?"

"*Extraordinary gall* touches the edges of its meaning. The

classic definition is the story of the boy who murders his parents and pleads for mercy because he's an orphan."

He sighed.

She poured wine into the two glasses (and into a clean ash tray for Bear).

"To life!" they said together (and Bear lapped his portion and wagged his tail).

Jonathan sighed again.

"Sweet Arianne," he said finally, "let me tell thee this: The corruption that besets this nation runs so deep that it will never be cleansed until someone comes and as his first act drives all the moneychangers from our temple."

MAY

*WHY DID ARGENTINA INVADE THE FALKLANDS?
To impress Jodie Foster.*

— *Graffiti in men's room,
Little Bear Bar,
Evergreen, Colorado
1982*

Dan Doherty put down the phone and pondered the strange predicament of the practicing journalist in the new decade.

He had just finished joining Jonathan Blakely in raising his voice to heaven in honor of the triumph of the "bizarre happenstance." He had sung a solemn song to the glory of "sheer coincidence," and while he was at it he had poured out paeans of praise for the latest in a series of accidental and remarkable events—no doubt easily explained—that suggest—but, he hastened to add, probably lack?—a causal relationship.

Vice President George Bush had made a few short trips out of the country since his inauguration on January 20, 1981. He enjoyed a quick in-and-out junket to the Dominican Republic, Colombia and Brazil, zipped down for a brief visit to Mexico City, went over the Pacific to deliver his memorable toast to Marcos in Manila, over the Atlantic for a few hours in Paris. Stuff like that.

He had not been out of the United States during January, February, March and most of April in 1982.

On April 27, the day the trial of John W. Hinckley Jr. finally began, the White House announced that Vice President Bush would go to China.

He had left the United States a few days earlier for Japan and South Korea. His official itinerary did not include China. It was reported that President Reagan had suggested in an April 5 letter to Deng Xiaoping, senior deputy party chairman, that Bush visit China. Bush went on to Singapore, Australia and New

Zealand—five countries in thirteen days—before arriving in China. As he left China on May 9 for a rest in Hawaii, Bush refused to tell reporters what had been accomplished by his visit. "I'm not going to elaborate on the details of any negotiation," the vice president replied somewhat testily when a reporter asked him to be more specific about the progress that he said he had achieved in China.

Four days later the *New York Times* editorialized on Bush's "emollient trip to China."

Dan Doherty burst out laughing.

"A soothing trip indeed," he said out loud, still laughing, when he thought of that editorial.

As was his custom, Doherty, currently unmarried, started the day with the *Washington Post* as his companion at the breakfast table. After the drive across the Potomac to his office in the National Press Building, he went through the *New York Times*, skimmed the *Wall Street Journal,* gave the preceding day's *Washington Times* the thirty seconds to two minutes it merited, quickly went through his own paper. Back in his early college days he had read nothing but the sports pages, dreaming of the time to come when he would be up in the press box covering the exploits of boys and men who remained boys. That dream had started to come apart when Jonathan Blakely scotch-taped the front pages of six or seven newspapers to the blackboard and began analyzing how the news of the world was reported. The dream ended the day the city editor on his first newspaper job pulled him out of the sports department—"You're too good to waste your time on games," he said—and dispatched him to cover the courthouse beat. Now here he was, chief of the Washington Bureau, covering the most spectacular trial in years. Spectacular: of or like a spectacle. Yea, verily, it was a spectacle.

He was still too good to waste his time on games, he thought, yet day after day he attended that farcical circus and reported it with a straight face, "objectively," as a good reporter should, "fairly" as a good reporter would. The grotesque was made plausible; the ridiculous was made seemly; the ludicrous made rational; the absurd—well, now and then he managed to convey a bit of the essence of the theater of the absurd that was performed in the halls of justice. But the desk back home wanted his copy free of the interpretation he had included in his first pieces from the capital. The message had been clear: Just the facts, Dan ol' boy, and do your interpreting at the Georgetown cocktail parties. He pointed out that what he was including was not opinion but reasonably documented background information, without which the story was incomplete—or in some cases misleading or false. For example, he would prefer to put aside childish things and open the Reality File in his Album of Memories:

There is George Bush in 1970, encouraged to enter the Texas Senate race by Richard Nixon, with a son of H.L. Hunt in his vanguard, losing in his second attempt to win that office. The Republican National Committee reported that more money was spent trying to elect him than was spent in any other state race.

There is George Bush replying to charges by Chilean President Salvadore Allende that the International Telephone and Telegraph Corporation had "launched a sinister plot" to prevent him from becoming president and that ITT and the Kennecott Copper Corporation had "dug their claws into my country." Bush was telling the United Nations that investment of American capital abroad was not intended to exploit foreign countries but rather was of mutual benefit to the investor and the people of the country in which the investment was made.

There is George Bush, chairman of the Republican National Committee, listening on May 23, 1973, as President Nixon explains his efforts to conceal his criminal activities in the Watergate scandal. There he is again, a few minutes later, along with twenty-one other Republican diehards from House and Senate, participating in a standing ovation for the president.

Look, there's Senator Frank Church in 1975 opposing President Ford's appointment of George Bush as director of the CIA, urging the Senate to "insist upon a Central Intelligence Agency which is politically neutral and totally professional." Turn the page: There is George Bush, director of the CIA, covering up some of the agency's dirtiest tricks.

Here's an interesting shot: CIA Director Bush in 1976 announcing that "effective immediately" he had stopped all paid or contractual relationships between the agency and full- or part-time employees of U.S. news organizations. (Unfortunately, it's a double-exposure; Former Director Colby years earlier had announced much the same thing.)

There's a good picture of President Reagan saying "Let George Do It" when Bush and Haig got into a no-holds-barred, knockdown-and-dragout battle over who would be the administration's "Crisis Manager" a week before Hinckley fired his shots. But next to it is a photo of the Argentine junta boss laughing when President Reagan suggested sending his vice president and crisis manager to mediate the dispute over Argentina's invasion of the Malvinas/Falklands.

Who's that man with George and why is he smiling? Why, it's the ruthless Filipino gangster who hesitates not a moment to imprison or assassinate his opponents, Ferdinand Marcos, and he is smiling because George has just told him—and the world—that "we love your adherence to democratic principles and to the democratic process." Even the *Wall Street Journal* gagged on that one, editorially chastising the vice president for taking "complete leave of reality."

Ah, there's George Bush a few weeks ago emphatically denying that he had ever uttered the words "voodoo economics" during his bitter fight with Ronald Reagan for the Republican presidential nomination. Now let's watch the NBC videotape of him saying it publicly.

Stare at this videotape, too: No one who saw the NBC-TV segment of Bush speaking at Tuskegee a few days after Hinckley attempted to assassinate the president will ever forget it. There was a haunted, harried, worried mien about him, especially when he referred to the shooting. Eyes darting, he paused and inserted the words, "The violent act of one man," followed by another pause and a nervous look around. For weeks afterward many Washington journalists privately noted how terrible Bush was looking. Ten months after the event an eight-year-old boy in Maine wrote to the *Bangor Daily News* that he hadn't been hearing about George Bush lately. "Did he quit his job," the boy asked, "or did he die? Do you know?" What Doherty knew was that once the trial was out of the way, the vice president would be seen in public more often....

Some trial. It's proving to be, as a fellow reporter put it, "the most elaborate and expensive extravaganza in the modern history of the insanity defense."

Let the old sports writer examine the lawyers:

In this corner, the substitute for the U.S. Attorney. The big man would have been in the corner if the bout hadn't been repeatedly postponed.

In the other corner, wearing silk trunks with satin trim, the challengers of the idea that a person who almost kills the president and gravely wounds another public servant should be punished. They boast of a long string of knockouts, of split decisions that went their way when judges disagreed, of an ability to get the ear of the commissioner on appeal. There have been rumors that they are experts at intimidation, that they gouge the eyes of their opponents with their thumbs, that they hit on the break. But only rumors; the fact, however, is that hardly anyone has ever laid a glove on them.

Another metaphor—and where is the sports writer who cares if it is mixed?—to tell the tale: Superlawyer Edward Bennett Williams isn't there, but four of the fastest thoroughbreds from his stable of approximately eighty were trotted out from the ten-story office building only a few hundred feet from the White House to look after the interests of their client's son.

Sidebar: "The President of the United States regrets that he will be unable to accept your invitation to be your guest at the opening game of your Baltimore Orioles baseball season because he almost died from wounds inflicted by the young man your outfit is trying to get off."

Ironies ooze from every pore of this afflicted corpus.

A color piece? "During his 30 years as a celebrated Washington trial lawyer, Mr. Williams has defended the likes of Senator Joseph R. McCarthy, whose Communist witch hunt brought him to disgrace; Teamster bosses Dave Beck and Jimmy Hoffa; Representative Adam Clayton Powell Jr.; the fugitive financier Robert Vesco; the mobster Frank Costello; former Treasury Secretary John B. Connally and Bobby Baker, the Lyndon Johnson protégé who went to prison for political corruption. Yet, so unshakeable is his position as a pillar of the Washington establishment that his client list has done little to tarnish his appeal among the nation's leaders. This is a town where quid pro quo is an accepted way of life." He would never write fluff like that; he had clipped it from the *New York Times* as an example of the kind of reporting generated by its Washington bureau. Especially the bland observation that Washington is a town where quid pro quo is an accepted way of life. That says it all, beautifully. To live in a town like that—what a damnable fate. He already was working at getting the hell out of there....

A Quote-of-the-Month? Ben Bradlee, of *Washington Post* fame and infamy, describes Superlawyer Williams as "a jock and a workaholic—a primitive man in the best sense of the word." Primitive, yes, but not just in the best sense of the word. Nixon said he regretted not hiring Williams when the Watergate felonies were revealed. Listen to the Superlawyer in one of his more widely-quoted assessments of law and justice: "I could have won it. The first thing, I would have told him to burn the tapes. I would have advised him, before they were ever called for, before they were ever subject to any subpoena, to make a public disposition of these things. It would have had to be premised on the fact that there were all kinds of state secrets, private conversations with heads of state that would be embarrassing to the United States worldwide if exposed. So the tapes would have to be destroyed for national-security reasons." Little wonder that Williams and some members of his firm are widely known as the "Georgetown Mafia."

A final word from Williams, the gospel according to the *New York Times:* A major criminal case trial takes "more creative talent than the production of a great motion picture."

"Right on, Superlawyer," Dan Doherty said to himself as he stuffed a folded pad in his coat pocket. "I'm off to cover a great motion picture," he said to the secretary as he walked by, "starring Jodie Foster, Travis Bickle, Judge Hardly and a cast of thousands of shrinks." She blew him a kiss.

Late that afternoon of the first day of May, after filing his story to his paper, he was on the line to Jonathan Blakely.

"Mayday! Mayday!" he shouted into the phone. "You won't believe what went on in the court today. Wanna feel the old adrenalin flowing, Coach?"

"After all that's happened this past year, nothing would

astonish me," Jonathan said.

"Try this bulletin from cuckooland," Doherty quickly replied. "The judge has ruled this day that the prosecution must prove beyond a reasonable doubt that Hinckley was sane at the time of the shooting."

"I'm astonished," Jonathan said quietly.

"In the name of all that's sacred, Jonathan, how can you prove anyone is sane beyond a reasonable doubt? Who hasn't done something crazy, especially in this town? If I had to prove in a court of law that Dan Doherty was sane all my witnesses, including the paid shrinks, would be people whose sanity I have questioned at one time or another. And the judge refused to apply a District of Columbia law requiring defendants who plead not guilty by reason of insanity to prove they were insane at the time. And Hinckley was charged with three federal crimes and ten crimes under the District of Columbia code. Judge Parker was persuaded by the defense lawyers that it would be too confusing to instruct the jury that the prosecution bears the burden of proof on the federal charges, but that the defense bears the burden on the D.C. charges. Can you believe that? Sometimes I think I'm going bonkers."

"Welcome to the club."

"And the prosecution is supposed to prove Hinckley's sanity with all the best evidence to prove how sane he is ruled out. The judge has excluded the testimony of three federal agents who said in pretrial hearings that Hinckley had seemed calm, cool, collected and in control of himself when they interviewed him after the shooting. Wanna know what Hinckley's first question was?"

"Sure. I like a good joke as much as the next fellow."

"He said 'Is it on TV?' Then a detective said that when he asked a Secret Service agent to spell 'assassinate,' Hinckley sort of smirked at him and said 'I'll spell it for you.' And he spelled it correctly. He answered all the routine questions clearly, asked for a hamburger and wanted to know the score of the basketball championship game being played that day. Then, get this: He asks if the Academy Awards had been postponed. This is all going on while the four men he shot are getting emergency treatment."

"I'm speechless."

"It's one of the few times, Coach, if I may say so. What makes the judge's ruling all the more remarkable is the fact that the federal agents repeatedly informed Hinckley of his rights to see a lawyer—they testified he was read his Miranda rights at least four times—and he was asked only for background information concerning his wanderings and whether he acted alone or in concert with others. For the love of Vince Lombardi, Coach, this country was in a crisis of gigantic proportions with the president out of commission. Even Haig lost his cool, remember? If ever there was a time that the authorities needed to know as quickly as possible as much as they could, this was it. And the judge and the appeals court threw out all the evidence of Hinckley's behavior after the arrest. He was questioned gently. He was not pressured to answer anything. No force was applied—or ever suggested by the defense. The fundamental idea in the Miranda decision was that the state shouldn't be allowed to extort confessions by beating, intimidating or wearing down suspects. What a miscarriage this is!"

"No, what an abortion this is."

"Here's another thing: Parker seems to be the CIA's favorite judge. You know how he gave Richard Helms that ludicrous little fine and a two-year suspended sentence for lying to a Senate committee when he testified that the CIA had not covertly tried to block Allende's election to the presidency of Chile. Well, Parker was the judge in several other cases in which the CIA had more than a passing interest. Then he bungled the Orlando Letelier trial and the conviction was reversed and then the Cubans charged with the murder were acquitted. That was probably the most significant of his several reversals. There was joy unbounded in Langley when the Cubans got off."

"I remember it well, as Frankie says."

"Hey, Coach, I can't resist this: On the wall behind the judge is a white stone statue of Moses handing down the Ten Commandments. No burning bush, though. He's in China."

Dan Doherty called often in the days that followed.

"Parker has a reputation for openly showing his displeasure when he is reversed by a higher court, but he has no trouble reversing himself," he said. "In December he ruled that the jury would be sequestered, but in an April pre-trial hearing he ruled against the prosecution and said the jurors would be allowed to return home after each day's court session, which is unusual in a trial of this kind. Not only that, but he originally told the lawyers he wasn't worried that jurors might see or hear a press account of the trial and uttered these words: 'If it's a straightforward account, what difference does it make if the jury's heard it in the box?' He also suggested that it would make no difference if they failed to obey his orders not to read or listen to a broadcast account of the case, and then when the trial got under way he said he couldn't be too emphatic in admonishing jurors to shun radio, television and newspaper accounts. How do you like them apples?''

''Pretty wormy.''

''Try these. Before the trial he didn't issue a formal ruling but he said he probably would allow the showing of videotapes of the shooting. Then, in the trial, he allowed the tapes to be edited, at the request of the defense lawyers, to exclude the shots of Brady and all the bloody closeups.''

''On the theory, no doubt, that in a court of law the Reader's Digest version is superior to the unabridged edition.''

''He reversed himself on the CAT scan issue, too. The defense lawyers had these computer-enhanced brain X-rays which they claim show that Hinckley has a shrunken brain. They claim it's proof of schizophrenia. At first Parker repeatedly barred putting the brain-scan evidence before the jury to support the defense contentions, saying there was a lack of general acceptance of it as a credible diagnostic instrument in connection with schizophrenia. But five days later he said that upon further reflection he decided to allow the evidence—or so-called evidence, to be more accurate. The prosecution said the jury might give undue weight to the scans, which even four of the defense shrinks testified were of no use in diagnosing schizophrenia in individual cases. A prosecution neuroradiologist testified that Hinckley's brain was perfectly normal, that there was no evidence of any significant abnormality whatsoever and that what the CAT scans showed was no more a sign of mental illness than premature baldness would be. It's peculiar how all the judge's self-inflicted reversals seem to favor the defense, but it was most apparent in the CAT scan scam."

Jonathan laughed. "That's a tongue-twister, isn't it?"

"Yeah, but worth it. One of the good doctors for the defense offered his professional opinion that Hinckley's shrunken brain may have something to do with the family home burning down in the third month of Mrs. Hinckley's pregnancy. One thing is clear—the kid's not dumb. He's said to have an IQ of 113, which puts him in about the eightieth percentile for men his age. I tell you true, Coach, we report the drivel of the psychiatrists and it's in newspapers the width of the country, more often than not on the front page. It's the same stomach-turning psychobabble I heard when I was covering the courts years ago."

"It's just as I feared," Jonathan said. "This isn't a trial at all. The defense has succeeded in making it an almost uninterrupted discussion about mental illness."

"Right. What you need in your article is a section headed *The Parade of the Paladin Shrinks*. Have gun, will travel. Shee-it, it's beyond belief. The guys for the defense, who incidentally are testifying for fees ranging up to $150 an hour for the time they're putting in on the case, have come up with—just a second, I've got it here—yeah, process schizophrenia, major affective disorder, schizophrenia spectrum disorder, pseudoneurotic schizophrenia, schizotypal personality disorder, pathological ambivalence—I think I'm suffering from that myself during this trial—paradoxical rage, paranoid personality disorder and borderline personality disorder. That's only so far. Also, the advocate of process schizophrenia admitted that none of the other seven shrinks shared his diagnosis. Now, on the other hand, the prosecution's paid shrinks contend that Hinckley suffers only from dysthymic disorder, narcissistic personality disorder, schizoid personality disorder and mixed personality disorder—none of which are on the serious end of the spectrum of mental illness. They conclude that Hinckley suffers from personality disorders that are common to millions of Americans. Obviously, when you listen to both sides delivering their dicta, those on one side simply have to be quacks. Schizophrenia is an extremely subjective matter. I think the person who has come the closest to diagnosing it is that noted philosopher, Lily

Tomlin, who said that if you speak to God, it's prayer, but if God speaks to you, it's schizophrenia."

He waited for Jonathan to stop laughing.

"Here's a little sidebar for you, Coach," Dan Doherty said. "Shrinks from the Harvard Medical School are testifying on both sides. I just finished filing a story to my paper that has obvious pertinence to what's going on here in the courtroom. Are you ready? The Harvard Medical School's faculty has twenty-five doctors who have failed to repay federal loans that helped put them through medical school. Of the thirty-seven medical schools that were checked, Harvard led the nation in delinquents. Of the 218 students who borrowed to attend Harvard Medical School, 143 are delinquent and they tied up $153,000 that could have been lent to other students. The defaults of all the delinquent doctors in the country have forced the government to deny loans to 3,000 students who could have been helped if proper repayments had been made. If the country's medical students want to march on Cambridge, I'd be happy to count cadence."

"Whew," Jonathan said.

"Pee-ooo is more like it," Dan Doherty responded.

"Have the lawyers been saying anything about Hinckley that has some significance?"

"The prosecution has been trying to sketch a portrait of a rich, spoiled, lazy, ungrateful malingerer who felt ordinary work was beneath him, complained that he had not received his inheritance, faked mental and physical problems, threatened suicide to wheedle money and sympathy from his parents, and carefully planned the attack, including using human silhouettes on a firing range. It seems that he cheated in college, lied regularly to manipulate his parents and even stole several thousand dollars worth of gold coins from them. His mother says that in 1979 John wrote a long essay saying that he was an all-out anti-Semite and white racist who thought the Jews deserved the Holocaust and Hitler was misunderstood. Now, on the other hand, the defense claims he assumed various personality characteristics of others, especially the title character of the *Taxi Driver* movie, lost his last tie to reality when he was kicked out of the family home, and then—hold on tight, Coach—inadvertently discovered an opportunity to shoot the president on March 30 as he passed through the city en route to New Haven."

Another call:

"Scott Hinckley testified he had not seen his brother in recent years except at family occasions and not at all in 1981—"

"What about that statement by the rock band leader who said he'd seen them together?"

"Search me. I'm just a humble reporter trying to get the facts, ma'am. It's not my duty to question why, it's my duty to let it die. Every time I've tried to do a little investigative reporting—or even a little interpretive reporting—I get snotty notes from my retarded managing editor back home. But ponder these items: Scott Hinckley testified he flew to Dallas in early March. He said he talked with his sister and her husband about having John committed to a mental hospital. He also testified that his family supported Reagan. No mention of the money they gave to Bush or the contribution to Connally when Big John was trying to cut off Reagan's balls."

And other calls:

—"Both the prosecution and defense are back to the old stalking theory. It seems to come and go, doesn't it? The prosecution showed a videotape of Carter in Dayton, Ohio, in which a man identified as Hinckley is seen in the crowd and Hinckley's lawyers also are suggesting he may have been stalking Reagan during that time. Nothing seems to get pinned down in this trial, but whether he was a stalker or not, he sure as hell ended up doing it in Washington, D.C., where there is a uniquely protective insanity law for the guilty and where close cooperation between the police force and the intelligence and federal law enforcement authorities is well-known. Could I interest you in Dan Doherty's Manchurian Candidate Theory?...."

—"Hinckley Senior said on the stand that he didn't know anything about the Jodie Foster thing until after the shooting. He also testified that his younger son had 40,000 shares of Vanderbilt Energy registered in his name but he didn't have access to the certificates. Worth close to half a million in the quarter before the shooting, according to SEC records, although it's worth only about $200,000 now...."

—"You know, they closed the courtroom to the press and public when they took secret testimony from Jodie Foster on videotape a year to the day after the assassination attempt. Also one year to the day, Jim Brady returned to George Washington University Medical Center for treatment of a blood clot in his left leg. Just a couple more interesting coincidences for your collection. Jodie was allowed to testify on tape because she's either working or playing in Europe—the stories vary—while the trial is on. Incidentally, Hinckley threw a pen or pencil at her—the stories vary—during her taped testimony when he didn't like something she said. He also said 'Jodie, I'll kill you,' which also was edited from the version shown the jury...."

—"Did you notice that both Sirhan Sirhan and Arthur Bremer came up for parole while this trial has been going on? Of course, they're not going to be let loose. It's something to keep in mind after this trial is over. Some of the lawyers around here are saying Hinckley will be out in a couple of years, more or less...."

—"The defense features this shrink who looks like a prophet out of the Old Testament and the prosecution counters with a doctor named Sally who is two years older than Hinckley. She saw him fifty-seven times at Butner. Hinckley greets her with a friendly wave when she takes the stand but then she testifies that Hinckley is so self-centered that three weeks after the shooting he was talking about writing a book about it. When she says Hinckley is a manipulative young man who rationally chose to shoot the president to make his mark, Hinckley starts mouthing a stream of epithets. Then she says that John's attempt—that's the way she refers to him, as John—to assassinate Reagan had multiple causes but that winning Miss Foster's love was not one of them. Hinckley says out loud 'You're wrong,' and lets loose some more hostile epithets. He appeared to be saying 'go to hell' and 'I hate you, bitch,' among other points of view. Later, Judge Parker lectures Hinckley on his conduct—I think this was the third or fourth time. The judge may or may not let him get away with attempted murder on the sidewalk outside the Hilton, but he sure as hell is letting him get away with murder in the courtroom...."

—"Hey, Coach, you'll love this. Today a shrink testified that Hinckley told him more than two weeks after the shooting that he had never thought about the parallel between *Taxi Driver* and him until he read about it in magazines. That's by far the most revealing bit of testimony in the trial thus far. The doctor said Hinckley has a strong tendency to incorporate into his accounts ideas suggested to him by others. Did I see you salute as I ran that one up the flagpole?...."

—"The judge blew up at one psychiatrist today, telling him that he's not up there lecturing with some intellectuals at Harvard. But there's something peculiar about what Hinckley gets away with. Parker's always pictured in the press as a crusty, brusque, cantankerous, no-nonsense judge who's quick to dress down anyone who fails to observe the strict decorum he demands in his courtroom. He's been tough on Hinckley now and then, but he's allowed Hinckley to walk out four or five times—only once with his permission. Judge Parker comes in slowly to the bench on metal crutches and Hinckley is obviously tardy in standing and noticeably hasty in sitting down. I've never seen a defendant get away with the contempt and arrogance that Hinckley gets away with...."

—"The bill to the taxpayers from one 33-year-old assistant professor of psychiatry at Harvard Medical School is $115,917. I agree with that past president of the American Psychiatric Association who likened shrinks who testify in trials to clowns performing in a three-ring circus. Some guy in the press row referred to the shrinks sotto voce as witch doctors, but I straightened him out during a recess. When you call these guys witch doctors you do the honorable ministrations of true witch doctors of several cultures a monumental injustice...."

—"You should have seen the look on Hinckley's face when a government-hired shrink testified that Hinckley didn't have a delusion about Miss Foster and that what he had was a longstanding interest in becoming famous without working...."

—"Coach, please, I beg of you, please don't think I've gone batshit. I'm not making this up: Today on the witness stand a man described in the press as an internationally known specialist in neurology who currently plays cornerback for the Harvard Medical School said that in addition to Hinckley's other fixations, fantasies, disorders and obsessions, he considers himself shunned by society like Elephant Man. Well now,

Coach, this shrink says nothing could be more painful to him than criticizing another doctor, but then he attacks the therapy prescribed by the Evergreen psychiatrist as disastrous and making things worse. He contends that Hinckley showed no ability to plan or premeditate an assassination and then he says 'My God, my sense of justice says absolutely not.' Later when the jury was out, Parker told the shrink that his sense of justice wasn't being sought in this court, which was entirely appropriate, but the guy next to me muttered that his sense of justice sure as hell wasn't getting any consideration here either. Oh, yes, the same shrink also said that in all humility—get that—he believed the prosecution psychiatrist who was the first to examine Hinckley after the shooting and later conducted fifty-five interviews had made an error in concluding that Hinckley wasn't driven by the *Taxi Driver* movie. The shifting sand on which the defense is based, Coach, is turning into quicksand...."

—"Hinckley's Evergreen psychiatrist testified today. Finally we got on the stand the only shrink who wasn't being paid by either the prosecution or the defense. The most interesting thing he said was that although he had seen Hinckley more than a dozen times between October, 1980, and February, 1981, he detected no symptoms typical of a mental illness. A pattern of depression and disillusionment, yes, but no suicidal, homicidal or aggressive tendencies. No hallucinations, no bizarre thinking. Their talks dealt mainly with the pressures Hinckley faced as the youngest and least successful of the three children in a wealthy family ruled by a strict and authoritarian father. He says the angriest he ever saw Hinckley was when Hinckley said he hadn't received his family inheritance when his older brother and sister received their shares. And listen to this: He testified it was their third session before Hinckley ever mentioned Jodie and it was only second on his list of obsessions—the first being his failed writing career, which obviously now has received a degree of satisfaction, thanks to *Newsweek* and the other supermarket sensationals. Then the doctor says he has a further statement about Hinckley's mental condition that might be useful, but after a bench conference Judge Parker promptly forbids it and excuses him. It was the government lawyers who objected. That seems odd as hell, but the transcript of the bench conference is sealed and there's yet another mystery to solve in this case...."

—"We got to see *Taxi Driver* today. Parker previewed it and said it should be shown to the jury. The reporter next to me said it should have been a double feature, along with *Reefer Madness*. The law isn't just an ass, Coach; sometimes it's a horse's ass...."

—"Hinckley told the judge that he won't testify in his own defense. He met with his lawyer Fuller in a small cell behind the courtroom and when they came out Hinckley looked agitated, as if he had been arguing with Fuller. I now present to you the wording of what Hinckley told the judge: 'I have just been advised by counsel that I have no intention of taking the stand.' The upshot is that we're going to have this case closed without the man who attempted to assassinate the president ever saying one word under oath and the case fraught with unanswered questions. Honest to God, Jonathan. *Honest to God*...."

And then:

"I worry about your article, Coach. I know you're not saying there was a conspiracy to assassinate Reagan. You've said it again and again to me, but you've got to put it in capital letters in the article. There's no question about the cover-up, that a lot of pertinent information hasn't been reported and that once the trial is over the unanswered questions remain."

"You know what Blake said?"

"All I know about Blake is a sentiment proclaimed on a poster hanging high in your office at school, that we should kiss the joy as it flies."

"And so we should, Daniel, so we should," Jonathan said. "But Blake also pointed out that *He who Doubts from what he sees Will ne'er Believe, do what you please*. I'm aware of that glaring fact of life...."

Dan Doherty sighed after he hung up the phone. He stared silently out the window for several seconds.

"He's probably right," he said softly to himself. "There are some subjects a lot of people just don't want to talk about—or even hear about."

JUNE

In the First Amendment the founding fathers gave the free press the protection it must have to fulfill its essential role in our democracy. The press was to serve the governed, not the governors. The government's power to censor the press was abolished so that the press would remain forever free to censure the government. The press was protected so that it could bare the secrets of government and inform the people.

—*Justice Hugo Black*

"Unbelievable!"
—Nancy Reagan

"I was shocked."
—Speaker Thomas P. O'Neill Jr. (D-Mass)

"It is deeply troubling to me when the criminal justice system exonerates a defendant who obviously planned and knew exactly what he was doing."
—Senator Strom Thurmond (R-S.C.)

"The verdict demonstrates again the need for responsible reforms."
—Attorney General William French Smith

"Just think about what we're saying to so-called crazies of the world regarding what they can do or not do as far as public figures are concerned."
—Treasury Secretary Donald Regan

"I don't find fault with the jury. I find fault with the law.... You can find a psychiatrist willing to testify to anything."
—Senator Orrin G. Hatch (R-Utah)

"I honestly don't think I've been a danger to society."
—John W. Hinckley Jr.

"The insanity defense is a rich man's defense."
—Senator Larry Pressler (R-S.D.)

"You couldn't even prove the White House staff sane beyond a reasonable doubt."
—White House Staffer Edwin Meese

"Well, that's what money will do for you."
—Secret Service Officer Timothy McCarthy

"Nobody really knows whether that boy was sane or insane except him and the Lord."
—Juror Belinda Drake

"He isn't crazy, he is a genius. He manipulated his family, his father and now us."
—Juror Maryland Copelin

"I've heard psychiatrists go through this routine.... The average Joe Blow out there on the street can't marshal the sort of testimony and evidence that was marshaled in the Hinckley case."
—Judge Barrington D. Parker

"Some legal experts believe that Parker's decision to make the government prove at Hinckley's trial the defendant was sane may have resulted in the insanity verdict."
—The Associated Press

"After I shot him, his polls went up 20 percent."
—John W. Hinckley Jr.

"Anyone who follows the psychiatric gibberish of the experts testifying for and against the defendant can be forgiven for concluding that the system itself is crazy."
—Columnist William Raspberry

"The outcome will be cynically viewed as another example of one kind of justice for the rich and another kind for the poor."
—Columnist James J. Kilpatrick

"Unless all the steam blows off in the whistle, this judicial travesty may be the shock treatment our society needs."
—Columnist Paul Harvey

"It's the system which found him innocent that's insane."
—Editorial, Denver Post

"On March 30, 1981, I was asking to be loved."
—*John W. Hinckley Jr.*

Jonathan paused. Should he use the next one? Was it fair? Why not?—after all, a columnist for the *Denver Post*, a very witty woman, had quoted it. She thought it was a collector's item, and Jonathan agreed. He pecked it out:

"And the quest for the chimera of perfect justice is subordinating the social good, including the rule of law, to the quicksilver axioms of a 'science' that is long on pretenses and short on testable assertion."
—*Columnist George Will*

Almost as good:

"Outrageous!"
—*The former president who had pardoned the man who had committed the unpardonable*

"All of us who are outraged at the idea of Hinckley going free in a short time should take some consolation in the fact that it is evidence of the high state of our civilization."
—*Columnist Andy Rooney*

"I'm deeply gratified by the thoughtful verdict of the jury. This is a triumph of fairness and common sense. It is also a victory for modern scientific methods in psychiatry."
—*Dr. David Michael Bear, Harvard Medical School*

And, by far, his favorite:

"Another day, another dollar."
—*Chief Defense Attorney Vincent Fuller*

Jonathan stared at the notes he had taken from Dan Doherty's phone calls a few days earlier, after the verdict:

6/22/82—Doherty:
Parker reversed himself again. Sed he wouldn't disclose

names of jurors—but while they're out deliberating he changes mind and releases names and addresses. He sed a New York Times reporter had presented cogent and compelling reasons for doing so (!)

A New York Times "News Analysis" published while jury was deliberating sed 2 of Judge Parker's instructions involving burden of proof "appear to make it at least a little more likely than it would be otherwise that the 27-year-old defendant will be found not guilty by reason of insanity." Also: Judge Parker, "who has been stung by a reversal in a major case before," took the "safer course of resolving doubts in favor of the defendant." (((I wonder which major case reversal the NYT reporter had in mind???))) Also: Judge Parker included an instruction to jury—requested by Hinckley's lawyers—concerning commitment to mental hospital if Hinckley found not guilty by reason of insanity.(!!!)

Parker so flustered after verdict he set date for sentencing—not a hearing, which crazy verdict calls for.

Nota Bene: Under a special act of Congress, applicable only in District of Columbia, Hinckley has right to petition for release within 50 days of verdict and every 6 months thereafter. (((A la Watergate: Did Hinckley know that?—and when did he know it???)))

Two jurors said they thought Hinckley guilty but pressure was so heavy they went along for acquittal. Something about being sequestered 4 days and wanted to hurry home.

One juror said he voted for acquittal because Hinckley "has some kind of problem but wasn't necessarily insane."

6/24/82—DOHERTY:
Hear a lot about Hinckley family wealth buying the verdict. Private lawyers estimate H Sr. paid $500,000 to $700,000 for the defense team.

(Hinckley Sr. on ABC World News Tonight assures us that if we had been in the courtroom, we'd agree with jury.) DOHERTY: "Purest horsehockey imaginable." Not a reporter there who wasn't surprised. Maybe Hinckley crazy, maybe not, but everyone has a capacity for craziness. "I hardly know anyone who hasn't had a tougher life than this guy, but he thinks he *can let go and get away with it. And he did. It sends a demoralizing message to everyone who tries to cope with problems."*

Jonathan heard the phone ring, and then Arianne was standing there.

"It was Homer Frook," she said. "He wanted to know if you'd be willing to give up some time on your day off to talk about the Dorothy Hunt plane crash. I invited him to dinner. That's all right, isn't it?"

"Sure," he said.

Suddenly Homer Frook had come into his life. Alonzo Schaeffer had brought the short, stocky man with the steel-gray eyes directly from the Placer airport to the table at the Royal where some of the *Tribune* news crew were celebrating a better-than-average paper they had put to bed a few minutes earlier. One day, it seemed to Jonathan, he had never heard of the man; the next day the man was an imposing part of his life. Homer Frook latched on to Jonathan as if it were a match decreed by the gods. It was fast, all right; a lot faster than Jonathan would have liked, but there it was: Homer Frook was very much in his life.

Frook was a member of the formidable fraternity of ex-Time Ink men who had gone on to better things. He had remained in the ranks of Henry Luce's legions for a couple of years, wrestling weekly with the unwritten laws by which the journalistic empire was ruled. He explained that he had managed through his time on *Time* to keep a relatively low profile, all the better to avoid the attention of the murderous aspirants to higher position who would gladly cold-cock him with a baseball bat if they thought it would further their ambitions. Frook explained how he had learned to visualize everyone in the Time-Life Building as carrying an invisible baseball bat in one hand, and had even mastered the skill of noting and remembering who was right-handed and who was of a doubly sinister bent. His aptitude for compilation was highly appreciated in the higher echelons, peopled primarily by sharp-elbowed writers whose most valuable talent was an ability to swing the bat on those beside, below or occasionally above them on the path to the top. Best of all, Frook explained, he had the essential physical attribute necessary for a career on a Luce publication—a strong stomach. He could eat and drink and witness what was going on about him and still sleep peacefully at night.

During the two years Frook had worked on *Time* he had formed a firm friendship with Alonzo Schaeffer. Jonathan was able to piece together a brief biography of Frook from the information he gleaned from the two former employees of the weekly newsmagazine. After their two years together in the warrens of Manhattan, Alonzo explained, Frook went on to become a successful free-lance writer. He appeared to be independently wealthy thanks to some prudent investments on which he confided he had received inside tips. He now lived on an island where he wrote occasional magazine articles commissioned by the *Reader's Digest,* which were placed in publications with amenable editors and then condensed and published in the *Reader's Digest* with all the big words taken out. The original articles eventually were gathered into books that were heavily promoted. Alonzo explained that Frook would come every year or so to the United States to check in with his publisher, drift slowly across the country to renew old friendships and nurture his elastic relationship with his native land.

While Jonathan had a justifiable suspicion of *Time* men, he had at least an equivalent compassion for ex-*Time* men. (He knew no ex-*Time* women, for it had been only in recent years that women had been regarded as anything more than munchkins fit to perform menial tasks, the management finally having been dragged, pouting and whining, into Henry Luce's American Century.) He had mourned for several promising male graduates who had been sucked into the Lucian vortex and then spewed out. It had been, in every case, a mean experience; to some humiliating, to others infuriating, to all disappointing.

Homer Frook obviously loved the Bitterroot. He drove there often, mostly in the afternoon or early evening, repeatedly proclaiming it one of the most beautiful valleys he had ever seen. Members of the *Tribune* news staff assured him that there were several valleys in the state that were its equal or perhaps even more breathtaking. But come midnight, after the paper was out, he would be back in Placer to join Jonathan and Arianne for an hour or two in their home.

For several nights the discussions centered on Jonathan's article, including the notes provided by phone calls from Dan Doherty concerning the remarkable trial in Washington. Homer Frook offered suggestions and corrections that Jonathan appreciated. But when Jonathan brought out his draft copy of "Strange Deaths and Other Tales," a manuscript reflecting years of research and writing, Frook was even more fascinated. He was especially intrigued by the chapter on the deaths of Dorothy Hunt and Michele Clark in a mysterious United Airlines crash at Chicago's Midway Airport in December, 1972.

Two days after Homer Frook had arrived in Placer and the day that Alonzo Schaeffer left early in the morning on an assignment for his newspaper, it was Summer Solstice, 1982.

Thus on Monday, June 21, at 11:24 a.m., a circle of nine was formed in the fenced backyard of Arianne and Jonathan Blakely. Holding hands, the nine welcomed the testimony that there is a divine order in the universe and that there is—or should be—an order in their lives. They had gathered earlier for brunch and champagne, welcoming Robert Robinson, who had taken an early lunch hour to join the celebration, and putting up with Donald Bitterman's good-natured pooh-poohing of what he contended was a pagan rite. Weenie Toole, with matching good nature, pointed out the message in Genesis 1:14 and suggested that the ceremony was both a religious and spiritual tribute to the intricate glory and power of nature. The vote was seven to one, Elaine Bitterman abstaining.

But she could not abstain on another matter, setting off a discussion that reigned until it was time for her husband, Deborah and the sports writer to go to work on the paper.

"I thought you said there might never be a trial," was the taunt she aimed at Jonathan.

"That's right," he replied. "I'm glad you remember where you heard it. I don't like to say I told you so, but I did tell you that—and there sure as hell wasn't."

Yes, that set it off.

"Jonathan here," the managing editor of the *Tribune* said especially to Homer Frook, "among his many other parallax views, thinks the press has been infiltrated and influenced by our intelligence services."

Frook squinted in the sunlight and sipped champagne. "It seems to me," he said quietly, "that anyone who thinks the press hasn't been deeply penetrated by the spooks has his head where the sun never shines."

Elaine Bitterman gave him a puzzled glance.

"Oh-oh," said Weenie Toole, "Jonathan appears to have acquired an ally."

"How much documentation do you need?" Frook asked, smiling at Mrs. Bitterman. "Bill Colby used to talk all the time about how his specialists in the CIA had locked up certain newspapers and magazines and the radio and television networks. 'Locked up,' he'd say. Hell, that's all in the record. And Colby told the Church committee that CIA penetration of the media was the highest, most sensitive cover program of all."

"It seems to me," Donald Bitterman said, "that you birds quake in fear of infiltration of the press by agents of our government but you close your eyes to the absolutely certain fact that agents of the KGB have poisoned the well with their disinformation. Haven't any of you read *The Spike*, for heaven's sake?"

"That's right," said Elaine Bitterman. "The president of the United States keeps the book on his desk. I read that somewhere."

"Was it something you picked up at the Safeway checkout stand?" Deborah asked.

"Yes, I think it was," Mrs. Bitterman answered quickly. "It was in *People* or *Newsweek* or somewhere like that."

Glances dart across the yard from several angles.

"I have no doubt the president likes that book," Jonathan said. "If he could have his way I'm sure he would bar the press from covering several government activities, especially in the military sphere. And I have no doubt that persons sympathetic to the aims and purposes of the international communist conspiracy have achieved positions of some journalistic importance. If they're engaging in treasonous activities or violating any law of the land, I'm the first to say that the bastards should be weeded out—that's what our federal law enforcement agencies are for. But that doesn't solve the problem of our own native bastards who poison the well in the service of the government by distorting and warping the news. The First Amendment wasn't put in the Bill of Rights for the government; it was put there for the people, to protect them from the government."

"Careful there, Jonathan," Donald Bitterman said, smiling. "That white steed you just rode through the yard has left some droppings."

"Then why did you step in it, Donaldo?" Jonathan said. "Look—I'd stake my minute savings account on a bet that there are a lot of people in government and in the press who know a lot more about this assassination attempt than has been put out for public consumption."

"And I think it's a simple matter of your news judgment versus the news judgment of competent and professional journalists, professor."

"Bullshit," Jonathan said, and Elaine Bitterman shuddered. "When a bunch of smaller papers put stories on the front page and the national papers and newsmagazines and networks don't touch them, it's more than news judgment and it's more than eerie coincidence. And I also think a lot of reporters and editors for dailies outside the so-called elite circle wonder why some of their stuff is never picked up by the wire services."

"Oh, that doesn't surprise me," the managing editor replied. "Lots of great stuff never gets picked up. That doesn't mean there's some sort of conspiracy out there."

"Then how come no one follows up on all the leads, Donald?"

"I don't know. Maybe it's because journalists have to eat, too."

"You bet, Donald," Jonathan said, his tone turning brittle. "That's a point I'd never argue with you. But Nat Hentoff answered that years ago. Sure, they have to eat—but eat what?"

It went right by Elaine Bitterman.

"I've been listening to Jonathan's stories for months," she said. "He still sounds a bit nutty to me."

"I don't think Jonathan's nutty," Deborah said with a jagged edge on each word. "The CIA has had years of experience infiltrating the press in other countries. That's all documented. Do you think Seaga would be prime minister of Jamaica if the *Daily Gleaner* hadn't been manipulated? It was consentual manipulation, but manipulation by any other name would never smell like a rose."

"That was a good one," the sports writer said. "Now we're rallying Shakespeare to our side."

Deborah smiled back at him and then went on: "And *El Mercurio* in Chile when they overthrew and assassinated Allende. What's so different about the United States? There are a lot of publishers and corporation executives who have seen nothing wrong with some horrendous covert operations and assassinations and were delighted to cooperate or to be manipulated. That may be the only thrills some of those old guys ever get."

Elaine Bitterman now was showing visible signs of stress.

"And it gets easier for the government all the time, with the new technologies," Arianne said. "I was reading the other day that nine major newspapers have folded in the last couple of years or so. The *Philadelphia Bulletin* went belly up just a few months ago after 134 years. The *Minneapolis Star* is gone. Fewer outlets, easier to control. And now we have corporations that have had nothing to do with journalism jumping in all over the place. Did you see that AT&T ad bragging that they'll be able to follow their technology wherever it leads? And they came right out and said they intend to make the most of those opportunities in what they call the Information Age. It's terrifying. What it all means is that we'll soon be getting the so-called news from giant conglomerates with no experience in journalism, with no idea of the history or traditions or obligations or the whole long struggle to keep the government from controlling the press. Jonathan is the farthest thing from nutty, Elaine."

"I think this is the appropriate moment," Jonathan said quietly, "to put an end, once and for all, to the notion that Jonathan Blakely is nutty when it comes to his warning that the American news media have been deeply penetrated by our intelligence community. Confirmation of everything I have been saying on that score came less than two weeks ago, and I've been waiting for just the right moment to pass it on. It comes from no less a source than the *New York Times*. I would like to say that it was the lead story on page one but, alas, as usual it was buried at the bottom of the fourteenth page of the second section on June 9. That story, my good and patient friends, reports that the Central Intelligence Agency, in order to settle a lawsuit under the Freedom of Information Act, reluctantly disclosed—those are the words of the good gray lady herself—that journalists have been used in a variety of roles and missions. Among other duties, journalists provided cover or served as a funding mechanism, some provided nonattributable material for use by the CIA, some collaborated in or worked on CIA-produced materials or were used for the placement of CIA-prepared materials in the foreign media. Some journalists had even served as couriers and as case officers who secretly supervised other agents. And some—oh, it's been a long time a-coming—provided assistance in suppressing what the CIA termed a media item, such as a news story. Ladies and gentlemen of the jury, the case, at long last, rests."

The silence was broken after several seconds by Homer Frook.

"We could use a lot more of that kind of intelligence," he said.

"Unfortunately," Jonathan added, "neither the CIA nor the story named the journalists or their employers or the countries in which they operated, but at least we have a description, for the first time, of the missions of what the company calls its elite assets. And the admission, for the first time, that the CIA gets assistance from people within our profession in suppressing stories."

"I'd like to see that clipping," Donald Bitterman said.

"No problem, Donald. I'll run a copy for you. And now," Jonathan said, raising his glass, "this also seems to be the appropriate moment to propose another toast. It is to the United Press International, which on this very day celebrates its seventy-fifth anniversary. That's the good news. Now this may be the bad news. It was sold nineteen days ago to a group of four who refuse to disclose any of the financial arrangements involved in the purchase of an international news organization that has been losing money for years. A toast, then, to one of our last best hopes—to free and aggressive and patriotic Unipressers everywhere in the troubled times to come."

They drank to that.

Weenie Toole sidled over to the bench where Homer Frook sat.

"You seem to like the Bitterroot a lot," he said. "I'm curious,

Homer." He grinned and winked his left eye. "The Bitterroot is famous for its beaver. Yes, sir, some of the finest beaver in Montana can be found by going down the Bitterroot."

Homer Frook grinned back. "No such luck, Weenie. I have friends down there. Hell, there's no secret. I know some of the Hmong who have settled there."

"So that's why you drive down the ribbon of death every day," Arianne said. "Jonathan, it's not the Bitterroot scenery Homer's interested in. It's the Hmong."

The old horse again heard the clang of firebells.

"That's interesting," Jonathan said. "Did any of you happen to catch that segment on Dan Rather's evening news the other night about the Hmong who've settled in Chicago? There it was—a microcosm of what's primarily wrong with news reporting today."

"Tell us about it, professor," Donald Bitterman said, "or will we have to wait for yet another article on the subject?"

"No, Donaldo, don't hold your breath. No more press studies for the old horse. But there was this CBS correspondent in Chicago's Uptown where the Hmong are shown working a community garden, trying to grow some of their native vegetables. That's the news peg, believe it or not. But not a word about why these poor people are suffering thousands of miles from their country or how they got here. That's the story that never gets on the networks."

"They're refugees, aren't they?" It was Elaine Bitterman who asked the question.

"Ah, but with a difference," Jonathan said. "Right, Homer?"

"I think I'll take a bye on this one," Homer Frook said.

Weenie Toole's eyes narrowed. "If they're friends of yours," he said, "you know why and how they got here, don't you?"

"Sure," Homer Frook replied casually. "When the war ended in Laos we brought a few thousand Hmong to this country as refugees. I once did a story on them. That's how I met many of them."

Weenie Toole was relentless. "Including the colonel?"

Homer Frook smiled. "Including the colonel."

Now everyone in the yard was even more interested. "What's all this about?" Elaine Bitterman asked.

"Ask Homer," Weenie Toole said, extending a bony hand, palm up, toward their recently arrived friend. "He's talking about thirty or forty thousand people who were brought to this country after Saigon fell."

"Well, I thought the story was fairly well-known," Homer Frook said. "A lot of Hmong tribesmen—we used to call them Meos back then—fought in a secret army against the communists. When they lost, many of them fled to Thailand and then were brought to the United States."

"That secret army you mentioned," Weenie Toole said, "was armed and advised by the CIA, wasn't it?"

Elaine Bitterman groaned and rolled her eyes skyward.

Homer Frook smiled. "That's pretty general knowledge," he said.

Weenie Toole leaned forward. "You know a man by the name of David Henry Collins?"

"No," Homer Frook said. "Should I?"

"Not necessarily," Weenie Toole said. "His obit was in the *Tribune* yesterday."

"He died in Bangkok," Donald Bitterman explained to Homer Frook. "An accident. They're shipping the body home for burial here."

"Yeah, the third guy in the American embassy to die in Bangkok this year," Weenie Toole said.

The managing editor of the *Tribune* was puzzled. "How do you know that? That wasn't in the obituary, was it?"

"Lots of things don't get in the paper, Donald," Weenie Toole said with a huge grin. "That's what I've been telling you for years. A friend up on the campus told me about it. He thinks Collins died in a very mysterious manner. However, I don't expect you to assign one of your reporters to the story. It might involve a phone call or two to the *Bangkok Post*, and I don't expect you could get approval from headquarters back there in the cornfields. You know, Donald, it's about time someone told you it takes money to put out a good newspaper. You're understaffed by six, the way I figure it."

"The way you figure it," Donald Bitterman said, "would put us out of business in a year."

"Good," Weenie Toole said. "Then maybe we could have a

locally-owned paper that spent its profits in Placer instead of distributing them as dividends far and wide."

"I won't dignify that with an answer," Donald Bitterman said. "Things are getting out of hand. Time to go. Thanks for the pagan ritual, Jonathan. Thanks for the delicious brunch, Arianne."

Then the guests were gone, with the exception of Homer Frook, who had been invited to stay for dinner.

Shortly after six o'clock the phone rang. Deborah, the same friend who had called to tell Jonathan that the president had been shot on March 30, 1981, was calling.

"I hate to spoil your Solstice celebration," she said, "but I just heard on the radio that Hinckley was found not guilty by reason of insanity."

He thanked her and hung up the phone.

Insanity! *Insanity?* Insanity!

"Those shrinks! Those shysters! And you can bet your ass that the American Bar Association and the American Psychiatric Association will do everything in their sleazy power to keep that fraud alive. There's no limit to their greed and mendacity when it comes to lining their lousy pockets. What a joke! Not guilty! Montana abolished the insanity plea and it ought to be thrown out of every court in the land as a defense. *Guilty but insane*—that's the verdict if the jury thinks the assassin is especially crazy. What a message to send to those kooks out there already fingering the trigger. It's enough to make a person puke!"

Five minutes later, Arianne had succeeded in calming him. He talked quietly and determinedly for hours with Arianne and Homer Frook, finally bidding their guest goodnight after the chimes struck midnight to end the Solstice day. While Arianne prepared for bed, he addressed a brief note to his son:

"I'm going to take my three-week vacation—or most of it—in Colorado and Texas, working on a story. We'll have to postpone our trip into the Bob Marshall Wilderness. (I don't need to tell you how much I want to see the Chinese Wall, too.) But another time. Hold off in California until you hear from me. You said some of your friends were planning a pudding after school was out. Go for it. Maybe we'll still be able to pack in for a few days if I get back in time. I'll send the plane tix. This is both serious and Roebuck. All my love, Dad."

And then he told Arianne that he would be leaving early in July. He planned to go to Denver and Evergreen, Lubbock, Midland, Dallas, Houston—wherever the trail led him—to try to answer at least some of the unanswered questions surrounding the events of the afternoon of March 30.

"I wish you wouldn't," Arianne said.

"I have to."

"I know. I've known all along that you'd have to."

"I'll be back as soon as I can."

She moved closer to him. Before he moved closer to her and for a time forgot all but the oneness of them, her apprehension flickered within him and then his own doubt flashed full.

"Let it be," said the Beatles.

"Let it bleed," replied the Stones.

JULY

*Whatever our personal frailties may be,
the nobility of our calling
will always be rooted in two commitments
difficult to observe:
refusal to lie about what we know
and resistance to oppression.*

> — *Albert Camus, Underground Journalist/Writer*
> *Acceptance Speech,*
> *Nobel Prize for Literature,*
> *Stockholm, 1957*

Bear knew something was wrong, and he knew that what was wrong concerned Jonathan. He had howled in the night after Jonathan left for Denver two days earlier, understanding the touch of sadness as his friend kissed Arianne a long goodbye at the Placer airport. Now his concern was evident as his sensitive antennae picked up the combination of tension and frustration that had overwhelmed Arianne.

"Why doesn't he call?" she asked—again—of Robert Robinson and Weenie Toole, who sat in the living room of the Blakely home and wondered the same thing. "It's getting close to 8. That's not like Jonathan. He said he would call around 6, when he got back to the hotel. That's when he called last night. Should we try again?"

"We've called three times today," Robinson said. "Alonzo said he would get in touch with Jonathan, too. If he got our messages he would call immediately. You know that. Let's wait a few more minutes, then try again."

"Maybe we should call the police in Denver," she said.

"That wouldn't help, Arianne. They couldn't find him any quicker than we'll get to him. He's probably out having dinner. He could have run into someone or—"

Robinson instantly wished he hadn't said that. The thought obviously crossed Arianne's mind at the precise moment it had struck him: What if Jonathan had run into "someone"? Or, worse, what if "someone" had run into Jonathan?

"Well," he said quickly, "he still has a lot of friends in

Denver. It could be anyone he knows. Or maybe he's staying late at the *Post*. You said he didn't get out of the *News* library until late afternoon yesterday, didn't you? Maybe he found stuff in the *Post* morgue to keep him there a little longer."

"Ten more minutes," she said. "Then we'll try again."

The roots were there, but the tree was gone.

Jonathan Blakely, as he walked down 14th Street, up 15th, down 16th and up 17th, knew that Denver no longer was his "home town." That afternoon he had seen in the neighborhood where he had been born and happily reared a transformation that was the customary price paid for "progress." Was he, he inquired of himself, becoming a victim of his mounting years, becoming that which he had promised himself he would never allow, turning against his youthful beliefs and taking on the deadening mantle of cynicism and conservatism too often the baggage of those nearer their end than their beginning? "Who is not a socialist at 20," a professor had once intoned, "lacks a heart." Then after a pause: "Who is a socialist at 40 lacks a head." Well, he had not been a socialist at either age, but the professor's principle had always nettled him. He refused to devour the ideals of youth and spit them up, primarily because he was convinced that the brightest of the young see most clearly before the dominant culture urges them to abandon their birthright in favor of the meretricious value system imposed from above. The dreams, too, then are abandoned.

And the reality? Trash littered the front yard of the home that once reflected his father's pride in a trim lawn and his mother's joy in hollyhocks and tulips, geraniums and roses. The tree that once served as the standard for the backboard and hoop of neighborhood basketball games had long since been cut down. The building that had been the big public library for the little boy was boarded and abandoned. Other landmarks of his childhood had been replaced by an exit ramp for the interstate, the only surviving cloverleaf in sight. His roots, still in that ground, had been covered with asphalt and concrete, the excrement of civilization.

Which explained, in part, the humidity. Try as he did to probe the deepest recesses of memory, he could not recall from his childhood anything like the sweltering heat of this day in July. What he did remember was that he had read somewhere that temperatures in urban areas rose appreciably when trees had been cut and earth had been paved, and there was no doubt in his mind that the fact was demonstrated here. Another influence had to be the pollution that made Denver the metropolitan area with the fourth highest number of days of unhealthful air in the country. Only the air of Los Angeles, the air of the sprawling complex of cities east of Los Angeles and the air of New York City were worse; the "Mile High City" in the preceding year had more days of unhealthful air than Pittsburgh (save the mark!), Houston (Texas), Chicago, St. Louis, Philadelphia (*et cetera, et cetera, et cetera*). Not even the puzzlement of the King of Siam, who could not fathom the idea that water could become ice, exceeded the bafflement of Jonathan Blakely, who knew that Denver had been in this century the promised land for tubercular patients because of the crisp purity of its air. Even his chosen new home could not escape the affliction of a pulp mill and the deadly blanket it often spread over Placer and the valley. Generations to come (perhaps, he thought, even the one just emerging into this world defiled with poisonous wastes, debased by man's refusal to live harmoniously with nature, rocketing toward an Armageddon more dreadful than any foreseen by any ancient Cassandra) would look upon us with horror.

He had spent the morning in the library of the *Denver Post*, studying the contents of stories clipped and stamped and inserted in brown envelopes. A former student, now an executive in the news room, had arranged admission to the paper's library. *Library*. He remembered when the room was called the *morgue*, before euphemism had saturated the society. When he left for the day, after looking at scores of news stories from which he was beginning to construct a loom on which to weave a pattern yet undefined, he thanked the person in charge for "letting me use the morgue." She looked at him uncertainly, so he had added, "That's what it used to be called—in the days of yore." When she nodded and said he was welcome, he added more: "Actually, I'm looking for where the bodies were buried and to see if there might be a skeleton or two in the closet."

He was delighted with her reply: "As your friendly undertaker, I hope you found both bodies and skeletons. That kid's lawyers were something else."

As he walked toward his hotel, between the monstrous buildings either reaching up or going up, he saw in the melancholy early evening the silent cranes perched high atop one building. During the day it had piled yet another floor to make the cavern below even darker, even more barren. He had stood for almost an hour on the corner where the old Cosmopolitan Hotel had stood and he thought of the vanished days described by his mother and father, when the downtown bustled with the energy of people living their lives, not just going to or coming from their jobs. As a child he had known a taste of that one brief shining moment when Denver, the D&F Tower a wonder to behold, looked unlike any other city on earth; now the steel and concrete and glass—oh, the endless glass—dwarfed the D&F Tower, left like a tombstone over the dead and buried city. Yeah, Frank, you're right: There Used To Be A Ball Park Right Here.

Now the town was a shimmering imitation of the characterless quality of scores of similar skylines. Just as the once-distinctive San Francisco downtown had been Manhattanized, so had Denver been Dallasized. The basketball team had passed to Texans, the baseball team had for a time been the chattel of a mean-spirited, hate-spewing Texas oil millionaire, and the Broncos had galloped steadily downward in the hearts of Denver football fans under the guidance of one of Tom Landry's Cowboy assistants. Jonathan remembered an article in a locally-published magazine that deplored "the latest in an ancient series of importunities by Texans who have always regarded this region as a sort of trendy colony where they can behave as they like." His friend on the *Post* had said at lunch that it was common to hear complaints of natives who found their favorite fishing streams closed off by the hordes from the southwest. "In the summer there are more Texans here than Coloradans," his friend lamented. And even more sadly he added a detailed account of how the once-thriving *Post*, victim of a corporate takeover, was now a clone of the *Dallas Times Herald*. The natives, no matter how restless, had become the colonials of the '80s, Jonathan concluded, and there yet was no sign of a determined and disciplined guerrilla movement....

He stood outside the Brown Palace Hotel, an architectural triumph and a monument to earlier and vanished days of glory when there were permanent residents, pleasant visitors, blue skies and expanses of flowered fields that stretched to Aurora, to Littleton, to Golden, Arvada, Greeley and Evergreen. Rabbits ran in the fields where the shopping malls subsequently were plopped. And he could not resist a smile at the irony of the hotel's honored name as he looked up at the cloud of brown smog that shielded the sky beyond.

The Brown Palace was everything the new hotels were not—dignified, stately, reserved. *Regal* is the word, Jonathan thought. They don't build them that way any more, as demonstrated by all the plastic warrens constructed or under construction or scheduled for construction all around the queen. When he walked into the distinctive square lobby he stopped to savor the elegance of the metal railings on the four sides of each of the six floors. He walked past the lobby desk—he had for many years preferred to carry his key with him rather than turn it in and later retrieve it—and past the elevators to the stairway he also preferred. He walked to the sixth-floor room he had requested, then decided to make a tour around the open square before entering his room. When he turned the key, opened the door, flicked on the light, his blood turned cold.

The chill lasted seconds as he tried to appraise the incredible situation. Sitting in a chair by the window, the drapes pulled shut, was Homer Frook, pointing at him an automatic with a silencer that glistened in the light.

Homer Frook smiled, then placed the gun on the table next to him.

"Come in, Jonathan," he said. "No sweat. The safety was on."

"Jesus H. Christ." Jonathan did not move away from the door. "Jesus H. Christ, Homer. That wasn't funny, damn it, that wasn't funny at all. You scared the hell out of me. How'd you get in here?"

"Sit down, Jonathan. You'll be all right. I brought along some Tio Pepe and Fundador Domecq. I've developed a taste for them in recent months. They'll settle your nerves. Sit down; I'll tell you all about it. There's a method in my madness. Come on, sit down; I'll pour."

As Homer Frook walked across the room to where the bottle of sherry stood between two water glasses, he pointed to the chair where he had been sitting. Then he pointed to the telephone, where the red message light glowed.

"You'd better have a couple of sips of this before you check on the messages. In the meantime I have some messages for you myself."

"You already gave me a big one, you mother," Jonathan said tonelessly from the chair where he had been directed. "No way, Homer, was that funny."

"It was not intended to be funny," Homer Frook said as he handed one of the glasses to Jonathan. "If it will make you feel better, I don't plan to ever do it again. That was my swan song."

"Some fucking song. I thought it was the executioner's song. I don't get a gun pointed at me every day, you know. That was the first time, and I hope the last time. Jesus H. Christ."

Homer Frook laughed. "Hey, Jonathan, catch your breath." He clinked his glass to the one he had placed in Jonathan's outstretched hand.

"To life," he said.

"To life. Jesus H. Christ," Jonathan said.

They sipped the sherry and stared at each other.

"Okay, Homer," Jonathan said. "What the hell is going on? How'd you get in here?"

"Picking locks is one of the more elementary skills I was blessed with in my early professional training." Homer Frook paused for several seconds. "You see, Jonathan, I'm a spook."

Jonathan took a long sip of sherry. He said nothing, letting the significance of that utterance sink in.

"Or, more accurately, I was a spook until yesterday in Placer. I'm now a retired spook."

Jonathan still said nothing.

"It's a long story. That's why I brought along the sherry and brandy. Let's order some dinner and I'll tell you the story. The gist is that my name isn't really Homer Frook. My name, Jonathan, is Anton Wojtas."

Alonzo Schaeffer poured himself another drink. No sense in trying to write the story he had come to Grand Forks to get. Four crumpled sheets of copy paper on the motel floor testified to the futility of that endeavor. He could think of nothing but the phone call he had received earlier that day from Robert Robinson—and of the memories it had set off:

...Homer Frook. Two years on the magazine and then he was gone. A good writer, but not a great one. He had joined the staff a couple of years after me, and we left at about the same time. We had become good friends as blowers of perfumed smoke for Henry Luce's fantasy machine. He never really said why he quit, although he often talked about a place he said he had on one of the Canaries—Lanzarote. He never said what he thought about why I quit (a combination of the steady disinformation pumped out during the war in Vietnam and an unwillingness to put up any longer with the magazine's interpretation of any event with which I was familiar. The pattern was always the same: part-truth, part-omission, part-fiction, part-inaccurate). Certainly it had been bantered about, mostly in bars in Rio and Buenos Aires, that Homer was a spook, but the same thing probably was said of me, even after I joined the Lady. Anyway, I had never thought he was, although come to think of it. . . .

...Yes, come to think of it, I thought there was something strange at the time when he asked me if I was going to be in Placer. He usually meets me in San Francisco when he comes through every couple of years or so. But this time he said it would be more convenient to meet me in Placer. . . .

...And then when Robinson said on the phone that Homer had stuck around town for about a week after I left—that was strange, too. This gets curiouser and curiouser. But above all, when Weenie found out Homer was headed for Denver, that was the clincher. I've kidded Jonathan unmercifully about his paranoia, but maybe the old saw is right—that just because you're paranoid it doesn't mean you don't have enemies....

...I've tried to get him three times. He ought to be calling me any time now if he's okay. What the hell am I thinking about? Of course he's okay....

...I ought to suggest that the paper do a fulltime investigation of the assassination attempt. We ought to force open all the sealed records, all the FBI reports, all the testimony that was barred from the trial. The People's Right To Know. That was a slogan of the press a few years back. But Jonathan said he'd go to work on that. We'll see what he finds first—it's his baby. But if he abandons the baby, I just might pick it up. Adopt it....

...I need another drink. If he doesn't call soon I'll be on my arse in a state that proudly proclaims Lawrence Welk as its most famous native son....

"The gun," Anton Wojtas said, "was for emphasis, Jonathan. I just wanted to make sure you got the point. The message was intended to be loud and clear: Turn around and go home. But before I go into the whys and wherefores of that message, you ought to take care of your message button. Your phone has been ringing regularly for the last three hours. I know, because I've been sitting here."

Jonathan took the three messages from the desk clerk: Robert Robinson at the *Placer Tribune.* Alonzo Schaeffer in Grand Forks, North Dakota (three calls). Arianne in Placer, Montana (three calls). The urgency was obvious; even the desk clerk was impressed. The young man had been a bit haughty during check-in, but Jonathan had learned long ago to pay no attention to the needs for ego gratification of desk clerks—or maitre d's, for that matter. He thanked the clerk for the messages that had been delivered almost obsequiously and then dialed his home phone number.

"Oh, thank God," she said. "Jonathan, are you all right? We've been worried sick about you. It's Homer Frook, Jonathan. We think he's someone else. We're not sure about details, but..."

"I'm fine, angel. Homer's sitting right here. We're sharing a bottle of Tio Pepe and discussing the state of the nation. This has been a fantastic day, like a kaleidoscope. My whole life flashed before me a couple of times." He laughed. "I'll tell you all about it—but later. How are you?"

"Oh, God, I was so worried. Are you sure you're all right with Homer there? I'm okay—now. Jonathan, we don't know what's going on exactly. Do you?"

"Well, tell me what you think is going on."

The story came tumbling out. How Weenie had gone to the funeral of David Henry Collins, honored by the Hmong community of Western Montana with a three-day ritual burial. At both the mortuary and at graveside, Weenie had been impressed by the deference and respect paid to Homer Frook by the Hmong, and especially by the Hmong colonel who rarely left Homer's side. And then, after the casket had been lowered into the grave, Weenie had heard the colonel address Homer Frook as "Anton." It was then that Weenie sought out one of the mortuary attendants.

"Let Clarence tell you," Arianne said. She placed the telephone in the extended bones of the man standing next to her who could barely control his desire for the opportunity.

"It was like this, Jonathan," Weenie Toole said. "At that point I was getting mighty suspicious of our friend Homer. You know how much time he spent with you, how interested he was in what you were doing, and all the stuff you showed him. I thought he was a little too interested at the time, but I didn't say anything about it. So when I heard him called by another name I became somewhat speeded. Then this fellow at the mortuary said that Homer had met the plane bringing the body and that the coffin was sealed shut. Add that to what we already knew and you have one of the strangest among strange deaths. Collins was getting close to busting the whole yellow rain story. If he committed suicide or died accidentally, it was one very convenient death for some people in high places. That's when I went straight to Robinson and told him what was going on. You sure you're all right there?"

"Absolutely certain," Jonathan said with a laugh. "Really, Clarence, everything is under control. Go ahead. This is fascinating."

"Okay. The day before you left for Denver the Hmong started this three-day ritual in honor of Collins. Homer didn't miss much of it. For a while I thought he was doing a story on it—him being a free-lance writer—but it got more peculiar all the time. Then yesterday, when the funeral was over, I went to see Robinson and told him what I knew. We both thought Homer's part in the funeral was a strange development, but nothing to bother you or Arianne about. That's the way it was until this morning. That's when Arianne called Robinson to tell him what a good editorial he had in the paper. But then she tells him Homer had called to say goodbye and to thank her and Jonathan for all the hospitality. Robinson immediately called me and I zipped right out to the airport and conferred with my good friend at the Frontier counter. He said Homer Frook had checked his baggage to Denver this morning. I wasted no time calling Robert, who called Arianne, and that's the story. If I told you I was mighty curious about all this, it would be the understatement of nineteen hundred and eighty-two."

"All I can tell you at this moment is that all is well with the world, Clarence, and that I have to hang up and call Alonzo."

"When are you coming home?" The tone made clear that Weenie Toole would experience great difficulty restraining his curiosity until Jonathan's return.

"I'll call Arianne in the morning and tell her the whole story. You can get the lurid details from her, Clarence."

Weenie Toole reluctantly accepted the verdict and relinquished the phone to Arianne.

"I love you," she said.

"And I thee," he answered.

Jonathan put down the phone and thought for a few seconds. Then he picked it up and dialed the number left by Alonzo Schaeffer in Grand Forks. Alonzo promptly expressed relief at hearing that Jonathan was in excellent spirits, confessed that he was "hanging one on in North Dakota," and concluded a few minutes later by extracting a promise from Jonathan to fill in the details of the whole tale the next time they were together.

Jonathan picked up the phone again, ordered dinner and wine for two, poured more sherry and settled back to listen to Anton Wojtas.

Before the knock on the door, Anton Wojtas told of his early years and the Nazi occupation of the land of his birth, the "liberation" of his land by the Red Army, his father's death and his flight with an aunt to his new home in Nebraska. He told how he worked on a weekly newspaper near Omaha, with the help of a bank bought the paper and ran it until he was invited to become an organizer for the national newspaper union and then was recruited to serve as an "adviser" to the labor movement being used to unseat Cheddi Jagan in British Guiana. Then he summarized the trials of two marriages and his years in the intelligence service as a case officer.

Jonathan answered the knock on the door and helped set the table for their dinner.

Over king crab and white wine, Anton Wojtas explained how a lovely woman on Fuerteventura had lured him away from martinis—"the vodka dulls your taste buds," she said—and brought him to the fine dry Spanish sherry he had purchased that day. And how she had helped to lure him away from a professional path that had led to a dead end.

Later, as Anton Wojtas rinsed the wine glasses before opening the bottle of Pedro Domecq, he explained how he had met and formed a friendship with Alonzo Schaeffer.

"We worked together on the magazine for two years. I was in deep cover—a mole with instructions to do nothing overt. It was clear that I was there just to learn how the operation works, make contacts that might be useful in the future, pass on anything I might pick up. No one specifically told me so, but it was obvious that the important work was being done at a high level, possibly even at the highest levels, although I have only limited evidence of that. There've always been close connections since Luce and Dulles first broke bread together. The agency always regarded the press as either an enemy force or a battery that could lay down friendly fire for us. Leaks, exclusives, confidential or secret documents—you name it—we used them all. How about that guy who got a Pulitzer for stories presented him in gift packages from the agency? And then he went to work for ITT. Interesting, isn't it?"

"Did Alonzo ever suspect anything about you?"

"No, I don't think so. We'd kid each other now and then. I

told him later, after I left, that I had a place on Lanzarote—that's the island next to Fuerteventura. I figured he'd never get there, so the cover story was safe enough. And he never knew what I was doing when I'd come through to see him every now and then. On my vacations I'd just go places where there were people I wanted to see. None of them knew what I was doing when I wasn't with them."

"Didn't you have to be careful? On guard all the time?"

"No, after a while it comes easy. I had my cover story memorized and I could live any fantasy I wanted when I was with these friends. It was great. I'd always go back to my post feeling pretty good."

"Did that fantasy life include women?"

"The fantasy life didn't because it didn't exist. But the real life was filled with women. A lot of women in a lot of places. Some of them I'd see pretty often if I was serving as a live drop."

"You mean you took messages, too?"

"Sure, in very important cases. Sometimes I'd be a live drop for a few months and then I'd take over the assignment. It could get tense. Sometimes the adrenalin would get pumping so fast I'd be in an unreal place. It was surrealistic. A natural high beyond description."

"And what was so important about the Collins funeral in Placer that you were sent there?"

"My final act. I told them I was quitting. It's a lot bigger than just his death—although that was a bit messy in itself. Ask Ted Koppel—he knows all about it. He's sitting on hours of tapes that the network won't broadcast. I was in Placer to make sure the lid stayed on."

Their conversation was interrupted by the ring of the telephone.

"I'm here at the Royal, at the end of the bar," Robert Robinson shouted into the phone, "and I have three things in mind. You got the time? I got the beer."

"Shoot, buddy. I'm sitting here with Homer going over old times we didn't spend together."

"Good. That's the first thing. You're an arrogant sonovabitch sometimes but I wanted to make sure you're all right. Now for the second thing."

There was a pause for a deep draft.

"The second thing, my good Jonathan, is that I promise never again to make a disparaging editorial reference to any conspiracy theory that may crosh—that's cross—my path. I know how pissed you get when I dismiss the possibility that the latest brainless scam out of Helena—like selling our water—indicates a conspiracy afoot, but I promise to mend my ways. As we all know, when we see clearly, everything in Helena is a conspiracy. Everything, you hear?"

"I hear you loud and clear. That's the least you can do, Robbie, to make up for your past sins."

"Oh, speaking of sins, that brings me to the third thing. At this very moment I have my arm around our newly employed environmental writer, a lovely damsel graduated only last month by our esteemed school of journalism, an addition to our staff, a nonpareil, a young lady of enviable beauty and wit, and I understand she can write, too. She has signaled that she wishes to greet you."

"Hello, Jonathan, I've heard an awful lot about you. When are you coming back?"

"It sounds as if you're getting a Royal welcome. I'll be back soon—I'm not sure yet. In the meantime watch out for that old lecher with his arm around you."

Robinson took the phone.

"That's all I have from here. When did you say you were coming back?"

"I didn't say. But I think I might be coming home sooner than I expected. I'm talking to Homer about that right now."

"Good. See you soon. Oh, Weenie's got a new one for you. Told it to Arianne and me before we left today. It's about Superman and Batman."

"Sorry, Robbie, I think I know that one. Is it the one where Superman tells Batman that if he thinks Wonder Woman was surprised, he should have seen Invisible Man?"

"That's the one. Weenie's going to be disappointed."

"Well, tell him I heard it years ago. At the same time I heard about the radio announcer who cured his hoarseness with a rare operation. Ask Clarence if he's heard that one. Thanks for calling, Robbie."

Robert Robinson put down the phone. He emptied his glass, nodded to the new environmental reporter, slid his glass five feet to the waiting hand of the smiling bartender, and walked out the front door of the Royal.

"You told me how you joined the company," Jonathan said as he refilled the glasses with Pedro Domecq. "How did you go about getting out?"

"There are a lot of people getting out. For most of them, like Ralph McGehee, it was a matter of growing disillusionment over many years. But for me it was a different experience. Mine came on all of a sudden. It was a combination of events that led me to realize that the dream had become a nightmare. I allowed myself to be made into an unwitting instrument by which thousands of people who wish us no harm and only want to be free of dictators have been tortured and imprisoned and murdered. That's the load I'm dumping."

"Look, Homer," Jonathan said. "I mean Anton. It'll take a while. The other day I called my wife 'Sarah.' I felt foolish about it, but she just laughed and said to forget it. Anyway, what I want to say is that we all carry around some loads we ought to dump—our mistakes of judgment, our miscalculations, our embarrassments, our cruelties both intentional and unintentional, our lies to ourselves and our lies to others. A lot of people I know are weighed down into misery by their guilts. No matter what, you can't let guilt get the best of you. You're doing a decent thing by getting that load off your back."

"I agree. I came to see that it's not enough to say that the end justifies the means. I found out there are better means to the end."

"Do you still believe in the end?"

"Hell yes. More than ever. I've never had a moment of doubt about that. The Soviet Union represents an unrelenting threat to us. And a lot of other countries, too. But we're fighting them with their methods, instead of the far better methods we have at our disposal. We're turning it into exactly what the Commies want—a class war. It's the poor guys, who have practically nothing, against the rich guys, who have almost everything and refuse to give up anything. And we're almost always on the wrong side. Hell, my father was a miner in the old country. What the hell good does it do to fight a totalitarian threat if we become a totalitarian state in the process? What we need is not less freedom, but a lot more freedom than that bunch in Washington wants us to have. I'll never stop fighting the communists. But I'm going to start fighting the fascists in our midst.''

"Welcome to the club, Anton."

"Finally, I was overwhelmed by the cynicism. At first it was from the hard-line guys, the fanatical types who condoned anything—and I mean anything—as long as it was part of the total war against the Soviets. I was with them. But then I came to see that the whole operation was controlled by cynics. I'd see these burned-out cases at Langley, pushing papers, staying out of trouble. They were technicians, pure and simple. Robots performing as they were programmed, and sure as hell never questioning anything. But underneath they were seething. And I couldn't blame them; they had a wife and kids and this whole standard of living that takes a lot of steady bucks to keep from going down the hole. They were terrified of a readjustment. Most of them couldn't hope to make on the outside what the government was paying. The whole operation was oiled with cynicism—and alcohol. Oh, the alcohol. You drop by the River Bend and the place is filled with cynicism and Scotch. And a lot of pain. Internalized pain, sure—but pain you knew was there. I stopped going, but that was one of the few places the officers could go without feeling that they had to watch themselves every second. When your life is centered on living a cover, especially in Washington, you don't feel comfortable when you're out in general company."

"You've touched the most sensitive nerve of all," Jonathan said. "I could have gone to the CIA at one point in my career. We both soon saw I couldn't live that way. I like to be open and honest with people"—he laughed—"as you may have noticed.

If someone asked me a question and I had to lie—I couldn't live like that. I think the whole mind-set gets out of whack. When you voluntarily enter into covert action you automatically enter a sleazy world."

"At the time I didn't think so. The director used to give us little pep talks about the dedication and discipline and integrity required by the anonymity and special demands of the intelligence profession."

"I don't knock the dedication or discipline or integrity or anonymity," Jonathan interjected. "But that bit about special demands includes not only lying but engaging in illegal acts. That's a commitment that destroys integrity. I could never do it."

"That part didn't bother me. At least not until a few months ago when a woman with more smarts than I possess came along just as I was beginning to question what I was doing. My two children made a difference, too."

"You hadn't mentioned them. You said you were married twice, but you didn't mention that you had two children."

"A boy and a girl. Both out of college now. They had been out of my life for years—by their choice, not mine. They caught a whiff of what I was doing back in the '70s and they wanted me to get out. I told them to do what they were doing with their lives and I'd do what I wanted with mine. What they were doing was working against everything I was doing, and a few months ago I began to see that they were right and I was wrong. I got a letter from them last March...."

He trailed off. Jonathan waited for him to start again.

"...It wasn't much of a letter. Just a clipping from a newspaper and a short note. The note said 'Dad, please read the enclosed. We love you. Yours with Yossarian.' The enclosed was an article about a former Air Force pilot who had been graduated second in his class from the Air Force Academy and was now a doctor in El Salvador, helping the peasants. He had gone through a lot to get there. It started with a real-life Catch-22 when he refused to fly missions in Vietnam because he saw how the government was lying to the public about what the Air Force was doing. So they said he was crazy because he refused to fly—exactly like Yossarian except this wasn't fiction—and they stuck him in a psychiatric ward of an Air Force hospital in Texas and then they stuck him with a medical discharge with a 10 percent psychiatric disability. After a while he went to medical school and was elected president of the American Medical Students Association. He fulfilled his residency requirements working at a hospital in California where most of his patients were indigent farm workers. That's where he got interested in El Salvador. He packed a 75-pound bag of medical supplies on his back right into guerrilla country, and he says he can't see much difference between the peasants there and the ones he treated in California. All of them were poor, innocent, civilian victims of what they were born into."

"Yossarian lives," Jonathan said softly.

"He sure as hell does. I got the point. The two kids are flying down to Mexico City day after tomorrow. It'll be the first time we've seen each other in nine years."

"That's beautiful. Their letter helped you make up your mind?"

"Well, yes, but something else happened that same day. That was the day I learned that Bobby Inman was going to resign as Deputy Director of Central Intelligence. When you've been getting messages for months from a woman you love and respect and then you get the same message from your children, and then you get the same message from someone you genuinely respect, it's time to listen to the messages. A lot of people think Admiral Inman is the outstanding intelligence expert in the world. For one thing, he believes we can have effective and legal intelligence operations abroad without limiting civil liberties at home. And I can testify that his concern about the extent of our covert operations can be found in substantial depth among intelligence professionals. Covert action is just a semantic disguise for secret proxy wars, torture, coercion, bribery, the spreading of lies and what Lyndon Johnson once called Murder, Incorporated."

"Don't those operations also interfere with the more important job of foreign intelligence collections and analysis?"

"There's no question about that. We've been using intelligence to support our foreign policy instead of using intelligence to make our foreign policy. You know, Goldwater wanted Inman to be Director of Central Intelligence when it looked as if Casey would have to resign. But those guys in the White House put out the word that if Casey was forced to quit, Inman not only wouldn't be his successor but he'd be driven out. I knew it was time not only for Admiral Inman to get out, but for me. And I bowed out gracefully, performing one last act of loyal service, making certain that all went well at the funeral of another man I respected. A lot of symbolism there, Jonathan, a veritable wagonload of symbolism. Enough to fill a novel, if you catch my drift."

Luis forced a smile as he watched Juanita and Simon pack their suitcases for the long trip from Fuerteventura to Mexico City. He already had given her the two tickets Anton Wojtas had purchased at the airport before departing. Yesterday, after receiving the cablegram, he had obtained confirmed reservations. Now all that was necessary to fulfill his final obligation was to drive them to the Rosario airport and see them safely aboard the plane that would take them out of his life and into a new life.

The house that Anton Wojtas had rented for more than three years now belonged to Luis. The purchase was a parting gift for loyal service, paid for with funds supplied by one of the extremely profitable proprietaries controlled by the company. "There's no more from where that came from," Anton Wojtas had told him, smiling, when he had bid him farewell—this time a final farewell—three weeks earlier. Luis, the deed to the house in hand, understood: This was the payoff. He was satisfied. He was extremely satisfied. He would live out his days along the beach, making enough round-trip runs to the airport or town to keep him in food, Winstons and Coca-Cola. He liked the United States of America. The United States of America had been good to him.

Jonathan put down the phone after ordering croissants and

coffee for two through room service, walked to the window and pulled open the drapes. "What time is it getting to be?"

"It's almost seven," Anton Wojtas replied. "You don't wear a watch, I notice."

"No, and I hope that fairly soon you won't be wearing one either. It's a chain around your wrist worn by slaves of a very uptight society. Toss it, Anton. Give it to the first guy who panhandles you."

Anton Wojtas laughed. "Maybe I will. You know, I never wore one when I was on the island. You're right, it's a drag. Now that I'm retired, I don't really need it. Maybe I will."

"There's one other matter we ought to clear up, Anton. What possessed you to believe it was necessary to slip into my room, sit in the dark until I returned and then point a gun at me?"

"I thought you'd never ask. It was simple, Jonathan. I told you I was trying to impress indelibly on you that you ought to turn around and go home. Don't snoop around here any more than you have and—especially—don't go to Texas. I've seen what you've dug up and you have enough. More than enough. Let others pick it up from here on out. You turn around and go live the good life in Placer. And if you don't mind another slice of unsolicited advice, burn your files."

Jonathan stared at him silently.

"The smartest thing you could do is burn your files." Anton Wojtas repeated the words slowly.

"I can't do that, Anton. There's too much at stake. I think there's a chance that we may be on the verge of millions of good and decent people gathering together and winning some elections and putting an end to this insanity we're going through. The polarization that's being promoted may turn out to be a blessing after all. I think there's still time to turn out the lunatics. Maybe 1984 will be close to what Orwell thought it might be, but it also may be the year when we start to turn things around. I still have faith in the majority of Americans. I want to tell this story, Anton. I may never write another word, but I want to tell this story."

Anton Wojtas nodded. "I understand. Then make sure you put everything you've got into this article and then burn your files. Could you accept that compromise?"

"I probably could live with that. No problem. I want to get this monkey off my back and give more time to my wife and my son and the good friends I've made along the way. There are a lot of other stories I want to write. This is a one-shot deal."

"As I said, you're safe if you go no further. Or farther. Don't get caught on the plains of Texas."

"Then you agree with me there's more?"

"I not only agree with you, I know it for a fact. I have been, for a long time, on the receiving end of the greatest information bureau in the world. Trust me. Go home."

Jonathan weighed the suggestion.

"Sure. What the hell," he said. "I can think of several thousand places I'd rather be than Texas in July."

"Right. Remember back in the '60s when *Ramparts* documented the collaboration between Michigan State and the CIA to train the South Vietnamese secret police for Diem? That broke through into the mass media. You've got to do the same thing and you've got a special problem because the mass media don't want to spread ideas like yours. A little bit of heresy goes a long way these days. I still think you ought to make it a novel."

"I couldn't do one of those fast-read blockbusters you see in the supermarkets. I wouldn't want to do that even if I could."

"No, not one of them. Write what's in your heart as well as what's in your head. What you know is true."

"A novel." Jonathan was suddenly more intrigued than he had been with the idea. "My beautiful wife has been trying to convince me of that for months. But I've almost finished the article and—"

"Use it. Tell the story of all these months since Hinckley shot the president. Feel free to tell my story, too, if you'd like. Change the names and places. That way you can write about a lot of other matters."

"I can't tell you how much I appreciate your assurances that I'm on the right track, Anton. Sometimes during these last fifteen months I thought I was embroidering clothes for a straw man."

Anton Wojtas raised his hand, palm toward Jonathan. "Don't apologize for what you've done or what you're doing. I agree with you without reservation that there was plenty of arrogance in the way the government handled the evidence in this case. We're right back to where we were before Watergate. We've got a bunch that doesn't fear the law and never hesitates to twist the law. A government run by people who don't fear the law is a dangerous government. Saint-Just said it all when he said that no one governs innocently."

"Which reminds me," Jonathan said. "I have to make another call."

It was two hours later in Washington, District of Columbia. Dan Doherty would be settling in at his desk after the deadly boring drive from Falls Church in the appallingly sticky heat. His familiar voice crackled over the wire.

"Doherty here."

"I'm in Denver, Dan. I wanted to talk to you before I headed back to Placer. It's all clear to me now. I'm going to write a novel, a kind of *roman à clef,* a different kind of *roman à clef.* And you're going to be in it."

"Great. In the movie, make sure Redford plays me. Send me some chapters, will you? How long will it take to write it?"

"About a year. Maybe a year and a half. Listen, Dan, I want to thank you for all your time and trouble. You've helped keep me going over some rough times when I wasn't sure exactly what I had. I'm still not certain, but I know I have a lot of unanswered questions to lay before my fellow citizens."

"Glad to be of assistance. One thing, though: Don't leave out the parts about what a sewer this town is."

"Not even a nice cool sewer at the moment, I'll bet. Don't worry. All those parts will be in there."

Anton Wojtas held his coffee cup in both hands and stared straight ahead.

"What it comes down to," he said, "is that you and I are trying to do the same thing. I figure we're both performing a useful public service."

"You mean you're going to tell your story?"

"As best I can. I'm going to put on the old writing harness when I get to Mexico. I'll have to submit everything for censorship because I signed the secrecy agreement when I joined the company. But I'll tell what I can. And I've got to get going. A plane to catch and miles to go before I sleep. Except that I'll sleep on the plane. It's been a long night."

"But what a night." Jonathan smiled. "A novel, huh? You've grabbed me by the balls with that one."

"Well, if Lyndon Johnson was right, your heart and mind are sure to follow. And this novel can have a happy ending. Here I am going to Cuernavaca to start a new life with an incredibly bright and beautiful woman and her little brother, and my two children are coming to wish me well, and for the first time in a long time I genuinely like myself. You're going home to God's country and Arianne and your boy beside you in the wilderness. All we need is a sunset to walk into." He thrust his hand toward Jonathan. "I've got to go."

Jonathan shook the offered hand.

"Thanks, Anton, for everything. This has been one hell of an experience."

"You and Arianne and your boy come help us celebrate in Mexico. I'll send my address as soon as we settle in."

"We'll make it. I promise we'll make it. I want to meet Juanita and Simon. But it may be a while; I think I'll take the time to write that novel. I may even quit my job to do it. But we'll get there."

"You do it. Get in a lick or two for me in the meantime." Anton Wojtas thought for a moment, tried to resist temptation, and lost. "Hey, Jonathan, how would you like a couple of other strange happenstances?"

"Collecting them has become my hobby."

"All right, ponder the fact that some of my friends in the FBI found on the person of one John W. Hinckley Jr. a pass that would allow him into the gallery of the United States Senate. That pass had on it the stamp of Senator John Tower, the well-known Republican from Texas who once said that the government's involvements abroad should be kept secret because the average American is not sophisticated enough to deal intelligently with foreign affairs. Now, since we know that Hinckley arrived on the bus Sunday evening, he could have obtained the pass only on the following morning, a short while before the assassination attempt."

"No kidding?"

"No kidding. And there's another striking coincidence I'd like to call to your attention. You seem to have forgotten that in the trial of the accused assassins of Orlando Letelier it was Judge Barrington Parker who uttered these words to the defense: 'I'm not going to let you put the CIA on trial in this case.' Then he issued a ruling forbidding the defense to cross-examine any of the government witnesses about CIA involvement in the assassination, although that appeared to be the key to the whole case. Just another happenstance, I'm confident."

They shook hands again and embraced.

"See you in Cuernavaca," Anton Wojtas said, and walked out of the room.

Jonathan went to the window, looked out on the city where he was born, and realized that his life had come full circle. He opened the drawer of the telephone stand and took out a sheet of hotel stationery and an envelope. He wrote a note to his son, telling him that he should come to Placer as soon as possible, that they would be going into the Bob Marshall for a couple of weeks after all. Then he opened the top dresser drawer, pulled out a sheet of blue paper and inserted it into his portable typewriter. He began to write about what had happened to him that night in a room on the sixth floor of the Brown Palace Hotel in Denver.

ABOUT THE AUTHOR

Nathaniel Blumberg grew up in Denver, where he was born in 1922. He has been a professor at the University of Montana School of Journalism since 1956 and served as dean from 1956 to 1968. He has also taught at the University of Nebraska and Michigan State University and has been a visiting professor at Northwestern University, Pennsylvania State University and the University of California at Berkeley. He has worked for the *Denver Post, Washington Post, Lincoln (Neb.) Star, Ashland (Neb.) Gazette* and the *Associated Press.* He is the author of the book *One-Party Press?*, editor of the two-volume *Mansfield Lectures in International Relations,* co-editor of *A Century of Montana Journalism* and the author of articles in several periodicals. He has served as an American Specialist with the Department of State in Thailand and the Caribbean area. He holds bachelor's and master's degrees from the University of Colorado and a doctorate in modern history from Oxford University in England, where he was a Rhodes Scholar.

ACKNOWLEDGEMENTS

The author gratefully acknowledges the support of family and friends who urged him to keep going, especially on days of doubt. For services far beyond the call of duty: Printer Bowler, Bill Forbis, Warren Brier, Robert McGiffert, Troy Holter and Douglas Bankson. Most of all, my thanks and love to my wife Barbara, who also considerably improved the manuscript.